Q's PROMISE

Q gently pressed his hand against Kitty's cheek and forced her to look at him. "I don't know exactly what's going to happen next. I don't know how, when or where the loop is going to take you, or what Leo will do, but if you want out, I need you to know something. You need to know this: No matter where you are, someone is on the outside exploiting and chiseling that crack on the outside wall, breaking things down. That someone is me. If you can just try to remember me always, no matter what happens, we're going to be okay. And one day...one day I won't even have to ask you to try."

Other *Love Spell* books by Liz Maverick:

WIRED
SHARDS OF CRIMSON (Anthology)
CRIMSON ROGUE
CRIMSON CITY
THE SHADOW RUNNERS

CRITICS RAVE FOR GROUNDBREAKING AUTHOR LIZ MAVERICK!

WIRED

"If Maverick's fast-paced, genre-bounding novel is any indication, Dorchester's new imprint, Shomi—which aims to hook a younger generation of readers—should catch an audience quickly. Maverick grabs readers from page one, throwing together romance, science fiction and cyberpunk....It's easy to get drawn into her world of twisting realities and shifting identities, especially with superb heroine Roxanne handling narration. This excellent piece of genre fiction shows much promise for both Maverick and the imprint she spearheads."

—*Publishers Weekly*

"The intricacy of a plot that could easily have devolved into a confused mess instead highlights the craft of an author at the top of her game, earning the tale the coveted RRT Perfect 10....An edgy, high-octane plot with anime-inspired characters and circumstances, check out *Wired* if you're looking for something a little unconventional."

—Romance Reviews Today

"*Wired* is easily the most interesting paranormal romance I've read in a while due to the fact that it aspires to break some new grounds and introduce some cyberpunk elements that are not dumbed down for romance readers."

—Mrs. Giggles

"This book kept me so captivated....Ms. Maverick's imagination is superb."

—*USA Today*

CRIMSON ROGUE

"This is the powerhouse conclusion to the exceptionally creative Crimson City series, launched by the versatile Maverick....With nail-biting suspense and fast-paced action, this novel is a spectacular finale!"

—*RT BOOKreviews*, 4 1/2 stars, Top Pick!

"This is a terrific conclusion to a stunning excellent romantic fantasy saga."

—*Midwest Book Review*

MORE PRAISE FOR LIZ MAVERICK!

CRIMSON CITY

"Shocking revelations, danger, and intense heat are ever present in *Crimson City*. For a fast-paced rollercoaster ride to hell and back, run—don't walk—to your nearest bookstore and snatch up a copy."

—Romance Reviews Today

"Maverick provides an intense tale with complex characters to kick off a new series set in an original, dark and fascinating world."

—*RT BOOKreviews*

"Liz Maverick's *Crimson City* is everything you could expect in a paranormal thriller. There's action, adventure, steamy romance, chills and thrills, and thwarted love. The action will keep you on the edge of every page and the romance is as hot as any summer day in L.A.... This is paranormal romance at its best!"

—Roundtable Reviews

"Ms. Maverick is a talented author who has penned a tale of love and vampires that I absolutely adored. I highly recommend it to fans of vampires and other things that go bump in the night."

—Coffee Time Romance

THE SHADOW RUNNERS

"If you like your heroines tough but tender, your heroes hard-edged and hungering for a better tomorrow, you'll love *The Shadow Runners*."

—Revision 14

"A winning addition to the *2176* series, *The Shadow Runners* is sure to please. Full of suspense, adventure, and an explosive romance, it is a book not to be missed."

—Romance Reviews Today

"This third novel in the gripping and explosive *2176* series moves along at a breakneck pace as another tough, strong woman does her part in the fight for world freedom. Ms. Maverick writes a unique, taut, exciting tale."

—The Best Reviews

LIZ MAVERICK

IЯ REVERSIBLE

LOVE SPELL NEW YORK CITY

LOVE SPELL®

October 2008

Published by

Dorchester Publishing Co., Inc.
200 Madison Avenue
New York, NY 10016

If you purchased this book without a cover you should be aware that this book is stolen property. It was reported as "unsold and destroyed" to the publisher and neither the author nor the publisher has received any payment for this "stripped book."

Copyright © 2008 by Elizabeth A. Edelstein

All rights reserved. No part of this book may be reproduced or transmitted in any form or by any electronic or mechanical means, including photocopying, recording or by any information storage and retrieval system, without the written permission of the publisher, except where permitted by law.

ISBN 10: 0-505-52778-2
ISBN 13: 978-0-505-52778-3

The name "Love Spell" and its logo are trademarks of Dorchester Publishing Co., Inc.

Printed in the United States of America.

10 9 8 7 6 5 4 3 2 1

Visit us on the web at www.dorchesterpub.com.

IЯ REVERSIBLE

PROLOGUE

Leonardo Kaysar raised his smartie and turned on the camera to snap a few shots of the disaster before him. Clothes lay all over the room, clothes his fiancée had bought on her own, that she wasn't supposed to wear, bought for purposes she wasn't supposed to have. Clothes and ridiculous trinkets spilling out of boxes and drawers all at once. Leonardo moved to the bureau and shot a still of the over-flowing jewelry box, again considering the excessive new purchases, most still with tags.

"Mr. Kaysar? We're here."

Leonardo shifted his gaze to the two girls waiting just over the threshold of the bedroom, Ariel and Deirdre. "Catalog the anomalies and get the cleaners here right away." He stepped past them back into the living room and surveyed the apartment with a practiced eye. "Bloody hell," he muttered. "How did she get so far off the base-line?"

Clearly flustered by Leonardo, Dee gestured to the en-tirety of the place, her stylus shaking between her fingers. "How soon before we bring in the next case? The apart-ment is going to need—"

"Flip it immediately. And make sure it gets a good cleaning. Get this crap off the floor."

Ariel bent down and carefully examined the parquetry, which was speckled with a dark, oily substance. Leonardo followed her gaze. The floor was oddly pitted, and the black squares of the harlequin pattern seemed to be buckling. The overall degradation of the apartment was completely incongruous with the woman who lived here, with her designer clothes and perfectly coiffed hair.

Leonardo tapped his wingtip against the floor, pressing down gently until the black square softened under the pressure. "Time is *so* unstable," he said with a sigh. "I can move it around but I've never been able to quite capture it." He looked up at Ariel, who was watching him intently. He pointed to his shoe and the stickiness beneath. "It's as thick and physical a thing as this floor under our feet, yet as thin and intangible as the air all around us."

Dee ran her fingers over the pockmarked floor. "Is this from her stilettos? This might be hard to—"

The sound of the door scanner echoed down the hall. Dee looked up nervously. Ariel seemed to steel herself. All three of them looked at the door; Ariel ushered Dee back toward the bedroom.

Leonardo's fiancée stepped over the threshold. "Baby," she cried in delight. "You're early!" The lovely brunette surged across the room and threw herself at him, the emerald chiffon of her summer dress floating like plumage in her wake. Leonardo managed to stay upright, but he did not put his arms around her tightly enough. She stumbled on her heels and fell into the wall, an awkward, embarrassing movement that left a smear of lipstick on the white paint.

Leonardo caught her by the elbow and helped her right herself; she saw her best friends, Ariel and Deirdre, standing in the doorway of her bedroom. "What . . . what's going on?"

"Mr. Kaysar?" Dee prompted with a quaver in her voice that she managed to control before asking, "Do you want us to step outside?"

The brunette looked at Dee and Ariel, and then back at

her fiancé. "Leo? What's going *on*? Ariel? Dee? Why are you here with Leo? Dee? Is something wrong?" She looked wildly among the three of them, becoming increasingly hysterical. "What did I do wrong?" she wailed, completely losing her self-control, as if a year of suppressed feelings were just bursting out.

Leonardo collected the girl in his arms. "Shush," he said. "It's fine. Everything is just fine."

Her rapid breathing slowed, and her shaking hands clasped tightly around his neck. She sniffed back tears and looked up at him uncertainly. Leonardo kissed her first gently on the lips, then harder as he pulled his finger-punch from his pocket. Behind her back, he flipped the lock and swiveled the syringe cartridge to the second position, then swiftly jammed the punch into the side of her neck.

Her fingers clawed into the fabric of his suit. Her body went tense. Her kiss drained of life. The crash of her body to the floor followed by Ariel's truncated curse emphasized the vast silence that followed.

A whimper escaped Deirdre's lips.

Leonardo turned sharply to the pale assistant. "Try to think of it this way . . ."

"Sir?"

"She was already dead."

Wide-eyed, Deirdre looked at Ariel, who just looked down at the body. She then nodded dutifully and shifted her gaze from her boss's face to the corpse. "I really liked her."

"Well, then, I suggest you work on that," Leonardo said tightly, moving into the kitchen.

When Dee swallowed hard and looked at her coworker, Ariel flashed a defensive palm at her and keyed her smartie. "Don't look at me like I'm on your side."

Dee chewed on her lower lip and moved tentatively to the brunette's side, taking care not to step on the luxurious hair splayed over the floor as she knelt. "It was such a good part. My first lead role. I've always wanted to be an actress. And I really didn't know that . . . I didn't know that you would . . ." Dee started to cry. "I'm sorry."

"Shut up," Ariel hissed, before turning her attention back to the call she was making. "Oh, hi. Yeah. I need the cleaners. Uh-uh. Not that kind. The other division. Yes, that's what I'm saying. I just said that. It's a body. . . . Then find the department that does!" In a much lower voice, she said, "Mr. Kaysar is in the next room. He just gave the order. Do I sound like I want to fill out some paperwork first? *Thank* you. I'm transmitting the location now. And do it fast, if you don't mind. He wants me to flip the room, stat."

She turned back to Dee. "Are you crazy? Stop crying before the boss sees you." Then she poked her head into the kitchen. "Sir, um, is there anything different you want done with the apartment, or is the next girl basically the same?"

Leonardo joined them in the foyer. "She's not the same at all. That is part of the point." Ariel flushed red as he stared at her. "You understand what you are doing, don't you? It's very important that everyone understands what we are doing, and why. If you don't believe it, why should our subject, whoever she is?"

"Mr. Kaysar," Ariel blurted. "I'm a hundred percent committed to my part!"

Leonardo smiled, then shifted his gaze past her to Dee.

Dee didn't answer. She just stared at him, stricken. Leonardo walked up to her. "Time is unstable, and the control of time therefore depends on how stable and predictable we can make it. To reduce the myriad possibilities inherent in the combination of free will and time, we stabilize what we can." He swept his hand out, gesturing to the whole of the apartment. "That is why we build in highly controlled situations with predetermined outcomes. We control what we can. For the rest, that which is in *here*"—

he ran his fingers across Dee's left temple—"and *here*"—he grazed her heart by drawing an invisible *X* with his index finger—"the rest we seek to control through meds and biotechnology."

"I understand," she said hoarsely.

"I don't think you do." Leonardo looked down at the spongy parquet floor, drawing her gaze along with his own. "This . . . whole set of situations is our lab. You are part of the lab. And that makes you part of something very special and important. When you auditioned, everyone was most impressed. You made us believe, Deirdre, because you believed. Make no mistake: this is not a simple exercise in the art of theater improvisation. You're changing the world. You're making history. And if you don't still believe, then by all means please visit Human Resources before I bring in my next fiancée and our next test subject, Katherine Gibbs."

Leonardo turned and knelt by his original ex-fiancée. Gently he swept the tangle of her hair off the floor and arranged it around her face. He laid his fingertips across her cheek and wiped the smeared lipstick from the corner of her mouth with his thumb. Then he stepped over her body and walked through her bedroom into the bathroom.

He opened the cabinet and surveyed the contents. Again, certain things shouldn't have been there. An amber-colored glass bottle rested on the upper shelf. He pulled it down and examined the label to confirm the date of issue, and then unscrewed the top and tapped the remaining pills into his hand. Shaking his head, he replaced them and pocketed the bottle.

Turning to go, he stopped short. He craned his neck to look at the bathroom wall. The white paint was streaked with thin gray rivulets, and as Leonardo Kaysar faced the wall head-on, raised his hand in the shape of a gun, and ran his index finger down the surface, on the other side of reality, one spin of the axis away, the nanoseconds of his present life were preparing to converge with those of his past. . . .

"I come bearing soup!" Katherine Gibbs announced triumphantly from downstairs. Roxy heard the door slam, followed by a ruckus involving the excessive banging of pots and pans far beyond what was probably necessary to heat up a can of soup. Roxy smiled, and then grabbed a tissue from the box at her side and sneezed loudly before falling back to her pillow with a groan.

"Hey, Rox!" Kitty barreled into the room waggling a brown lunch sack. "Feeling better?"

Roxy scrunched down farther under the covers and tried to look as pathetic as humanly possible. "I still god a code."

"Good news, then," Kitty replied, fiddling about in the sack and pulling out a small purple vial. "I stopped by Potions and Notions and had them mix up some essential oils that I really think will help recenter your wa." She uncorked the vial and tipped the top against her thumb.

"I dode think by wa is askew. I just god a code."

Kitty suddenly lurched forward and pressed her thumb against Roxy's forehead. Roxy yelped and dodged, only to give Kitty easier access to smear something behind her left ear.

"Gah!"

Another fruitless dodging attempt left the right ear in the open. "Aah! Stop!"

Kitty calmly stuck the stopper back in the bottle. "Roxanne. I have been dealing with your various illnesses—including the ones you make up—for how many years now? Decades. It's been decades. And are you still alive?" She threw up her arms in fake shock. "Look at this! I do believe you are."

"Maybe two decades. Less nod exaggerate," Roxy said, rubbing at what she considered the nonessential oil that was probably going to get all over the covers now. "If I could smell, I bed it'd smell bad."

"It smells like eucalyptus. You like euca—Hey, something's not right. Oh! Oh, no, you don't." Kitty bolted for the windows. "There will be no cocooning in excessive darkness. And absolutely no wallowing."

"Bud I like it dark," Roxy said with a sniff. "Udderwise I cand seep." She coughed for good measure and craned her neck toward the brown bag to see if Kitty had brought something more promising back from the store. Like chocolate.

With a violent snap, Kitty opened the curtains behind the headboard and ushered in a bright shard of light.

"Ack! That's so wrong!" Roxy ducked under the comforter and made some clogged snorting noises.

Downstairs, a timer went off. Kitty left to fetch the soup, leaving Roxy basking in the fun of being sick enough to be pampered and waited on, but not so sick that she couldn't enjoy it.

Kitty returned with a lap tray, the bowl of soup front and center, a spoon, a napkin . . . and a small bar of chocolate. "In case you can still taste," she said.

Roxanne Zaborovsky grinned up at Kitty, then sat up in bed and eagerly accepted the tray. "Dude, you're, like, the world's best friend ever. . . ."

Roxanne Zaborovsky opened her eyes. It was dark. There was no soup. It didn't smell like eucalyptus. And her *wa*— whatever the hell that was—was definitely askew. She'd dreamed of something that had happened more than a year ago.

She sat up in bed and glanced at the empty spot next to her; Mason was already up. Roxy suddenly sneezed and grabbed a tissue out of the packet on the side table. She blew her nose and threw the wad of tissue across the room in the vague direction of the garbage can, and then slumped back in bed. There'd been no soup, no motherly fussing, no stupid New Age potions in some time. For that matter, there'd been no shopping, no late-night movies, and no excessive ice cream eating, either. And there'd certainly been no talk of dreams for the future or laughter and wincing about the past.

I miss my friend.

Roxy grabbed a second tissue from the packet and used it to mop up the tears suddenly streaking down her face. She crumpled the tissue into a wad and threw it as hard as she could after the first one, and then slumped back again, only to need another. But instead of cocooning or wallowing, Roxy forced herself to get out of bed. With a yank, she opened the curtains and let the sunlight blind her.

Hey, Kitty. Are you still alive? I do believe you are. . . .

She yanked down the hem of Mason's baggy workout shirt, swiped at the tears with one sleeve, and shuffled downstairs toward the smell of coffee and cooking oil wafting up from the kitchen. Angus looked like he needed some breakfast, so Roxy tapped some flakes into his fishbowl from the shaker, then proceeded to cross the living room floor for the sole purpose of staring at the living room wall.

"Why do I always look *sooo* good on you," Mason Merrick said as he came out of the kitchen with a spatula in one hand. He wrapped his arms around Roxy and plopped a sloppy kiss on her neck. She turned and burrowed her head into his shoulder, and he pulled her off him to study her face with one arched eyebrow. "Hmm . . . bad dream again?"

"Knowing Leonardo Kaysar is out there still makes me want to . . . makes me want to . . ."

"I know." Mason glanced up at the wall, then back at Roxy. "I *know.*"

Roxy managed a smile. He wasn't just saying that. Mason felt it every bit as much as she did. Leonardo Kaysar had come into their lives once before and nearly succeeded in taking everything away from them. That should have been the end of it, but it wasn't, and now they were going to have to go into his life and finish what he'd started.

Roxy raised her hand and pointed her index finger, then pressed it against the wall as if she could just poke it and knock the whole thing over. "We beat you once before, Leo." She raised her thumb and turned her hand into the shape of a gun. "Kapow."

CHAPTER ONE

There is the future. There is the past. And, of course, in between there is the present. Simple enough for the average person, but not for a wire crosser, someone who could cross and splice versions of life and assign people different realities. Those in the time-manipulation business knew that whether one was past, present, or future at any given moment really depended on one's point of view. Well, one's point of view and some particularly clever technology.

Unfortunately for Katherine Gibbs, she didn't actually have a point of view; someone else was having it for her. She couldn't have known that she was an ordinary present-day girl stuck in Leonardo Kaysar's extraordinary version of her future world, and that he was running her through one highly controlled week in this new life over and over and over again. He'd looped her mind, and the kicker was that she'd never been happier.

The condo next door to Katherine's had been empty the entire time she'd lived in the tony housing complex. It had remained empty for so long, she never even considered that eventually someone would move in. But apparently someone had, because on this night, as Katherine stood at the bathroom sink listening with her mouth slightly agape, there was noise. Something more than your average sort of noise. In fact, it seemed the new neighbors were hacking away with some sort of blunt instrument at the wall separating her bathroom from their living room. It was the sort of blunt-instrument hacking that would be borderline inappropriate at any time, really, but which was particularly inappropriate this late in the evening.

Glancing over her shoulder, Katherine uttered the word *clock* loudly in the direction of her bedroom. A gauzy blue light illuminated the bedroom wall, superimposed with numbers in thick black. She noted the time and sighed heavily.

Such a fabulous day it had been. Such a perfect day. Good karma all around, then suddenly this. Katherine hesitated . . . but, really, it wouldn't be unreasonable to ask the new neighbors to postpone demolition until the next workday. Though it was true such meetings were best done with fresh cherry pies in the light of day, Katherine decided that she couldn't wait, and if she couldn't wait, the best approach would be a friendly offense. She'd just pop over and put a face on things so at the very least these people would think twice about making more noise. Katherine's face had an excellent batting average in this sort of situation, and she was lucky enough to still be wearing full makeup, so she slipped her shoes back on, grabbed her smartie, and stepped into the hall.

The electricity had been all screwy lately, and even when Katherine tipped her head back and ordered a fix using regulation tone and perfect enunciation, the light filament in the hall outside continued to frizzle and spit. If she hadn't been living in one of the nicest buildings in the city, the effect would have been downright creepy. She lifted her smartie to her mouth and recorded a note to inform the manager.

Her heels pressed down into the rich, cream-colored carpet lining the hall as she walked over to her neighbor's door and paused. Katherine didn't know anybody else in her complex. There were only a few units per floor, as each luxury condominium took up quite a bit of space; the high ceilings and long hallways gleaming with decorative arcs of steel and polished inlaid wood took up the rest. This wasn't the sort of building where you popped next door for a cup of sugar, so it was with some reluctance that Katherine raised her smartie to activate the doorbell.

She then realized that she couldn't hear the offending sounds anymore—not from the hall, anyway. Perhaps they'd stopped. There was nothing less effective than complaining about a metaphorical barking dog when the dog wasn't barking. She waited a few moments, then turned away from the door with a sigh.

Tink.

Katherine turned back.

Tink. Tink. Tink. Tap.

Blam!

She placed her palm on the door and leaned in to listen—

The door unlatched and slid open and inward of its own accord. Katherine went with it. Horrified, she immediately lurched back, but alarm sensors didn't go off. Nothing went off. There were no angry neighbors. No lights. From her spot just over the threshold, she could see that the unit was just like her own one-bedroom: it opened into a small entryway and sported the kitchen, bedroom, and bathroom to the right, with the dining and living room areas center and left. And just like her own one-bedroom, this was furnished, with a black-and-white parquet floor and swanky deco-futuro furniture and trim.

Blam! There it was.

"Hello?" Katherine called. "Hello?"

Blam!

The only light in the place emanated from the streaks of moonlight burning through the windows. Katherine stood for a moment, taking in the familiar gray trapezoidal fabric pulled back with clips on either side of the frames. It was not mysterious in the least that apartments in a furnished complex should be decorated in exactly the same way, but still it was something of a surprise. To see her personal space duplicated made her feel as if someone had stolen her property and put it on display.

Design was Katherine's vocation. She might be a clothing designer, but it was hard to imagine she wouldn't have made over her own apartment to her unique tastes. And yet . . . here it was again for somebody else, and she couldn't remember whether she'd decorated it for them or they'd just copied the design from her. With a sigh, she shrugged off this latest reminder of the blankness that never stopped plaguing her and stepped gingerly over the threshold.

Dust particles swirled in the light. *Tink. Tink.* Katherine peered through the murk toward the living room, which was shut off by a familiar set of French double doors.

"Anybody here?"

Tink. Tink. Tink. Blam!

The apartment lurched. The floor shuddered, knocking Katherine to her knees. She scrambled forward and grabbed the double doors for stability, clutching them until the reverberations died away.

"Hello?" she called out again, a quaver in her voice. She slowly pushed the doors open.

Tink. Blam!

With a gasp, she sat back on her heels, staring at the . . . well, there was nothing happening in here at all.

The sounds continued; the apartment rumbled beneath her. It was very clear that whatever was happening was happening right there where Katherine knelt on the tile. She was not experiencing residual noise and jolting from above, below, or next door; it was immediate. Katherine knew this, though she couldn't have explained why—or why she could see nothing out of the ordinary. Her eyes teared up, and for the first time she could ever remember, fear crawled from the pit of her stomach and fluttered through the rest of her in waves. She wasn't scared of what she was witnessing; she was scared of something she sensed but couldn't recognize within herself. Something that wasn't supposed to be there.

Stumbling to her feet, Katherine bolted from the condo, slamming the door behind her. She made quick work of the small distance between the two units and squirreled herself safely behind her own door.

It made her feel much better to be home. Much, much better. In fact, within mere seconds she'd managed to calm herself, and when the odd, loud noises started up again a moment later, she simply ignored them, stepped out of her shoes and dress, and washed her face. But as she carefully refolded her towel and tucked it back on the bathroom rack, Katherine still sensed something just wasn't quite right, something that couldn't be ignored.

A minuscule inkblot on otherwise perfectly white paint very low on one's bathroom wall might escape the notice of a normal person, but it was just the sort of not-quite-right detail a girl like Katherine would catch. As she contemplated the blot, a fragment of plaster popped out of the wall with a *tink* and wafted like a snowflake down onto the black tile at her feet.

Katherine looked at the snowflake, then at the wall. With another dainty *tink*, a second snowflake projectile fluttered to the ground. And as she stared at the chips with blank curiosity, a crack began to form in the wall, radiating sideways from the mark with a shushing sound, as if she were crumpling paper.

Another crack formed and radiated upward this time, and without further warning a patch of plaster practically leaped out at her, smacking her on the forehead. Katherine lurched and fell, then immediately rose up on her hands and knees. The funny sensation she'd felt next door was threading its way through her system again, and, still on her knees, she crept forward. She ran her fingers from the top of the crack down to the roughest crumbly area; they came away smeared with plaster dust to reveal a walnut-sized hole.

A sucking sound, like that of a deep breath, whistled through the hole. The vague notion that every inhalation inevitably had a matching exhalation passed through Katherine's mind, but that thought scattered as the blunt force of some tool smashed through her bathroom wall from the other side. *Blam!* Katherine yelped as the vibrations from the blow slammed through her knees and body. Then all went still and silent.

Crouching awkwardly in her underwear on the slippery tile, Katherine slowly ducked her head down, kept a reasonably safe distance, and looked through the hole.

By all logic, what she was supposed to see was a dark living room and furniture matching her own, but Katherine had to blink hard against a bright, cheerful light. And when her eye finally adapted to the change, she found herself watching a goldfish swimming merry circles in the confines of a fishbowl. She automatically reached out to touch, only to yank her hand back when the light flickered and something much darker obscured her view.

It took her a moment before she realized it was another eye. Somebody's plain brown eye was blinking rapidly, apparently trying to focus. "Kitty?" a woman's tentative voice asked.

Katherine screamed at the top of her lungs, scrabbled backward across the bathroom floor until she managed to recover control, then shot up and ran to the bedroom to grab her smartie off the bed. Holding the gadget to her chest, she stood between the two rooms and waited for something else to happen. Nothing did but a long stretch of silence. After a moment, as her pounding heart calmed and the exact details of the strange and impossible event began to fade from her compromised brain, Katherine peeked around the doorframe and looked at her bathroom wall.

The paint on the wall was completely normal, untouched. No hole, no radiating cracks, certainly no goldfish or brown eyes or strange voices. Katherine stared at the wall for a moment, trying to keep straight what all this was about and why her heartbeat was skittering, but the situation seemed a bit silly somehow. Forgettable. And, indeed, within a few more seconds of quiet, she'd completely forgotten about any of it. Katherine glanced into the mirror over the sink, double-checked, then fished tweezers out of the medicine cabinet and perfected her right eyebrow with an expert flick of her wrist.

CHAPTER TWO

On the other side of reality, on a parallel wire but in present time, no one was certain about anything. If anyone thought that what had transpired when Kitty's eye had first come into view was a failure, no one was willing to come out and say it. At least they'd made first contact, and the team was a hundred percent committed to getting more of Kitty than just her eye.

The team consisted of four (five, if one counted the goldfish). There was L. Roxanne Zaborovsky, recently recovered from a bad reality hangover and now happily ensconced in her apartment in the present with her boyfriend, Mason Merrick. Mason was a professional wire crosser, trained in the future to manipulate fate and reroute different wires of reality. Then there was Louise—Mason's sometime partner in the future, and Roxy's former roommate from the past—and also Vesper, the enthusiastic wire-crosser intern born in the future, who attended J-SWAT there for weapons and tactical training, but who played varsity soccer and track at a high school in the present.

Of course, with Kitty's life in the future happening in real time on a parallel wire, it too was a kind of present—when you happened to be physically there. So the team had developed a specific vocabulary and agreed to refer to Roxy's apartment in San Francisco as home base and life there as "the present." And when Roxy's brain started to implode from thinking too hard about future-present and past-present and parallel-present and the physical versus virtual issues inherent therein, and she wanted to just give up and spend the rest of her life under the blankets in a dark room, she remembered why they were all there crowding into her apartment every day in the first place: to save Kitty from their nemesis, Leonardo Kaysar, and bring her home.

With this single goal in mind, Mason and Louise had forgone paying jobs in the present's nascent and quasi-secret time-manipulation industry, Roxy had stopped taking on freelance tech jobs, and Vesper was interning for free. Now they had made their first contact with Kitty—and at least they knew what they were up against.

Kaysar had once held Roxy hostage in a version of reality that separated her from Mason because she'd had a piece of technology he'd wanted. It had been the most unfair torsion in a life that had seen some pretty amazing twists and turns created by the reorientation of time that Roxy had managed to best Leonardo only at the expense of her best friend, Kitty Gibbs. But somehow they'd get everything put back to normal.

It was for that reason that Roxy and Mason's apartment in the present had been morphed into a kind of team headquarters: "Rescue Central," as it were. Cartons of office supplies were stacked in the corners of just about every room, and the kitchen counters were crowded with bulk purchases of everybody's favorite foods. Massive boxes of Froot Loops warred for space with a crate of oranges and double-length packages of sandwich bread. A bag of freshly ground coffee contained enough of the stuff to keep an entire battalion of wire crossers out of bed. The floor leading to the living room was deeply scuffed where chairs from the dining table had moved back and forth so many times, and ink stains and loose staples had marked up the living room couch.

Despite the wear and tear, there was nothing depressing about the place. Fresh flowers always sat by the fishbowl on the counter, and the red cushions on the new bar stools Mason had bought for the kitchen breakfast bar perked things right up. More even than any physical thing, a sense of purpose and optimism set the tone for this center of operations.

Upstairs, the only real change over the course of the past year was that Kitty's old room had been cleaned up a bit so Louise or Vesper could crash there when they needed. Roxy had balked at the idea of actually boxing things up and moving them to storage. She'd made it clear they would all operate on the pretext that Kitty would be home soon, and so they all did.

Right now, as Roxy processed seeing Kitty again after so much time—well, she'd just seen Kitty's eye, really, and some blond hair—she thought about the moment when they'd first figured out where her friend had gone, and with whom. Roxy remembered laughing hysterically, all the while feeling a tremendous pain in her chest. More than a few people had told her to give up. They'd said she'd be wasting her time, that Leonardo Kaysar was simply too good—the best, in fact—and unfortunately it was true: he *was* the best. But she'd made a promise to herself and to Kitty, and she was going to keep it. Mason had promised to help too.

Which was what he was doing at the moment, in his way. He was poking madly at his smartie with a stylus, as he'd been doing for the better part of an hour while pacing the room. Roxy scowled at the smartie. As if it had all the answers. As if the stupid little piece of equipment cared. Damn smarties.

The Personal Communication Reader—or "smartie," as slang would have it—was *the* device of the future: the one that did just about anything and contained information on just about everything. The programs that came preloaded—these were all the things one would expect in a future iteration of today's standard handheld device. What made this evolution truly amazing came from specialized chips developed by private parties. There were supplemental programs for just about everything under the sun.

The technology behind both the cartridges and the smartie itself was patented by Kaysar Corporation in the future, but thereafter compromised and reverse-engineered by the government and associated freelancers. It was this technology, used in tandem with other innovations, that first allowed humans to cross the wires of reality and leap through time. It was this technology Leonardo had tried—and failed—to steal back from Roxy and keep to himself.

"Rox, it was just the first go. It's going to be fine," Mason said, coming up next to Roxy and putting his arm around her waist.

Roxy nodded. "I know."

"If she really did recognize us, we'll take that into consideration when we make contact again," Mason said. "Maybe she'll be more receptive."

"I'm telling you, she recognized me," Roxy replied. "Why else would she scream?"

"Point," he said, his mouth twitching with amusement.

Roxy rolled her eyes. "That's not what I meant."

Mason didn't return the volley, and she followed his gaze to the living room wall. It was significant in its complete and total lack of wear and tear. The hole they'd made was gone, and not because of any stucco or wood repairs. The particles of time and matter had simply morphed back into place as if they'd never parted, as if the team had never seen Kitty through the time chasm in the first place.

"What are you thinking?" she asked.

Mason managed a sad smile and took her hand in his. "I want to have all this over with in time for our anniversary. I just wish I could walk up to Kaysar and have it out with him and be done with it once and for all, you know?"

"I know. But we've done it this way for a reason." She looked back at the wall and imagined it in the future. "We've done everything for a reason."

It was true. Mason and Roxy had dealt fairly with Kaysar in the past, even if they'd stymied his plans to alter time. After that, Roxy had decided that Leonardo could have the future if he wanted, as long as he left her and Mason alone in her own time. She had persuaded Mason that they shouldn't move into the apartment Mason had anonymously bought in the future, and he'd agreed to allow all of Kaysar's temporal felonies to be handled by other wire crossers except for the ones directly involving himself and Roxy.

Of course, Kaysar had not been content to leave them alone in return. According to Louise, in the future he'd purchased the run-down parking lot that was all that remained of Roxy's less than impressive apartment building in the present. He'd erected the condos there that now housed Kitty, and it consequently was no accident that the apartment in the future that Mason had anonymously bought was one that bordered the condo in which Kitty lived now.

It wasn't just next to Katherine's in the future—it was also parallel in time to the one they were standing in now.

And if Roxy were in the habit of taking the half-full point of view, she would have noted that Leonardo's desire to avenge his failure against her and Mason was really the only reason Kitty wasn't where Leonardo had originally left her: on the floor of Roxy's apartment, where he'd shot her dead.

So good news: Kitty had been technically unmurdered. Bad news: Kitty wasn't exactly Kitty anymore.

Roxy looked down at their clasped hands, their fingers intertwined, and gave his a bit of a squeeze. "We'll still have a nice anniversary." He leaned in, tucked a bit of loose hair behind her ear, and pressed a gentle kiss to her forehead.

Louise suddenly appeared, hovering above the two of them with the distinctly displeased look of someone who feared being left out of an important meeting. As team leader, she was responsible for coordination, communication, and anything related to making sure young Vesper didn't accidentally die in the project. If anyone was having a spontaneous idea somewhere in the apartment, she certainly wanted to know about it. And while sometimes it was hard for Roxy to reconcile Idiot Roommate Louise, her inaccurate recollection from her past, with Highly Functioning Project Manager Louise in the present, when push came to shove Roxy could only be grateful for the woman's unwavering dedication to getting Kitty back.

"Are we ready?" Louise asked, and then proceeded to clap her hands and tell everyone to "Gather 'round" at the dining room table. "Mason, break it down for us, please."

He granted her a smile in exchange for the pun and sat down. "Well, this is it. We worked hard just to locate her, and I think we should . . . well, acknowledge that as a success."

He paused, but no one said anything until Vesper nervously blurted, "Yay?"

"Go on," Louise said.

"And we did a pretty amazing thing last week. We reduced the amount of space between two completely different layers of time and actually broke through from one to the other." He looked around the room and nodded. "I mean, that's no small feat. Do you realize how few people have been able to do what we've done so far? And it's not like that's all we've got."

Vesper nodded enthusiastically, and Roxy managed to smile. Louise, all focus, chewed on her thumb cuticle.

"Unfortunately, since we can't be *on* the other layer in the future to explain to Kitty that we're not, you know, space aliens or whatever with intent to kill who are invading her bathroom, we didn't get very far." Mason raised his index finger in the air. "But we did kick some ass."

The rest of the team loosened up a little as his words sank in. "We did kick some ass," Louise admitted.

Roxy nodded. "Mason's right. We've come a long way."

Vesper made a fist in the air. "Let's kick some more!"

Mason grinned. "Absolutely. Okay, that's enough patting ourselves on the back. Here's the drill. I've spent some time analyzing the data from that last attempt. I'm going to take it and multiply it threefold so we'll have a really strong GPS layer crossover. This is going to be more than a hole." He turned to Roxy. "You're going to need to be ready. Don't panic. Remain calm but focused. She's your best friend. You'll know what to say."

"So Rox and Kitty chat and—" Louise began.

"That worries me," Mason said.

"What?"

"The word chat. Don't use the word chat. We may be talking about mere nanoseconds for Rox to connect with Kitty. We have no real experience with time chasms between layers. Anything could happen. We need to connect and get out."

"What if it's a black hole we open?" Vesper asked chirpily.

Three heads swiveled in her direction. None of the expressions of the faces on those heads looked pleased.

"Let's just say black holes are generally not good," Louise said, gesturing for Mason to continue.

He nodded and ran a finger over the stubble on the side of his jaw. "Rox? Do *you* have any questions? We're stuck between needing to be as quick as possible versus needing to be careful of the unknown. We just don't know what exactly we're going to find between the layers of present and future."

"I understand," Roxy said, going a little hoarse. She tried to focus on the fact that they weren't entirely out of their league; this attack plan was similar in some ways to the usual manner in which wire crossers traveled between layers of time, using smarties and punches. The usual method was like a finger snap, though: you're here . . . and, boom, now you're there. This new way was a much more complex version, with the potential to take the time-travel process to another level by moving the layers of time around on multiple axes at once. The tricky part was that it meant the team didn't just have to worry about the end points but also about what was—or wasn't—in the space between.

Save for the *tippity-tap* of Vesper setting up a fresh template on her portable computer to document the upcoming attempt, the room was silent as Mason dropped his smartie on the table and reviewed his calculations.

"Let's get into position," Louise said, watching the time.

Mason lifted his head, and the rest of the team leaned forward. He nodded. Everyone got up and moved to their places. Louise and Mason slipped on pairs of protective gloves. Roxy squatted down next to Mason, one hand hovering over a nearby toolbox.

"Charge unit," he said. Roxy took the safety off the charge and untangled the tiny, multicolored wires, then handed it to Mason, who set the charge in place against the wall and hooked together the wires. He took a deep breath, released it, and very deliberately pronounced, "Crowbar."

Roxy picked a high-tech tool shaped like a crowbar out of the box and slapped it into his hand. He positioned the tool against the wall with a *tink* sound, twizzled some knobs and futzed with some wires, repositioned it with another *tink*, and then plugged coordinates into his instruments.

"Mallet," he said.

Roxy slapped a mallet into his hand.

Blam! Tink. Tink. Blam! "What the hell?" Mason said, stilling his work. "Drill!"

He'd never asked for the drill before. Roxy placed the handle of the tool in Mason's palm. He glanced at it and handed it back. "Other bit!"

Roxy rummaged around in the toolbox and pulled out something bigger.

"The *other* one!"

She almost started to say that there wasn't another option when she saw the thing in the bottom. It was the mother of all bits. She handed it over.

"Visor?" he said.

She nodded and grabbed herself an eye shield from the toolbox, but when he set off the charge, the room became so bright that she closed her eyes anyway. Mason shouted words that were unintelligible and something exploded, sending debris and dust flying. Roxy raised her forearm to her visor and opened her eyes.

Mason had created a much larger breach this time, to say the least. He'd managed to blast an enormous hole in the wall; it was obscured by flying dust and was clearly much harder to maintain than the last one. His muscles straining from their pull, he had drilled holes in the layer, clipped hooks through segments of the wall, and was working several bracing ropes like the anchor in a tug-of-war. Louise ran up and added her weight to the task. The ropes jerked and the gap in time and space contracted. The dust and paint from the area seemed to fuse into a kind of liquid opalescence. Mason and Louise held fast, and when the opalescent cloud dissipated, there, for only the second time in a year, stood Roxy's best friend, Kitty.

It wasn't just her eye and some hair visible this time; it was her in her entirety, head to toe. Unable to speak, Roxy just reached across the void.

"Roxy, be careful!" Mason yelled.

Roxy ignored him, holding her arm stiffly in front of her. It was impossible to determine how wide the chasm truly was—optical illusion could have camouflaged a massive stretch of time—but Kitty didn't even reach back to her. She stared at the team and scratched an itch on her earlobe.

Hyperconscious of Mason's earlier warning about getting through and getting out, Roxy tried to explain: "Kitty, it's me—Roxy! I'm here to rescue you. You're living—"

"*Who* are you?" Kitty asked, with a note of irritation in her voice. She cocked her hip, and Roxy tried not to panic.

"It's me. Your best friend. Roxanne Zaborovsky. You're living the wrong life, in the wrong—"

"You're my best friend?"

"Roxy, make her believe!" Mason gasped.

Roxy lunged forward, nearly losing her footing as the optical illusion of solid black between them gave way to the fact that it was only just air and time. She grabbed her friend by the wrist and pulled as hard as she could. "This isn't your life. You're not living your real life. I'm here to save you from—"

Kitty leaned sharply back against the weight, a look of indignation on her face as she stared down at Roxy's hand wrapped around her wrist. Then, instead of commenting on, say, the incredibly bizarre rift in time between them, she gave Roxy a rather pedestrian look of disdain. "How thoughtful of you to want to *save* me," she said with a withering glare. "But I don't need a rescue. What I'm living is my life. The best damn week of my life. Any real best friend of mine certainly wouldn't try to take me away from that." She tugged her arm back, but Roxy planted her heels and wouldn't let go.

"*Really*," Kitty said, "I'm going to have to call security if you keep this up."

Roxy's mouth went completely dry. She couldn't see any of the Kitty she'd once known in this woman who stood before her. Well, sure, their physical bodies were the same. To be honest, this Kitty looked better and healthier than Roxy remembered, which was nice. But she didn't sound like herself. She didn't give off the same vibe. And Roxy wasn't sure whether somewhere deep inside, this Kitty was a completely different person.

"Try something else," Louise begged.

Roxy clutched harder at her friend's wrist. "You don't get—"

"Let go of me," Kitty said, her fingers curling into a tense claw.

Roxy desperately held on, but she could feel her luck slipping away along with her hold.

"Hurry," Louise said behind her.

"Can't . . . hold . . . on." Mason grunted, the strain of holding the ropes that kept the rift open gumming up his words.

"The coordinates just unlocked," Vesper yelped. "Five hatch marks to disengagement! Five . . ."

Roxy stared into Kitty's eyes, and it was sort of like

watching her house key fall toward the crack between the elevator and the outside world.

"Four . . ."

It had happened once, not long ago. She'd been afraid to make a grab for fear that she'd actually knock the key straight down into the crack, so she'd done nothing. The chance trajectory it followed was straight down and through.

"Three . . ."

"Kitty! Kitty, it's me!"

"My name is Katherine," the woman said, wrenching her hand away. Roxy's arms windmilled as she hopped back and struggled to regain her balance.

Kitty took a step back, planting her stiletto like a flag in Leonardo's territory, and rubbed her wrist.

"Two . . ." Vesper said. Roxy looked back at the intern, who was staring with a hangdog expression at Mason's smartie screen, then pulled herself together and moved to his side to help him maintain evenness as he slowly gave up the chasm.

The wall between realities had almost entirely morphed back. Roxy watched in a kind of daze as Kitty turned again to her mirror and finished with the lipstick she'd been about to apply, while that same milky opalescence spread over the hole in the living room wall. And then, without ceremony, the rift closed with a *pop,* the opalescence seemed to get sucked into a vacuum, and what remained was a massive, jagged hole in the side of Roxy's apartment.

"And . . . *one,*" Vesper announced, adding rather unnecessarily, "We've disengaged."

The four of them stood in the living room for a moment, not quite making eye contact with one another. Mason rubbed his forearms and flexed his biceps, wincing as he stretched out his cramped muscles.

"Oh, my God," Roxy finally said. "That was so . . ."

"Lame," Louise said, sitting heavily down on the couch.

Lame would not have been Roxy's choice. Lame couldn't begin to describe what she was feeling. Surely she hadn't expected it to be easy. But she had depended on its being possible.

Roxy quickly swiped at the tears in her eyes, unwilling to let the others see her losing faith. Could they outthink Kaysar? They'd tracked Kitty along many realities, all the wires that he had twisted and tangled. They'd known Leonardo couldn't go back along the very wire they'd ended with last time, and they'd guessed right that he'd spliced an offshoot. He'd therefore run the offshoot wire of her life along a line of reality adjacent to theirs. He'd gone utterly parallel with Katherine, but cleverly maintained continuity with the past by moving her to a future layer of time: the one he himself was living on. It made Roxy's mind melt.

She bit down on her trembling lip. Sensing her anguish, Mason went to her and wrapped his arms around her in a huge bear hug. They stood there for a while, just trying to process; then he marched her over to a chair facing away from the living room wall and, in some misguided effort to get her all cozy and comforted, wrapped an enormous blanket around her until her head just barely poked out the top.

The minute he walked away, she hopped in her blanket cocoon over to a couch facing the living room wall. The wall was definitely torn up, fully smashed in spots, with puffs of insulation and a broken wooden rib below the hole through which she'd grabbed Kitty's wrist. Roxy stared at it and swore. All that time they'd spent—she, Mason, Louise, and Vesper—the four of them, all crammed in this apartment she had once shared with Kitty, studying and calculating and searching . . . That an endeavor of such importance could end up with nothing more than a pop and a "lame" was beyond horrific.

Kitty had looked at her as if she were a complete

stranger. What had Leonardo Kaysar done with the wires that the most important people in her life were now alien and Kitty's destroyer himself was all Kitty knew? Roxy leaned her head back on the edge of the sofa and stared miserably up at the ceiling.

It's my fault, she told herself. *It's all my fault.*

Roxy shifted her focus to the clomping of Mason's sneakers upstairs. They couldn't really move forward, the two of them, until Kitty was back. It wouldn't be right. Mason had hinted more than a few times about their future, and Roxy couldn't help but grin as she thought about the last time he'd tossed out his wire-crosser version of a marriage proposal. He'd suggested casually over a bowl of leftover spaghetti, "Maybe we should think about making things as permanent as permanence can get . . . relatively speaking."

Thinking about that bowl-of-spaghetti discussion always made her stomach flutter in the most delicious way, but there was something too awful about even contemplating a happiest-day-of-one's-life without one's best girlfriend by one's side, particularly if you were the one responsible for that girlfriend's murder. Even if—or maybe *doubly not* if—that girlfriend had subsequently turned up wire-crossed, alive, and engaged to her murderer.

With a scowl, Roxy thought back to her own strange relationship with Leonardo Kaysar. He'd once made her think well enough of him. She'd fancied him, and she could remember kindnesses from him that had seemed real enough. Though she'd never bring it up with Mason, it did sometimes cross her mind that there were versions of reality, a few wires at least, on which Leonardo Kaysar wasn't entirely the nightmare he'd turned out to be in this version of the present.

But that was irrelevant. For this present and the known future, he was still the literal and figurative bane of Roxy's and Mason's existence; he was everything that stood between them and a happily-ever-after. Kaysar's path would never have crossed Kitty's if not for Roxy. He'd called himself a sore loser, and this was his response—his revenge, even. Kitty was now his prisoner, his creepy experiment. He could have used anybody; he'd picked Kitty. So, how could Roxy possibly get engaged or married while Kitty was trapped? She couldn't. And so, in their own way, she and Mason were caught in a loop like Kitty's.

Roxy watched her fingers drumming nervously on the sofa cushion, then almost violently threw the comforter off her shoulders. *I don't get to be happy until you are again, too. It's only fair. We've just got to get you out. We've got to.*

The lilt of measured voices, Louise and Vesper communing in the kitchen, wafted through the apartment. Mason's clomping upstairs grew more frenzied, and Roxy followed the path of his noise with her eyes as he made his way from one room to the next and then down the stairs. His feet hit the landing with a dull thud punctuated by the sound of smashing glass. "Damn." He finally came into view with a hugely long, thick piece of plywood under one arm and a regular old hammer in the other. He pinned a box of nails to his upper chest with his chin and neck, and marched straight to the wall. "I'll get you a new one," he said. "Sorry about that."

Roxy shrugged it off, but then she realized what he might be talking about and leaped up like a madwoman to check the spot where the fishbowl used to sit. It was still sitting on the counter, and the fish, Existential Angst— Angus for short—seemed perfectly fine. The vase of flowers that used to sit right next to his bowl, however, was not.

She grabbed a dustpan and broom from the kitchen and started cleaning up the mess. "No big deal."

"You feeling any better?" Louise asked, coming out of the kitchen with a brown grocery sack. Vesper trailed behind.

"Meh."

"Mmm. Well, then, let's do something about it." Louise held out the sack, into which Roxy dumped the swept-up glass. "Plan A didn't work," she continued. "No matter. We put it behind us. We take what we learned and we move on to plan B."

Bam!

Bam!

"Mason, if you would be so kind?" Louise snapped.

Mason froze in the middle of swinging his hammer and looked at Roxy. She nodded, so he ditched the tools and headed over. Leaning against the breakfast nook countertop, he unintentionally revealed a swath of tan skin above his low-slung jeans that made Roxy feel a lot better.

Louise handed Vesper the sack of debris for disposal, then waited for the intern to come back. Then, with a flourish, Louise pushed her heavy black spectacles up the bridge of her nose and cleared her throat.

Roxy took a deep breath and moved to the kitchen table, pulling up a chair and grabbing a pen and a pad of paper from a stack. "Brainstorm?" she asked as Louise settled into the chair next to hers.

Louise blinked at her over her glasses. "Well, there's really only one thing to do. We need to bring in a specialist."

"What kind of specialist?"

"A time-anomaly specialist. Someone who understands how Leonardo Kaysar thinks. Someone who's up on the leading time-based technology that Kaysar is likely to use on us when he figures out that Kitty's out of sync. Stuff that Mason and I don't even know about."

Mason harrumphed.

"She's not out of sync," Roxy said. "She's tragically *in* sync. She thinks nothing's wrong."

"Trust me," Louise said. "Slip a second in, pluck a second out . . ."

"But having seen her routine . . . all we did was delay the application of lipstick by five minutes," Vesper spoke up.

Louise gave the girl a severe look. "You have no idea how that can snowball."

Roxy drummed her fingers against the table. "So, we hire a specialist and we tell the specialist to do what, exactly?"

Louise clasped her hands on the table and leaned forward with a look of authority. "To perform an extraction."

Mason snorted with laughter, but he shut up abruptly as Roxy gave him a quelling look. "An extraction," she repeated.

"She doesn't know that she wants out. In fact, she's resistant. Hence, an extraction."

"An extraction," Roxy echoed again in a monotone, even as her emotions boiled through her insides.

"Precisely," said Louise, unwitting.

Roxy leaped up, arms flailing. "We're not cleaning out her pores, for God's sake! This isn't a facial! We're trying to save her life!"

"Roxy," Mason crooned, gently pulling her back down into her seat.

Roxy put her face in her hands. "Sorry. Sorry." She took a deep breath.

"Do you have a specialist in mind?" Mason asked.

"He's the best," said Louise.

"Is he expensive?" Vesper asked, probably running their finances through her head.

Louise shrugged. "He said he'd do it at a discount."

Mason looked at her suspiciously. "You've talked to him? Why? Who is this?"

"Because he's my brother. I'll get the friends-and-family discount."

Mason rolled his eyes in the awkward silence, and Roxy looked at him. "Have you met him?" she asked.

"He's always had a pretty good rep," he admitted, look-ing incredibly unhappy. He opened his mouth again to say something, closed it, then began again. "Okay, look. We've entered an area I'm just not familiar with. This is alpha and beta tech stuff—anomalies, experimental time loops, personality changes. . . . It's not what I do, and this *is* Leonardo Kaysar we're working against. If we need a spe-cialist, let's get a specialist, but I'm telling you, he'd better be really good."

Roxy stared at him, completely torn. Mason had always been a brilliant wire crosser, and few could touch him when it came to the mental and physical requirements of classic, straight-line jobs. But as he said, this was something else. The team had realized a while ago that they were dealing with technology that wasn't in any training man-ual. That Mason would come out and say that they needed someone else to handle the situation drove home how se-rious it was—and how badly he wanted the problem solved. What they really needed was a skilled hacker who could compromise other people's supposedly secure technology.

It melted Roxy, no question, that expression on Mason's face. And that he'd trade personal pride for his love for her. *I'm so lucky to have you.*

Nonetheless, Roxy didn't want to expand the circle. There was something to be said for discretion, for running a tight ship. It was hard to keep a secret, and if Leonardo discovered they were onto him before they actually man-aged to get Kitty out, it could blow the whole project. And there was another issue in there as well. People who had the ability to manipulate reality were seriously scary. Sometimes it was hard to know what was the truth and what was a lie. Roxy had believed Leonardo's word over Mason's once, and the fear and guilt she still felt over that hadn't entirely gone away. Inviting someone else with time-manipulation skills into her world didn't thrill her at all.

"It's just a bad idea," she blurted. And suddenly she couldn't stop. She babbled on that such a move would be a mistake, that it was inappropriate and foolhardy to start trusting and adding outsiders willy-nilly. She then went on about how there would be plenty of *I told you so*s, and how the group would all rue the day—and there was a bit about how this would be the biggest calamity they could possibly manufacture for themselves, and that they would have to live out the rest of their ruined, meaningless days suffering regret of a magnitude beyond what any of them had previously experienced in their entire lives combined.

But that was before Roxy actually saw the specialist in question.

CHAPTER THREE

"Morning, Katherine."

"Good morning, Ariel!"

Ariel Fallola turned to the kitchen bot, stated her name for voice recognition, and ordered her usual. The bot went off to whip it up, and Ariel turned back to her coworker. "Oh, what *happened?*"

Katherine lowered her coffee mug. Ariel had backed up against the countertop of the break room, a look of horror on her face that gave Katherine no cause for concern whatsoever, given that horror was Ariel's natural expression. If there was drama, Ariel would either be the cause or the conduit for all relevant information.

"What's that on your wrist?"

Katherine turned her wrist, nearly upending her coffee while doing so. She slid her mug onto the counter. The passing refreshment bot immediately picked it up, wiped the bottom as well as the countertop, and placed the mug back in exactly the same location.

Her wrist did look strange, actually. Ariel moved in and grabbed her hand, and the two women glanced down at Katherine's skin, then back up at each other. Ariel used her other hand and gently maneuvered it over the surface of Katherine's flushed wrist. Her fingers covered four small-ish bruises; her thumb found the fifth.

"When did this happen?"

If it was odd to have bruises in the shape of a hand; it was perhaps odder yet that Katherine had absolutely no idea where or when she might have gotten them.

"Maybe the transport driver?" she mumbled. A normal bruise, something more along the lines of a random blob on the thigh or the side of the arm, had an explanation: you'd run into something; you were clumsy. But this, a hand applying enough pressure to make marks on your skin, was something entirely different. Both Katherine and Ariel knew it.

"Oh," Katherine said. "*Oh.*" Something was beginning to form in her mind. *My wall.* She waited for the refresh-ment bot to hand Ariel her order. When the bot disap-peared to attend something else, she leaned over to her coworker and said, "Can I ask you something?"

"Of course. What's up?"

Katherine lowered her voice to a whisper. "It's personal."

Ariel made an invisible *X* across her chest with her in-dex finger. "You can trust me."

The refreshment bot returned and began booting down to standby, and Katherine waited for the orange light on it to start blinking. She took a sip of her coffee, her eyes flicking to and fro over the rim of the cup. When the bot was down, she again leaned toward Ariel, tipping her head just slightly, and said out of the corner of her mouth, "I think maybe someone's trying to break down my walls."

Ariel's eyebrow arched. "Literally or figuratively?"

Katherine considered. "More literally. At home. What do you think about that?"

"I don't know what to think," Ariel said slowly. "Do you mean like . . . like a construction worker or like some sort of . . ." She paused for a really long time, as if she didn't want to have to finish her sentence. Finally she uttered, ". . . a time hacker? You don't mean a time hacker, do you?"

Katherine shrugged, her face grim. "It's possible. I'm not sure. Well, I'm sure it's not a construction worker, because there's no evidence of anything."

"No evidence? A time hacker is still incredibly rare." Ariel moved in close and said under her breath, "Most people outside this place don't even have a clue how much is really possible regarding time travel and time manipulation. And if there's no evidence . . . how do you know it happened?"

Katherine took a sip of coffee. "Well, I remember that this hacker or worker or whoever cracked my wall to bits."

"Which wall?" Ariel asked.

"The bathroom." Katherine grimaced, new implications of the location dawning on her. "Oh, and that's just gross."

Ariel put up a palm. "Let's not get excited. Give me all the facts. What did this person use to try to break it down?"

"I'm not sure," Katherine said. "I think something with a narrow edge. Like . . . a crowbar, maybe. It had a sound like a *tink* and a *blam*."

"When did all this happen exactly?"

"I think it was last night."

Katherine's coworker chewed nervously on her lower lip. "Wait a minute. You said you *remembered*?"

"Well, see now, it's very strange. I didn't remember . . ." Katherine's eyes grew wide and knowing. ". . . and then I *did*."

"*When* did you remember?"

Katherine suddenly felt as if she were being questioned as though *she'd* been a stupid time hacker. "This morning, just a moment ago, I guess. So do you think I should call the police or something?"

"Definitely not." Ariel glanced through the door of the break room into the hall, then back at Katherine.

It confused Katherine that Ariel should be so very certain when she herself was so very . . . not. "Okay. But, um, why shouldn't I?"

"One, because reporting what you've just described to the regular police without any evidence is going to make you look like a psycho; and, two, because it was obviously a dream." She paused. "But if you want, I'll file an internal on it for you."

Katherine Gibbs had been in the fashion industry in her old life, and it had made perfect sense for Leonardo to place her there in the present, as it was one less variable; she had nothing to learn and nothing to forget. So he'd assigned her to the Bot Division, designing clothes for the bot models. Researching, developing, and manufacturing bots was the more obvious bread and butter of Kaysar Corporation. The commercial demand for bots to do any manner of things never wavered, and the profits from that division poured money into his personal projects in the time-based-technology side of the business.

That the corporation was intricately involved in heavy-duty temporal research wasn't a secret. In spite of the fact that Katherine spent her days at the company creating mix 'n' match outfits for what were essentially dolls, the Kaysar Corporation as a whole was classified by the government as a weapons systems developer and manufacturer. There was a government squad beyond the "regular police"— albeit one that was fairly under wraps—for investigating issues related to the burgeoning time-manipulation industry; it wasn't an urban legend, as some people believed.

All of this information was in the employee manual, so

it seemed a little odd to Katherine that Ariel would gloss over reporting an incident like the one Katherine had described—well, assuming it had really happened. Odder still was the idea that Katherine couldn't file her own silly internal paperwork because of a smidge of a bruise, but Ariel was a sweetie, really, and perhaps she was just trying to be helpful under unnerving circumstances.

"You dreamed it, Katherine," Ariel said firmly. "Just forget about it."

Katherine stared at the undreamlike bruises on her wrist and then up at Ariel. "Right." A little uncertainly she added, "I think maybe I *have* had some odd dreams lately. I guess that's all it was."

Once Katherine agreed with her, Ariel seemed to relax very quickly. "Just a dream. It was definitely a dream. What you experienced was absolutely, unequivocally a dream. It's probably your subconscious trying to . . . spur your creativity. I mean, we're in the middle of fall and it's almost time to start the next collection. In fact, I think this dream of yours is actually a really positive event. And I think you're fabulous. And I really love that wrap dress you've got on!' "

"Oh, you are so sweet," Katherine said, her focus switching immediately to the object of Ariel's attention. She swished the fabric of the skirt to show the pattern off to its best advantage. It *was* a lovely wrap.

"Well, it's true. You're the best, Katherine. You really are. There's nobody as fabulous as you. Seriously. You're *special*. And you know, you can always talk to me about these dreams of yours." Ariel's face was bright as she patted Katherine on the shoulder. "Anytime. Anything strange, any weird dreams, anything that seems . . . out of place, definitely come to me."

Katherine smiled, trying to hide her confusion as the dream began to disappear on her again. "Thanks, Ariel."

And, deciding to treat herself to the new zero-calorie-same-great-fatty-taste cream, she asked the kitchen refreshment bot for a coffee refill.

She returned to her desk, humming and gliding as if a weight had been removed from her shoulders. Which it sort of had been. Because the dream explanation seemed completely logical, and, in fact, she couldn't quite remember the dream itself. Something about a goldfish . . . ?

Ariel, on the other hand, did not hum and glide back to her desk. She sat down heavily in her cubicle and exchanged glances with Deirdre across the aisle. Dee leaned in. "Is she okay?"

Ariel peeked over the top of her cube to the large space at the back of the room, where Katherine had already moved and was now cheerily examining a line of evening wear presented on a row of bots posing in lockstep. "I dunno. She described someone trying to break down her bathroom wall but says there's no evidence. . . ."

Dee's eyes widened. "Literally break it down?"

Ariel gulped at her coffee and shrugged. "It's either a dream . . . or she was targeted by a wire crosser."

Dee and Ariel looked at each other, then exchanged almost imperceptible nods. Ariel dialed a connection to Mr. Kaysar's office.

Katherine returned to her desk, pointed her smartie at her screen, and wired in her notes from the design review of her pet project, the evening-wear line, suitable for blending in hostess bots at parties and important events. The fabrics were absolutely gorgeous, the lines of the new patterns cutting-edge but inspired by eras gone by. That was what everyone wanted: to feel as though they were in a kinder, gentler era in a time when everything wasn't so cold. Oh, how satisfying it all was! And how she loved the beaded fringe and the drop waists! Leo would be delighted. Well, he'd be delighted once he

they made love in almost brutal silence save for the electronic clicks marking when the emergency stop would
reset itself and the camera would switch back on. The clicking quickened; the blue light fired up. They came together
as the light pulsed faster.

Leo pulled away, his eyes locked with hers, and they re-
arranged themselves, hurrying against time. "Everything
all right, then, darling?" he murmured into her ear,
straightening his tie.

She nuzzled her face into his neck. "Of course."

"Nothing bothering you?"

"Nothing at all," she said, planting a fleeting kiss on his
lips.

"What happened to your wrist?"

Katherine blinked in confusion, then looked down.
"Good Lord. Did you just do that?" She glanced up at
Leonardo. "Naughty boy!"

He studied her face, really studied her face. "I'll try to
be more careful next time," he finally said.

The camera made a whirring sound and switched back
on. The blue light extinguished. The elevator doors opened
and a bunch of suits stepped in. Leonardo didn't look back
at Katherine as he exited at the next floor.

Leaning back against the wall, Katherine closed her eyes
and rode the elevator to the bottom, smiling the whole way
down. She had no idea how she'd gotten so lucky as to
land a boyfriend like Leonardo Kaysar, but he was definitely the perfect accessory to the rest of her fabulous life.
What she'd said to him about nothing being wrong was
true. The wrist thing didn't bother her. Ariel's comments
didn't bother her. None of this bothered her, because she'd
already forgotten. The wrist, the dreams, Ariel's funny
reaction—none of it was within the parameters of her
schedule.

This was the best week of her life, the peak of her

personal and professional success; Kitty hoped the feeling
would never end.

Leonardo Kaysar stared out the window at the Scotch ad-
vertisement blinking across a nearby hover-ad. It featured
a gorgeous woman who'd either been airbrushed within
an inch of her life or who'd actually gone and been plasticked, tits to toes. He reflected that Katherine Gibbs
hadn't needed any plasticking; she had the luck of natural
beauty.

"Mr. Kaysar, sir?"

Without moving a muscle, Leonardo shifted his gaze to
the right side of the window, where a vague reflection of
the open door told him everything he needed to know.
"What is it?"

"Did you want to postpone the meeting? Everybody's
ready. I just haven't called them in yet." Deirdre didn't
move from the doorway. She acted like a scared little mouse,
which was essentially how everyone acted around him.

"Move it to ten, and bring me the latest QA reports.
And please close the door behind you."

"Yes, Mr. Kaysar, sir." She took a quick step back from
the door and carefully closed it.

So boring, this excessive display of deference, but necessary. Distance was necessary. That was what it took to run a
corporation well and remain a true power, which was something he intended. He'd never actually get his father back or
reclaim the inventions that the Kaysar Corporation had
originally created and that were stolen by the government;
he'd come to terms with that. Too many wires intersected,
too many lives as well; there was absolutely no good purpose
to manipulating time and reality given the risk. He'd been
stymied. But there were other things he could do.

Yes, the past was dead to him now, but all hope was not
lost. Everything Leonardo did, everything he breathed,

was now about the future. If he could not bring all that he'd lost back from the past, he would instead rebuild the Kaysar empire into something that would last until the end of time. Mason Merrick and L. Roxanne Zaborovksy were really beside the point, a fact that gave him rather a good bit of pleasure. More than he'd be willing to admit out loud.

Yes, they'd beaten him. They'd found a way to defend against almost every move he made—or at least to escape his traps. One had to come to terms with one's failures, and they'd certainly beaten him. Of course, there was no actual intelligence in what Mason and Roxanne did, nor in how they had done it. It was infinitely more difficult to create than it was to destroy, and all this pair could do was deflect his tricks, destroy, decamp. All brawn, Mason. No art.

Leo was a creator. He fancied himself a bit of an artist, really. For that reason, he wasn't too hard on himself for losing his grip on Roxanne and her smartie code the last time he'd gone up against Mason Merrick. That code would have put the ability to time travel and wire-cross solely in his hands, true; but his failure had reaped other rewards. Incredible ones. Processing what he'd done wrong and how Mason and Roxy had managed to best him, he'd created ingenious workarounds. And stealing Roxanne's best friend, Katherine, for beta testing and refining his brilliant innovations more than made up for the nastiness of losing the previous struggle.

He'd wanted to see what inventions he could create out of his new ideas, learn how the human mind and body could be manipulated, and vice versa. Katherine wasn't suffering. Leonardo had simply understood how he could make her want him, and she enjoyed their weekly sex—same time, same place—as much as he did. More, since she was in love with him. He could have any woman he wanted, of course, but it was so nice to have *her*. The way she felt about him . . . it sometimes felt so damned good that every now and then even he forgot it was all a lie.

He hadn't connected with the first girl the way he did with Katherine. If the current experiment didn't pan out to his satisfaction and he had to bring in a third girl, at least he'd have a better understanding of whether it was the underlying personality of the subject or the technology itself that made a difference.

Leonardo went back to the elevator in his mind. Those bruises on her wrist . . . they were odd. He'd seen nothing like them in all the previous weeks he'd been using her in this experiment. It was important that everything be as exact as possible. He'd have to bring up the necessity of continued and meticulous vigilance at the upcoming meeting. It was a tricky business to provide the right parameters to keep the subject on the straightaway, and repetition in any situation had a way of yielding to sloppiness over time. He'd have to talk to the engineers about tightening the screws on the loop, as it were.

Another knock at the door. He glanced at the panel on his desk and saw Deirdre waiting on the other side, files tucked under one arm.

"Open door," he said to the panel. Deirdre entered, placed the papers on his desk, and quickly scampered out again with a nervous smile and a mumbled, "Sir."

Leonardo shuffled through the documents until he found Katherine's continuity report, and he studied the quality-assurance data. There was nothing out of the ordinary, but now was as good a time as any to bolster certain parameters. He didn't care for that wrist. It could have come from a random accident, a simple physical misstep, but the placement of the bruises . . . he'd have someone try to suss that out. It could have been something bigger—something related to a shifting in her mind, perhaps—which was exactly what he wanted to prevent.

He took in the quiet hum of his wall clock, its gauzy blue glow reflecting off his white-lacquered furniture. His office was soundproofed, of course, and the overall effect of intensity and security and pressure was by design. But despite the bright white furniture and massive windows, sometimes he felt as if he weren't getting any air at all.

Leonardo slumped back in his office chair, the suspension gears shifting easily to accommodate the change in the distribution of weight. His eyelids fluttered, and he nearly dropped off to sleep, but the weight of his head falling to the side woke him. He stood, trying to shake the weariness that clung to him like cobwebs, and forced himself to channel all his focus. He'd taken the company to the peak of efficiency and had hired the most talented executives to handle the daily grind of research, development, and production, freeing his mind to think and dream and invent. With the corporation running smoothly, he'd allowed himself to indulge as much as he wanted in his pet project: the ability to manipulate increments of time in ways and at levels heretofore unimagined. If anyone had asked what his primary goal was in the pursuit of this project, he would have answered without hesitation: the maintenance of Katherine Gibbs's loop and the information he could draw from that.

CHAPTER FOUR

Roxy fretted about the hiring of Louise's brother for the entire three days it took for him to free himself from his previous freelance assignment. Nepotism was a lovely concept, siblings helping siblings and all, but when it came to saving lives, she wasn't sure she liked the idea of hiring somebody's kid brother just because . . . well, just because he happened to be somebody's kid brother. But Walter

"Q" Sheffield was already on the way, and time, as always, was of the essence.

Apparently it had been some duration since Louise and Walter had hung out, and she kept stepping into the hall to look for him, as if that would make him arrive faster. But after the fourth time, the rest of the team heard a squeal and followed her out.

Louise glanced over her shoulder. "Vesper," she said sternly, "this is not some sort of spectacle." She gestured to the paperwork in the intern's hand.

Roxy tried to stay out of Louise's business, but she couldn't imagine a boss keeping a tighter grip on an employee; the woman kept Vesper awash in paperwork and kitchen duty. All the poor girl wanted was to see some action, but Louise insisted her inexperience would mess things up. This time Roxy gave Vesper a look that said, come along, because there was nothing here that could possibly get messed up, and what was approaching down the narrow corridor certainly qualified as a piece of action.

A small squeak leaped from between Vesper's lips as the specialist sauntered down the narrow corridor toward the apartment. Actually, *sauntered* didn't describe what he did; he *owned the corridor.* He sucked a little more oxygen from their lungs with every step. He wore all black, cargo pants and a T-shirt, sported a wire cable slung diagonally across his chest, carried a huge metal box in one hand, and swung an enormous bazooka in the other. The pheromones were everywhere, unavoidable, clogging the air in the best possible way.

Vesper couldn't stop gaping. Roxy kept a more businesslike demeanor, careful not to reveal in front of Mason how insanely attractive she found this other man. It wasn't personal; anyone would find the specialist attractive.

They watched the family-reunion moment play out, then invited Walter in. With Louise fussing over him, he removed his equipment and weaponry and carefully lined it up along the back of the sofa.

"So, why do you think they call him Q?" Roxy whispered. "Because of the gadget thing? He's big into gadgets, like the guy from James Bond movies?"

Vesper gulped. "No. Because you can't call a man that hot 'Walter.'" She fanned herself with an invoice, her sweaty fingers smearing the ink. "Please don't let him be a total dumb-ass," she added, her eyes going buggy. She crossed her fingers. "That would just so kill it for me."

The only person in the room unaffected was Louise. "Hey, hey, bro," she said, slapping him vigorously on the back, continuing her welcome.

He ruffled his sister's hair, then turned to the rest of the team. "Hey. I'm Walter," he said. "Or Q."

Roxy stuck out her hand. "Roxy."

"Mason," Mason said, a little tightly, perhaps.

"You're Mason Merrick," Q said with a nod. "I know the name. Obviously." He looked at Roxy, and then back at Mason. "You're one of the best straight-line wire crossers in the business."

Roxy felt Mason tense up a little in spite of his smile. Working in straight-line versus anomalies was viewed as the difference between being a commercial pilot and a jet fighter pilot.

Q turned to Vesper. The intern didn't move. He cocked his head and looked at her, then offered a handshake. Vesper didn't seem to notice. Roxy poked the girl discreetly in the small of her back, and the intern thrust her arm out, grabbing the specialist's hand with her gaze glued to his eyes. "Blurg" was all that came out of her mouth.

He smiled and tried to pull back his hand. Vesper didn't let go, so he unfurled her fingers with his other hand and gently lowered her arm back to her side.

From the corner of her eye, Roxy saw Mason flex one bicep, an unconscious movement meant to reassert his superior manhood. She found that flash of vulnerability adorable: he wasn't used to having alpha-dog attention diverted from him. Of course, he was already with Roxy, so to the other women in the room his deliciousness was beside the point.

"Hey, Mason, can I talk to you for a sec?" Without waiting for an answer, she grabbed Mason by the hand, dragged him into the other room, grasped the back of his head, and pulled his mouth down on hers. The kiss ended in a blaze of fire, so she planted an extra smack fleetingly on his lips and gave him a look that said no man—not even the one outside—could ever take his place. Mason replied with a sort of monosyllabic caveman sound, and they returned to the room grinning like a couple of high school kids exiting the janitor's closet.

Vesper, Q, and Louise were seated at the large table where all of their files were kept, poring over the documentation binder. Or, rather, Louise and Q were. Vesper's eyes bored into the top of Q's head as he studied everything they'd accumulated about Kitty's situation over the last year. He glanced up at Vesper, and the teenager hiccuped.

"And you say she didn't want to leave this artificial construct, this 'weekly mental loop'?" he asked, his brow furrowed. "Had no idea she was even in a loop? Interesting." He leaned back in his chair and looked at Mason. "I would have done the same thing you did, for starters. . . ." He raised the binder and scanned the top page again. "But that obviously would have produced similar results. Which means . . . I need to dip into my bag of tricks."

Roxy actually bounced up and down in her chair for a second. "You know what to do!"

"Uh, I didn't say that."

"Oh."

"But I'm used to finding workarounds for anomalies, so there are some other things we can try."

"Well, great," Roxy said, trying her best to keep up the enthusiasm. "Let's just do them."

The others all looked at her. "Do you want to discuss—" Mason began.

"What? What's to discuss? He's a specialist; that's why we hired him. He knows what he's doing." She looked at Q. "You know what you're doing, right?"

"One can never know exactly what one's doing before one's doing it, not in the anomalies game," he said, looking over Roxy's shoulder at his sister. "Do you want to discuss this in more detail?"

"Nope," Roxy said, answering for all of them. She looked around the table and tapped her watch. It was old-school—a Casio she'd bought long before she even learned about wire crossing. She appreciated its old-fashioned early-twentieth-century geek chic. "I want to get this going before Leo makes things even harder on us."

No one argued with her, so after a few moments of silence, Q raised his palms and said, "Okay, then. The rundown is this: we're going to open the chasm again, but this time using much stronger equipment, and we're going to back that up with something that's called a brain freeze and—"

"A brain freeze? Tell me you're joking," Roxy said.

"It's just a slang term. It requires a prototype that's not even out on the market, but I've talked to a guy who had good results. If we can freeze some fragment of time on your friend's layer in the future while maintaining normal, linear time on ours, it gives us the opportunity to hack the subject clear off the layer. It would make any protest or incomprehension on her part irrelevant."

"Theoretically," Vesper said.

Q looked at her in surprise. "Well, yes. Anything is possible in theory."

"Has it been done in practice yet?"

"I know the one guy who has."

"So . . . it worked?" Vesper asked hopefully.

Q cleared his throat. "No. It failed, actually. But like I said, he had good results. Excellent experiment. But that's why they call these things anomalies. Because these are instances where we can't predict behavior and we can't predict solutions. If we could, you wouldn't have hired an anomaly specialist," he said pleasantly. "And you know what else?"

"What?" Vesper asked, leaning in, agog.

"These questions seem to be making Roxanne very nervous."

Vesper lurched back and looked at Roxy. "Sorry."

" 'S okay," Roxy said. "But maybe we could just get on with it. I just feel like now that we know where she is, the longer she's there . . ."

Q put a comforting hand on Roxy's shoulder. "I understand." He went to the box he'd brought, pulled out an enormous pump bottle of SPF 165, and asked everyone who was planning to stay during the procedure to apply said sunscreen liberally. While Roxy was busy doing that—and muttering about the impersonal use of the phrase *the procedure*—Q rolled up his sleeves, jumped a couple of times while shaking out his limbs, as if this were some sort of track meet, and then picked up his bazooka.

Built into the weapon's back section was a control panel; Q tapped in some information as if he were texting someone. Roxy opened her mouth to ask a question, but Louise shushed her before the words could materialize. Roxy kept her mouth shut while Q performed a series of mathematical calculations on the bazooka's flicker screen.

"There is something very attractive about a hot man solving complex math problems," Vesper whispered.

Q finally pushed away from the table, donned a metal fabric glove, and stood up. "You need to stand back."

The four teammates took a step away.

"No, I mean *far* back. Anyone who is not critical to this

operation should step out of the room—or out of the apartment complex if possible."

The four of them took another step back.

Q glared at Louise, then faced the once-again-pristine living room wall. He cocked his head, stared at the white paint, then moved forward to press his hands against it, those hands forming a triangle. He appeared to be examining angles; then he compared the bazooka's flicker panel to his smartie screen and carefully set the weapon on the floor within reach.

"Should we remove the plywood?" Roxy piped up, her heart inexplicably beating out of her chest, part with excitement, part with terror.

"That won't be necessary," Q replied. He took a sledgehammer from his toolbox into his right hand and tested the heft by lifting it off the ground, smoothly raising and lowering it, the muscles in his arm straining. Vesper made a slurping sound, as if she'd just saved herself from drooling on the floor.

Q looked over his shoulder. "Visors." He waited until they all had their shades in place, then slipped a pair of blast glasses over his own eyes and turned back to the wall.

He widened his stance, raised the sledgehammer, and began looping it in a circle in the air. As momentum built, the hammer swung faster and faster, smoother and smoother in its rotation. Mason threw his arm out in front of the girls like a seat belt—a really ineffectual seat belt, but a lovely protective maneuver nonetheless—and ushered them back against the far wall and to the side, out of the reach of any miscalculation that might send the blunt instrument careening in their direction.

And then it was just Q and his hammer and bazooka facing the wall, Kitty in the future somewhere on the other side.

With a loud prehistoric-sounding grunt, Q let go of the hammer. Roxy saw what he meant about it being unnecessary to remove the plywood; the explosion was so intense it pulverized an entire section of the wall, almost up to the ceiling. A brilliant white line stretched across the wall like a horizon, emanating a tremendous, almost painful glow. Plaster dust swirled thickly everywhere. Q stood backlit, a black shadow of strength, his right hand held up at a forty-five-degree angle, his fingers curled into a fist. The upper sleeve of his opposite arm smoked and caught fire, but he merely looked down and brushed out the flames, then curled his hand back into a fist.

The color of the blast changed to a bluer tone. Q looked over his shoulder at the rest of the team, then un-curled his fist, giving the go-ahead with his index finger and thumb. Roxy ran forward; Mason grabbed the end of the cable behind Q to anchor the imminent rift. Louise stayed back, holding on to Vesper, who seemed to think jumping into the middle of things would be helpful.

Roxy teetered on the edge of the growing rift, taking in the strip of black below and between, and also what was in front of her eyes: the normal apartment bathroom of Kitty's future. Kitty stood inside, beyond, across the black void, toothpaste splooging onto the floor from the tube in her grip.

"Kitty?" Roxy said faintly.

"Damn," Katherine said. "I seriously need to see a therapist." Then she turned back to the sink and started to brush her teeth.

"Kitty, it's Roxanne!" She stepped forward, intending to get as close as possible this time, in case she needed a better grip, but her forehead struck an invisible wall.

Roxy yelped in pain, and Q moved quickly to her side, palming the surface with one hand. The rift between the two apartments widened. As the continuity of the two dwellings slipped a little, Roxy's floor rose slightly above Kitty's, a void still in between.

Q quickly grabbed his bazooka, flipped up a harpoon

attachment, and pulled its trigger. The projectile went flying into Kitty's bathroom, its hook crashing against the wall
and leaving white, powdery scratches in a trail as it failed
to take hold until it was at towel-rack level. Kitty froze
midbrushstroke, and she stared at the hook jiggling and
tugging against its meager hold. The splice in time began
to weaken. She took a deep breath, looked back at herself
in the mirror, and calmly spat her toothpaste out into the
bowl.

Total chaos was erupting on Roxy's side. Q had wrapped
the cable around his metal-gloved hand and, while Mason
commandeered the back of the cable, he used his other
hand to strike at the wall with some sort of electronic
pickax, struggling to chip chunks of opalescence out of
the surface before him.

"She's double-, maybe triple-insulated. She's trapped in
some kind of box," he grunted in explanation.

His feet lost traction and he gave ground; Louise let Vesper go, and both women grabbed the bazooka cable to try
to keep the rift from closing and Kitty's reality from slipping farther away. Q took his pickax with both hands and
just started whaling away at the wall, prismatic slivers flying in every direction.

Kitty languidly dabbed a towel against her mouth,
looked at the frenetic activity across the way, and said, "A
television wall? Awwww, Leooooo," as if she'd just realized her delightful boyfriend had secretly installed a fabulous present. She pulled her smartie off the side of the sink
and checked it, then sat down on the lid of the toilet and,
with a delighted smile on her face, proceeded to watch
them flail.

"Change channel," she said loudly, frowning when, of
course, nothing happened but the team slipping farther
backward and off-kilter, sweating, panicking, and shouting
all at the same time.

Roxy was yelling her name again, trying to explain at

the top of her lungs in the midst of the chaos that, no, this wasn't a "television wall." And then the oddest thing happened. Kitty looked at Roxy and the others and then looked at Q. She stepped in front of him.

Q shouted instructions over his shoulder to Roxy as Kitty walked right up to the wall, the toes of her shoes actually hanging over the precipice. He turned back from the team to face her, and the two of them made eye contact. Kitty sucked in a quick breath of air and reached out to touch his sweaty face. He froze. And then, without warning, the cable they'd been trying to anchor for so long in an effort to keep the chasm open and the layers of time aligned snaked through everyone's hands.

Q reacted first. He took the pickax and, swinging with all his might, slammed its point as hard as he could into the invisible wall, clinging to it while everyone else went flying backward in a disorganized pile of bodies. Katherine stared at him, hanging as he was by one arm and the handle of the ax, then completely freaked. She grabbed her smartie and frantically pressed at the screen.

As she watched the team react she slowly became more hysterical. "Pick up, pick up, pick up," she babbled into her smartie as they rose and dusted themselves off. Tears streaked down her face. She bent over at the waist, looking as if she might hyperventilate. Roxy called out to her again, to no avail.

And then the chasm finally collapsed, the bouncing-around sounds of displaced time crashing around them all as the pressure ripped a horizontal line from Kitty's bathroom all the way to the end of her adjoining bedroom. Q turned his head away to shield his face but held fast to his pickax, while everyone else struggled to grab and hold down the harpoon cable, which Louise had managed to retrieve. They began to lose ground.

Kitty screamed at the top of her lungs and got into the bathtub. She bobbled her smartie, swiped her forearm across her face to clear off the dust and the tears, and said. "Redial . . . Leo, Leo, Leo, Leo, please wake up. Where *are* you?"

The top halves of Kitty's bedroom wall and Roxy's living room wall collapsed. Plaster blew out so far it puffed back across the bathroom's open doorway and spilled across the ground.

"Leo!" Kitty screamed into the smartie one last time, then seemed to give up on him. Roxy was crying as she watched her friend's frightened face, and she was still watching when something in Kitty's expression changed. It was as if Roxy were actually witnessing the wheels in her friend's head turning—or screeching to a halt. In the bedroom, the glowing blue screen flickered, and the wall clock switched to 11:58.

Everything seemed to go quiet. Kitty sniffed quietly, her body relaxing. She stared down at her smartie, and it looked as though her eyes were fighting to stay open. It seemed as if the destruction around her didn't exist, as if she were somewhere else—somewhere in the spot between a second before midnight and the first moment of a new day, a speck of time so tiny you could never really count it; it would have passed before the thought was even complete. Roxy watched the clock in stunned silence as it turned to 11:59. Her lids half-closed, Kitty got out of the bathtub and walked into her bedroom, moving through a cloud of plaster dust. Then, almost as if someone else were directing her, she lifted her arms like wings, closed her eyes, and dropped gently backward onto the bed, her hair and the silk robe billowing around her in angelic quiet. She was fast asleep by the time the wall clock read 12:01.

"Disengage!" Q yelled. He let go of the pickax stuck into Kitty's reality, and the team pulled as hard as they could, dislodging the harpoon. The projectile snaked back into the living room, and, like celluloid in a film projector snapped and gone horribly awry in the middle of a screening,

Roxy's apartment seemed to fly straight down while Kitty's
went up. Roxy couldn't have said who really moved, or if
everyone stood still, but the image of Kitty suddenly became very small and faraway, and then the rift went black
and Q, Mason, Louise, Vesper, and Roxy were flung across
the living room floor.

Without a word, the five untangled themselves. It took
some time before they'd collected themselves enough to
reassemble around the table. Louise, who'd been looking
as dazed as the rest, seemed to force herself to focus, at which
point she sent a pointed look Vesper's way. The intern retreated to the kitchen, returning with a pitcher and a stack
of plastic glasses. "Um, orange juice, anyone?" she asked,
looking woefully at her boss.

Roxy nodded and accepted a glass to wash the dryness
out of her throat. No one really spoke; everyone was still
processing. She gulped the juice, fixating on the way Vesper was sulking over her orange juice duties.

Roxy's gaze shifted to Louise. Obviously, the woman
felt responsible for the kid's safety, but there had to be
more to it than that. Mason had described Louise's upbringing, the Sheffield family's emotional sterility; people
came and went and nobody seemed particularly in charge.
Roxy wondered if Louise's behavior toward the girl had
more to do with a familial desire for Vesper to be looked
after and protected, rather than a professional interest. It
reminded Roxy a little of the way Kitty always used to
fuss over her.

She put her glass down, the juice suddenly tasting too
acidic. With tears pricking at her eyes, she looked away
from the rest of the team, not wanting them to see how
frightened she was that their attempt had been rebuffed
when Kitty had seemed so close. They'd tried three times,
now. Leonardo Kaysar must have some inkling that things
were not normal with his experiment.

Roxy reined in her emotions and turned back to the

group in time to catch Louise shooting daggers at Q with her eyes. Vesper had abandoned the orange juice pitcher and was dabbing a wet paper towel over the cuts and blisters covering the specialist's arms. "Bummer about the pickax," she said, wrinkling her nose as she crumpled the paper towel in her hand.

Q finished downing his second glass of orange juice in one continuous swallow, at which point Louise took the glass out of his hand and literally dragged him to the side of the room. Vesper caught Roxy watching and repeated, "Bummer about the pickax, huh?" But Roxy didn't answer; Q and Louise were arguing, and she wanted to hear.

"What is this?" Louise hissed. "I put my reputation on the line for you. You've always been worth it in the past."

Q brushed plaster dust off one shoulder, and a white cloud rose around the two of them.

"What happened?" his sister pushed. "You lost focus, didn't you? Did you let up? Why?"

Roxy pretended to be fully engrossed in shaking out her own clothes, but really watched the siblings. Q's brow furrowed. He seemed lost in thought and a little . . . awed, perhaps?

Louise cocked her head and stared at him. "What happened?" she asked again, though in an entirely different tone. "Are you all right?"

"I think so. That girl . . ."

"Kitty?"

"She touched my face."

"Uh-huh. And?"

"She was very . . . present."

Louise arched an eyebrow.

"I don't know what else to call it." Q took a deep breath and seemed to snap out of his daze. "You know I've done a lot of time hacking. Granted, I've never pulled someone who was firewalled onto a parallel layer in a completely different time frame, but . . . well . . . it's just that the subjects don't normally feel so 'present' until they're on the same layer as you. She felt . . . different. I mean, I could really feel her hand against my face."

"I see," said Louise.

Q took his sister by the shoulders. "No. Seriously. This is special. This is a special case."

Louise looked abruptly at Roxy, who totally failed at concealing the fact that she'd been listening. "Rox," she said. "What did it feel like when you took Kitty's wrist the time before?"

"What do you mean?"

"When you had hold of Kitty's wrist the time before this attempted extraction and you were trying to pull her over, what did it feel like?"

Roxy didn't remember it feeling like anything in particular, so she just shrugged.

Louise looked at Q, who'd gone all introspective again, and then her face seemed to soften, as if she'd just had some sort of epiphany. She did her clapping-schoolmarm thing. "Could we gather 'round, please?" she called to the rest of the team.

Mason came back from the kitchen with damp dish towels and passed them around. Roxy cleaned off her face while studying the fairly catastrophic damage in the wall on the far side of her living room, feeling an impressive amount of detachment.

Louise flapped her arms and cleared her throat and paraded around as if she were going to make a big speech; then she simply said, "Okay, so that didn't work."

Hooray for stating the obvious, thought Roxy. "What do you suggest next?"

"Well, obviously, this is no ordinary hack job. Kaysar's no amateur. He's invented half of the technology and probably ninety percent of the improvements used by everyone in the profession. We have no idea what new tech or variables we're up against, or what he's going to come up with next."

Roxy struggled not to snap at Louise. She preferred a little less analysis and a lot more rescuing. "We're in better shape than most would be." Between Mason's and Louise's connections with the government—necessary, considering their previous jobs had been to keep time lines as they were originally intended and lived, or as close as possible— and Louise's brother's knowledge of the underground freelance community, at least this team had the best smartie cartridges money could buy, and the most tricked-out readers themselves. That was something. Wasn't it? *Wasn't it?* She sighed and tried her best to remain Zen.

"My point is that after several failed attempts, where we've gone wrong is in not fully understanding the nature of the beast. We need to slow down."

"Slow down?" Roxy yelped. "There's no slowing down. There's definitely no slowing down. Who knows what Kaysar has planned for her? What if he knows we tried to hack his loop? What's he going to do next? What if he moves her?"

Q nodded. "I'm with Roxy on this." He picked up his bazooka and began dusting it off and examining the damaged harpoon attachment.

"All you're going to do by hacking into her world again and again like this is make her think she's completely insane. I personally think a Katherine Gibbs in a sanatorium in the present is not much better than a Katherine Gibbs in an endless loop not of her own making in the future," Louise said.

Q looked nonplussed. "So, what do you suggest?"

His sister cleared her throat. When she looked at him this time, it was more as if she were looking at his ear than making actual eye contact. "The first stage would be to develop a deeper relationship with her. She's blank, and she's not even aware of it. She's clearly *been* blanked somehow. But if we postulate that whatever was in her before is still in there, then she just needs something or someone to draw it out. What's stronger than a weapon?" She looked around.

"Is that a rhetorical question?" Vesper asked eagerly.

"No. What's stronger than a bazooka, a smartie, and a crowbar? Those things have a specific action-reaction relationship, a generally consistent one. You blast a bazooka at a person's head, that head will explode every time. Cause and effect, always the same. But when we're looking to create a personality shift as well as a time shift . . . well, people can influence and be influenced by"—she stuck her index finger in the air and nodded—"*other people.*"

Q sighed. Everyone waited.

"Not bazookas. *People,*" Louise repeated. She narrowed her eyes and studied each of her teammates carefully, pausing with her stare locked on her brother's face. "Or *a person.*"

He looked up at her, and his eyes suddenly widened.

Roxy took that moment to speak—or, rather, spew. "Louise, we agreed about this before we made our first contact: even if we figured out how, we aren't allowed to enter her loop. We discussed it a million times. Believe me, I'd like nothing better than to go in after her, to find her future and redevelop a relationship with her there, but I thought everyone said ours and Kitty's pasts are too intertwined to share that reality, and that by extension any such attempt would throw us all onto random wires in random realities and—"

"Breathe," Mason said, gripping his girlfriend's shoulders.

Roxy exhaled. "Sorry. Tense. I'm very, very tense."

Louise nodded. "I'm not disagreeing with you. That is all true. That is why I'm proposing using a third party without past attachment."

"Hey, that's me, right?" Vesper asked, leaping from her chair. "I've never met her. I'm a third party!" The girl's face fell as she watched Louise's head swivel in the direction of her brother. "Oh."

Q's hands froze in midcleaning of his bazooka. He stared at his sister. "Louise? Are you kidding me? I don't do relationships," he said. He looked around at the rest of the group. "Do you know what this would take? I'm just a . . . just a . . . For God's sake! What do you think I am?"

"She said you were the best," Mason remarked quietly. "And we need the best."

The two men studied each other but didn't seem to come to any happy conclusions.

"For God's sake!" Q blustered again, apparently too gob-smacked by his sister's suggestion to come up with anything else.

Louise waved a dismissive, languid hand in the air. "He had a bad experience."

"I don't do relationships. I'm a simple mechanic," Q repeated. "A time mechanic, an anomaly specialist." He raised his bazooka and everybody ducked. "When they say I'm the best, they're not talking about dance moves. They're not talking about small talk."

Louise waved off his objections. "Get to know her before you take her dancing. And as for small talk—"

"Oh, you are *kidding* me!" Q waved the bazooka erratically in the opposite direction. Everybody ducked again.

"Do I look like I'm kidding?" Louise retorted. "Listen, we just need to find one teensy-weensy moment in her week where Kitty is not under Leonardo Kaysar's absolute influence. When we find that downtime, you step in. Talk to her a little. Get to know her. She'll start trusting you; she'll *like* you; she'll start listening to what you have to say. And then . . . boom! She has a context for understanding why people are breaking into her bathroom trying to take her to another place and time. And because of you, she'll get why this is a good thing. Then we can bring out the tools and you can start blowing things up again. Okay?"

Q stared at his sister with an incredulous look on his face. "No. Uh-uh. Not gonna happen."

Roxy leaped up and went to him. "Please," she said. "Please help us." She put her hands on his.

Vesper gasped, clasping her own hands. It was the last sound for a while, as a hard silence fell over the room. Q looked at Vesper, whose eyes looked like they were going to pop out of her skull. Then he reluctantly looked at Roxy. Roxy sniffled. Q softened. Then she blinked.

"Oh, shit," he muttered, glancing in terror at Mason.

Mason shrugged, knowing the power of his girlfriend's eyes.

Q looked back at Roxy. A single tear slipped slowly down her cheek. She totally had him.

Just then, an enormous rumble passed through the apartment. The top portion of the entire side of the unit crumbled and collapsed inward, and the roof above the hole buckled and bowed.

"That's unfortunate," Louise said in the understatement of the year.

Roxy glared at her.

Q pulled out his smartie and punched something in. "I've got some guys who handle this kind of repair and cleanup."

A pall fell over the room. The window of opportunity had collapsed like the wall, closing in on the likelihood of his accepting the new terms of his job, and Roxy knew it. She began to cry for real. Mason turned away without another word. Vesper sat down in her chair with a *thunk*.

Only Louise seemed unperturbed. And she apparently knew her brother best, because after he'd dialed up his cleaner friends and made his request, heaved an enormous sigh, packed up the last of his equipment, and done just about everything else there was to do except say good-bye and walk out through the door, he very pointedly cleared his throat.

"Okay, I've given it some thought," he said. "And, frankly, I don't feel particularly happy about the outcome of plan A. I'd like to see this thing through. I'll do what we have to do."

Roxy squealed. "I knew you weren't the sort of man who just waltzes in, blows out a wall, and takes off!"

"I said I didn't dance," Q warned.

Everyone, of course, burst into cheers, doing ridiculous things like slapping him on the back with glee. All except Mason. But as Q held up his hand, the women all fell silent again.

"I just want you to know, however, I'm doing it my way. First of all: Lou, you're going to have to let me use Vesper on the future layer. This is a complicated project, and if you don't want me to bring in an unknown assistant, she's the only party here without ties to Kitty's past wires."

Vesper screamed at the top of her lungs, then slapped her hand over her mouth as she caught the look in Louise's eyes. Her boss folded her arms across her chest, but to her credit, she didn't automatically say no.

Roxy would have liked to scream too. *She* wanted to go and assist. *She* wanted to do the work to get her friend out. A smartie coupled with a powerful nanoliquid transmitted via a mechanism called a "finger punch" effected the most powerful known method of time-wire travel available, and it had been the original plan, not busting through the walls of time and space. The downside was that the finger-punch method was incredibly hard on the body and required ultimate fitness. Roxy had spent hours—*hours*—at the gym to prepare herself, only to find that she couldn't be directly involved in the rescue the way it might now take place. Mason felt similarly horrible, she was sure, being unable to do the grunt work. When they'd first started trying to recover Kitty, they'd had no idea what they'd be up against. In hindsight perhaps it had been silly to ignore the possibility that their relationships with Kitty were far too close for the tech to function properly without all sorts of devastating ripple effects.

At least I have really tight abs, Roxy thought forlornly.

After a really long silence, Louise glanced at her brother and then the intern, and she said sternly, "One mistake and I'm pulling you out; you got that? When you're in the future, you do only—but everything—Walter asks you to do. When you're here with me, you do what I tell you. If there is even one argument or one screwup, it's over. You got that?"

The intern enthusiastically raised her fingers in a Boy Scout salute. "I swear, Louise. I swear it. You are going to be seriously shocked and awed—in a good way, though! I mean that in the best possible way. You are going to be *so* proud."

Louise made a show of rolling her eyes at Vesper's overblown earnestness, but she crooked her elbow around Vesper's neck and gave her something close to a hug.

Q cleared his throat. "There's something else. I don't know what you have in mind to get Kitty to talk to me once I'm in her world, but let me make this clear: I'm not doing myself up like Leo. No metrosexual makeover, no etiquette coaching, no bullshit. You can just get yourself someone else if you don't like what I have to offer, or if she doesn't want to have anything to do with me."

Vesper choked on her own spit. "I can't imagine *that* will be a problem," she whispered.

"A lot of unimaginable things happen every day," Roxy replied, though trying to stay optimistic.

"Don't worry, Rox," Vesper said, her eyes glued on Q as he talked plans with Mason and Louise. "Just think about how psyched your friend's going to be after we get her out of this mess. Leonardo Kaysar, you're going *down*."

Roxy followed Vesper's gaze and watched Q shake hands with Mason. "I hope so. Because friends don't let friends marry guys in the future who murdered them in the past."

CHAPTER FIVE

"Vesper, be on time," Q muttered, willing his smartie to ring. "Don't let me down." He'd hoped for a call by now. This whole thing could easily degenerate into amateur hour. He wasn't exactly bringing his own pro game, playing to his strengths. Not by choice, of course.

Finding Kitty's "downtime" had taken some doing. Q had analyzed her daily schedule quite thoroughly and, opposite what he'd expected, she did indeed have several pockets of freedom. Granted, these pockets were lodged in between extremely important appointments, suggesting that as long as those appointments were securely anchored, no one needed to worry about the rest. He wondered if maybe that was the point, that maybe the wiggle room was specifically designed to see how the subject would react.

In the end, Q had decided to set up an intersection with Kitty in the outside world, away from her apartment, for obvious reasons. But, as the thwarted rescue attempt proved she didn't adapt well to the wholly unexpected, he'd figured the best approach was to develop a plausible scenario that he would make her think was scheduled in her smartie.

Since he'd started tailing Kitty in the future, he'd watched carefully from afar as she went about what appeared to be a carefully structured week. She'd become engaged to Kaysar on three consecutive Thursdays, and on three consecutive Fridays had gone into some dance hall to celebrate each "special moment." He'd kept his distance so far, but he guessed that once inside her engagement party, she celebrated each week with all the innocent enthusiasm of someone experiencing that joy for the very first time. He'd noted her patterns, followed her schedule, memorized her routes. He had photos of her entering and exiting every building she visited in the week, had become familiar with what she wore each day, and could even anticipate some of her movements based on a mixture of recollection and simply knowing her body language.

The only snippet of inconsistency Q had so far detected that was put forth by the experiment itself was when Kaysar sent her to a psychologist named Dr. Greeley. It wasn't always at the same time, and since Katherine didn't spend a lot of time in his office when she went, it seemed like it might be an "as needed" sort of thing related to keeping her mind compromised. By the beginning of his fourth week of research, Q felt as though he could have lived the week for her. But whenever the repetition started to seem intolerably ridiculous, he simply had to get close enough to catch a glimpse of her open, trusting face to remember how tragic and serious the situation truly was.

A wave of adrenaline swept through Q's system as Katherine Gibbs came into view. He tucked himself a little farther back in the alcove of the unleased building he'd been using as his vantage point, and watched. Kitty wandered down the street just ahead, then stopped short and stared into one of the shops midway down the block.

As far as he could tell from all of this reconnaissance, this was one of a handful of time slots when no one seemed to expect her to be doing something specific. Whether this gap in her schedule was an oversight or part of Kaysar's research plan, Q couldn't know. What he could posit from the girl's almost robotic nature was that Leonardo wanted her as blank as he could possibly get her. Sticking Kitty in a controlled week that looped over and over made for a pretty useful study subject. No variables to worry about cluttering up the results.

The most interesting free slot was Friday, when Kitty walked home, having left early from work to get ready for her engagement party. Interestingly, in that free time, the girl still seemed to keep to a schedule and do the same things. She went window-shopping on Grant Street and stood in front of the New Age crystal shop, with its weird little bundles of herbs and vials of oils, and stared through the window for what seemed like an oddly long amount of time for no particular purpose before she continued down the street toward the high-end jewelry stores, looked briefly at the jewels, and then headed home.

"See the shop," Q muttered, watching the way her purse swung carelessly in her grip as she focused on the storefronts lining the block. "It's fascinating, but you don't go in. Don't know why, but you never, ever go in. Check your smartie. There you go. Aaaannnnd . . . walk briskly, now; don't want to be late." He tapped on the screen of his smartie and made a quick note that today's beginning was almost—if not precisely—the same as always.

Slipping from the alcove to the sidewalk, Q kept a measured distance from the girl, refusing to rush. He knew the team was chomping at the bit back in the present, and there was definitely danger in waiting too long: there was a reason the wall between Kitty's bathroom and Roxy's living room across the two layers of time had been strengthened, last he'd checked it. He'd be willing to bet that Leonardo Kaysar didn't know that a rescue attempt had been made by people actively trying to extract Kitty, but the man must have suspected that something in his technology was compromised. The last thing the team needed was Kaysar getting more suspicious.

Q slowed down and let Kitty disappear from view. He knew where she was headed, and he knew that Vesper would be intercepting her this time before she got in a motocab to go home. He knew a hell of a lot about this girl—he had to, if his sister had pegged the situation right and this job was less about who had the better tech than who had the better link with Katherine Gibbs's mind. How ironic: with the success of the project entirely on his shoulders, Q was arriving on the job feeling more clueless than he'd ever felt in his life. He'd be forced to stretch himself.

Part of Q rejoiced. It was unlikely he'd ever get another chance to go up against the best. The challenge appealed to him, not to mention the value of whatever technical skills he might learn during the project. He'd already seen some new factors and tech in that first attempt at extraction. That being said, Q was also pissed off. What he was being asked to do here required many talents only tenuously connected with his actual skill set and past experience—and not only that, he was being asked to develop a relationship with this woman. He'd been *guilted* into doing that. The whole thing felt way too personal.

Of course he had emotions; of course he had *feelings*: he was empathetic, he was sympathetic, he was intuitive, and, frankly, he was something of a softy. He didn't swagger about his day, maintaining a screw-everybody blankness in his expression and speaking in terse sentences. He was not that kind of guy. But the required connection in order to correctly extract this victim from her loop . . . frankly speaking, it required an untenable violation of his personal space.

Q now stood casually across the street observing from behind an adapter kiosk. He ran through the options in his head once more. They wanted him to get inside Kitty's brain first before pulling her out, but the more he thought about it, the more he considered all he'd seen in her repeated week, the more he wanted to simply cut to the chase and just try a classic time-travel punch. They hadn't been able to pull her through the wall across the wires, as they'd originally hoped, but there was little reason to believe there'd be any problems with jumping fully back and forth with her in tow—not with him doing the dragging, at least. He'd just get her out of the future and into the present; then they could all work on restoring her true self and removing the influence of Kaysar.

Of course, knowing Kaysar and his protections, that might not work; there could be some sort of new temporal defenses guarding Kitty and keeping her locked on this wire. He'd seen some definitely odd things while trying to pull her across that void. But if he couldn't get her off this slice of time right away, he still might be able to do it if he could get her away from her normal routine, away from Kaysar altogether; it was possible that the protections were time *and* space based.

Yes, he would try that. If a jump didn't work—one attempted when Kitty wasn't in Kaysar's immediate area and power—then and only then would he go that extra mile and get inside Miss Katherine Gibbs's brain, gaining her trust and hooking himself into her consciousness until he could convince her of what she did not see on her own— that her reality was an elaborate fake, a facade of a world and a time line that she lived over and over.

Q turned toward the sound of heavy pounding on the sidewalk behind him. Her black hair flopping in an uncombed mass behind her moto helmet, Vesper ran up the street. Panting between words, she doffed the helmet, thrust a bulging shopping bag at him and said, "One size fits all."

Q checked his smartie. "Nice timing. Are we ready with the set?"

Vesper's face glowed. "The office is good to go. Just for future reference, I think I'm gonna need a larger, ahem, discretionary fund. You know how it is. Bribes, threats, the usual."

He had to work to keep a straight face when he told her

to talk to Louise about that. Then he pulled a plastic-wrapped square from the bag, tore it open, and removed a lab coat. He shook the garment out, slipped it over his T-shirt, then raised his arms for Vesper's inspection.

"Yeah," she said with a pleased nod. "Looks good."

Q took off the coat and stuck it back in the bag before he took Vesper by the shoulders. Her eyes widened.

"Are you ready?" he asked.

"Absolutely."

"This is very delicate."

"I know," she said. "But we've talked it through a billion times."

"She needs to believe in you as someone in her normal network," Q said. "We want to get to the point where—"

"She knows that when I come into the picture to take her somewhere, she thinks she's supposed to go. I got it, I got it!" Vesper plunked her moto helmet back on. "Let's go. How tough can it be?"

"No." Q grabbed Vesper's arm. "Listen to me. You need to be focused. This isn't training; this is the real deal. You've *got* to be subtle enough, and you have to be that way from the start. You tell her that you were sent from the Kaysar Corporation to relay a schedule change, and that you're supposed to deliver her to a new appointment. Just like we discussed. That's it. Stick to the plan."

Vesper nodded, obviously intent on showing him she could be calm and serious, a professional. She followed him to the rented moto and got on behind him, handing him the spare helmet from a back hook. Q stamped down hard on the accelerator, and they took off in the direction Katherine Gibbs had walked. They passed her within five minutes, drove a couple extra blocks, and stopped. Q turned the moto and helmet back over to Vesper and put the lab coat back on.

"You've set your timer?" he asked.

She raised her smartie. "Yep."

"Door codes?"

"Yep." She wired the information to him.

"Go ahead. Go on and get things started."

Vesper grinned, then blazed off down the street, and Q turned toward the main entrance to the unassuming building in which the intern had leased them an office. A few more costume elements would be helpful to complete the effect, he decided. He clipped his smartie and a mini Maglite to his belt, and went in to prepare for Kitty's arrival.

The hallway leading up to the office was quiet. Q wondered if there were any other tenants on this floor, though it didn't matter either way. The office door opened without a problem. Desk, chair, sofa, coffee table. It was furnished in a modern style, clear acrylic and metal. No retro here. Probably cost too much for the developers to bother. At least the sofa, with its white plush cushions, looked sort of comfortable. It was neither sterile enough for a medical doctor's office nor homey enough for a psychiatrist's den, but hopefully Kitty wouldn't notice or have an opinion either way.

Q moved the chair to a different spot, then pulled from Vesper's shopping bag the rest of the props he'd been given, raising his eyebrow at the selection of odds and ends she'd obviously rushed to buy: a bottle of water, two cheap drinking glasses, a box of empty files, and some floral potpourri cubes that he immediately tossed into the trash can.

His smartie beeped: a text from Vesper indicating her arrival—and Kitty's. There wasn't time to set up any voice recognition with the tech here; she must have texted from the stairs, because the door-scan chime followed within seconds. Q froze, looking around at the office. He flung the dust protectors off the furniture and crammed them between the wall and the back of the sofa, rethought the potpourri and rescued the cubes from the garbage can, then tumbled them on the corner of the desk, smoothed down his hair, and opened the door.

Katherine Gibbs stood in front of him, just over the threshold, with only a hint of puzzlement in her eyes. Just a few inches of air swirled between them. No wrinkle appeared on her flawless face. No sign of real anxiety. No sign of recognition, either. Q recognized her, however. He thought of the feel of her palm against his cheek.

Vesper broke the spell by whipping something out of her cargo pocket behind Kitty's back—a small sign—and pressing it against the wall by the door. Kitty stepped into the office and Vesper closed the door, leaving Kitty and Q alone.

"Doctor," Kitty said, although in a way that suggested a question. She obviously didn't recognize him, but something inside of her from all those weeks of repetition must have felt that seeing a psychiatrist was an accepted and normal thing to do. It reminded Q that she still retained a sense of the familiar; his job was to make the things that seemed accepted, normal, and familiar those that were actually real.

They stood in silence for a moment. Was she always waiting for a trusted source to take up the leash and lead her to the next encounter in this life? Was she waiting for him to take the next step? The number of nanoseconds that had passed between them would have seemed very strange, uncomfortable between most people. But Katherine waited for him to do something; he waited to see what she'd do.

Finally her eyes flickered with a sudden realization, and she pulled her smartie from her bag and reviewed the screen. She looked up, a little wrinkle creasing the middle of her forehead. "Oh." She stared at him. "I'm supposed to . . . I have an appointment?" She looked around in confusion.

"This was a supplementary appointment," Q said gently.

She looked relieved. "Oh. I thought I'd messed something up again for a minute."

It was too easy. She waited with a hint of a calm smile upon her mouth, her expression clear and open. She was obviously willing to trust him.

"Do you want to begin? Should I sit?" she asked.

"Uh, no." Q cleared his throat, then unclipped the mini Maglite from his belt and switched it on. He hoped this didn't seem too ludicrous, too little like a real doctor's office. He backed her up until she was resting against the desk. "So . . . look at me."

She opened her eyes wide as he swept the light across her face. He was amazed how eager she was to help blind herself. Blanked. How horrible.

He clipped the Maglite back on his belt and removed the stylus from his smartie. "Say 'ah.'"

"Aaaaah."

Using the stylus as a tongue depressor, he glanced down Kitty's perfectly normal throat. As he removed the stylus she asked, "Did you sterilize that thing?" She looked around the room. "You're supposed to be a psychiatrist."

Good. She still questioned things. Q slipped his punch glove on his index finger. Mason had programmed the straightest line to their wire into his smartie, and Q prayed it would work now. He was going to do something a little against plan.

He placed his thumbs on Kitty's temples and pressed gently. "Does this hurt?"

"No."

"How about this?"

Her eyes followed his movements as he walked back and forth in front of her, surveying her, though she kept her head perfectly straight. "Uh-uh." But when he ran his fingers down her throat, her eyes went wide and she shivered. She said, "Sorry, you just gave me the chills is all."

"I'm sorry, too," he said. Then he punctured her neck with the needle.

The result was not what he expected. A fizzing sizzling

like the noise of a frying egg sounded, then a pop, and Q's smartie started smoking. Kitty's legs buckled, and Q helped her sit on the top of the desk.

"Nurse!" she yelped.

Luckily, Vesper did not appear. "Er, sorry . . . a little electrical problem," he said.

"Is something wrong?" Kitty was sniffing the air and looking confused. "Is something . . . frying?"

Hopefully not your brain, he thought.

She giggled. "I see funny things."

Q ran his hand over her forehead, brushing the hair away from her face. She felt warmer than she had. He went to the coffee table, opened a bottle of water, and moistened his coat sleeve with it, then pressed the soaked fabric gently against her skin.

"What do you see, Kitty?" he asked as he led her to the sofa and eased her onto the cushions. He lifted her feet up and stuck a throw pillow behind her head.

"Roxy's got a date with Leonardo, but he's too busy shooting me dead!"

Q's hand froze. "Who's Roxy?" he asked.

"I have no idea!" she burbled, giving a trill of laughter. Her mirth broke off, and she suddenly frowned. "Hey. There's Mason. Why is there a fishbowl on his head? Hey, there's me! Wait a minute, where am I? What's happening? Make it stop. Stop the moto! Stop the moto! I don't want to take this trip!" Kitty struggled to sit up. Q tried to push her back down, but she struggled against him, panicky. "Who are you?"

"I'm Q. I'm a friend."

She became very still. "I don't feel good," she said in a small voice. She blinked rapidly several times; then her expression went through myriad changes once more. "Take your hands off me," she said, her voice like steel. "Take your hands off me and step away. This. Second."

Q pulled his hands back and retreated.

Katherine stood up and steadied herself against the wall. She stared at Q with a woozy expression. "You." She swallowed and swayed a bit. "You are a *fake* doctor."

"You are perceptive," he said, meaning it.

She contemplated that, and, oddly, the corner of her mouth quirked up. "Thanks."

"My pleasure." Then, realizing he should try to maintain an air of authority, he added, "I am a *kind* of doctor, though."

"Oh. You are . . . most unusual."

"As are you."

"Yeah. My head's totally messed up," she admitted. She seemed to be recovering a little. The swaying had stopped, and her eyes looked just a little bit clearer.

"You're aware of this?"

"Of course."

"How aware?" he asked, noticing that the fear and suspicion she'd displayed moments earlier was already evaporating.

Kitty sat down on the sofa and crossed her legs. "Well, it's more like being aware that I'm . . . *not* very aware of things."

"Can you be more specific?"

"I wish I could. It's just all . . . black, what came before. Isn't this all in my files?"

"Of course," Q hurried to say. "I was just checking on your progress. For Leo."

Damn, the idea of this poor girl unwittingly (albeit happy in her ignorance, theoretically) screwing her own murderer disgusted and saddened him on the most fundamental of levels. His presence and experience during the burgeoning time-travel boom had shown Q how easy it was to lose control of one's destiny. He'd seen how easy it would be to lose the things that mattered most with just a flick of a wrist, a jab of a needle, and the application of some as-yet-unknown work of brilliance issuing forth from the Kaysar Corporation. And this girl was now proof.

Q made a show of tugging his lab coat back into place to remind her he was a doctor; then he sat down next to her on the couch and pulled her wrist toward him. He pressed his fingers against it, checking her pulse. They stared at each other as he counted.

He looked down and smoothed his thumb across the underside of her arm. When he finally let go, Kitty pulled her hand back close to her body, looking up at him with bewilderment. Staring into her eyes, he thought about how he'd come to this place: sitting in this office with some girl, pretending to be someone he wasn't. It wasn't guilt or social pressure that had sealed the deal; it was something more. This attempt to extract Katherine Gibbs from Kaysar's loop experiment was about saving one particular girl, yes. But when he really thought about it, as he'd thought about it the first few nights after he'd agreed to take on the case, Q knew that the quest was more than that. He was attempting to save the world. The loop technology imprisoning Katherine Gibbs was the beginning of the end; Kaysar was stretching too far. That was why Q had *really* agreed to do this, whatever it might entail, whatever it required of his mental and physical abilities. If he could figure out how to save Katherine Gibbs, he could figure out how to save everybody from such meddling.

She was still staring at him, waiting for some kind of response—waiting for a cure, as it were, though she didn't know it. "Your pulse is normal," Q lied. Her heart was racing, which was only normal, considering she'd almost just had her brain fried. His own heart was beating fairly fast.

"You see a lot of messed-up people. Bet you're not messed up, though," Kitty said.

He laughed and remarked, "I've got a whole grocery bag of issues. Whether or not I'm 'messed up,' though . . .

you'd have to ask my sister." He was trying to think of some other pretext on which to examine her that wouldn't earn him a slap and a lawsuit before his brain reminded him that this was all about developing a rapport. This was about the mental, not the physical. For some reason it was tough to keep focused. He kept wanting to touch her.

Kitty considered. "Maybe you have issues, but you're very handsome."

"And you're very sweet. But everyone tells you that," he replied.

"Yes, they do, don't they?" she muttered in a bored voice, her vibe turning negative.

It was time to change the subject. "I'm going to run some cognitive tests here," he said on a whim.

"Okay."

"Tell me about your week," Q suggested.

Kitty did a double take. "My week?"

"Yes. Start with Monday. What did you do on Monday?"

"Well, Monday I will go to the—"

"No, what did you do *last* Monday?"

She shrugged. "I really don't remember. That's part of my problem, you know." She regarded him carefully. "You have my file."

"Of course. Go ahead, then. On Monday you will . . . ?"

"Um . . . on Monday . . . hold on a second." She went and retrieved her smartie, poked it with its stylus, and pulled up the schedule of her week to come.

Q held out his own smartie, indicating she should share the information. "Could you . . . ?"

She looked a little taken aback. "Do you think this will help?"

"No question. I have a new idea for helping you fix your brain. It involves . . . memory practice."

She brightened. "I'd be very interested in that," she said, pointing her smartie at his and transferring her schedule.

He punched and twisted buttons and dials, made his way through her listed week. The details were incredibly sparse, mostly a peppering of references to waiting for a receptionist to call her down to waiting motos. There were notes about the level of formality of each event she was to attend, but not descriptions, save for a suggested outfit for each.

Q finished scanning the info. "No plans at all for the week after this one? Any thoughts about what you'd like to do?"

"That week I'd like to . . ."

He glanced up. Katherine's mouth was slightly open. Her eyes narrowed as if she were searching for thoughts that wouldn't come.

"That week . . ." She looked up at him and said in a small voice, "I don't know."

"You're drawing a complete blank about any plans whatsoever for the following week?" he prompted, then watched her carefully as he formulated his next sentence. "Maybe you'll just do the same things you're doing this week? Any thoughts?"

"I don't know *what* I'm doing that week," she said huffily, "because next week hasn't happened yet."

"What did you do the week before last?" Q asked.

She didn't answer.

"What's in your smartie?" Q asked.

"It doesn't keep that stuff."

"What?"

"Smarties don't keep track of what's already happened, silly."

"Yeah, Kitty, they do," he replied.

They contemplated each other in silence. "Why would you call me Kitty?" she whispered, standing up.

"It suits you more than Katherine."

"Nobody calls me Kitty."

"Your real friends do." Then, suddenly unsure what to

say and worried that he was going to lose her, he blurted before he could stop himself, "You're really stunning—gorgeous, you know that?"

"Yeah," Katherine said dismissively. "I know that. But my brain is still on the fritz."

"You could say that," he agreed sadly.

"Bummer." She looked up at Q. "You're a man," she said at last.

He cleared his throat.

"Can you think of any reason why someone might . . . love you less if you were more?"

"If you were more?" he repeated, not understanding.

"Yeah. Something's been bothering me." She hesitated. "Let's say that my brain gets fixed. Would I be a different person?" She hesitated for a moment, then: "Would my boyfriend still want me? Would Leo still love me?"

He doesn't love you now, Q wanted to rant.

"Because I'd really like to grow a personality, but I'm not entirely sure it's worth it." She stared off into space, her manner changed.

Her smartie alarm beeped, and she glanced at the screen. "I have to get ready for my party," she said.

Q shook his head, put his finger under Katherine's chin, and raised her face to his. "It's worth it, Kitty." Then, realizing he wasn't behaving the least bit like a doctor, he rose and stepped away from her.

"Listen, Kitty. I can tell from my . . . ministrations . . . that it's all in there. Your original personality, your memories, your emotions, et cetera—it's all just compartmentalized in there. Here's the important thing: keep an open mind. Embrace the unexpected, and things you don't understand. Be kinder to yourself. Stop thinking there's something wrong with you. Instead, embrace the possibility that something inside of you is being unfairly held back, and if you just let go . . . if you just let go . . ."

Kitty was looking at him with a kind of wonder on her face.

"Er, just let go," he finally said, not sure how far he should push.

"All right, Doctor. I can try."

"Just one more thing."

"Yes?"

"Don't tell your friends or your fiancé—"

She glanced down at the rock on her finger.

"Don't tell *anyone* what you are thinking. It needs to be an organic process without any external influences. Just let yourself . . . find yourself. Do you understand what I mean?"

Kitty frowned. "I think so. I mean . . . this sounds very promising."

"Just be willing to believe in what you once were."

She nodded, but fear was now faintly etched into her features.

Q impulsively took her hand, then covered the confusion that swept him by turning the gesture into a hearty doctor-patient double-grip handshake. "You're going to be fine, Kitty," he said softly. "You're going to be fine."

And then he was staring into her eyes. They were the bluest he'd ever seen. And before he could think, he began to wonder what her lips would feel like on his. She was dating someone in this reality; she was taken; but it was only her enemy. She was in Kaysar's power and deserved so much more.

He leaned forward, and Kitty didn't seem to object, and he was just about to—

"Dr. Van Heusenfleugen!" Vesper crashed through the door with a bang, a nurse's hat falling over one eye. She righted the cap and cleared her throat. "I think we're done here," she said. She shoved a smartie at Kitty, who seemed happy to give a fingerprint for ostensible payment verification. Vesper gave Q a pointed look and beamed Kitty an electronic business card. "Call this number if you need anything."

"If you need *anything*," Q echoed, trying not to want to stay.

Katherine nodded, collecting her coat and purse. She turned at the last minute. "What did you say your name was?"

"Dr. Q . . ." Trying not to roll his eyes at the ridiculousness of it, he muttered, "Van Heusenfleugen."

"That's funny. I don't remember . . ." she said, cocking her head and staring into space. Then she gave up and looked back at Q. "Whatever. Good-bye, Doctor."

"Until we meet again," he replied.

Looking woozy, she vanished through the front door.

He immediately turned on Vesper. "You weren't supposed to come in yet," he growled, unsure exactly why he was so annoyed.

"But my entrance was perfectly timed," the girl said, flapping her smartie in front of Q's face. "We want her to get home at the same time she'd get home if she'd done her full walk, right? The motocab driver is right downstairs waiting for her to come out. We're exactly on time. *Exactly*."

"I . . . I wasn't finished with her. You have to allow for unforeseen circumstances," he lectured.

"Unforeseen circumstances? Is that what kisses are?"

Q stopped in his tracks. "I didn't kiss her. There was no kissing."

"You would have. You were moving in."

"I was not 'moving in,'" he snapped.

"Dude," she replied. "You *so* were."

Q just glared.

Vesper cocked her head, not giving an inch. "Oh. You're actually kind of pissed, aren't you?" she suddenly realized.

Q cleared his throat. "Okay, you know what? You're right. Yes, it's possible I was . . . 'moving in.' If I was, this is a good learning experience. This is an excellent example of how business and personal sides of life come into close contact. *Never* cross completely over—that's something we should all know. So . . . thank you. Thank you, Vesper, for stopping me in the event that perhaps I was leaning in more than I realized."

Vesper gave a brilliant smile. "No worries."

They continued walking to the moto.

"That being said . . . what the *hell* was that about a 'Dr. Van Heusenfleegen'? The name we discussed was Dr. Fulton. You cannot change things up on a whim like that."

The intern swallowed hard. "I knew she wouldn't know the difference, and I just wanted to put my own spin on things." She raised her index finger, trying to look convincing. "Mind you, changing the name did not affect the placement of nanoseconds, and I thought such a foreign name gave the whole gig more of an air of authenticity."

"A foreign name . . . a name I can barely pronounce? I might have laughed. That would have been completely inappropriate! Not to mention it takes at least an extra nanosecond to get it out of my mouth."

"Your mouth was thinking about something else," the intern muttered.

"What did you say?"

"Oh, nothing." She grinned at Q, her normal jovial nature clearly recovered. "By the way, it's Heusen*fleugen*. There's an umlaut—or was in the original. Two umlauts, actually. You need to kind of purse your lips to get the pronunciation right."

Q didn't smile and Vesper's face fell. "Sorry. It won't happen again," she said. "Are you going to tell Louise? She'll say I messed up."

"I'm not going to tell Louise. But this is a really serious

matter. Do you understand? I shouldn't have to worry about whether you're going to stick to the plan. It's incredibly dangerous."

Vesper nodded. "I understand." Then she pulled out her smartie and her nanoliquid punch. "You coming back with me, or are you just going to send a report?"

Q clicked his own smartie and positioned his punch at his neck. "I'm coming. I've got issues." He looked over and studied the girl's face. "You've been traveling a lot, by the way. How's your body holding up?"

"Hey, I'm fine. No worries." She socked him in the arm with her elbow. "I bet I'll smoke you on the way back."

"Front door?"

"You got it."

He grinned. They raised their smarties and their punches simultaneously, faced each other, and: "One . . . two . . . three!"

CHAPTER SIX

Q lay on the couch, trying not to look exhausted while the rest of the team discussed the project behind him. Beating Vesper back to the present had taken more out of him than he'd expected. He didn't normally do a lot of business in the present and wasn't used to making this many trips in a week, much less multiples per day. While he explained what had happened with Kitty, he'd actually had to work to conceal that he'd gotten slightly out of breath. He would definitely have to take a look at supplementing his diet and making sure he was stretching enough in the mornings. Maybe a few extra trips to the gym would be in order. Maybe—

"Fine?" Roxy repeated for something like the fourth

time since he'd come over to the couch, her voice raised. She was talking to Louise. Q glanced over his shoulder in time to see her storm over to the fishbowl and tap some flakes into the water. Again. "*Fine?*"

"Didn't she already feed Angus this morning?" Vesper whispered nearby.

Mason nodded. "When she's especially worried about Kitty she feeds the fish or changes the water."

"That can't be good for his life span."

"This fish has had as many lives as I hope Kitty still has left." And, raising his hand to shield the volume of his voice, Mason added, "I'm not actually sure it's even the same fish, given all the wires that have been crossed."

"*Fine?*"

Mason took a step forward, extending his hand with the palm up, as if he were approaching a rabid beast with a stun gun. "Don't freak out, Rox."

She froze, took an enormous breath, exhaled, and calmed herself. "I'm not freaking out," she said glumly. "I'm just saying that he took some unwarranted chances, and now, without any medical proof at all, he says she's fine."

Q sighed heavily and eased himself off the couch to grab his duffel bag.

"Electric-shock therapy wasn't exactly what we had in mind," Roxanne said pointedly to him. "Do you want to run this whole thing without any input from us?"

Louise rolled her eyes. "Rox, please."

Roxy turned from the fishbowl and put her hands on her hips. "He said the smartie was smoking after he tried to punch her out of that time. As in, there was a burning substance. *Smoking.*"

"Yeah, the smartie. Not her head," Louise said.

"It wasn't ideal," Q agreed, "but we learned something important. Her body chemistry is also firewalled. That's why the nanos in the punch couldn't activate properly."

He stepped in between the two women and put his arms around their shoulders. "I had to try it. You would have tried if you were around. There's nothing worse than going for a complicated solution, only to realize that the simplest trick of all would have saved a lot of headache."

"Fine. Well, your trick didn't work. So what's next?" Roxy said.

"I'll need to do a little work on this," Q said. "I'll clean it up and run Kitty through the psychiatrist drill a couple times. I want to see how much she retains from our meetings and which details are particularly sticky."

"Good idea," Louise said. "If we can pinpoint the soft spots in her memory, we're on our way to an effective punch-out."

Roxy chewed on her lower lip. "How long is this going to take? I mean, can you do the doctor thing more than once a week?"

"She gave me the general template of her week on her smartie, and I've been there for it, too, remember. I've figured out several times she's alone when I think I can get her away from Kaysar without suspicion. Of course . . . her smartie was practically empty. I think they come and get her for a lot of it. Or they're depending on the repetition to guide her."

The team broke up, and Mason headed for the kitchen while Louise started going through several files. Vesper came bounding down the stairs and slumped dramatically onto the sofa.

Q chuckled. "Don't you have homework of some sort?" he asked.

She stuck her index finger into her nurse's hat and tried to spin it like a basketball. "It took me, like, five minutes. I'm done. And I'm bored." She suddenly narrowed her eyes and leaned in close to him. "Hey, is there anything cool I could do to help? Something that doesn't involve chauffeuring or squeezing citrus fruit? Is there some, you know, *espionage activity* I could perform?"

"You're lucky Louise has allowed you to do as much as you've already done," Q said, giving her an annoyed glance as he rummaged around in his duffel bag for his minikit.

"She thinks I'm going to mess things up. I don't understand the point of getting an intern as brilliant as me and then not bothering to take advantage of my capabilities."

There was a pause and then Q said, "You know that my sister gets on your case because she believes in your potential, don't you? She only yells because she cares."

"She must care a lot," Vesper grumbled.

Frustrated beyond belief, Q reared back on his heels and dug both hands back in the bag for another look.

"Did she tell you I'm at the top of my class?" Vesper asked.

"If you only spend five minutes on your homework it's not going to stay that way."

She huffed. "Whatever."

Hearing the disappointment in Vesper's voice, Q looked up and softened. "It doesn't surprise me at all that you're at the top of your class. You're a smart girl, and you've done well for me so far—apart from the Boygenfloygen thing." He kicked his bag, and yelled, "Did somebody take my smartie minitools?"

Everybody looked up; nobody answered. Mason, Roxy, Louise, and Q all looked at Vesper. Louise got up from the table and went to Vesper with her arms crossed over her chest.

"Oh, crap," Q muttered, sorry to get the intern in trouble again.

"Vesper?" Louise asked.

Vesper hung her head. "It's still in my backpack. I needed it to jimmy the scanner on the moto."

"Why did you jimmy the scanner on the moto?" Louise asked in a scary-calm voice.

Vesper swallowed hard. "So we wouldn't leave a smartie trail. I fixed it when Q was done. Well . . . I think I fixed it."

Q struggled between admiration for her abilities and forethought, and a desire to join Louise and admonish the girl for her thoughtlessness. Louise seemed to have it covered.

"What if he'd needed it in a tight spot?" Louise yelled. "And how could you be sure that your smartie adjustments weren't leaving another trace of some kind or maybe triggering an alarm? That's not okay. It's just not." She suddenly collected herself and took a massive breath of air, releasing it in a slow, noisy gust. "Let's discuss this upstairs."

Vesper nodded and followed Louise up the stairs.

Q went to Vesper's backpack, unzipped it and could only sigh as he easily found the tools.

Roxy leaned against the bar next to him. "Q?"

"Yeah, Rox?"

"About earlier? I'm sorry if I'm being—"

"Don't worry about it." He gave her a smile.

"No, it's just . . ." She cleared her throat. "Kitty's really important to me. She was there for me in my absolute worst moments." She took him by the arms, and her gaze was a laser into Q's eyes. "She needs someone to protect her now. And that's you."

Q nodded, a little uncomfortable with the intensity of Roxy's emotions. Worse still, the woman suddenly launched herself at him and gave him a huge hug. "Thank you. Thank you so much. I wish I could do this, but since I can't, thank you so much. Please let's just get this done."

"Uh, of course." Q watched Mason staring at him from the kitchen with a sandwich in his hand, the lunch meat about to fall out of the bread and onto the floor. Under his displeased gaze, Q managed to detach the increasingly hysterical Roxy from his body, place her arms at her sides, and give her an awkward pat on the shoulder.

She managed a watery smile. "Sorry. That hug was, like, way too long. I just can't believe how close we are to pulling it off. When Kitty is home and safe and happy . . . well, then Mason and I can get on with our lives and everything's going to be amazing, and you're the guy to do it. You're the man."

Q watched Mason's eyes narrow, and then insult was added to injury as his meat slipped from his bread and hit the floor with a small *splug*. Mason swore, and Roxy turned and went to him.

Q shook his head. There were just way too many feelings in this project for it to be normal. He was used to working alone, acting impartially, and being ready for the unexpected. It wasn't as if he were the cold, emotionless sort; it was just that he was more used to compartmentalizing. Not in any ridiculous I-am-such-a-tormented-and-solitary-human-being sort of way, either, but in the kind of way that made it easy to get work done and not have to worry so intensely, like Mason and Roxy did about disappearing on each other. He worried about his sister, Louise, of course, but that was why they rarely worked on the same project: partly so that if one were in trouble, the other could get them out. Here she'd gone and begged him to do a project that involved getting, well, all involved. It was so unlike him. It was so unlike *her*. He wondered if it was due to the fact that her old partner, Mason, was the one doing the original asking.

They'd come to terms with their fairly cold lives, their few close human interactions, he and Louise. Their decisions to lead such lives had been made independently, of course, but being siblings with the exact same upbringing had made their like attitudes fairly predictable. People disappeared; they went away; they didn't come back. That was how it was growing up in the nascent stage of time travel and wire crossing, and that was the line of work they'd both chosen—wire crossing and time anomaly, where reality was precarious and life and love could be gained and lost in a time particle. It had taken him a while to realize that they'd likely chosen their jobs in the industry because it justified their choices to turn their backs on the very thing Mason and Roxy worked so hard to keep: intimacy.

Q watched Mason and Roxy start laughing as they replaced the dropped sandwich meat, and Mason held half out for his girlfriend. Roxy got a blob of mayo or mustard on her nose as she took a bite, and Mason sucked it off or kissed it off, or whatever it was exactly that happened before Q turned away feeling crankier than ever. Maybe *that* was why Mason was so hostile. He'd had to fight hard to get Roxy; he'd had to fight harder to keep her.

A lot of goddamn drama, Q thought. And before any of it could irritate him further, he grabbed his bag and punch and looked around for his smartie.

Mason caught him before he could head out.

Just great, Q thought, taking a seat.

"Can I talk to you a minute?" Mason asked, plunking down on a barstool, clearly not expecting an answer. "Your sister might be yelling at Vepser, but frankly, I think you deserve a little of the medicine."

Q narrowed his eyes and slowly leaned forward toward the other guy. "Excuse me?"

Mason shrugged his shoulders. "You went off plan. You went off plan and practically fried her. That's not what we discussed."

"If you're a halfway decent freelancer, you should know that much of what we do is determined in the field."

"I don't like what you're suggesting," Mason growled.

"I don't like what *you're* suggesting," Q answered.

Mason craned his neck, ostensibly to figure out whether Roxy was listening in; then he turned back to Q. "I trust

Louise," he said. "But I don't know you. I'm here to protect my girls, and my eyes will be on you twenty-four/seven." He tipped his head to one side. "Fair warning, is all." With that he got up and walked away.

Stupid smartie had better have enough juice left, because Q couldn't wait to get back to the future. "Why did I say I'd take this job?" he asked no one in particular,

"Because it's the right thing to do," Louise said, coming down the stairs. She took Mason's seat. "What was that all about? Everything okay?"

Q shrugged. "He's pissing on his territory, that's all. Speaking of which, maybe ease up on the kid."

"Vesper needs to understand that her ego could kill us all."

Q had to smile at that.

Louise pushed her brother's shoulder. "Maybe ease up on Mason. Give him some credit for getting out of your way as much as he has. It takes a lot of pride, you know."

"I'm just doing what I'm getting paid to do," Q said tightly, as he stood up and a wave of light-headedness nearly took him back down.

"You okay?" Louise asked.

"Yeah. I'm great."

She studied his face. "You're sure you don't want to stay here?"

"You know I'm not much for the present," he said, managing a smile. "I've got my place."

"You've got a coffin. It's not healthy."

"It's a *capsule*, Louise, if you don't mind. And don't pretend it's a weird, darkly meaningful choice when you know it's common for guys like me."

She drummed on her lips with the pads of her fingers. "I wonder about us sometimes. Wire crossers. Specialists. Why do so many of the guys like to live in coffins and the women like to live in . . . well, like normal human beings? Most curious." She shrugged. "At least take some vitamins. You're beginning to look a little gaunt. I worry about you."

Q hotkeyed his smartie and raised his finger punch. "Have a stiff drink. I worry about *you*."

Katherine lay curled up on her bed, the sumptuous pin-tucked charcoal satin comforter wrapped around her like a cape. She wriggled her toes against the fabric and burrowed them deeper as she watched Leonardo pick through the room, still buttoning his shirt.

Leo swept his fingers across the top of the walnut bureau, his quick eyes taking in the details of the room. He opened her lingerie drawer and carefully lifted out the contents, patting his hand across the lacy garments, then closed it and repeated the process with every drawer.

"I'm not trying to push, darling, but did you get a chance to look over my proposal for the bot formal-wear line?" Katherine asked as Leonardo moved to her closet and pushed the hangers aside one by one, dedicating a second to look over each article of clothing before dispatching it.

"I'm sure it's excellent," he said. "You know I trust your taste. Go ahead and requisition whatever resources you need."

Katherine sat up and plumped her pillow to use as a backrest, trying to see the bright side of his trust in her aesthetic sense rather than feeling a little let-down by his lack of interest. He was currently using the toe of his wingtip to tally the shoes lining the bottom shelf of her shoe rack. He finally turned away from the closet, voice activated her wall clock and looked straight over her head at it.

Katherine turned, sending a cascade of blond hair over one shoulder. "Come back to bed," she purred.

He'd already disappeared into the bathroom; she could see him taking inventory of the contents of her medicine cabinet.

"Can't you stay, Leo?" she asked loudly, unable to mask the quaver in her voice.

He looked straight into the medicine cabinet mirror, his eyes blank. "Not tonight, darling."

He left the bathroom and walked straight past her out of the bedroom. Katherine could hear him in the kitchen, opening and shutting drawers. Sudden tears pricked at her eyes, and the sensation of sadness shocked and scared her, and she simply didn't know from whence it had come. Her heart palpitated. "Leo!" she screamed, his name erupting from her lips in a cascade of terror.

He was at her side in a moment. "Good God, Katherine. What's wrong?" She grabbed at his arm, pulling it to her as if afraid that if she let go she'd lose him forever.

"I just feel scared. I don't know why. I wish the doctors could figure out what's wrong with me and fix it."

Leonardo reached out and stroked her cheek with his knuckles, but he said nothing.

"Make me feel safe," she begged.

Leonardo blinked, then moved forward and brought her in close. Katherine closed her eyes, but as she sat there with his arms around her and her face crammed into his armpit, she didn't feel any more secure; she just felt like someone with her face in somebody's armpit.

She pressed her face forward harder. Leonardo patted her on the shoulder blade, and Kitty pressed herself deeper, desperately seeking . . . the comfort that just wasn't there. She looked up at him.

"Leo, is something wrong?" she rasped.

He raised an eyebrow. "No. Why?"

"You just seem . . . like you're somewhere else."

"I'm the same as always." He lifted her chin and gave her a smile that seemed a bit tight. "I think you're imagining things, darling. This is all so unlike you. Did you take your pills today?"

"I always take my pills," she mumbled automatically. She didn't want to take them; she just wanted to feel better. She moved closer to him, but he took a step back.

"You should get some rest." He turned and grabbed his suit jacket, and Katherine watched him slip his hands through the armholes.

"Don't you think it's strange we never sleep in the same place? I'm always here, and you're always there. When do we cuddle?"

Leonardo seemed uncharacteristically taken aback. Finally he said, "There will be plenty of 'cuddling' when we're married." Then he finished his walk-through of her condo, came back to her side, kissed her forehead . . . and left her alone in her pool of gray satin.

CHAPTER SEVEN

Three loops of the same blank response were beginning to drive Q positively mad. It was necessary to run the drill several times to see what—if anything—changed in Kitty's reaction, how events and memories might change from any of the previous iterations, and to what about him—if anything—she seemed particularly responsive. He'd lived the same damn experience through with Kitty so many times—*Was it five? Six?*—he'd learned to pronounce "Heusenfleugen" like a native speaker of German, double umlauts and all.

He now lay in his capsule, lolling with his hands behind his head, wishing he hadn't managed to close out his prior freelance job so quickly. It had been a simple matter of repairing a wire of reality that someone had cut badly, causing an unusual ripple effect that moved a dog to a different owner. In the end, the right lady got her dog back, intended reality was restored without sending any new problems up or down the line, and Q walked away feeling warm and fuzzy—albeit a little sheepish that all of his skills and brainpower were being used to chase poodles going the wrong direction down a figurative one-way temporal street.

He'd done enough research. Enough watching. He needed to figure out how to draw Kitty out of her shell. Literally.

At first it hadn't bothered Q that, when she would come to see him, they'd talk for a few minutes and he'd ask her questions to ascertain her state of mind or figure out what she had planned; then the next time she'd forget everything. Being a man, he had even thought once or twice—well, maybe once or twice before he started to get to know her better—that theoretically she was the perfect one-night stand: there'd be no trouble in the morning, because she'd have already forgotten whatever happened. But now the forgetting thing was really beginning to irk him. He couldn't tell whether she was forgetting less, or if her forgetting was taking longer than it had the first time their paths crossed. He couldn't tell anything except how frustrating it was to see her and not have her remember him after more than a month.

And the truth of the matter was, the frustration Q was experiencing was on a personal level rather than a professional one.

From a personal perspective, it shouldn't have made a bit of difference. What should he care what she did or didn't think about him, as long as her thoughts were actually her own? His job was to extract her, not appreciate her. Except he did appreciate her, and he couldn't figure out why. How could he appreciate a manufactured set of feelings and behaviors, no matter how hot the package?

Bots were getting better and better, but there was still no mistaking a bot for a human being. Well, until now, he thought with no small amount of nausea. Maybe that was what Kaysar was trying for. The Japanese had been going about it all wrong: instead of trying to get a bot to behave more like a human, what about simply getting a human to behave more like a bot?

Q sighed, completely unenthusiastic regarding his need to go out. He reached over and ran his index finger absently across a gouge in the side of the plastiglass enclosure. Capsule, coffin, or cocoon, he wondered. *What am I hiding from?*

I'm not hiding, he thought angrily. He lurched up suddenly as if to prove the point, hitting the crown of his head on the plastic ceiling. Swearing a blue streak, he slid out and stalked into the locker room to change for his first appearance at Kitty's engagement party.

It was to be a formal occasion, his meeting tonight. Q wasn't one of those guys who made a big deal out of donning a tuxedo; he rather liked it, actually. On a professional level, it was easy to blend into a room full of tuxedo-clad men. Louise had snagged the invite from a regular attendee, a Kaysar employee who was all too happy to be paid even more than usual to stay home. It seemed there were malcontents at every company.

Arriving at the party, Q handed his invite cartridge to the man behind the velvet rope. The faux bouncer loaded the chip into his smartie, then waited for the clearance beep before removing the chip and tossing it into a bin already piled high with similar squares. "Have a nice evening, Mr. Chan," he said. Q nodded and slipped beyond the velvet rope. He made his way into the building.

"Blah, blah, blah," someone said loudly on his right. Q turned to the source, a woman next to him, rolling her eyes at her date. The man answered, "And a 'blah, blah, blah' right back atcha." They both laughed, took swigs of their drinks, and then looked around as if this were the most boring party ever, in spite of the raucousness Q saw surrounding Katherine on the other side of the room.

Suddenly the woman caught Q looking and blanched. Q raised an eyebrow. The man cursed under his breath.

"You're new," he said.

The woman elbowed him and added, "She can't hear or see us from up there." She looked scared, but raised her chin and asked, "Freshie or plant?"

"New hire. Freshie," Q guessed, thinking being the former could explain away any number of discrepancies in his behavior.

The couple relaxed instantly. "What group are you in?" the man asked.

"Sorry?"

"What group?" He glanced at his watch. "Almost nine thirty. Do you know your mark?"

"Yeah," Q said.

"You start back here too and then wind in?"

"Uh-huh," Q said, watching the man's eyes and taking the cues.

The man nodded. "We've been Party Murmur on Fridays for months now. Gets a little dull, you know, same thing each week. Sometimes we just have to joke around with it a little bit."

He nodded and turned back to his date. The two drank in silence.

After a moment there came a flash of light from inside the woman's slightly translucent evening bag, and an almost simultaneous flash from just inside the man's breast pocket. The man looked at the woman and said in a complete monotone, "Geez, darling, you look so pretty tonight. Is that a new dress?"

"No, my dear," she answered in an equally bored voice. "I just haven't worn it in so long. I'm so glad you like it."

"I do like it."

"I'm so glad. I haven't worn it in so long."

"Well, you look so pretty tonight. Is that a new dress?"

"No—"

They went on and on, repeating the same concepts over and over, changing little. Q took a step back and watched them in the context of the rest of the room. He examined their faces and those of the other partygoers. From this close he could see that they were all acting, but from the place where Katherine was, just out of earshot, everyone's rehearsed speeches on display at the same time, the ebb and flow of the "conversations," the higher-pitched laughs and the low-edged chuckles, the expressions of surprise and the sounds of a snipped anecdote holding other listeners in silent rapture—it all combined to form the perfect storm of a party. These professional partygoers created the layers-deep facade of people having a fabulous time in honor of a couple that was universally adored.

But, Q knew, nobody was having a fabulous time, and the couple wasn't universally adored.

He turned away and strode to the bar. "G and T, please." He drummed his fingers against its marble top and watched the guests party on. It was like a circle radiating out, with the people at the outermost ring the least enthusiastic. On the inside stood Katherine with some friends and Leonardo. Q felt a little breathless just watching her, though he knew she couldn't see him yet. He prayed that, if there was any change in her mind and what she remembered, she would not let on that he was anything other than what he pretended.

Despite the danger, he was tempted to move a little closer.

He turned back to the bar to find that the bartender hadn't moved. The youngster just stood there, his face flaming red with a look of terror. "That wasn't on the list," he said, his voice cracking. "G and T is not on the list."

"What's *that?*" Q asked, pointing to the bottle of gin on the rack behind the bartender's head. "What does it say?" The boy took the bottle down, looked at it, and reported, "It says gin, sir."

"Right. It says gin. And what's that?" Q pointed to the bottle of tonic water through the glass refrigerator door.

The boy looked where he pointed. "It says tonic water, sir."

Q pointed to a highball glass up on the shelf. "Use that. Now put that . . . and that . . . together," he said, making a swirling motion with his fingers.

His hand shaking so badly that he had trouble keeping everything in the glass and off the counter and himself, the bartender made a gin and tonic and handed it over. For show, Q scanned the panel embedded in the wood of the bar to collect tips—his rented smartie wasn't activated, so the bartender would sadly get nothing—and walked to the wall with his drink.

He pocketed the handheld and took a swig of his gin and tonic, eyeing the crowd, and kept sipping even though his first sip had revealed a nasty surprise: it was just water. He should have brought something with him.

At the far end of the room the band abruptly stopped playing. Leonardo Kaysar walked up on the stage, resplendent in a black tie and tails. He tapped the tip of the bandleader's microphone; the scratching noise and high-pitched hiss got everybody's attention. All went silent immediately. Q noticed that not one person needed to be quieted further.

"I want to thank you all for this lovely, lovely party," Kaysar said. "That Katherine and I should celebrate our love and union in this way . . ." And he continued on, his prepared speech filled with witticisms and gallantry galore. The man was smooth, too smooth. Everybody was.

Q glanced around, really concentrating on the faces in the crowd. A nasty prickle crept up his spine. The people were all real, obviously. He knew how to tell a bot from a human, and these were the latter. But there was a certain malaise in the air, a sense of weariness that he couldn't quite pinpoint. He hadn't noticed it so much when he was just watching the play of events, collecting data and not interacting.

"Are you supposed to be here?"

Q turned toward the voice. A beefy man with what looked like a real Scotch in one hand and a flesh-colored earpiece not quite concealed in the depths of one ear looked him up and down.

"New hire," Q said, meeting the man's eyes with his own.

The Scotch drinker slowly nodded. "Got your script on you?"

Q raised his eyebrows. "Didn't know I was supposed to. Don't have many lines."

"Yeah, well, I think you're off your mark. Newbies start out in the back."

"Right. Sorry. Didn't really think of it," Q said, "but you're absolutely right." He looked over at the stage, where a flutter of white organza darted up the steps. When Leonardo held out his hand, Katherine had joined him.

The Scotch drinker's hand clamped down on Q's shoulder. " 'S all right, boy. Happens to every guy here. She's damn hot. But go find your mark before the other section guards get riled up."

Q nodded, mumbled his thanks, and headed back toward the side of the room. Damn. This was like being in the bleachers. He couldn't see Katherine, just a flash of blond, a laugh floating across the room, that crazy construction of a dress that an average girl could never pull off.

"Here we go," said the woman he'd seen near the door, her date nowhere to be found. She put a hand on Q's back and pushed him gently forward into what was a kind of whirlpool of people moving in spiral fashion closer and closer to the stage. He saw clumps of guests lurch together and form groups, groups headed supposedly naturally in Leonardo and Katherine's general direction. But Q saw a pattern, a controlled eddy of humanity working its way in and out, to and fro, near and far from the object of everybody's interest.

As they'd come partially down from the stage, he could see only the tops of Katherine's and Leonardo's heads, shining gold and dark ebony, but he could still hear her peals of delighted laughter bubble up again and again. He was drawn irresistibly forward.

"Do you have a line?" the woman asked.

"Mmm," Q said noncommittally.

The sea of people parted before them, and then there they were: the night's golden couple, ablaze in a spotlight. Katherine stood in profile, handing off a female friend to her fiancé. She turned to receive the next well-wisher. Q raised his smartie, snapped a picture, and pressed the button for the date and time stamp. As the second well-wisher was thanked and passed along, Katherine turned to Q. And all he could do was stand before her as she focused in on him and he became once more, as he had fruitlessly attempted to describe to his sister, "unsensed."

Katherine looked like a bride—or at least as beautiful as one. Q wondered if she felt like one. He wondered if she really felt anything at all, joy at her "recent engagement," or if her mind was just taking her for yet another ride.

When she moved, the beads of her dress shifted, flashing like silver all around her. Her blond hair was pulled up in some fancy hairdo, and her blue eyes stared at him. Behind Q, a woman hissed in his ear, "Say your line or you'll throw it all off. The whole point of this is consistency."

Katherine held out her hand. Q raised his own and wrapped his fingers around hers. They just stared at each other for a moment. And when someone gave him a small shove from behind, he lost all track of things and leaned

forward, bringing his lips close to her ear. She turned a little, her eyes questioning, and a few strands of loose hair
brushed his cheek.

"Congratulations," Q said, watching closely for a sign
of recognition. It never came.

He pulled away, stepped back into the swirl, and passed
in an orderly manner toward the outer ring until he was
once more in the back of the room; then he watched her
from afar for quite a while until at last she headed for the
door.

He followed, slipping into the narrow hall just outside
the women's restroom. He looked around and saw no one,
so he pushed the door ajar and peered in. Katherine sat at a
dressing table, looking into the mirror, arranging her gauzy
skirts carefully to avoid trapping the fabric under her
chair's legs, and then dumped the contents of her clutch
on the sleek marble. Humming a tune under her breath,
she powdered her nose and touched up her lipstick. Then
she rose, tipped her head to one side, and smoothed the satin
fabric of her bodice. Turning around to survey her back-
side, she was apparently satisfied, for she put the makeup
back in the clutch and headed for the door.

Q moved back into the hall and intercepted her as she
came out. He was suddenly at a loss for words, and she
didn't seem to know what she should do, either.

"Are you happy, Kitty?" he asked.

She might have laughed at the question, and should
have answered, "Of course." There were a hundred different responses possible other than remaining entirely speech-
less. Which at last she ceased. "Nobody ever asks you that,"
she said. "They just tell you that you are."

Spontaneously, he took her hand, cradling it between
her palms. "You deserve . . . to be happy," he said.

"Of course I'm happy," she replied—too late, though
she now wore a smile.

Two women hurried up, obviously coming to check on their charge. He'd delayed her too long; they could expect no more freedom.

"Katherine, come back to the party!" the brunette said gaily. "We miss you terribly." She hooked her arm through Katherine's and dragged her away. Katherine looked at Q over her shoulder, but he couldn't see her expression; the redhead was standing before him with a most suspicious look, blocking his view.

He pulled out his smartie and gave her a terse nod, pretending to check something off with his stylus. "Everything seems as it should. Do you have anything you want to report?" he asked.

Her face relaxed. "Oh, I didn't realize there was an audit tonight. No, she's acting normal."

Normal? What a joke. But he pretended to scan a list. "Sorry, which one are you?"

"I'm Ariel. The best friend? It's a lead role," she snapped. Tossing her hair back, she turned and flounced back into the main room.

Q shook his head and rejoined the party, waiting until a large group of celebrants headed for the door. He slipped in with them, then backed into the shadows as they got into a waiting line of motolimos and took off.

Exit stage left, he thought to himself.

Q took a moment to breathe in the fresh, cold air. He felt dirty. That whole experience had just made him feel that way—and it had made him more determined than ever to get the girl away from here. Moving quickly from the nightclub, he grabbed his real smartie and made some notes. They'd been going about things all wrong; he could see that now. They'd been going about it all wrong, and he was going to make it right.

CHAPTER EIGHT

Q was just now hurrying down the sidewalk.

"You're late," Vesper complained.

Q didn't answer; he just approached her motolimo and stared at her through the open window.

"Has something happened?"

"No," he said gruffly. "I wish." He looked up and down the street, checking to see if anyone was around.

"Nope, no one," she informed him. "But, if nothing happened, what's with the look on your face? What are you thinking about?" She was trying to squeeze her finger under her safety belt to scratch an itch as she spoke.

"The job," he said—very unhelpfully, Vesper thought.

"You have a sneaky look," she said as he walked around the motolimo and got in the passenger side.

"A sneaky look?"

"Like you're a man with a plan. Is it a nefarious plan?" she asked. "Does it involve weapons? Do you need help?"

"Nope," he replied. "But I've had an epiphany. I've been an idiot. I've been doing all the wrong things."

"No, you haven't!" Vesper said. He was the only one letting her do *anything* useful. She prayed he wasn't regretting that choice.

"Yes, I have. A complete idiot. Everything I've been doing has probably reinforced the rigidity of Kitty's mind. The way we've been working, trying to fit in . . . I'm just another repeat episode in her life. No wonder I'm not getting anywhere being Dr. Van Heusenfleugen in her doctor's office every week. I've got to set things apart. I've got to go in there and jolt her out of her fog, make her really look around and say, 'What the hell is going on here?' Then we bring her back in and see what we've got."

Vesper breathed a sigh of relief, nodding vigorously. "That makes sense." Twisting in her seat, she got up on her knees and reached behind it for her bag.

"Sorry, Vesper," Q said, stopping her with a hand on her shoulder. "Just me." She slowly turned back and dropped heavily into her seat. "I need you to tell Mason I'm moving in next to Kitty, though, and get whatever I need to make that happen." He raised his smartie, and she automatically raised hers to accept his transmission. "Here's security clearance for my locker and capsule. Please take all the clothes from there that I need to blend into Kitty's week—and only those clothes, Vesper—and move them into that apartment. Get it livable in time for tomorrow. Just the absolute basics. Don't spend a lot of time on it."

Vesper nodded. "Anything else?"

Q's head jolted up. "Oh, would you mind . . . I need a tuxedo dry-cleaned."

She had to stifle the urge to roll her eyes. *Et tu, Brute?* "Yeah, okay. Oh! What about toiletries?" She wondered what sort of toiletries a man like Q used.

"I'll pick up everything else," he said, disappointing her. Raising his smartie again, he said, "Rental code?"

She flashed her best fussy-baby look, but it was to no avail, so she transmitted the motolimo's startup and security codes.

"Thanks," he said. He got out of the motolimo and walked around to the driver's side. "Vesper?" he said through the open window. She hadn't moved.

She frowned and clenched the steering controls with both hands.

"*Vesper*."

She sighed and let go, stepping out of the motolimo and then reaching back inside for her bag and pulling it out. Q got into the driver's seat and ordered the appropriate seat and mirror adjustments.

"Enjoy the walk," he said with a wink. "Exercise is the best thing a time traveler can do for herself." He reached through the open window and patted her cheek before stealing her chauffeur's cap and placing it atop his head. "Your day will come, kid," he added, subsequently flicking the accelerator with his thumb and leaving her in a cloud of geetane.

Vesper waved the fumes away and hiked to the capsule hotel. When she got there, she did exactly what Q asked her to do. Well, exactly what he told her to do and a little extra. It occurred to her as she pulled his Kitty Week's "costume changes" from his storage unit that since she was already here and had access to the place, thanks to Q's entry code, she ought to take advantage of a little networking. This hotel and sports club was a de facto hub for freelancers in the business. She glanced at her smartie, calculating that she had just enough time to introduce herself around before making it to the dry cleaner's with Q's extra tux.

And that certainly wasn't any kind of interference Louise could be upset about. It wasn't like shaking somebody's hand messed up the wires of reality or anything. In fact, it was the sort of initiative that would *please* Louise. Vesper carefully placed the clothes she'd just rolled up back in the bottom of the storage unit and closed the door. Then she walked straight into the men's locker room just for fun to see who she could meet.

When Q reached the pickup zone at the Kaysar Corporation, he slowed down, watching the building exit so that he could time things perfectly. Kitty emerged through the revolving doors in one of his favorite outfits: the yellow, wasp-waisted suit. She was a vision, a ray of sunshine dripping down the cold, dark stone stairs.

She'd just descended to street level and looked around in confusion the moment before Q drove up.

Q scanned the sidewalk, watching the passersby for any unusual signs. He slipped a pair of shades over his eyes, and then got out of the motolimo, leaving his smartie plugged in and running.

"Katherine!"

She turned and gave him a confused smile. It was obvious she had no idea who the hell he was.

Q palmed a knife from the side of his cargo pants, and after casually throwing his arm around her shoulders and giving her a friendly squeeze, he pressed it up against her throat. "Get in the motolimo."

Her eyes widened, but to her credit she didn't scream. A tiny little squeak was the only sound she gave as he pushed her head down and pushed her through the driver's seat to the passenger side.

The doors were hardly shut before he peeled off into traffic, one hand clenched around her wrist, his eyes scanning the rearview mirror.

"Are you my appointment? Do I always get a ride?" Kitty asked, the expected element of fear—or at least suspicion—conspicuously absent.

"I'm your appointment," Q said. So far, no one seemed to have noticed that Kitty was being absconded with into an unsanctioned event. At least, that was Q's impression. He prayed it was the truth. In any case, he wasn't planning to take her anywhere really fresh—they'd just go for a "ride" and, depending on her reaction to that, he planned to stop and take her into that New Age store and make her buy something, just to see what he could trigger.

He turned his head to the side. Kitty turned her head toward him and smiled. "Hello," she said.

"Hello," he replied, trying not to let her beauty disarm his caution.

She glanced down at her smartie and poked it with her stylus before looking back up at him. "You're taking me to my brain appointment," she decided. "Who am I seeing today?" She stared into his eyes, clearly expecting some kind of answer.

"It's not listed," he said.

She frowned. "I thought everything was listed."

"Not everything." Hadn't he looked at her smartie the other week, and hadn't it been mostly empty? Unless Kaysar's minions were in the habit of updating her smartie as things went along.

"Really?" she said. "I didn't know that. Do we do this often, take a ride?"

"We've never done this before," Q said pointedly, glancing back and forth between her face and the moto tracks unfolding before them.

"Oh!" She looked rather excited, and then her smile became uncertain. "Is this okay, then?"

A small chime sounded from her purse.

"What's that?" Q asked.

"What?" Kitty asked.

"I just heard that a second ago. Is that coming from you?" He glanced at the vehicle's control panel.

"Oh, that's my smartie. It's telling me I'm supposed to be doing something."

Oh, shit. "Give it to me."

She handed it over without a fuss and then looked around. "I don't suppose you have some water," she said.

Q steered with one hand while he checked all the functional programs on Kitty's smartie for a GPS component. He couldn't find anything of interest staring back at him, but that didn't mean something wasn't there.

He whipped around and stared at Katherine. "I don't suppose you'd know if you were GPS-chipped."

She gave him an incredulous stare. "Chipped? That's absurd. I'm not a bot."

"Not on purpose, anyway," he muttered. "Do you have any scars?" he asked, even though she'd obviously have gotten plasticked if she had.

"Of course not. I'm perfect. Do you have any water?" she asked again, pulling a glass bottle full of tablets out of her purse.

Q looked over. "What's that for?"

"My head."

Q stared at her in disbelief. Being kidnapped was giving her . . . a *headache*? No screams or dramatic outbursts. Just a flatline sort of acceptance about everything and a freaking headache.

One eye still on traffic, Q reached into his bag behind him and pulled out a half-empty water bottle. Kitty hesitated, then uncapped it and stuck it between her knees while she shook out a couple of pills.

Q went back to scanning her smartie.

The scream Q had expected out of her earlier suddenly came out of Kitty's mouth at the top of her lungs. He looked up and dropped the smartie into the foot well, wrenching the steering wheel to one side to avoid hitting the moto that had just stopped short in front of them.

They went careening into the emergency lane like a couple of kids strapped into a bumper car, their motolimo's rims catching on the track edge. The emergency struts engaged and inflated, sending a wireless signal to the struts lining the emergency lane; the motolimo was pulled immediately away from oncoming traffic and sucked hard against the safest edge.

Kitty's purse, the pills, the water all went flying into the well at her feet. Q's bag flew forward as well, the heavy tools pitching against the back of his seat.

Then it was still and quiet. They sat facing the wrong way in traffic, but safe in the emergency lane with their safety struts popped up all around the motolimo. Q's arm was still frozen in its original reflexive motion across Kitty's chest; he could feel her heartbeat, and it was definitely racing. But when he dropped his arm and look at her, she still seemed . . . unimpressed. She was pale, yes, but more subdued than terrified. Q just shook his head. She'd been kidnapped at knifepoint, thrust into a car with a strange man and driven off to God knew where, experienced a potentially life-threatening car accident, and all she could do was stare forlornly at her feet.

"Kitty? Are you all right?"

The corner of her mouth turned down. She cocked her head a bit and continued staring at the floor.

Q followed her gaze. At her feet was a soup of glass and pills and spilled water, all of it soaking into the leather of her purse. And then he saw the side of her foot, where a needlelike line of blood ran across her anklebone. By any interpretation it was a minuscule cut.

"I broke the bottle," she said, looking at him with a worried expression.

"What?"

"The bottle." She pointed at the mess at her feet. "All the pills spilled out."

"Forget the damn pills," Q said roughly, reaching around and messing through the jumble of his bag for the small plastic first-aid kit. He grabbed it, nearly sent it all flying in his haste, and wrestled out a small tube of antiseptic. He delicately dabbed a smidge of ointment on her foot, and then unwrapped the smallest bandage he could find and stuck it over the cut.

"Ah, shit!" Q blurted, completely disgusted with himself. *Continuity*. They might not notice a cut that small, but they'd certainly notice the bandage. "Sorry." He slowly pulled the bandage off again and tossed it on the floor with the rest of the mess.

Kitty's smartie rang. Before Q could stop her she

answered the call; if they were trying to track her where-abouts, they'd just hooked right in. With one hand he held her wrist down to keep the smartie away from her mouth and with the other he pressed the strut release, and the safety mechanisms rimming the car began to retract. "Tell her you wandered off and got lost, but that—"

"Kitty?" a tinny voice called out from the smartie speaker.

"Gotta get this," Kitty said. "Hi, Ariel, what's up?" she said into the phone.

"What's up?" That was all she had to say? "Tell her you wandered off but that you're getting into a motolimo and you'll be right there," Q hissed. Kitty did no such thing. The Ariel person on the other end started talking a tinny blue streak. Q shook his head and focused on waiting for the motolimo to finish its postaccident checklist and issue him a go signal. The green light flashed, and he immediately made a three-point turn within the confines of the emergency lane, and then signaled to merge back into traffic. *Strange man with knife. Car accident. Cut on foot. And all she can say is, "Hi, Ariel, what's up"?*

The blue streak stopped and Kitty opened her mouth to speak. Hitting the accelerator, Q grabbed Kitty's wrist. "Tell her—" he whispered urgently.

"I'm in a motolimo on One-oh-one, level three," Kitty said blithely into her smartie. ". . . Dunno. I'm really con-fused. I think I got in the wrong one. Oh. Yeah. That's what I'll do. I will. Of course. I'm coming right back." She hung up and looked at Q. "I got in the wrong motolimo. Can you take me back downtown to the Kaysar Corpora-tion, please?" Then she reached out and adjusted the tem-perature of the air coming from the passenger-side vent.

The calmer and blander she became, the more worked up Q felt. "Do you even realize you've essentially just been kidnapped?"

Kitty looked at him. "Well, that's semantics, really." She looked out the windows and shrugged. "We're just driving."

He gave her a look as if she were insane. "The difference between just driving and a kidnapping is *not* really one of semantics."

"If you think about it, it kind of is," she argued.

Q gripped the steering component and sat back, wondering how a seasoned veteran of time battles known for his powerful intellect and technical know-how could be so snowed by a fashion designer with holes in her gray matter.

"It *is*," she insisted, staring through the windshield at the traffic ahead. "I mean, you're taking me where *you* want me to go. But while you can call this trip by whatever name you want, you're not going to hurt me."

Q turned his head very slowly to look at her. "How do you know that?"

Kitty raised her hand and studied her manicure. "I just do. Things pop in and out of my head, and this I just know. Happens all the time."

"Does it?"

"Uh-huh."

Q contemplated her matter-of-factness.

Kitty looked at him and rolled her eyes. "Look, if you want me to fake being scared, why don't you just say so?"

"I don't want you to fake anything!" Q yelled, throwing his hands up in the air. The motolimo swerved, and he grabbed the steering component again, trying to collect himself.

"No offense, but you really need to pay more attention to the road," she said.

Q shook his head, furious. "Does *nothing* rattle you?" he burst out. "Do I have no impact on you whatsoever? Are you completely numb? There's no damn point in taking you to sniff a punch of herbs and potions; you probably don't even have a sense of smell! You *are* a goddamned bot."

He stared in horror as her eyes watered, but a moment later she sucked the emotion back before tears could fall. "Why are you so mad at me?" she asked, clearly genuine in her bewilderment.

Q stared at her in silence, then finally blurted, "I don't know." Suddenly more than happy to abort the mission, he stopped several blocks away from the Kaysar Corporation, leaned out the window, and flagged down another motolimo. "I've got to get this car back to the garage. She's headed to the Kaysar Corporation."

The motolimo driver gave him a lazy nod, reset his meter, and pulled in at the curb just ahead.

Q stopped the vehicle and got out, jogging around to Kitty's side to open the door for her. She put her hand in his and he carefully helped her avoid the mess at her feet. She went for her purse, but Q stopped her and pulled it out of the broken glass himself and shook it off as best he could. Most of the water had already sunk into the leather, and the headache tablets were just a mess of dissolving muck plastering the floor. The water stains in the black leather weren't obvious; Q just hoped he hadn't missed any shards of glass.

Kitty's smartie alarm beeped again, but she just ignored it and got into the new motolimo. Q stared at the cut on her ankle as she pulled her legs into the vehicle. Q shut the door, and she smiled up at him in the instant before the driver drove back into the traffic stream. Q watched her drive away; Kitty never looked back.

Q got back into the rented motolimo and took stock of the mess. The pills had completely dissolved into the mat, a white foamy mass covering the floor. So much for the damn deposit.

He curled his hand around the steering component and gripped it tight as a wave of nausea swept over him as if he'd just inhaled fumes. He ordered the window down and breathed the fresh air deeply into his lungs. How strange. How extremely strange. Bracing himself against a head rush, Q thought that if the anomaly herself hadn't just left the car, he'd swear he was in the middle of one right now. Q glanced through the windshield and looked up at the sky. Nothing but the hover-ads buzzing quietly to and fro.

I have no impact on her whatsoever, he was thinking when a giant fist suddenly came down hard on the window. Q lurched backward, then clued in to the cacophony of horns behind him. "You're holding up traffic, asshole!" the guy pounding on the driver's-side window yelled.

Q nodded and hit the accelerator; he thought he'd still been parked, but there he was idling in the middle of traffic. *Look at that, Kitty. Lost time. Happens to everyone.* Heading for home, Q suddenly felt more tired than he could remember feeling in a long, long time.

Slipping into the capsule hotel, Q directed a cursory nod at the ragtag group of freelancers playing poker in the common room. He was not looking forward to moving to the apartment tomorrow. This place might give Louise the willies, but Q felt at home here. He'd rented it for as long as he could remember, and it was one of the few constants in his life—besides his sister, of course. He pointed his smartie at the barcode on the outer door of his capsule, looked inside to make sure everything was fine and that Vesper had collected what she needed, then made quick work down the rungs of a nearby ladder to the workout level. There he sidled down the narrow rows of lockers to find his own.

After an instinctive glance over his shoulder, he unlocked the metal compartment with a flash of his smartie and opened the door. He raised his hands and, with a violent sweep of his arms, separated the hanging clothes to reveal a drop-down interface. He punched in his vault code, adjusted his smartie to unlock the second level of security, then flashed the gadget one last time. A click and a hiss of a vacuum seal, then the back panel slowly flipped down. Beyond was a second locker.

He stowed his tool kit on the revealed platform, ran his fingers across several tools and weapons lining the real back wall of the cabinet, and chose a couple to swap out for what he'd been carrying. He pointed his smartie at the vault's closing-and-locking mechanism and clicked, then closed his locker proper. Grabbing a proffered towel from a passing hostess bot, he automatically glanced at the manufacturer's code under her ear to confirm that it wasn't a Kaysar Corp. model, then strode buck naked toward the baths. He wrapped the towel around his waist as he went.

The wide underground space was vast, a designed combination of decaying mosaics and Romanesque ruins where burbling water flowed. The burbling masked most of the already limited conversation that went on here in the baths. Q tossed his towel to the nearest bench; then he climbed into the water in his customary corner where the few anomaly specialists tended to hang out. This was a solace, a hideaway from his problems.

Across the way, disappeared-persons detective Ace gave him a silent nod, but a black eye and puffed-up lip were likely making any more communicative facial expressions painful. Nearby, Q's time-anomaly peer Roderick sat on the edge of the pool. Roddy was still wrapped in his towel, his legs soaking in the hot water, a bloody bandage around his neck. Last time they'd compared notes, the guy had mentioned he was working on something to do with leap year and said the case was busting his balls. At least he was able to lift a couple of fingers in greeting.

Another man was also present. He raised his gaze and gave Q a terse nod, a faint hint of a wince passing over his face as he shifted in the water and raised his enormously muscled arms: the movement raised the top of a metal chest brace just above the waterline. Before being slammed between two wires of reality a couple of months ago, this man formerly known to his pals as Sam had moved off the main wires—the time-based battlefield—to focus on edges, research, the minutiae of parsed nanoseconds. They'd been calling him Professor ever since.

Q and his peers soaked in silence for a while, shifting their weight off their more injured limbs or working out the kinks in their sore muscles. After a few minutes, however, the sound of a snicker pierced the mist.

Q dislodged his unseeing gaze from the nearby statue of Venus, whose head lay in white plaster chunks at her sandaled feet. He glanced at Ace, who said nothing, his expression carefully blank. He looked at Roderick next, who looked right back at him. Then he looked at the Professor.

Q would have liked to get some advice from the other experts in his field, but it was a tricky business. He couldn't trust anybody 100% and he wasn't even sure how much he wanted to reveal or how to begin. He needn't have worried about *that*.

Ace pressed his finger experimentally against the purplish bruise around his eye. "Heard you're on kind of an unusual assignment."

"Every job's different," Q said, sinking a little lower into the water to aim a pulsing jet against the spot where his tools had slammed against his back. He didn't much want to talk about it.

"Lots of rumors," the Professor added. "I heard you're working with a Kaysar subject."

Q ran his fingers through the water, watched currents flow over his skin. "No comment. When it's case-closed, I'll give you the rundown, as always."

The guys here who shared their line of work also shared their approach, and some of their information. Things got sticky only when two desired outcomes contradicted each other, and that had happened only a few times—and only once with major repercussions. One of the two guys had left the business altogether as a result. Ace was the other, and he'd never quite been the same.

Someone cleared his throat. Q shook his head. "If you know I'm working on Kaysar, you know I'm not going to say a thing until it's over. No comment."

The three other guys looked at one another. The Professor took the ball and ran.

"Look at him. He's obviously getting his ass kicked." He stared at Q. "Isn't that so? You getting your ass kicked on the job?" He tried to rally the others. "Hey, Mr. Perfect's finally found a snare he couldn't handle. Give us details, will ya? None of us is working on anything with a direct link to Kaysar right now." He looked around for contradiction and got none. "And we're all friends here."

"We're not *that* good of friends," Q quipped, knowing that they would take it in the spirit it was meant. You just didn't share *specifics* of a job. If one was discussed, it was discussed in the abstract, with hypotheticals. Sure, they were always comparing notes to make sure they weren't working against one another, but specifics, especially Kaysar specifics, were something else.

He shrugged and said vaguely, "Something happened at work today—it's happened over the last few weeks, actually. I'm just not sure what to make of it."

No one said anything. He wasn't surprised, but he also wasn't happy. Truth was, he wouldn't mind getting some other points of view.

He flexed one of his aching knees and cleared his throat. He'd have to give more information. "I kidnapped this girl today, and she didn't react properly."

"What's your definition of the proper reaction to a kidnapping?" asked Roderick.

"You know: screaming, escape attempts, knees to the

groin, crying, whatever." Q waved his hand expressively in the air. "Proper."

"What *did* she do?" asked Ace.

"She told me she wasn't scared because she didn't think I'd do anything bad to her." Q looked vaguely at the ceiling. "I set up an action scene, and the woman was unimpressed. Demoralizing, to say the least."

The Professor looked at the other guys, then shook his head. "You, my friend, obviously need to start with a little more excitement. I myself like to put unpredictability in the game from the get-go, so there's no need for her to say anything about it. If you get to the point where someone's saying they're bored, that's the beginning of the end . . . in my opinion."

Q stared at him in bewilderment. "What the hell are you talking about? 'Action scene' was not a metaphor. I really meant *action scene*. I'm not asking for relationship advice. I haven't even kissed this girl."

"I think you've just diagnosed your problem."

"Wait, what are we talking about?" Q looked wildly at his friends through the steam. "Hey, I'm not talking about my sex life. I'm not asking for advice about my sex life. I have no issues with my sex life. She would not be unimpressed with the sex; let me make that clear!"

Laughter wafted back at him.

"Oh, man. This is so wrong," Q muttered.

"Okay. If you don't want to talk about it . . ." The Professor placed his palms on the edge of the bath and lifted his body out, sitting himself on the edge of the pool. He grabbed a towel, carefully wiped water off his abbreviated left leg, which looked like it had been cleaved down the middle and closed up with plastiglass, unwrapped a metal prosthetic from the towel by the side of the pool, perfectly curved in the shape and width of the missing piece, and snapped the gleaming metal into place. "Plug and play," he said with a wink. Then he stood and limped off. "Catch you later."

The usual comfort provided by the hot water, and the usual friendship provided by the other freelancers, was missing tonight; they clearly thought his problem was personal and that he didn't want to get into it. But it wasn't personal. Not really. And since talking sex when he wanted to talk work and technical difficulties was fruitless, Q bade his pals a good evening and retreated to the locker room. From there he made a quick departure for his capsule.

In the main hall he had few words for the regulars, but then he sealed himself in with such haste that he almost felt he was running from something.

The lid shut above him and he released a long breath. Some—his sister, for example—might find this capsule claustrophobic, but Q found it therapeutic. No external sound pierced the curved walls lined with strip lighting; in here, he could think without distraction. Not to mention it was always nice to live in an armored space if you were going to let your mind wander.

He had just enough room to maneuver, and Q leaned over and unclipped his boots, placing them alongside his bag beside the mattress. Then he lay back and clasped his hands behind his head and stared up at the ceiling, where he'd stuck a stickerphoto he'd printed out from his smartie. It was Kitty looking happy and radiant at her engagement party.

Why are you so mad at me?

He still didn't know. But math and logic wouldn't help him find the answer.

CHAPTER NINE

Q tried to ignore the flutter that swept through him as he passed Kitty's apartment. Inside the apartment next door, Vesper had done a bang-up job indeed. She'd piled a couple boxes of supplies in the entry, opened the curtains to let the world in a little, and had filled a basket with all manner of bits and pieces, details she thought he might need. *How like Louise,* he thought, knowing his sister had helped pack— especially since he'd asked Vesper to grab only his clothes.

He pulled out a handful of items including miniature scissors, a tube of antibiotic, and a blank smartie chip, and gave Vesper an amused nod. Then he headed into the bedroom and dumped his duffel out on the bed. His stuff scattered over the blanket.

He pulled out a handful of items including miniature scissors, a tube of antibiotic, and a blank smartie chip, and gave Vesper an amused nod. Then he headed into the bedroom and dumped his duffel out on the bed. His stuff scattered over the blanket.

Opening the closet, Q saw how she'd carefully draped everything in plastic and hung it up according to the days of the week, ending with a tuxedo for the engagement party on Friday. Q looked over his wardrobe. Vesper had also hung up an assortment of other outfits, some of which looked vaguely familiar and seemed to match what he remembered from other people who populated the scenes in Kitty's life. A waiter's apron, a maintenance worker shirt, a lab coat . . .

"Did Louise tell you to get all this together?" he asked.

Vesper didn't look up from the list on her smartie she was ticking off with her stylus. "Just in case," she mumbled.

He wandered back out of the bedroom and walked through the rest of the apartment. Never in his entire life had he lived in a place this nice. Nobody needed this much space. Of course, he lived in a capsule.

Looking out the window, which spanned almost the entire back wall of the living room, he had a fantastic, bird's-eye view of the city. Motoways stretched and curled like ribbons, the tramlike motovehicles proceeding across the span like dots and dashes of Morse code. Advertisements at this level were almost entirely in the form of fiber-optic lighting, if designed with an eye to nostalgia for eras gone by. If you kept the curtains open when the sun went down it would probably be like living in a neon speakeasy.

"Nice digs," Vesper remarked. Q turned to find her watching him.

"It smells and looks fake, just like everything else," he snapped.

"You don't like him, do you?" Vesper asked.

He shook his head. "What do you mean?"

"This," Vesper said, obviously thrilled to have proprietary information to which Q wasn't privy, "is Mason's apartment."

Q raised an eyebrow.

"Oh, yeah," Vesper went on. "He bought it during the time he was working to get Roxy back. Their present-day apartment was demolished, and the complex became just a dilapidated basketball court or something. I guess the neighborhood sucked. He bought it before the next wave of gentrification and all, playing the wires, but all within legal ways."

Q had to appreciate the cleverness there; this was actually

the same damn apartment in the future as in the past, albeit with a slightly different floor plan and temporal coordinates.

"I've gotta run," Vesper said abruptly, heading for the door.

"Why?" Q asked, scanning her face.

She kept her head down and didn't look at him. "I have a test soon."

"You never study."

"Uh . . . well, if I want to be valedictorian, you know . . ." She turned at the door.

"Hey, kid. You getting into something I should know about?"

She looked back at him over her shoulder, her eyes all wide and innocent. "Me? Of course not." Then she tapped the wall with her palm as a parting salvo and left.

Q sighed and slumped down on the sofa, looking around at the furniture. Then he got up and wandered into the kitchen to see if there was anything interesting. He found nothing. Then he walked to the far end of the apartment and opened the double doors leading into the bedroom. The wall clock was turned off, and the only sounds in the place were his own breathing and the scrape of his clothes as he walked toward the wall that abutted Kitty's apartment.

On this floor, in this room, sharing this wall on a completely different layer of time in the past, was Mason and Roxy's apartment. For Kitty, her friends were so close and yet so far.

For Q it was the same. Only it wasn't just his friends.

It wasn't just demoralizing that Katherine Gibbs never seemed to remember him; it was downright embarrassing—on a professional level. He had little to show for their continued interaction, other than her report of the vague sense that, as she put it, he wasn't going to hurt her. Whether that was due to naive idiocy or something he'd said to her, he couldn't know or guess. He'd been brought in as a specialist, someone who always got his man or woman.

Demoralizing, depressing.

Another thought struck him, as he forced himself to be honest: Kitty was lovely. She was so beautiful—and so blank about him. He couldn't decide whether his reaction was depression simply because nobody liked to go unremembered, ignored, treated in passing, or if it was that Kitty didn't remember *him* specifically, which really shouldn't have mattered. Q wasn't supposed to be taking any of this personally, of course. It wasn't even as though *he* knew *her* that well.

Most likely the biggest problem was, it rubbed Q wrong that somebody could take such sweetness from anybody— from everything he'd heard about Kitty from Roxy, she was a loving and warm woman—and so successfully erase it, mold it into something sterile, emotionless, and frankly creepy. In a situation like her engagement party, with everyone supporting and pushing her story, she seemed entirely in her element, happy . . . and she was at her blankest with Q. Even ignoring her interaction with him, how could a kind and loving person be happy with an engagement to Leonardo Kaysar, no matter the other factors in her life? And when he'd asked her if she was happy, she'd flipped out. There was *something* left of her original personality, and that crushed him.

He had made some progress, he reminded himself. Those times when he'd pretended to be her doctor, when she confided in him, when she saw him as an authority figure who had the answers—or at least a possible cure—he'd at least gotten trust. Q wanted to believe this was some sort of cumulative impact from their interaction. And that one comment, when he'd asked her why she wasn't scared when a perfect stranger kidnapped her, when she'd said she'd just somehow *knew* he wouldn't hurt her . . . there was something to that. Q needed to exploit it.

Yes, he wanted to believe that Roxy and Mason's Kitty still existed. And there were hints, clues that the person she was was still part of the person she'd been, despite being buried deep and trapped in this endless choreography that steered her thoughts. Louise was probably right: if he could just break through to her, get deep enough and then somehow keep the door open, the loyal, caring, enchanting friend of Roxy would still be there.

Q groaned and leaned forward until his forehead hit the wall, then banged his head against it a second time. There was only so much you could do with words. Everyone gave Kitty words. Leonardo Kaysar had his lines; her friends had theirs. What if it really took something beyond words to break through the barrier? *I'm so not the man for this. I don't want to be the man for this,* he groaned.

He stood at the wall, imagining the plane on which he stood in the way Vesper had once described it: overlaying that different time where the rest of the team gathered around their table. Then he turned that reality back on its axis to imagine Kitty just over there on the other side, standing across from Roxanne and the others, brushing her teeth and waiting for someone to save her.

She was waiting for *him* to save her.

Q turned and sat down heavily on the bed. A small poof of dust came up from the long-disused coverlet. He waved it away and stared down at the panel of his smartie as time inched forward.

The more I pretend to be someone I'm not, the more I become like everyone else in her life: a liar. Which is not who I am.

Damned if I do, damned if I don't.

He stood up, pacing the small space with his hands on his hips. "I don't want to do this," he said aloud. He stopped short. "I said I don't want to *do* this," he repeated. But neither Louise nor any other member of the team was there to let him off the hook, and if they had been, they wouldn't have understood.

No, there was no way around it. The professional response was to try all of the options in the order in which they made the most sense, to attempt every angle to free his quarry. *Just go over there. Just go over there and do something. Snap her out of it. Snap her out, rile her up, find a way in. The answer here can be found only in the unexpected. Consistency will always be her downfall.*

Q threw up his hands, silently cursed whatever gods might exist, then stuffed his smartie in his back pocket. He stalked across the room, out into the foyer, back out the front door, and down the hall to Kitty's front door, where he purposely shunned scanning the bell with his smartie in favor of a sharp rap on the wooden door.

For a moment all was silent; then he could hear the distant clicking of high heels across the floor. The sound seemed to amplify in his ears, though it only took a few moments for her to get to her destination. He heard her command—"Open"—and the door slid aside.

Q found his heart pounding; the door seemed to slide open with excruciating slowness, revealing Kitty in fractions of pixels. And then suddenly she stood before him, her blandly cheerful expression revealing that no ground had been made, no forward motion experienced. Her fingers curled around the door frame, and the perfection of that shellacked pink color on her nails just sort of did him in.

You always come back fine. A hundred percent repaired. Damn you, he thought, gritting his teeth.

Why are you so mad at me? she'd asked once before. He could hear her say it. He remembered the tone of her voice, the lilt at the end, the intonation and cadence of her speech. Here he stood, a bundle of raw emotions, battling demons he hadn't wanted to admit he even had, things that he'd managed to keep down for so long, just like Louise, and Kitty was bringing them all out of him. The irony of that, the bitter irony: the blankest, most emotionless girl in the world was breaking down all of his defenses . . . and she didn't even remember doing or saying anything to him in the first place.

IRREVERSIBLE

"Excuse me. How can I help you?"

He flashed a jaunty smile. "You don't remember me."

Katherine reared back a bit, her forehead crinkling as she considered his face. "I'm so sorry, I don't."

"Didn't think so."

Q reached out, grabbed her by the arms, slammed her against his chest, and executed a graceful twist and dip, bending her dramatically over his arm. He was going to shock her into progression. And she reacted correctly: she looked like a doll taken from a box marked, Surprise, with her wide eyes and mouth in the shape of an O. He pressed his lips down on hers, and the O closed even as she struggled against him.

The idiocy of the move and the clarification in his mind that he was behaving like a complete asshat sank in almost immediately—who was *he* to feel privileged to a lip-lock with this amnesiac beauty?—and he was about to release her, except that a fraction of time passed while their lips met, time enough for the kiss to sink in and for Kitty to completely stop struggling. She returned the kiss, and it wasn't without passion.

It was only a fraction of a moment, but that was all he needed. He kissed her again, this time not quite in the name of saving the world. Somewhere in the middle of soft lips and damp tongue and warmth radiating off her skin, with Kitty in his arms and her hair flowing over her arm and the fabric of her dress brushing against his skin and the lovely faint scent of her neck, he completely forgot himself. He kissed her. Oh, God, how he kissed her. And when he slowly pulled away and stood her upright, the only meaningful thought inside his head was something like: *Good Lord.*

The next breath they took together seemed to repair the flow of oxygen. Kitty came to her senses, pushing away from him at the same time he let go. She stumbled back like a drunk and caught her heel in the hem of her dress, sending her arms thrashing in midair for balance. She righted herself, two bright red spots shining on her cheeks, her eyes enormous in her head to the point where Q wondered if you could kill a person with a kiss.

She inhaled loudly, and then she exhaled even louder.

Insert automatic response, Q thought, refusing to allow himself to duck out of the way in the fleeting speck of time before her entire body relaxed on the exhalation and she raised her hand and slammed her palm across his face. His head snapped to the side, the blow stinging. It hurt way, way more than he'd expected.

"You won't even remember it tomorrow," he growled, momentarily forgetting that he actually deserved the slap, and maybe something harder.

Kitty couldn't seem to find the words she was looking for. "You're disgusting," she said at last. "Get out."

Q looked at her with a kind of rising horror—had he really done what he thought?—but he couldn't quite seem to make himself move. She slowly raised her arm and tentatively reached out.

Q couldn't move; he couldn't even draw his gaze from her eyes.

She was shaking as she stepped forward. Her extended hand scraped across his shirt, tingles exploding down his chest. She placed her hand there, lurched forward and . . . pushed him back from her threshold.

"Kitty—" he began.

The strange spell between them faltered. Her expression shuttered for good. "It's Katherine," she snapped. And then she ordered her door shut in his face.

Q rocked back on his heels. He stood there, listening to the click of her shoes fade back into the far rooms. In a kind of shock, he felt a sudden wash of tears fill his eyes. He blinked back, confused and embarrassed, then turned and walked woodenly down the hall to his own door. He went inside and shut the door behind him, then leaned against it, biting down hard on his trembling lip.

Yes, I know why I'm so mad at you. He reached up to where her palm had made contact against his chest, and pressed his own palm over the spot. *Because caring about you hurts.*

CHAPTER TEN

Q unwrapped a piece of Roxy's gum, grimaced at the prospect of the bland, old-school flavoring, sniffed it, stuck it in his mouth and chewed, then decided it wasn't as bad as he'd expected. Louise sat beside him, drumming her fingers on the arm of the sofa.

Q studied her impatient digits, then looked at his sister. "There's really not much change," he said, purposely fudging. It all seemed so exhausting. So . . . disappointing. "Like I said, she's just not retaining."

"She hasn't shown *any* sign of remembering you from one meeting to the next?"

"No."

"Well, just because you can't tell doesn't mean it's not happening," his sister mused. "Can you ratchet it up a notch?"

"What does that mean, Lou?" he asked wearily.

Louise slumped back against the couch, the computer on her lap falling against her stomach. "I don't know. Let's just get the report in and we'll start talking about different tactics." She tapped the space bar to make the screen saver go away. "So . . . you played doctor again and got the same result as usual. And you're saying there was nothing different from the last time. That's what you're saying, right? So I'm basically just going to reference her last visit with you and—"

Q shifted uncomfortably in his chair.

"What's that mean?" Louise asked, when he didn't respond otherwise.

"What's what mean?"

Louise waggled her fingers in the direction of his uncomfortable shifting, which made Q that much more uncomfortable.

"I tried something new," he said, feeling that same strange anger well up inside him again. The anger at being emotionally connected but impotent. *Just pull the damn Band-Aid off and explain.*

Louise's hands hovered over her keyboard. "Oh?"

"I kissed her," he said nonchalantly. "And she—"

"Are you kidding me?" Louise asked, unable to stop a painfully goofy grin from crossing her face. When Q refused to smile in return, she dialed it back and said in her most professional voice, "Why don't you tell me about it. I'll record it directly into the file, and it'll save you the trouble of having to write up the report."

"There's a report?" Mason's voice boomed out as he crossed the apartment. "Did something happen?"

Q lolled back on the cushions, smacking his gum and generally exuding the air of one who couldn't care less. "I realized I was simply becoming part of her loop. I needed to start changing things, make our time together more irregular. I wanted to really try to prevent repetition of any sort, hoping to get the random access memory in her brain fired up again. So I made a small adjustment."

Mason came around and sat on the coffee table. "What was the adjustment?"

Attempting to control the irritation that Mason Merrick always seemed to generate in him, Q made a big show of resituating the throw pillows lumped against his side. He slumped back again, completely aware of how lame his explanation was going to make him sound.

Louise leaned sideways and nudged his shoulder with hers. "Well?"

A great clattering erupted as Roxy came bounding down the stairs and into the living room. "You're just in time for Q's special report," Mason said, reaching out to her. She settled on his lap.

"Awesome. Go ahead."

Son of a bitch. Fine. Q grunted. "I was trying to . . . how should I put this? Shock her system without actually frying her brain."

"I'm all for that," Roxy said cheerfully.

Q picked at a loose thread on the seat cushion next to him, then pulled himself together and looked Mason straight in the eye. "First I pretended to kidnap her, and when that didn't elicit a reaction, I moved in next to her. As you all should know. Then I . . . went to her apartment."

Everybody leaned forward.

"I knocked, she opened the door . . . *anIisseder.*"

"What?" Louise prompted, laughing. "They can't understand you."

Q sunk lower in the sofa. *"Ikisster."*

"What's he saying?" Roxy asked, looking around in bewilderment. "What's that he's trying to say?"

"I kissed her!" Q yelled. "Now, can we all please behave like adults?" He shifted his gaze to Roxy's face and then Louise's, completely aware that he was behaving the least like an adult of all of them. This was excruciating.

For a moment no one said a word, much less a mocking word. Sadly, the respite was not to last.

"That's the report?" Roxy asked, the corners of her mouth twitching.

Q shrugged. "I never said it was a special report," he growled. "It's no big deal."

"No big deal? It sort of is. How did she respond?" Roxy asked.

Q hemmed and hawed for a moment; then he said, "She slapped my face and shut the door." He held up a finger. "Which I take as a positive sign in the most important respect. Unlike the kidnapping, it wasn't just a bland, vague response. There was passion behind it."

Again, all was silent. Someone snickered. It sounded like Louise. Roxy bit her lower lip. Mason coughed. And then he chuckled.

Q glared at him. "That's not what I meant. I meant there was the kind of intensity of emotion that we're looking for. Not that there was *passion*. Not that there wasn't passion, either. Not that . . . Oh, hell."

Mason started full-on laughing, which only made things worse as the hilarity became contagious.

Q tried to be a good sport about it. "You know what? You're absolutely right. It's funny. You *should* laugh," he said.

"Wait a minute," Louise replied, her face becoming slightly more serious. "I don't think this is as funny as we'd like to believe. I mean, it *is* . . . but maybe it had an impact. And maybe that impact was negative. Maybe she'll store it in her subconscious, and the next time she sees you she'll think that you're somehow dangerous and bad."

A slow grin swept over Q's face. "Well, maybe I *am* dangerous and bad."

"You're not dangerous and bad." His sister laughed. "You're an iron marshmallow. And why you're pretending to be a cocky bastard I have no idea. It's completely ridiculous. What are you hiding?"

Q smacked his gum, pretending that he was a cocky bastard who didn't care, which couldn't have been farther from the truth. Still, it was safer. "Nothing. I'm just saying . . . I could tell her I'm in love with her and it's not like she'd care or believe me."

Louise cocked her head and studied his face.

"What?" Q asked.

"Nothing. Your comments have been noted. Moving on. Actually . . . Roxy and I've been working on something that will help alleviate the pressure on you to—"

"Go around kissing women like a complete jerk?" Q suggested.

"Exactly."

"Rox? You want to take this one?" Louise suggested.

"Sure." Roxy got off Mason's lap and went over to the dining room table. She shuffled through a stack of papers, then turned back to the group. "We're just trying to make this work. If the idea is to get you to gradually sink into her consciousness and become embedded in the reality there, we can't afford to have her associating you with negative vibes. Louise and I have been brainstorming some Pavlovian response techniques that will counteract any onetime ill effects, and these will be useful in neutralizing those you might have lodged in her brain with this business. I think the next step is to give Kitty some triggers. Some *positive* triggers."

"I thought Q was going to be the trigger," Mason spoke up.

Roxy looked at him. "We want to reinforce her subconscious memories as well. We need to give her sensory cues to associate with Q so that she thinks of him and anything he's told her even when he's not actually there."

"So . . . what are we talking about?" Q asked. "A color? A sound?"

"We may need to try different things."

"A sound, I think," Q mused. "Something very distinct that can't get confused with anything else. Nothing gets into your mind like a song."

"I like that," Louise agreed, removing her glasses and carefully wiping the lenses on her shirt. "And it should be some auditory stimulus that happens for the first time when you're with her. We just have to figure out now what sound it will be—and what it will mean. Let's think about it."

"I'm also going to work on putting together a little album," Roxy said. "You know, like some photos and some memorabilia or whatever. Those would be great triggers at the right moment." She glanced at Q. "Don't worry; it'll be something small enough so you can carry it with you until you need it."

The team broke, and Louise waited for Roxy and Mason to move on before dragging her brother to the opposite side of the apartment. "Anything *else* you want to share? I'm always on your side, you know."

Q frowned.

"You want to tell me what really happened?"

Q rolled his eyes. "It happened how I said it happened. It was a simple situation. I just kissed her to try to give her a shock."

Louise stared at him for a moment. "It's . . . it's just not like you. Why'd you decide to try *that?*"

He stared at her, but didn't manage to speak.

"I think Mason might be right," his sister said slowly, glancing off to the left. Then she looked at him again and added, "But since I know you guys aren't particularly fond of each other, I know that saying that Mason might be right will likely piss you off, and I don't really care—"

"Mason's right about what?" Q interrupted.

His sister sighed and patted his shoulder. "He said you were likely acting as a total asshat, and no girl in her right mind would find your behavior attractive. I said, 'Lucky for him she's not in her right mind,' but I only said that to defend you. The truth is . . . you're acting like you'd normally act with a girl, and what we need you to do is to act in a way that a girl might find appealing."

Q chewed his gum more rapidly. "This is ludicrous," he muttered. "How did I get involved in it?"

"Listen. You don't have to like her," Louise said. "Like

her, don't like her, I really don't care. You just have to *pretend* to like her."

"I've got issues," Q muttered.

"Comes with the job."

"Tell me something I don't know."

"How about this: I know that you know that I know that you're really only acting like an asshat because you *do* like this girl and you're afraid of it. So what you need to do is to pretend to yourself in real life that you don't like her in order to be able to successfully pretend that you do in fake life."

Q blinked, confused, the working of his jaw slowing. "I *don't* like this girl, Louise," he said. "Just because she's pretty, and just because she's got Leonardo Kaysar messing up her life, doesn't mean that I have any emotional attachment at all."

Louise slung her arm around him and gave a squeeze. "See, now? If you just keep telling yourself that, this is going to work out just fine."

CHAPTER ELEVEN

It was difficult to focus on what Dee and Ariel were saying; everything at brunch seemed so *interesting*. Katherine stared down at the table setting, taking in the curlicue details in the bottom of the flatware and the painfully inane country flowers bordering the dishes. The country flowers really bothered her. She kept staring down at the rim, wishing the pattern weren't so faded and the flowers were a bit more delicate. How remarkably *interesting* that the pattern was faded and the flowers ugly. She looked around, surprised that the restaurant was a bit . . . tacky. Why hadn't she thought so before? Why on earth did they eat here all the time?

"Miss?"

Katherine looked over at the menu being flapped at the side of her face, and she took it in hand. Dee and Ariel made their choices immediately, without bothering to look at their menus. Katherine studied the choices but kept stalling out every time her eye reached about a third of the way down: it was just about there that she felt the overwhelming compulsion to order organic granola with genetically modified yogurt. The trouble was, she was actually in the mood for pancakes. Pancakes with a tremendous amount of syrup. She looked up and watched Dee and Ariel order. They always seemed so sure of themselves.

"And for you?" the waiter asked.

Katherine sighed, and all three looked at her.

"Organic granola and genetically modified yogurt?" the waiter asked helpfully.

She looked at the waiter, struggling against a natural instinct to agree, and finally forced out the word, albeit in a crazed, high-pitched tone, "Pancakes!"

His stylus failed to make contact with his smartie. "You mean the granola and yogurt?"

I want pancakes.

Katherine didn't know what to do. She stared down at the menu and the word *pancakes* blurred by someone else's greasy fingerprint. The seconds ticked by in an almost physical way; Katherine felt as though her mind were literally pushing through time that was pushing right back at her.

"Katherine, you know what you want," Dee said. "Order the granola and yogurt."

Katherine looked up, and it felt as though it took a massive effort to keep her eyes open.

Dee and Ariel looked at each other. The shape of Dee's lips distorted in slow motion as she formed some sort of word that, judging by the scowl on her face, was not likely pleasant.

"Go ahead and order," Ariel pleaded, as if the fate of the universe had come down to Pancakes versus Granola, No Holds Barred.

Katherine shifted her gaze back to Dee, the lateral movement so slow she could almost hear the tick-tocks of the nanoseconds themselves. Ariel was staring down at the way Katherine's fingers gripped the cheerful red-and-white-checked tablecloth.

Katherine loosened her grip, took a deep breath, and relaxed into the words: "I want pancakes."

Dee flinched. Ariel just looked scared. And Katherine's heartbeat accelerated so quickly it knocked the breath right out of her.

Gasping for air, Katherine found focus in her peripheral vision; it seemed as though the entire restaurant had reacted simultaneously to some hidden instruction. Katherine blinked drowsily, trying to hang on before the edges of her vision were completely blurred. For a moment it seemed as if the medicine she'd been taking was working; the blur focused once more. But it wasn't the table setting and her girlfriends she saw before her; it was a man's face. Again and again he approached in her mind's eye, his body crowding hers, his face too close, his mouth coming down on hers. In that one moment he stepped forward, touched her, kissed her. She saw her hand slap his cheek, then rewind and slap it again, rewind, slap, rewind, slap.

"Oh, my God," Katherine whispered. She looked up at her friends in terror.

Ariel reached out and gripped the side of her arm. "What's wrong?"

Katherine felt the compulsion to strip her friend's hand away. She looked to the side, trying to focus her thoughts, trying to come to terms with the fact that she might never be free from this state of confusion. "Would I ever cheat on Leo?" she asked.

The mouths of her friends dropped open in shock.

Then Ariel calmly pushed her chair back and stood. "I have to make a phone call. Excuse me."

"Dee, what's happening to me?"

"We've been through this before," Dee said. "You had an accident."

"I remember that part. I don't remember what kind of accident it was."

Dee looked over her shoulder. Katherine followed her gaze to where Ariel stood having a very intense conversation on her smartie.

"What kind of accident did I have, Dee?"

"Um, the kind that blows your memory away." She took Katherine's hand. "You have brain damage. Your memories are blanked out."

Katherine sat back in her chair. "I *am* blank. And that's so . . . *tragic*."

Dee nodded. "But everything's fine now. You're fabulous. You've got a fabulous fiancé, a fabulous job. Katherine, you have a fabulous life." She took Katherine's hand and looked her straight in the eyes. "There is absolutely nothing wrong with you."

"Yes, but I don't seem to have a personality. I find that troubling." She stared down at their intertwined fingers and had an odd sensation of personal space violation. She pulled her hand loose and shook it out, then caught her two friends staring.

"Did something happen?" Dee asked.

"What do you mean?"

"Did anything unusual happen to you on the way over here?"

Katherine thought about it. Dee waited silently across the table.

"Is there anything *wrong* with Leo?" Katherine asked.

"No." Dee looked as if the question could not have been more insane. "He's got it all."

"Right." Katherine glanced over at Ariel, who was still

talking a blue streak into her smartie. "I don't think Ariel would understand, but I think I had a sex fantasy and Leo wasn't part of it. What do you think it means?"

Dee's lips moved but didn't formulate a sound. She looked a little terrified, her gaze darting in Ariel's direction and back.

Katherine turned her head to the side and attempted to sort through the massive amount of fog in her brain. "You don't think it means I doubt Leo's love for me, do you? Or my own for him?"

Dee looked relieved to hear that question. She patted the back of Katherine's hand. "There's no reason to doubt. You have him wrapped around your little finger."

"I do?"

"Absolutely."

Kitty relaxed. "Just as long as it's not the other way around," she said with a little sass. Her friend went suddenly silent, so she felt the need to say, "Oh, don't worry! It's not that big a deal. I was just talking aloud. I think maybe I'm having cold feet or something. But that's normal, right? I mean, that's pretty normal."

"She's sick," Dee muttered to Ariel, who had just returned.

"She's tired," Ariel replied.

Katherine looked at them both, wondering how they felt they could talk like this in front of her. "I'm fine. I just . . "

Ariel ignored her, instead leaning into Dee and whispering in her ear. Dee nodded and pulled a small bottle from her bag. She broke the safety seal and shook out a couple of pills. She reached across the table and put them on Katherine's plate, then got up and walked around behind Katherine, pushing a glass of water against her mouth. "These will make you feel better."

"But I didn't say I felt bad," Katherine said.

"Now, Katherine, you're having an episode."

"I am?"

"Take the pills."

Katherine looked up from the plate, startled by her friend's steely tone. She took the pills in her hand and watched them slide into the depression between her fingers. She shrugged, then popped the pills onto her tongue, tipping the water in after them. She swallowed half the glass along with the medication, then set it down and looked at Dee. "Okay?"

"Great."

The waiter put his finger up to his ear. "Stand by . . . she's almost down," he said.

It was as Katherine suddenly Magnavoxed back in her chair that the couple seated at the table behind her stood up and began changing the table setting in front of her. Dee and Ariel both put down their spoons and leaned back in their chairs, extras flowing forward around them and re-setting the scene.

"God, I'm tired," Ariel muttered. "Did a double yesterday and filled in for a friend."

"Oh, man, I'm sorry."

"It was just Party Murmur, but still . . ."

Dee nodded. She looked at Katherine. "Do you think this was just a glitch, or do you think she knows she's being Truman-ed?"

Ariel shrugged. "If she does, she's about to forget again."

Dee studied her smartie. "How do you want to make up time? I could cut out the anecdote about the feral cat."

"Yeah, okay." Ariel stared down at her smartie. "We're over by fifteen minutes, thirty and nine . . . I'll just keep interrupting. We'll hit the next topic and keep going until we time out right."

The waiter nodded. Dee stood up; Ariel adjusted herself to hover just above the seat cushion. "Three . . . two . . ."

He pointed his finger at the girls . . . and they sat down and started the morning over again.

Katherine emerged from a state of nothingness, the buzz and the thump and the emotions that had seemed so vivid earlier almost immediately losing their richness, as if pixels were dropping from a digiframe photo until the pieces were nothing more than colored dust at her feet. She stared down at the table, pristine in layout, the napkins untouched, water glasses not yet filled, and the slate in her brain began to fill up . . . with words she wasn't quite sure were her own.

"And for you?" a male voice asked.

Katherine looked up at the waiter and smiled. "I'll have the organic granola with genetically modified yogurt, please."

CHAPTER TWELVE

"I'd wanted pancakes," Kitty said. "And for a while I didn't even remember that I'd wanted pancakes but asked for granola . . ." She walked up to Q, sitting in his "doctor's" chair, with the labcoat slung over the back of the seat and leaned over his desk. Her eyes widened. "But, *then* I was sitting there in work looking at lace trim and suddenly . . . I thought about *pancakes* again."

"And what do you think the significance of that is?" Q asked.

Kitty frowned and stood up straight. "The girls said there was just a mix-up with the order at brunch last Sunday. But then, they keep telling me I've always preferred granola."

"But you . . . don't."

Kitty rolled her eyes in a "keep up with me, here" sort

of way. "Sometimes I like one, and sometimes I like the other. That's not really the point."

Q smiled. Actually, it was the point.

She suddenly drew into herself a little, eyeing him nervously. "This is going to sound a little . . . crazy."

"It's probably not. And if it does . . ." He shrugged. "So what? That's what I'm here for."

Kitty cleared her throat. "So, sometimes I feel like there are two me's. And one me does all these things right and people don't get all worked up about it. But the other me . . . the other me sometimes wants *pancakes*." She went silent.

Q nodded, but she didn't go on.

Kitty suddenly plopped down in the chair in front of him and clasped her hands. Then she leaned toward him and whispered, "Maybe it's not so bad to want pancakes. Because deep inside? Wanting pancakes felt . . . right. I've had that rightish feeling before, with other things. It kind of catches up with me a little sometimes."

Q tried not to look too excited by this news. "So you actually remember going to a brunch several days ago and wanting pancakes and getting granola."

"I think so. I'm not sure. I mean, I don't know how much of what I remember actually happened and I don't know that I would have remembered any of it were it not for . . ." Kitty turned and grabbed her purse, then pulled out a soiled paper napkin. The word *pancakes* was scrawled on it in rose-colored crayon. "I think I made a note to myself."

Q peered down at it, then raised his eyes to Kitty's lips. She moistened them with her tongue and he gave himself a mental kick to stay on point and focus less on their lovely little bow-shape and more on the fact that the color of her lipliner was similar to the color of the writing on the napkin. "You wrote this?"

"That's how I write my esses."

"Why didn't you type this into your smartie?"

"I have no idea."

Because deep inside you know something is wrong besides what they tell you is wrong and you didn't want them to know about it. If I can just bring what's deep inside of you to the surface . . . Q took the napkin and stuck it in his pocket. Not a good idea to chance that her friends might see that she was still thinking about something that happened days ago.

"I haven't shown it to anybody else. Wasn't going to," Kitty said, walking around the fake doctor's office, picking up Vesper's props, examining them, and putting them down. "I've decided to stop asking my friends about what is and isn't reality so much." She looked up at Q with her clear blue eyes. "It's incredibly embarrassing. I mean, I don't even tell them half the things I'm really thinking these days because I don't know if any of them have actually happened. You're the only one I tell."

From his seat across the room, Q followed her every move. He straightened in his chair. "Do you tell *me* everything?"

Kitty paused with a paperweight in her hand. Her eyes downcast, she slowly set the rock down on the table, looked at her hand, and cleaned it by running it down the side of her skirt. "If I think of it, I do." She looked up at him, and Q saw the fear in her eyes. "It's not as confusing when I tell you things."

So, she remembered she'd told him things before. "Why is it less confusing?" he asked.

"Because you never tell me that things I think happened didn't happen, or that things I didn't think happened, happened. You just believe that what I think happened must have seemed to me to have happened, and therefore they must have happened." She giggled. "Well, you know what I mean."

"You trust me," Q said quietly, more to himself than to her.

She studied his face and smiled. "More than anyone."

Q tried to conceal his reaction to her words, the nause-ating sense of wrongness that swept through him. He must have revealed something, because she frowned watching his face. She'd misunderstood his reaction. Blinking rapidly she added rather dully, "Except for Leo, of course."

"Of course," he murmured. He climbed to his feet.

She chewed on her lower lip. "Can you help me.?"

Q tried not to stare at her mouth. He failed.

Kitty pressed her fingers to her temples. "Do you really think I can go back to being what I once was?"

Q took her hands and brought them down to her sides. Kitty looked down at their entangled fingers, and then up at Q and swallowed hard. She pulled her hands away. "I think there's something wrong with me. Where you touch me, my skin gets all . . . fizzy."

"That's good. It means you still have . . . feelings." Q lowered his head. "Have you considered that . . ." He wanted to tell her that Leonardo Kaysar was pure evil, that Kaysar didn't love her, that he never had. That she was no more and no less of an experiment than the alpha and beta bots for whom she designed dresses. But it was too soon; she was still harnessed to the loop, and as long as something in her felt that Leonardo Kaysar was her savior, any truths he gave her would be minimized down to a he-said/she-said. He needed her to be able to prove to herself that Leonardo wasn't who she'd thought, not merely because someone said, "He's lying, believe *me*."

"Have you considered that your friends and your boyfriend have been . . . underestimating you?" he suggested.

"Yes, but they are looking out for me," she replied.

"Well, Kitty, I think you are capable of much more."

"It's Katherine," she said, but without any particular emphasis. "If it weren't for Leo, I don't know where I'd be. I mean, I forget everything, with the brain damage and all."

Q laughed. "You don't mean that literally, right?"

Katherine wrinkled her nose. "Of course I do. Everybody knows I have serious brain damage. That's why I see you!"

"Everybody knows, do they?" Q muttered, his temper threatening to flare. "Well, let's think about this. What do you think is going to happen to you if all of these people leave you alone? Do you think you're not going to know what to do with yourself? Do you think you're going to forget where you live or confuse your right shoe with your left? Have you ever thought about what might happen if you just . . . let things happen on their own?"

Katherine took a step back. "Dr. Van Heusenfleugen, you're turning red. I think you should consider taking a Valium."

"This is me getting very, very, very angry," he said.

She flinched. "I can't imagine I've said anything to—"

"It wasn't you. God, Kitty, there's nothing wrong with you." He took her by the shoulders and she reared back a bit, her eyes wide. "Look at me. It's one thing to tell someone they're muddled up and need a bit of straightening out. To tell them they're actually sick, that they have brain damage and that they must rely on others . . . that's wrong, don't you think?"

"It's not wrong if it's true," she said uncertainly.

"I wish I knew how to make this sink into your brain. If there is one thing I wish you to never forget, it's this: you are *not* brain damaged. You are not *anything* damaged. You've done nothing wrong, and there is nothing wrong with you. And I'm not talking about your perfect life or your perfect friends or your perfect clothes or your perfect job. I'm saying that what's already perfect is what's buried in there under layers of lies and pretense. There is nothing wrong with *you!*"

They didn't say anything to each other for a long time. She looked up at him, her eyes searching his. "But everyone knows that's not true."

"Everyone's wrong." He gave her a little shake. "They're lying. Everyone, Kitty."

"Everyone . . . but you?"

An innocent question, a soft voice. It sliced right through him.

"Doctor," she whispered, backing up against a wall, flattening herself against it.

Q slowly moved closer. Her eyes locked on his, and his peripheral vision caught the quickened rise and fall of her breathing, the slight tremor in her hands. He stopped just in front of her; there was nowhere for her to go. She raised her chin a bit, as if something in her knew the right thing to do was to try to escape, but everything else wanted to be right here and nowhere else.

"I'm lost," she said.

"I know."

"I'm . . . blank."

He didn't answer.

"I'm stuck."

He nodded.

"I don't know why I feel this way. I just know that it's no good telling anyone."

"It doesn't matter. It's Wednesday. You won't feel this way on Monday." The cumulative effect that built up over the course of the week was always compromised after the Sunday night reset.

"I'll feel . . . better?"

"Yeah," he said bitterly.

"How do you know?" she asked. Her voice was small.

"Because I've been watching out for you."

"Watching out for me, or watching me?"

"What would the difference be . . . to you?"

She shrugged. "I'm supposed to be happy *now*."

"Yeah, you are."

"I don't feel happy these days."

"That's not a bad thing, actually."

"It doesn't feel good." She leveled her blue eyes at him. God, they were powerful. She moved nearer, one hand out for balance, stopped a few centimeters away, just where he could have rested his chin on the top of her golden-haired head. She looked up at him, searching his eyes with her own. "Aren't you going to check my vitals?"

"Not today," Q managed to say.

"How do we know if I'm getting better?"

Q swallowed. "I can tell."

She looked up at him, and Q's mind went spinning off into the wild; all the powerlessness and rage that had been building up in him over the past few weeks just swamped him. She was so close, he could smell the faint perfume she'd delicately swiped down her décolletage. Her eyes were curious—if he'd been thinking straight, or at least somewhat rationally, he'd have caught the struggle in the depths of that gaze, the recognition that even in her ignorant state, the one thing she wasn't forgetting was that she was capable of so much more.

A new look passed over her face. She wet her lower lip, still looking as though she were processing $E=mc^2$. She paused. Her mouth curled at the ends; she seemed forever lost in her reverie.

Maybe if I just . . . if I did it properly . . . if I just . . . Q reached out and took Kitty's arm, adrenaline roughening the movement.

"I'm still scared!" Kitty yelped.

He froze and immediately let go, taking a step back.

"I don't feel like I'm getting better. I actually think I might be getting crazier," she said. "And I can't say anything because they'll—" She stopped abruptly.

"They'll what?"

"They'll give me extra pills," she whispered.

"What did you say?" Q asked.

"The pills I take for my brain. I don't like them. They make me feel spacey, and I haven't been taking as much as

I'm supposed to." She looked down at the floor. "I guess they figure spacey is better than crazy."

That son of a bitch, Q thought. "May I see the pills, please?"

She pulled a small bottle from her bag. A number of capsules bobbled around in the bottom of the amber glass. Q stared at the bottle for a moment, and then took it from her and wrote down the information off the label. He dumped a couple of the capsules onto the desk beside him, closed the bottle, and handed it back.

He took a deep breath, wondering for the millionth time what had possessed his sister to think he'd be good at this. "Look, Kitty. I want you to trust me. I mean, you have to trust me or I'll never get you out. So, tell me what would prove to you that I mean no harm and am trying to help." A laugh escaped from his mouth. "Really, I'm trying to save your life. You've got people who love you waiting for you."

His last words seemed to really strike a chord. "People who love me." Her eyes bulged a bit. "I . . ."

"Are you okay?" Alarmed, Q grabbed the water bottle and dumped half of it into a nearby glass.

"I . . ."

"Drink this."

"No!"

He reared back. "Okay." He set the water glass down on the counter next to her and waited.

Kitty stood there, her hands curled into fists, a look of total misery twisting her face. "I don't always love Leo!" she finally said. She exhaled a deep breath and closed her eyes and seemed to will herself to relax.

He'd have to tread carefully here. He could try to lead her to a conclusion she felt was unnatural . . . but it would be like walking a tightrope.

"Something's very wrong," she said. Q could see her struggling to find the words. "I don't always love Leo," she blurted again. "I'm not sure I love him. I don't know if I love him. He doesn't always love me," she babbled desperately, running circles around what she must have suddenly realized was the truth.

He pleaded with his eyes, not daring to interrupt, not daring to impose his thoughts.

"Is it real?" she finally asked. "Any of it?"

You know it isn't.

She took a handful of his shirt, squeezing the fabric, gripping at him without really pulling him toward her. She wouldn't look away from him, and the look in her eyes was excruciating. "Is it real?"

He felt the muscles in his jaw working, but still he waited for her to look inside herself for the answers. *You know it isn't. Say it, Kitty. Just say what you know to be true.*

A sound of pure anguish slipped from her lips. "Leo's a lie. He and I are a lie. My life is a lie."

Q didn't know what to think. A strange elation filled him from the inside out, and as her face crumpled and she burst into tears, he pulled her in tight, closing his own eyes as her warmth sought his.

This was what he'd meant to avoid. This gorgeous feeling, always so fleeting, never lasting, better off avoided in the first place. Because some things you could never forget. Some losses you could never forget. He didn't want to care about her only to lose her in the end. And that was how it was in his business. That was how it was in life.

He held her close, tilting his head at an odd angle to keep his face as far from hers as possible.

Her sobs eased and she phased into periodic sniffles. He loosened one arm with some difficulty, because she didn't seem to want him to let go, and managed to obtain a Kleenex from his pocket, which he slid through the small gap in their embrace. She blew her nose, and the wad of tissue came back through the crook of his elbow. He tossed it into the trash.

She squeezed her arms around him tighter. Q stared

helplessly up at the ceiling, trying to focus on anything but the feel of her against him. Everywhere her body touched him was a combination of angel and devil.

Her head burrowed against his shirt and her breathing began to slow and grow steady. He cocked his head to catch a glimpse of her face. Her eyes were closed; her expression was relaxed and something like contentment settled in there. She burrowed deeper into him, and at the gap of skin where her hand weighed down his shirt, her tear-dampened mouth pressed against him.

In all my life . . . in all my life . . . he thought. Nothing had ever touched him so gently and so fiery all at once, as her mouth on that bit of his skin.

"I'm going to take you home," he announced, standing taller, which had the effect of jolting her back a bit.

She looked shocked for a moment, as if he'd interrupted a deep reverie. Then she lifted her chin. "Absolutely not."

Q looked at her in surprise.

"I said absolutely not."

"I heard you. I just thought you might need some time to—"

"I have opinions, you know. I have feelings and opinions, and there are things I want to do and things that I don't want to do, and so that's how it's going to be now."

Q unfurled a slow smile. "I think that sounds terrific," he said quietly.

"You do?"

"Of course. How do you think it makes me feel when you disappear on me?"

Her eyes widened. "When I . . . How *does* it make you feel?"

Q took a step back, fumbling a little. "Well, I . . . I mean, it's really . . . frustrating . . . to . . . have to start over." He looked away, confused by the sudden rush of emotions sweeping him.

"Do you miss me . . . when I'm gone?"

"Well, of course," he said, dismissive. "Leonardo might not care, but I do."

She started in surprise, and Q realized how careless he'd been.

"But Leonardo hired you, didn't he?" she asked. "Isn't that why you're . . . Wow. He *didn't* hire you." She blinked in confusion. "How did you know I needed you?"

He studied her face and realized that this breakthrough was just the tip of the iceberg. She hadn't clued in to Roxy and Mason or anybody else. She hadn't clued in to much other than that she wasn't supposed to be where she was.

"I just knew," he murmured. "Some friends of yours were worried. They asked me to look after you. They . . ." *Tread carefully.* "They don't quite see eye-to-eye with your boyfriend."

"What friends? Ariel and Dee?"

Q shook his head. "Friends from before your . . . accident." He didn't dare mention Roxy and Mason for fear she'd get confused, blurt their names to Leonardo at some point, and clue Kaysar in that everybody was in the game.

Kitty went very, very quiet. "It's very strange, what you're saying." She looked sharply up at him, and in a voice that climbed higher and higher, said, "What you're suggesting is very strange. Leonardo looks out for me, helps me with everything in my life . . . and it's just very, very odd for you to suggest that Leo might not care about everything I do. I mean, really, it's outrageous."

He knew what she must be thinking. She'd already revealed she was no longer 100% certain that the ones who were supposed to love her the most had her best interests at heart. If she really accepted that, it would probably feel like her world was crumbling around her.

"If there is anything you have lied about or concealed

or pretended, you'd better tell me right now," she said in a steely voice.

"I'm not a psychiatrist," Q said immediately. "I'm not a doctor. Not the usual kind."

Kitty frowned, and then fidgeting with her bracelet, she asked, "Then why do you make me tell you all these personal things?"

"Because I do rescue people. I'm a specialist in time anomalies and with you, it's necessary to take into consideration the psychological effects of time."

"You're not a doctor," she repeated unhappily. She looked away. "You're telling me I've got these friends who sent you to me and that you're in the time-technology business . . ."

"That's the truth."

"Right, well, think about what that means for me? My fiancé is the best there is in the time-technology business and you're not working with him to help me, so you must be working . . . against him." Kitty threw up her arms. "What am I supposed to do with that information?"

Q placed his hands lightly on her shoulders. "You are supposed to do whatever you feel like. That's the point. Tell you what. You go with me on this ride a bit. Let me show you some things, tell you some things . . . then you make your own choices. That's what I'm here for. To help get you back to the point where you can make your own choices." It made him a little queasy, knowing that his words were manipulative in their own right. Were they really giving her a choice? Or were they just pulling her back into the version of life they wanted for her.

"I could turn you in to Leo so easily. He could make you disappear just like that," Kitty said haughtily, snapping her fingers.

"Let me help you fill in the blanks, Kitty," Q murmured. "If Leo's world is what you choose in the end, so be it. He won't have to disappear me. I'll just go."

She frowned. "Oh. You make it all seem so easy."

Q would have liked to imagine it was the idea of him leaving that bothered her. "I'm not going to pretend any of this is easy. I'm not going to pretend anything with you from here on out."

She thought about that for a moment. "Is there anything else you want to tell me?"

"Yeah. My name isn't Dr. Van Heusenfleugen. Everyone just calls me Q."

"Q," she echoed. "Just Q?"

He smiled. "Yeah. Try to remember that."

She reached for her purse, dug around, and then pulled out her lipliner and wrote on her inner wrist.

He would have protested, but the letter Q she'd drawn there was so tiny and faint, it wouldn't pose a threat before it smeared into her skin and vanished.

"Hey." Q touched Kitty's cheek gently. "It's going to be fine."

She nodded and then pushed back her shoulders and lifted her chin. "We can go to my apartment now, if you think it will help me."

Q arched an eyebrow at her.

She grabbed her coat and walked right past him and out the door, turning back when he didn't follow and holding it open for him. "I *trust* you."

CHAPTER THIRTEEN

He drove her back to her condo complex in silence, her trust in him making him feel all prickly inside, as if he were doing something wrong even though the plan couldn't have been going more right. He followed her to her apartment, painfully enchanted by the small details in her movements, quirks and habits that he hadn't noticed were missing before but that must now be amplified by virtue of her having a longer leash than the one Leonardo had wrapped around her neck.

Kitty flipped her hair back away from her eyes in that certain way he'd become fixated upon, and she pressed her index finger to her lips, almost like a shush. "So what do we do now?" she asked.

Q readjusted his focus, doing his best to shift his attention from her personal details to the greater magnitude of her overall problem. "Your brain has become overly accustomed to repetition and continuity. It has learned to accept—and expect—certain things. But what if we could provide a trigger that would tell your brain to expect and accept things that are different from what you've been experiencing . . . ?"

Kitty didn't know the extent of Leonardo's experiment; she didn't understand that he was really nothing to her, and that nothing he wanted for her was anything she should embrace. Therefore, instead of finishing his explanation with ". . . different from what your fake friends and fake fiancé have been stuffing down your throat," he said, ". . . to kind of jolt you out of patterns of blankness and give your mind an excuse to start turning its wheels again."

"I'm game," Kitty said; then she disappeared into the bathroom.

Q followed her to the doorway and watched her check her makeup, even though it was already the end of the day. He wondered how many of her habits were really hers and how many were affectations relating to what the people around her wanted her to be, what they had forced her to do.

"The concept I want to work with has a solid foundation in the old Pavlovian experiments. You know, where the dog begins to associate the bell with food, that type of thing." Q looked around the apartment and found the entertainment center on the far wall. "Nice rack," he said, going over and checking it out.

"I never use it," Kitty said, coming out into the living room.

Q peered over the back of the multitiered system. It was incredibly dusty. He checked the plugs. It was designed in a walnut-encased art deco shelving system. There was even a replica phonograph player. A stack of records lay flat on one of the shelves, thick with accrued dust.

"How often does your maid come?"

"Oh, I don't know. The concierge handles that."

Kaysar handles that.

"You have any favorites?"

Kitty looked surprised. "I don't think I've heard any of them."

Q shuffled through the choices. It was a retro pack, obviously purchased together in bulk and set out for show. Inside the faux-worn sheaths, blue metal rounds glinted. He lifted the top of the phonograph and placed a round on the pad. "Music on," he said.

A row of green lights lit up; the arm of the system lowered but did not touch the round, but the music began to play. Q sat down on the sofa and examined the album sleeve, which listed a medley of Broadway hits dating back to the 1920s. Neither he nor Kitty nor any of his friends had existed then, not in any linear sense of time, but these songs appealed. And it was nice that the relics were still available.

" 'I've Got a Crush on You,' " he murmured as he listened to the lyrics. It wasn't a particularly long song; he ordered it to loop, and for the next while he sat back and let George Gershwin's music play and play and play. . . .

". . . but you had such persistence,
You wore down my resistance:

I fell, and it was swell
You're my big and brave and handsome Romeo
How I won you, I shall never, never know
It's not that you're attractive
but, oh, my heart grew active
When you came into view . . ."

"Is this where we segue into an impromptu foxtrot?" Kitty asked. She was standing off to the side.

"Uh. Actually, no," Q said, alarmed.

Kitty's nose crinkled as she frowned. "Oh. Then, um, could we turn the music off? We've listened to the same song about twenty times now."

"You don't like it?"

"It's not that I don't like—"

"'Cause I really like it," he said cheerfully, trying to keep himself focused. "'I've got a crush on you, sweetie pie . . . All the day and night-time, hear me sigh . . . I never had the least notion . . . that I could fall with so much emotion . . .' It really speaks to me. Ya know?"

Dear God. A traditional metal band from Mason's collection would have been a much better idea. Wouldn't it?

"Yes, but—"

"How 'bout a couple more plays and then we'll take it off."

Kitty sighed and sang in a monotone, "'But you had such persistence, you wore down my resistance . . .'"

She turned and looked at him. They laughed.

"'I fell and it was swell . . .'" he sang, clowning it up.

Kitty clasped her hands together melodramatically over her chest. *"It's not that you're attractive . . ."*

"Oh, yeah? So that's how it is." He grabbed her by the hand and twirled her once, then released her.

"I was just kidding," she said—then added: "'You're my big and brave and handsome Romeo. How I won you, I shall *never, never know . . .* '" The Gershwin tune faded on her lips, and the two of them stood in silence.

"What's supposed to happen with the song?" she asked.

"It's going to get your brain moving. Thinking outside of what everyone else is telling you."

"Isn't what everyone's telling me true? Why are we trying to get away from that?"

He'd forgotten that she wasn't quite on the same page about the relative merits of Leonardo Kaysar, so he amended, "It's supposed to make you think of me." *Instead of . . . him.*

In retrospect, Q would have liked to argue that what came next was the logical thing to do: a musical trigger, a true emotional response and all that. But the reality was that he *wanted* to do it. He wanted to kiss her. Properly. So he shut his brain off from the sort of logic that would make a man think twice, took a step forward, and brushed his lips against hers.

A tiny sound escaped her mouth. She didn't move.

He slipped his hand up the side of her cheek to caress her face, closed his eyes, and slowly pressed his mouth against hers. Gently, so gently, he bit at her lower lip with his teeth, and when she relaxed into him, responding with the soft press of her mouth to his, Q let his tongue slide sensuously into her heat.

For once in his life he completely lost track of time. It took the jolt of Kitty stepping away and the loss of her body heat against his skin to pull him out of the moment. When he opened his eyes, Kitty was staring up at him, her face incredibly pale.

She swallowed hard, her eyes like saucers.

Q took in her expression with alarm; absolute misery was written across her face.

"I have a fiancé," she whispered, her eyes filling with tears.

He should have been happy to see her brimming with

emotion, to see that he'd had an impact on her. But all he could think was, *What have I just done? I'm so sorry.* He looked at her, helpless. "That was nothing," he said woodenly. "That thing that happened there . . . it was nothing. You'll forget it."

She blinked uncertainly.

"It never happened. If you ever asked anyone about it, they'd tell you it wasn't true."

She didn't answer, just pressed her hand to her mouth, running her fingers back and forth over her lower lip.

"Kitty?"

"I'm awfully tired," she said, more surprised than anything else as she stared down at the bedspread. "I didn't wash my face. Why didn't I wash my face?"

"Wash your face? What do you mean?"

"It's time for bed. Why didn't I wash my face?" Kitty couldn't seem to control her limbs anymore. She swayed and started falling over.

Q grabbed her. "You've got to stay awake." He took her by the shoulders, but her head flopped over on her neck, a tangle of lush golden hair spilling over her features. She was lolling as if she were drunk.

Kitty looked up at the man with her; he looked as if he were fighting back tears. She smiled. "For me?" she asked, but the question was garbled by her uncooperative tongue.

"Nobody deserves this," he said, and then a flicker of light from the changing wall clock passed over his face.

Kitty looked up. The blue light from the clock blurred with black as the seconds accelerated. She blinked, obviously trying to focus on the numbers. The blur vanished and the time stood still, the numerals indicating seconds on the clock readable at last, though they jumped and flickered from the weight of the infinite particles of time that were always moving. They'd just fast-forwarded toward midnight.

She swayed, suddenly woozy again, and then she fell into his arms.

Q held Kitty in his arms for a while, just gazing down at her face. Then, slowly, cradling her gently, he lowered her to the sheets and rested her head on her pillow. He removed her high heels, covered her with a blanket, and sat on the other side of the bed, wondering if he was somewhere in her dreams while she slept.

CHAPTER FOURTEEN

Q could not have been in a fouler mood if he'd tried.

His sister leaned back in her chair and asked, "So, how did it go?"

Everyone looked up expectantly, which served to annoy Q that much more. He shrugged. "There's something different about her. I mean, there's no way she could be doing everything exactly the same every nanosecond from week to week, so the amount of variation I'm seeing could be something entirely natural and explainable within the confines of her loop, or it could be something else. Let's hope it's the something else, because if I can break through a little, I can figure out how to break through a lot."

"What happened? Did something happen?" Louise asked eagerly.

He *so* wasn't in the mood. "Nothing. Well, nothing permanent," Q hedged. "It's just . . . I mean, she's been in contact with me a couple of times now, you know, so there's a little bit of memory sticking. I hope."

" 'I hope' isn't really the sort of phrase I like to put down in the files."

"What do you think is causing things to stick?" Roxy

asked. "What exactly do you mean by 'she's a little different'?"

Vesper coughed, and Q glared at her. "Well . . . it's like there was a little spark down there and it's ignited," he said. "Her memory, of her personality, I mean," he rushed to add.

Louise purposely and pointedly did not look up. "You kissed her again."

"Er, yeah. But not like an asshat," he growled at her. "And even though it wasn't like a . . . well, like a big, dramatic thing, you know, it was . . ." He sighed, supremely put out that, with all of his expertise and skill, debriefing came down to his explaining the efficacy of his seduction techniques. "It was . . . it seemed to . . ."

"It seemed to 'take'?" Louise finished.

"Right. That's exactly what it was like."

Roxy leaned forward. "You ignited her!" She looked very pleased. "That's wonderful." She leaped up and grabbed some sort of book off the counter next to the fishbowl, then dropped it on the table with a loud thunk. "I finished," Roxy said excitedly, pushing a small photo album in front of Q. "I picked photos I thought would best trigger her memories. And I also stuck in some random stuff I thought might help." She opened the cover and pointed at an envelope slipped into the side pocket. "And that's a letter I wrote to her. I tried to explain things. Whenever you think she's ready, just . . . lay it on her."

Q picked up the album and tossed it across the room to the top of his duffel bag slumped against the wall. "Thanks."

"Oh, and I left some blank pages in the back if you think of anything else. Just let me know." Roxy looked around at the others with a wide grin. "This is working. We're going to get Kitty back." She looked back at Q. "You're a genius, whatever you're doing. Louise, you were so right about hiring him."

Vesper frowned and pointed at him. "So, why doesn't *he* looked pleased?"

They all looked at Q, and Louise burst out laughing. "Oh, this is rich. This is so rich."

"What now?" Q groused.

"You're pissed. Oooh, baby brother. You kissed a girl and it didn't go any farther." Louise laughed harder and punched Q in the biceps, which must have hurt her knuckles, because she shook her hand afterward. "You should probably worry. It's not the situation; it's that Kaysar must be a way better kisser."

"You can shut up anytime, Lou." Q said, in retreat.

"This is the best day of my life," Louise went on. Roxy couldn't help but giggle too. Mason tried to look disinterested, but he was still chuckling under his breath. Vesper looked with woeful eyes at Q getting his dressing-down. He appreciated her support.

"I'm *not* pissed about it," he growled, "because—"

"Because you don't do relationships," his sister finished.

"That's right," Q agreed, his voice tight. He turned to make a show of rummaging for something in his duffel bag and dusting off the bazooka; then he returned to the table holding the weapon. "But there's no way Kaysar's a better kisser. Of course, I'm just saying that. Because it's not like there's any jealousy or whatever, because that would obviously be stupid."

"Hello, stupid," Louise said, reaching over to mess with his hair.

The group just laughed harder. All except Q and Vesper.

Q slipped his bazooka strap over his chest, causing the weapon to career around the side of his body. The laughing stopped abruptly as everybody ducked.

"Oh, sorry 'bout that," he muttered, but they could tell he didn't mean it. Then he paced the living room. "I don't want to do this anymore."

Louise looked at her brother. "Oh, please. Stop acting like a child."

Q crossed his arms over his chest, which made him look even more petulant. "I'm not continuing with this line of action. It's wrong. It's just wrong. There's got to be another way."

"Oh, for God's sake. We get this far and you bail out?" Mason looked at him in disgust. "I had the balls to tell them to call you when I knew I couldn't do what needed to be done. If you can't pull this off, have the balls to say so clearly."

Q stood up and squared off with him. "Don't try to outballs me on this. I have ethics. A moral code. I'm not just a guy with a toolbox and bills to pay. I think that—"

"I'm not paying for failure."

"I wouldn't take your damn money if you tried."

"Well, I'm not trying!"

"Well, I still wouldn't!"

Roxy and Louise stepped in and took the men to opposite corners of the room.

"Okay, little brother. Spill," Louise said.

Q turned his head away, glowering at Mason over his sister's shoulder. "He doesn't know what the hell he's talking about. He hasn't stepped one foot into the actual situation."

"Okay, let's go with that theorem. Mason doesn't know what he's talking about and you do. So, talk to me."

Q leaned back against the wall and traced a crack, trying to verbalize something that had been bothering him—besides becoming emotionally attached, which he wasn't. At least, not too seriously. "It's wrong. This tactic is flawed from the inside out." He looked at his sister head-on. "We hypothesized that Kitty was empty in a false world, and that if we could replace the empty with something meaningful, something that's real, she would know it and choose meaning over facades."

"That's right. So?"

"And I'm supposed to march in there and supply her with that meaning."

"Uh-huh."

"And then what? We'll drop her in the middle of our reality and say, 'Yeah, congrats, have a ball'?"

"Well, she'll have all of us. And Roxy's her best friend."

"But she'll know that I was a fake," Q burst out. "I was lying to her. I *am* lying to her. I told her that from here on out I wouldn't pretend anything. She actually told me she trusted me. This is . . . I won't do it anymore. I can see what I'm doing . . . well, I'm telling her that reality with all its pain is better than the prison of a perfect albeit artificial life. But we can't guarantee she'll be happier in real life. Maybe she won't be. She was happy in her loop. I saw it before we started messing around. You saw how she fought. She was *happy*, Louise. Louise?"

Louise had gone white. "Are you really saying this? And besides, she's falling for you. That's how you're persuading her to see what's real. We both know it."

"Fine, so I make her fall for me—assuming someone can fall for someone like me. But then she comes to her senses and embraces reality. That's when I pull the rug out from under her and say, 'Oops, sorry, beautiful, but I was just faking it so you'd want to embrace what was real'? 'I used a lie to get you to embrace the truth'? That's twisted! That's as heinous as it gets. I don't want to do that to her. I just want her to be happy. And if that means she stays in her loop and only thinks she's happy, so be it. What's the difference between being happy and thinking you're happy, anyway? Maybe Roxy's being selfish. Maybe this is all wrong."

"What's the difference? It's the difference between being human and being an uncontrollably drooling, bobble-head version of yourself. Snap out of it, Walter! Jesus." Louise put her hands on her hips and stared at the wood grain in the floor for some time. Finally she looked up. "This is a job, little brother. You took the job. Finish it."

Q drew back in surprise. "That's . . . not what I thought you'd say."

"Well, you need to grow up." Louise raised her arms and let them fall back to her sides in a gesture of futility. "There are no easy choices in this line of work; it's true. Slip a second in, pluck one out—who knows how any of us is gonna end?" Her voice started to get louder and louder as she continued: "We can only make our best guess and do the best we can to help people. That's what we do. But at least we're trying to maintain the integrity of time and not twist it to our advantage like Kaysar. What we do is *moral*. It's ethical. And at the end of the day, we're taking Katherine Gibbs back to where she should have stayed all along. There is nothing to be sorry for in that."

"But—"

"I'm not done!" she yelled, shoving Q down in a chair. "If you break Kitty's heart to restore her life, that's a sacrifice that's worthwhile. We all have our hearts broken sometimes. This is the job."

A muscle in Q's jaw pulsed. Louise pressed the back of her hand to her forehead. "Got a little worked up there," she mumbled, then did a double take as she realized that everyone was staring at her.

Vesper gaped at brother and sister, her wide eyes settling on Q with a look of sympathy. He smiled bitterly at her. When Mason chuckled, everybody looked at him in surprise. He shrugged his shoulders.

"What's so funny?" Q asked.

"You're not even close to objective, are you? You, the 'specialist.' I thought you 'didn't do relationships,'" he remarked, making quotes in the air with his fingers.

Three heads swiveled to look at Q, awaiting his response. Q felt as if his head were about to explode. Through gritted teeth, he burst out, "There's no goddamn relationship! I'm doing a job! Just because I want her to be happy—*I don't date bots.*"

The room was silent. Mason's jovial look faded.

"Ouch," Roxy said, a pained expression on her face. "Please don't call her that. She's a wonderful person. She was bubbly and silly and loyal and the best friend any of us could ever hope to have. She's not a bot. She's a victim." She stood and walked to the stairs.

"Nice," Mason said to Q, curling his lip.

Q stood, his chair slamming back to the floor behind him. "Let's have this out, Mason." He flexed his muscles. "I'm sick of your bullshit attitude. You lounge around here while I'm on the front lines; then you have the nerve to get in my face and sneer at me all the time? Let's see what you've got." He danced a bit like a boxer, raising his fists in the air.

Mason's eyes narrowed into slits. "You go ahead and float like a butterfly." He raised his fists. "I'll sting like a bee." He jabbed his fist out, hard and fast; Q dodged, but the blow grazed his temple. Q's return was fueled by the fury of the day, and it caught Mason in the nose.

"Not fucking again!" Mason yelled, swiping at the resultant blood. "Always with the nose."

"Boys! Don't you dare bleed on the paperwork!" Louise yelled. "Vesper, upstairs! Go sort something."

"But, Louise—"

"Upstairs!"

Vesper looked like she might burst into tears, but she headed upstairs. The party was over anyway. With a great roar, Mason pushed the rest of the chairs aside and sent himself flying into Q's chest, taking him down like a linebacker would a quarterback.

"No holds barred," Q growled into Mason's ear, and he put him in a choke hold.

"I wrestled in high school," Mason gasped through the

grip. "State championship." And he pulled a release move, sending Q sprawling over his head.

Q untangled himself from the fringe of the couch throw. "Magna cum laude, time-leap PT training," he growled, throwing himself atop Mason. And then there was a tangle of arms and legs; grunting; and chairs scraping across the floor.

"Bench lift two-fifty!"

"Three-minute mile!"

"Fuckwit!"

"Moron!"

"Stop!" Louise separated them, then pulled Q to one corner of the room while Roxy dragged Mason to the other. "You have got to be kidding me," she snapped.

Q looked sheepishly at Mason over her shoulder. Mason looked sheepishly back.

"If it's any consolation," Mason said, "I think it's out of my system. Don't be pissed."

"I'm beyond pissed," Roxy spoke up. "Totally turned on, but seriously pissed." She dragged her boyfriend up to the second floor.

Louise pulled Q into the kitchen and proceeded to address his cuts and scrapes, her lips pressed in a tight line. Q stared glumly out the window. His sister's dabbing and bandaging stopped.

Q pressed his hands over his eyes. "I know, Louise, I know. I'm sorry. I know she's not a bot. I know this mission is important—and the right thing. It's just . . . what is the *matter* with me? I'm all . . . I'm just . . ." He dropped his hands and looked around at his sister, saw her expression. "Please don't—"

"I'm not going to give you crap," she said quietly, bending the corner of the bandage wrapper in her hand back and forth. "You don't have to be sorry. I've pushed you really hard on this one. Maybe too hard."

"No, I'll fix this," Q said desperately. "I don't . . . I

don't know what's going on here, Lou, but this is not . . . This isn't . . ."

"I know it's not."

"I—"

"Hey." Louise took her brother by the shoulders and made him look her in the eyes. "Hey. I know it's not normal for you. And I know you'll fix it."

He nodded.

"So, it's fine." She suddenly lurched forward and gave her brother a hug.

"Do you think we've been going about this all wrong, Louise?" he asked into her ear. "Our lives?"

She slowly released him and stepped back. "What do you mean?"

"Not forming attachments, not doing relationships because the time lines change so easily and then they're gone. Do you think Mason and Roxy have it right?"

Louise crossed her arms in front of her. "Look, there're two ways to go in our line of work, and we picked one. Seemed reasonable to me at the time." She gave him a jaunty wink. "Go get this girl out of her loop so we can go back to some *normal* freelance jobs. This one's giving me a migraine."

Q nodded, disappointed but unsurprised that his sister hadn't given him a straight answer. He sighed and headed for the door, stopping to grab his jacket and jam the photo album into his bag.

"You're not going to jump back now, are you?" Louise asked in alarm. "I think you should relax."

"I just need some air." Shouldering on his jacket, he remembered the pills in the pocket and walked back to Louise. "This is what Leonardo's getting Kitty's 'doctor' to prescribe to her. He's got her convinced she's had some sort of accident that's damaged her brain and this is critical medication. I'll make a full report of what all went down."

"What is it?" Louise asked, leaning down and peering at

the pills. She pulled a ziplock bag from the counter and dropped them inside.

"No idea. We'll need a full chemical workup."

Louise's eyes lit up as she bent over the unassuming tablets once more. "I'll get the team started right away."

"Fantastic," Q said, in a voice devoid of emotion as he headed out the door.

Outside, he might have wandered in any direction to think, but he knew exactly where he wanted to go: the path to the local convenience store was well-worn— infamous, really. He walked to the spot where Roxanne, Mason, and Leonardo had first tangled, way back when. That rope of their tug-of-war—the wire that eventually became their time line—had ended up being more like a wick to a stick of dynamite, for it was here that the events originated that blew Kitty all to hell.

Q pulled the collar of his jacket up around his neck against the chill. Newspapers and trash swirled in eddies just above the pavement. Darkness was beginning to swallow the sun, daylight fading as evening descended, and the 7-Eleven sign down the street glowed brighter in contrast.

He walked past the nearby gas station and turned toward the convenience store. *That must be Naveed,* he thought, watching through the window as a man rang up a customer. Louise had given him the entire download; after all, Mason and Roxy's file was crucial to Kitty's case. But as Q thought about Naveed's complete ignorance regarding the different versions of his life, all changed because of wire crossers, it weighed hard upon him.

The losses mounted; they grew and grew and finally took their toll in making the last thing you wanted a relationship—until you realized that your life was barren without one. But the only people who could possibly understand what it all meant, how it all felt, were the ones who did the same thing as you—and these were the ones most prone to disappearing. It was a lose-lose situation. There was a reason that "Let's not go there" was one of the most often used phrases in the business.

Q didn't "go there." He never had. His sister never had. Vesper didn't know enough yet not to go there, but she'd learn soon enough. Everyone did.

Of course, in all fairness, Mason had made it work. It hadn't been easy to keep track of Roxy, what with forgetting she even existed a couple of times. But he'd managed to build things and tie wires so that he got what he wanted—Roxy's love—and kept it.

Louise was the only one Q had taken a chance on again and again. She was everything. If she asked him for anything, he was there. But was she enough?

Q turned away from the shop and headed back into the street, still aimed away from the apartment in favor of walking a bit more. He gazed up at the sky and thought of the future, of what he wanted and what he'd have. Would he be happier if he'd never met Kitty at all, if he didn't know she'd ever existed? Just look at what he and the others were going through—and who knew if they'd ultimately be successful? Look at how tied up Roxy was in getting Kitty back.

It took a fragment of a nanosecond to disappear, and the rest of everybody else's life to get over it.

Vesper barreled out of the apartment with her fists clenched. She didn't blame Q and Mason; she wouldn't mind working a little steam off, too. She looked around for something good to kick, but then decided it probably wouldn't have the same impressive dramatic effect from Louise's vantage point up at the window.

Argh! This was all *so* not what she'd had in mind when she'd accepted the internship. If it wasn't about orange juice and housekeeping for Louise in the present, it was about endless runs to the store, driving a motolimo around town, and being at Q's beck and call in the future. She got to play his nurse assistant once a week, but he never wanted her to come into the office anymore when Kitty was there, so what was the excitement?

To add insult to injury, Mason had asked her to shop for Roxy's anniversary present. How pathetic was that? Okay, well, he really just wanted her to suss out some cool ideas, since he couldn't go to the future right now, but *still*. Any minute, Roxy was going to ask her to pick up some dry cleaning or something.

I'm not even getting paid for this. If I were a real girl Friday, somebody would be remunerating me for this.

Vesper crossed her arms with total disgust. She'd show them. She'd wow them to bits, and they'd be, like, falling over themselves wishing they'd sent her to the front lines when they first had the chance.

Or . . . yeah! She'd do something *amazing* to prove she was ready for more responsibility, and they'd make her a full member of the team. She'd be the youngest professional time-travel expert—male *or* female—in the world. After she'd helped get Kitty back, everyone would thank her, and some other poor scrub would start making the orange juice.

She'd . . . she'd . . . she'd do no such thing. Vesper sat down on the curb. Louise would take it all wrong. Louise just didn't understand what Vesper was capable of. Not yet. But one of these days. One of these days . . .

CHAPTER FIFTEEN

Katherine stood in front of the bathroom mirror, staring into her own eyes as she used a brush to curl in the ends of her hair.

A man, a kiss . . . a dream that just wouldn't go away. Katherine wasn't sure whether she should be pleased that something new was sticking to her brain, or horrified by what she'd dreamt.

Every time it popped back into her head, it seemed so *real*, so intense that thinking about it actually gave her goose bumps.

Her hand with the brush stuck halfway down, mid-stroke. In her mind she again saw the man . . . and then the curve of his lips . . . and then it dawned on Katherine that the kiss might have only *seemed* real, but the sensation of emotional vibrancy buzzing through her body *was* real. It should have gone away! Or at the very least, she shouldn't have remembered it this long.

This was definitely a breakthrough. Katherine stuck the brush on the sink and leaned closer to the mirror. She looked deep into the blue eyes staring back at her. There was a difference between remembering a thing and re-membering a . . . sensation. How extraordinary!

Katherine took a deep breath and closed her eyes as she exhaled, waiting for her brain to conjure up the images that would bring that marvelous feeling back to her. The man's face slowly revealed itself. His sensuous lips parted and his eyes darkened with a passion that sent a shiver through her body even now.

With a gasp, Katherine opened her eyes and lurched back from the sink. *I know who that is, that man who makes me feel so real. I know who he is.*

Oh, my God. I kissed my psychiatrist. A storm of thoughts raced through her brain. Katherine clamped her hands to-gether in front of her in distress. *Did it really happen? Or was it just a fantasy? If it was real, then I'm cheating on my boyfriend. But if it was just a fantasy . . . but Leo is better than any fantasy and he's never made me feel quite that way. I don't think. I would know. I'm sure I would know somehow.*

Wait a minute. Wait a minute! Katherine gripped the edge of the sink and collected herself, scanning the image of the kiss in her mind once more. *I did* not *kiss my psychia-trist; my psychiatrist kissed* me. *He's moving in on* me. *All I did was . . . let him. No, wait. It wasn't even really a kiss. I remem-ber now. It was a sweep. A brush. A scan. A mere whisper.* That's *what it was. Just a whisper between us.*

It's all right, Kitty. You didn't do anything wrong. It was just a dream.

Pressing the palm of her hand against her forehead, Katherine shook her head as if to clear it. She'd been like this all day. Probing her mind for what was real and what was nothing but a dream. When she found the answer she thought she wanted, a minute later a streak of fear passed through her and she told herself to believe something else.

This was nuts. She'd passed through her day at work practically on autopilot while her brain bounced theories around—luckily, everybody seemed very happy with her performance, which was lovely, since everything had seemed even more higgledy-piggledy than usual.

Work was over, but neither her mind nor her body seemed willing to let the issue go. Leo would be here soon, and Katherine wondered how much she should tell him. Well, not about the other man in her fantasy, but maybe about how her body seemed to be more . . . alive than be-fore.

Of course, he'd have more fun figuring that out for himself. After all, there was no reason not to take advan-tage of her buzzing sort of hot-and-botheredness.

With a bit of a smirk at her reflection, Kitty put down the brush and went to the bureau in her bedroom. She rummaged around and pulled out something a little racier than the pale blue silk nightgown she was wearing: a clas-sic black push-up bra-and-garter set. Leonardo would think he'd died and gone to heaven. Glancing at the time, Kitty quickly changed from angel to vixen and waited for her fiancé's arrival.

She thought she might just burst right out of her skin

with excitement, and the moment Leo came through her door, Katherine launched herself at him.

The blaze in her surged as soon as their lips touched. *Yes!* And then . . . *oh.* The spark just blew out, and the buzz from her dream vanished, leaving only a dull hum in its wake.

She kissed her boyfriend harder, tried to ratchet up her passion, but it was a bit difficult with him pushing her off him. "Katherine!"

She looked up at him, feeling hurt and a little embarrassed, which was odd, considering how long they'd been together.

"What are you wearing?" he said—but not in that ooh-la-la sort of way she'd expected. She looked down at herself, at her incredibly hot body, and simply couldn't understand how she'd managed to mess up again.

"Where's the blue?" he asked.

"Is it important?" she asked glumly, and immediately wished she could take the words back. He just stared at her. For a really long time he stared at her while she stood trying not to cry, mostly naked and completely embarrassed in her trashy lingerie.

Finally, after Leo had stared her into a kind of humiliation she couldn't remember ever experiencing, all he could say was, "You always wear the blue," and then he moved past her into the living room.

The most peculiar idea lodged itself in her brain just then. *It's Tuesday. We don't have sex on Tuesday. On Tuesdays I wear the blue nightgown and he wanders around my apartment but then just goes home. I'm so stupid! There's no sex on Tuesday!*

Katherine ran into her bedroom, ripped the hot black lingerie off her body, and put the blue nightgown back on. "Leo! Of *course*." She ran into the living room. He was a darling, helping her keep to her schedule, to keep things on the straight and narrow so that she didn't get confused or feel upset about her condition. "This is so much better. This feels so much better. The black was . . . just . . . was just *not right,* was it?"

He looked at her and took her in, in a way that he really hadn't before, acknowledging her beauty with a much more genial flick of the eyebrow and lick of the lips. "You look gorgeous in that color," he said. But rather than pick her up and toss her on the bed and make a night of it, he simply went back to examining the contents of her apartment. *Because there's no sex on Tuesdays.*

But that's . . . really odd.

With that thought, that stale, unpleasant thought, something else stale and unpleasant occurred to Kitty. She realized that she didn't mind that it was Tuesday. She didn't mind at all. And after a while when it seemed liked Leo had looked over every room in the condo twice over, she started wishing that her darling, perfect boyfriend would stop poking about the place and let her go to sleep already so she could start dreaming about a man and a mouth and a delicious shiver throughout her body that seemed impossible to ever forget . . .

Kitty woke up to the sound of music playing from the phonograph across the room. She stayed in bed listening to the strains of a song that seemed to be stuck on repeat. It was a lovely song. The nanoseconds drained away as she lay in bed listening to the entire piece once more before she ordered the music to stop. The fake sound of a nonexistent record player arm rising off nonexistent vinyl was followed by the fake click of that nonarm settling back in. In the ensuing silence she sat up in bed, and the first thing that popped into her head wasn't: *eggplant suede peplum jacket with short black skirt and tall stiletto boots, ponytail hair.* It was: *What do I feel like wearing today?*

She grabbed her smartie and clicked over to the calendar. In the spot next to the date, it told her to wear the eggplant suede peplum jacket with her short black skirt with tall stiletto boots and to put her hair in a ponytail. She scrolled through the rest of the week, noting a similar specificity each day. Some days held descriptions for two outfits. Friday night called for a formal dress—the white organza. Clicking through, she found a listing for a place called the Cotton Club for eight-thirty p.m. and a more detailed description of her evening hair, makeup, and accessories. Nothing said what it was for. If it was so formal, it must be a very special event; why didn't she know?

It bothered her all morning, really bothered her. She showered and dressed in a complete daze, just thinking . . . well, everything she could. She'd been doing so well with the whole cognizance problem. Every day she seemed to be learning just a smidge more about herself. Maybe . . . maybe she could be late to work. Just this once. After all, she was dating the boss. It wasn't like anyone was going to knock her for it.

Feeling positively giddy, instead of going straight to work—and without even realizing that she was making a critical alteration to her daily schedule, the magnitude of which had never before been logged in her spreadsheet over at the Kaysar Corporation—Katherine Gibbs walked straight out of her life and caught a motocab to the Cotton Club.

When it stopped at the curb, Katherine thought the driver had made some kind of mistake. But the GPS coordinates she'd sent him were glowing red on the meter, and the awning over the door did say, THE COTTON CLUB, in what looked like gold letters that had lost a bit of shine.

She let the motocab go and had a look around. Finally, after staring for some time at the building in front of her and the carpet below, she realized what this place represented. It was the event hall where her friends had thrown a party for her. She couldn't remember when. Still, it was so odd, that such a nice-sounding place with such swanky

parties would be in what seemed so . . . warehouselike a
building. She couldn't remember anything she'd visited
before seeming similar. The grungy thing beneath her feet,
the sort of soiled reddish black mat, was the red carpet
she'd walked. In the night, with the lights just so and the
people all dressed up and the excitement of the occasion,
everything had seemed so majestic and glamorous. But it
wasn't glamorous at all, was it? No.

The sidewalk in front of the venue remained empty,
bleak now, without any well-wishers or even passersby.
Katherine stood at the spot where she'd once stepped out
of a limo, and noticed marks on the ground, little white
slivers in various places and in pairs forming ninety-degree
angles. She glanced around, then bent down to the sidewalk and ran her fingers over one of the sets of marks. It
was some sort of adhesive tape. She stood up, wiped off
her hand, and walked toward the entrance. The velvet rope
was gone and the place looked abandoned. Katherine
looked over her shoulder at the walkway and closed her
eyes.

In her mind's eye, the red carpet was laid out, her friends
blew kisses from either side of the walkway, and . . . She
tried to picture the faces of all the people behind them.
She'd really made eye contact with only Ariel and Dee.
What friends of hers stood behind them waving and con-
gratulating? They must have just been Leonardo's friends.

Katherine stepped up to the landing and peered
through the tinted glass of the door. The club was dark
except for a lamp at the bar, where a beefy guy seemed to
be replacing champagne glasses. She pushed through and
stepped into the bar, pausing as she waited for her eyes to
adjust.

"I'm so sorry," she said, with her face bent down over
one hand a bit, letting her blond hair spill forward. "I've
lost a cornea jacket. Can I use your bathroom?"

He didn't answer right away, and it was all Katherine could do not to run away.

"I can't," he said uncertainly. "It's a security thing."

"Oh, please, help me out," she said sweetly.

"It's really not—"

"I'm in real trouble here," she said, lifting her hand slightly so she could bat at least her one ostensibly healthy baby blue at him.

He hesitated, but she had him in the end. "I'll give you five minutes. And come right back through this way when you're done. Got it?"

"I promise," she said, and moved quickly to the bathroom. She remembered being in here. She remembered it being more impressive, but she still remembered. Katherine waited a few moments to make her excuse more realistic, then stepped out again. She waved in thanks to the bartender and said, "I'm done," then walked right past him.

He called out his good-bye, and she opened the door and let it slam shut without actually going through. With her heart pounding so loudly she could feel it in her skull, she flattened herself against the side of the coat closet, where he couldn't get a direct line of sight, and waited for a few more seconds. The sound of crystal glasses chiming together gave her courage, and when she'd decided he was safely behind the bar, she slipped along the side of the coat closet and headed down the darkened hall.

Kitty looked around. In the day, the place looked much shabbier than she remembered. Of course, Leonardo had kept refilling her champagne flute. The emergency exit at the end of the hall opposite the door leading back into the bar was ajar, and was obviously not up to signaling an emergency of any sort. It led to a courtyard.

And . . . there was a retractable roof. Like a western movie set it was, the place built in a square with boxes of costumes and storage and garbage and tables and chairs and wardrobe racks and a GPS screen on one wall and a mural and some switched-off bots wearing Katherine's designs. The mural looked familiar. Katherine walked up to where it hung suspended on storage hooks at one end of the square. She reached up and ran her palm across the surface, accidentally dislodging one of the hooks and sending the metal to the ground. It struck with a ringing noise.

"Hey! Hey, girl! Are you still in here?"

Before Katherine could move, the door behind her swung open. The face of the bartender came into view. The angry face. She started inching backward.

He glanced to the left, where a hotline was mounted on the wall; he was going to call security.

Katherine glanced around for the nearest escape and saw that her only real shot was across the square and out the back.

They looked at each other. *One . . . two . . .*

He reached for the phone; she took off running and started dodging set dressings like a steeplechase. Beefy guy made his call and was soon in pursuit. Katherine ran up the back steps to the building on the right. Grabbing the handle and jiggling it with all her strength did no good—the door was locked. She climbed under the handrail and headed for the next building.

"Don't go in there!" he yelled, attempting to cross the distance with his considerable girth.

Up the steps. Grab the door. She fell into the building, picked herself up, and started looking for the front entrance. There was no one in here, and the place was completely dark. She stumbled into a low table, knocking a lamp over with her thigh. Scrabbling against the wall, she found a knob and opened it—stuck her hand in, making a racket as she knocked against a handful of wire hangers. A closet, but at least it had a light switch. She grabbed the switch. It snapped up out of her hand but fortunately it illuminated the fact that she was in a food storage room.

Her idiot pursuer was inside the building now. Katherine switched the light off and crawled behind a box of canned goods.

"I'm not gonna hurt you!" he called.

And you're not gonna leave me alone, either. Katherine breathed shallowly, did her best to ignore her burning muscles, and waited.

"Girl! Uh, lady! Lady? I didn't mean to scare you. Let me help you out." His bullshit was punctuated by deep breaths. Katherine didn't move. He swore a blue streak, and she heard doors slamming. He was checking out rooms. She shrank as far into herself as she could go and put her head down on her arms.

Please leave me alone. The tears she'd held back began to flow. Katherine cried silently into the eggplant suede, a button on her cuff pressing painfully into her face.

The door swung open and the light went on. "Lady?" the guy asked in a voice that seemed to expect no answer. He breathed like a freight train as he started moving boxes. She heard a tremendous "oomph," and then something slammed into the ground. Katherine instinctively reached out to stabilize herself, managing not to touch anything or make a sound. "Son of a bitch!"

Katherine stared at the cardboard box in front of her, the light blue stamps on the brown surface blurring through her tears. She blinked them away.

DEIRDRE MARTIN'S FRAPPUCCINO MIX

She saw this on another box that slammed down on the ground. The case of Deirdre's frappuccino mix shifted to the side, making Katherine's precarious situation even more so.

"They do not pay me enough for this shit!" the guy bellowed. He left the room muttering and cursing the Kaysar Corporation.

Kaysar? Leo?

The light went out. Katherine didn't move. Doors continued to slam outside of the room; she rocked with her arms around her knees. And then, after some time had passed, she allowed her muscles to relax and her body to settle. She reached out and laid her palm on the box, letting that funny settled feeling soothe her a bit. Why would there be a box of frappuccino mix with her friend's name on it? What kind of company stocked up for one person like that? The kind that knew she would order it over and over again, apparently. Talk about customer service.

She looked between her splayed fingers at her friend's name on the box and just shook her head. Finally, the silence tempted her too much, and she uncurled her body, stood up, and babied her aching limbs. After a minute of just standing there in silence she finally reached up, felt around for the old-school light cord, and pulled.

The light went on. Katherine looked down at the box that said DEIRDRE MARTIN'S FRAPPUCCINO MIX. It was next to a box marked KGIBBS-ORGANIC GRANOLA, which was on top of ARIEL, NOV. CANNED HASH.

Does she know her hash comes from a can? was her first thought, followed by *Oh, my God. She knows her hash comes from a can. She probably barfs when she gets home every Sunday afternoon. But then again, she gets paid for it and stays a size two.*

Followed by *They must think I really, really love organic granola. Oh, my* God. "No," Katherine murmured, shaking her head. But the cloud of evidence was beginning to take shape in her mind, made out of all of the little fragments of her life that never seemed to make complete sense.

A smartie that tells you what to wear: costumes. A schedule that tells you where to be: call times. People on sets ready to tell you when you get your lines wrong and to remind you that your character wants granola instead of pancakes . . .

Maybe she didn't need people to tell her what to do and what to think. Maybe they were damaging her more, rather than helping her recover from damage. If they just let her alone, what she wanted to do and think would just . . . happen. Her psychiatrist had told her as much. Or maybe this right now, these thoughts were just Katherine being crazier than ever.

Katherine stepped out of the closet and took a good look around. Personalized blue stamps covered all the boxes, and some of them had notes scrawled on them. She tiptoed to the door. An electronic reader hung on a hook there. Katherine took it down and turned it on. It opened a file labeled CONTINUITY. A checklist of things started with, *Only small spoons; bring serrated spoon with KG grapefruit. Left side plate, face up, point angle ten degrees away from center KG.*

That's brunch! That's brunch with the girls! She pressed her finger against one of the thumbnail images along the side of the text. The image enlarged, taking over the screen as the first in a slide show. It was a still of Katherine and her friends. Deirdre was leaning forward, her mouth twisted in one of those in-the-moment shots. Katherine and Ariel were leaning back in their chairs laughing. But most significantly, the picture's focus was not the girls. It was the tabletop.

With a pounding heart Katherine scrolled through the slide show. They were all different angles and zooms of the brunch table, and then some were close-ups of the three girls—each taking in different shots of their clothes, purses, tote bags, and jewelry.

She turned the reader off, put it back on the hook, and walked out the door. Two supply rooms and a prop room later, Katherine opened a door and stepped into the restaurant itself. Almost in a daze, she walked around the deserted tables until she reached the one she sat at every Sunday.

If what she'd just discovered, that her life was nothing more than a stage-play in which she struggled to remember her lines and take her cues properly, if that was true . . . then Katherine had no real friends, her lover didn't love her, and her entire existence was nothing more than somebody else's monologue in a drama with an infinite run.

Suddenly cognizant of the fact that her daily schedule mattered more than she'd ever before imagined, Katherine checked her smartie, and then went racing out the front of the restaurant to the street.

As she climbed into a motolimo and asked the driver to take her back to Kaysar Corporation, one thing seemed absolutely, positively clear to her now.

That feeling, that sensation I had . . . that was 100% real. It wasn't a dream and it wasn't a fantasy. I did kiss that man and that feeling never, ever went away. It still gives me a thrill.

Katherine stared down at her hands in her lap, and then she suddenly turned over her left arm and stared down at her inner wrist. There was nothing marking her skin, but an incredibly distinct memory emerged and she saw herself writing on her wrist with her lipliner, of all things.

With a shocked gasp, Katherine saw the pieces come together in her mind. She saw the man. She closed her eyes and replayed the snippets of conversation that were suddenly flooding back like a movie on fast-forward.

Oh. Oh, wow. That was not my psychiatrist. His name is Q, and he is real. He kissed me and I kissed him back and the biggest thing of all is that I know that I really wanted to.

But then . . . oh, Leo. Leo. What are you doing to me?

CHAPTER SIXTEEN

She was so paralyzed with fear, Kitty couldn't concentrate at all on ribbons and edging and buttons and trim, hemlines and colors and accessories and the rest of the frippery associated with her job. She let Ariel and Dee come up with the ideas they liked, and she agreed with everything they said while she waited and waited and waited for her smartie to give her permission to go home for the day.

She almost failed to see Leo's name blinking on the call panel. Catching it just before the final ring, she ducked her head down closer to her desk for privacy and whispered, "Hello, baby."

"I can't stop thinking about you," he said, his British accent winding around her senses like a delicious perfume. "I want you."

Katherine froze. The giggle she managed to direct at her microphone came more from a sense of hysteria, but hopefully he'd find it . . . flirty, or something. "*Leo*. I can't. I'm working."

There was a long silence on the other end of the line. "I don't understand," he said, a peculiar edge to his voice.

The stupid song from that morning popped back into her head, and without warning a tremendous wave of guilt washed over her.

"Katherine, are you still there?"

"I'm here," she said, trying not to reveal how frightened she suddenly felt, and then compounding it all with the notion that her darling Leonardo was the last person she should be hiding her feelings from.

"Katherine, I don't understand," he repeated, colder now. *I don't either. I have no idea what—Oh, God. Maybe I do.* "I'm just joking, darling," she blurted in a panic. "Where should I meet you?"

Another pause, and then a frigid response. "Where you always meet me."

"Of course," she said, hanging up with the distinct sensation that she was being . . . tested in some way. She looked around self-consciously, then beelined to the bathroom and pushed the button for the zoom mirror. Her makeup was still perfect, her hair fabulous, her dress as flattering as any piece of clothing could get.

She should have been happy, but when she tried to find her smile it was a struggle, and she didn't want to leave the bathroom. She went into one of the stalls and sat on the toilet seat with her arms around her knees, acutely aware that her fabulous boyfriend was expecting to screw her in the elevator. And what the hell was more thrilling than that?

Katherine made a humming sound with every exhalation, to stop herself from crying; then she got up and blew her tingling nose and walked as fast as she could to the elevator. When the doors opened, Leonardo was already there, alone.

"I've been riding this bloody lift for two minutes. What the hell's the matter?" he snarled under his breath, glancing up at the corner-mounted camera.

Katherine looked into his eyes. They were breathtakingly dark but did little for her.

They went down a couple of floors; then Leo looked at her. She was supposed to be getting butterflies, but there was no electricity in the air, nothing between these two pairs of eyes looking at each other. He stared at her like a specimen of sorts, and suddenly Katherine was frightened.

"Well?" she asked, trying to sound seductive, forcing her mouth into a smile.

"Leonardo Kaysar. Camera off. Emergency stop," he said—very distinctly, so that the voice recognition would pick it up. The elevator lurched to a halt. Leo didn't move; he just stared at her.

"Whatever is the matter?" Katherine said with a laugh, pulling him roughly toward her. His mouth took hers. Katherine went through the motions, thinking of another face, another body, another time. The brutality of the act was not lost on her, and she counted down the seconds, keeping time by the electronic clicking of the emergency-stop reset timer.

"Did you . . . notice something different?" she asked loudly, trying to conceal her shaking hands in the act of repairing her attire.

He turned to her in surprise, repairing the knot of his cravat. He finished setting himself to rights. "Yes," he said tightly.

"I didn't take my pills," she said, hoping it would explain away everything.

His gaze snapped to hers.

She moistened her dry lips. "I thought maybe I was getting better and I wouldn't need them so much, but . . . now I don't know."

Something in him relaxed. He cupped her cheek with his palm. "I think it's best to do what the doctor suggests, don't you think, darling?"

It wasn't a question, and Katherine didn't answer.

"Let's go back upstairs, shall we? We'll get you back on your medication."

The camera made a whirring sound and switched back on. The blue light extinguished. The elevator doors opened, and a bunch of suits stepped in. Leonardo didn't look at

Katherine again as they rode back up together. Leaning back against the wall, she closed her eyes and focused on not throwing up.

Well, she'd bought time. He had reason to believe she was acting "off script" because her medication was erratic. Continuity was going to be a struggle, or at least she assumed it would: the more free will she could exert, the less she'd know about what she was supposed to do.

"You are so right, Leo. What was I thinking? Everybody knows you don't just stop taking your pills. And now I feel ill." She didn't have to fake the hot sweat covering her brow and upper lip. "I think I might be sick. I'll take the pills in a minute."

They walked back to her desk, where she left Leo to dart from her cubicle to the restroom. Ariel and Dee followed, but waited outside like sentries.

She didn't have to fake her symptoms of nausea, and she certainly didn't have to fake the results. But did she feel guilty because she'd cheated on her fiancé, or because she'd just had sex with him? The taste of sick in her mouth was overwhelming.

Crying, Katherine ordered the toilet to flush and went to the vending machine. She hadn't brought her smartie to swipe, so she just voice-ordered. "Katherine Gibbs," she said. Her voice registered in the system. "Toothbrush, toothpaste, gum, fresh wipes," she enunciated. After a moment the packets were dispensed. Sniffling and crying, she brushed her teeth, ignoring the knocking on the door. In the mirror she watched Dee come in and walk up beside her.

Katherine finished brushing her teeth. She washed her face, then went back into the stall and cleaned Leo away as best she could. She came back out and washed her hands for a really long time, just scrubbing them with soap and water until Dee finally reached out and turned the water off and dried her hands with a towel.

When everything was done—when Katherine was

washed and dried and fluffed and folded, made perfect for another day of theatrics, of lies—Katherine saw Dee's hand move toward the counter and lay down two capsules. Katherine stared at the funny little orange-and-blue pills.

"What if I don't want to, Dee?" she asked in a clogged voice. Dee didn't answer, and Katherine looked up. "Would you tell him?"

Dee's gaze flicked to the side.

"Well," Katherine lied cheerfully, "they'll make me feel better than I feel now." She took the capsules and popped them in her mouth, followed them up with a cup of water, then stuck out her tongue at her friend.

Sniffling again, she wrinkled her nose. Dee handed her another hand towel, and Katherine smiled, putting the towel to her face, blowing her nose, and letting the pills roll out into the cloth.

Dee held the door open for her. Katherine put the wadded towel up to her face again, pretending to wipe, then crushed everything in her fist and stuck it in her pocket. When she turned to smile at her friend, Dee still hadn't mustered the nerve to look her square in her face.

CHAPTER SEVENTEEN

Roxy looked down at Mason, who was flopped on the sofa with his eyes glued to the television set, and then up again at the countdown clock that was scrolling its way toward half-time. Biting her lip, she forced herself to wait it out like a decent girlfriend.

The minute the quarterback tossed the ball to the ref and headed for the sidelines, she plopped down on the couch next to him and entwined her fingers with his. Mason smiled, and then leaned over and kissed her gently on the mouth.

"Babe," she said nervously.

"Mmm?"

"I can't get this off my mind. And I know you hate bringing Leonardo up in this sort of context, but I need to just come out and say it and get it on the table." She waited for his response.

He looked down at their clasped hands, perhaps trying to hide the pained expression on his face. "Go ahead, Rox."

"I can't believe I ever believed there might be something between Leonardo and me. That I ever believed he might be better than you."

"You couldn't help it," Mason said. "He crossed those wires on us, and you couldn't do anything to stop it."

She reached up and pressed her fingers against his jawline, gently pushed his face toward hers. "Do you really believe that I couldn't help it? Or do you just say that? Because if we're going to have a future, we've got to be completely honest with each other. I mean, I did kiss the guy."

"Ouch. You really don't have to bring that up again. I don't forget things like that."

"Sorry." Roxy chewed on her lower lip, afraid all over again that Mason would disappear from her life the way he had long ago—but it'd be on purpose one day. "It's just that . . . he can make anyone believe anything, you know? That's how I know it must be hard for Kitty."

After a pause, Mason added thoughtfully, "And for Q."

Roxy nodded and had to swallow hard against the lump forming in her throat. "I just wanted to make sure there isn't something left over from all of that, that maybe you don't know how absolutely, positively certain I am about you."

"Well, that's the thing. The only part that matters to me is how you feel now. Kaysar can turn the world upside down if he wants. But we loved each other before he crossed those wires, and I love you still. The only question that remains is: do *you* love *me* now?"

Roxy grinned. "I love you now, and I'll love you for the rest of time."

"That's all I need to hear."

He kissed her again, this time not so gently. "Now, for the love of God, can we not mention your kissing Leonardo Kaysar ever again?"

Roxy answered with another kiss. Then: "Um, babe?"

Mason kept pressing kisses into her neck.

"Babe?"

"Mmm?"

"You're going to patch things up with him, right?"

Mason sucked on the side of Roxy's neck until she squealed and wriggled away. "Who?" he asked.

She ducked out of reach as he tried to kiss her more. "I'm *serious*. He wants to make up, but he acts like a boy and doesn't know where to begin."

Mason leaned back, an amused grin on his face. "You are so full of crap."

Roxy snorted her laughter. "I know, but . . . you *know*?"

He sighed. "For you, anything. But after the game . . . and after . . ." He moved up and pressed her down into the sofa, one finger under her bra strap and pulling it up over her shoulder.

"After," Roxy echoed. "Excellent idea. Maybe we should go upstairs."

"In a minute," Mason mumbled.

Louise glanced over her shoulder toward the sound of excessive giggling coming from the vicinity of the sofa, then slipped into the kitchen where Q was fastening the end of an ACE bandage around his knee. "Hey," she said, taking up post against the counter.

"Hey," Q replied. He pressed the bandage clip in harder

for good measure, then grabbed his spent coldstay pack off the floor and tossed it over Louise's shoulder into the sink.

"Fix the thing with Mason," she said.

He gave her an irritated look. "He has to want to."

"No, he doesn't. But it just so happens he does."

"Oh? Let me guess. You and Roxy put your heads together, and you've come up with an idiot scheme to make us each think the other person wants to apologize."

"Something like that."

"Fine. Whatever. I'll fix it. No reason not to. It was dumb to begin with, and it gets in the way of team progress."

Louise cocked her head and smiled. "You're such a sensible man."

Q grunted and avoided his sister's eyes. "I just want to get Kitty out. That's what I'm here for. That's what you're paying me for. Fighting with Mason was totally unprofessional. So I'll fix it. Okay?"

"Speaking of Kitty . . . I was wondering if you wanted to talk," Louise said.

Q looked at her suspiciously. "What about?"

"You *do* like her. You know . . . about that," she said softly. "And how we shouldn't go around denying it. There's nothing wrong with liking someone."

Q looked around the room. He wasn't sure what her point was. "Is there something going on here I need to know about?"

"Oh, shush. You have abandonment issues. We both do. Maybe we should talk about it."

Q grimaced. "I'm a guy, Louise. I don't 'talk about it,'" he said, using air quotes. "You're acting really weird. Last time I brought up . . . Oh. *Oh*." He shifted uncomfortably. "*You* want to talk about it. Has something happened?"

"Yes, it's very annoying!" she blurted, suddenly flustered and not making eye contact.

He just waited.

"Roxy and Mason all kissing everywhere. I mean, this place isn't that big, okay? I mean, the walls aren't that thick, you know? It's Roxy this and Roxy that, and Mason this and Mason that, and all they ever want to talk about is how great life is going to be when we get Kitty out and everyone can finally be happy. . . ."

Q raised an eyebrow. Uncharacteristic bitterness had seeped into his sister's voice.

"And for God's sake, he won't shut up about how to propose to her and what kind of ring he should buy. I have no idea why he's asking *me*. Hell, I understand why you went after him!"

Q stared at her. "You're his partner. It's like with cops—you're supposed to sit around in cars and share intimate details of your love lives."

Louise rolled her eyes. "We're not the police! We're just business partners. Business partners don't share intimate details," she said, grabbing a dish towel and thwacking her brother on the shoulder. They stared at each other for a moment and then started laughing.

"You had to sleep in the same bed as him for two years trying to take down Leonardo. Remember when you were posing as his girlfriend while trying to help Roxy? Remember that? What the hell *did* you talk about all that time?" Q asked, incredulous.

She heaved a sigh. "Leonardo. Roxy. Sports."

Q shook his head. "Well, maybe you should think about changing your policy. It's time, perhaps. You seem to want to. Do you want me to tell you it's all right? Just because I'm who I am, having issues, doesn't mean—"

"Maybe we *both* should think about who we are," she cut him off. "I don't know. I just know I'm jealous that everybody else has somebody."

"Until they get disappeared," he said. "Which is the risk. But you know, I was thinking . . . Vesper made me think."

"Vesper?" Louise asked in surprise.

Q leveled her with a look. "You don't give the kid enough credit. Also, nobody here needs to drink as much orange juice as you force her to make. Ask yourself what that's about."

"You're changing the subject," his sister snapped.

"Fine. You want an answer? We like to think we're all screwed up because we had bad models growing up. Dad dies, Mom bails, it's you and me and a couple of major relationship complexes. But Vesper never even *had* parents. She went from a petri dish to the academy system. And she's not screwed up at all. Have we just been indulging ourselves with all this 'can't do relationships' stuff?"

Louise went quiet, thinking for a moment. "Does make you think, I guess."

"I mean, is it better to have nothing and not miss anything, or to have had something that was taken away?"

She studied Q's face for a moment, then folded the dish towel back into a proper square and placed it in its correct spot. "Familiar sentiments, little brother. Sounds an awful lot like, ''Tis better to have loved and lost than never to have loved at all.' But are you sure you were really thinking about Vesper?"

"Of course I was thinking about Vesper."

Louise gave him a disappointed look, then glanced at her smartie and said, "Where *is* Vesper?"

"At school?"

"What's the sudden interest in school?" Louise asked.

"You want her to skip?" Q asked with a grin.

"I just like to know where she is, is all," Louise said, before turning and leaving him in the kitchen.

He stared at the counter. "See? There I was thinking about Vesper," he muttered to himself. "Nothing to do with Kitty. We were talking about Vesper." He turned his head and yelled over his shoulder, "Hey, Louise, you know we were talking about Vesper, right? Louise?"

There came no answer, just the uneven sounds of Mason's sports show on the TV. With a sigh, Q headed toward the sound.

Roxy's fiancé sat on the couch, his blackened eyes taking in the game, a white butterfly bandage across the bridge of his nose. Roxy apparently had done her part, because he hoisted his beer and said, "Nice half nelson, man."

"Nice uppercut," Q replied. "Sorry about your nose."

Mason shrugged. "Not the first time. Have some grog."

Q went to the fridge, got a beer, grabbed a bag of chips off the counter, and then came back and sat down an appropriate distance away from Mason on the couch. He wasn't entirely sure where to begin.

Mason looked over, gave him the old chin-up nod.

Q responded with the same; then he turned to the screen where little images of men were throwing themselves into one another for the sake of an oblong ball. Thank God this shit didn't exist in the future. It was excruciating. Then again, as a meditative device without the sound, perhaps . . .

He was interrupted by a moment of paranoia, though it was delivered casually. "You touch my girl, I'll put her stiletto through your scrotum," Mason said before calmly taking a swig of beer. "I mean that in the nicest possible way. You know, just to kind of make things clear." Then he gestured with his index finger to the screen. "He was totally offside."

The referee blew the whistle for a penalty.

"Nice call," Q remarked.

"Did you hear what I said?"

"Uh-huh. Not interested in your girl," Q admitted. He took a swig of beer.

Mason turned away from the TV and studied his profile.

"It's possible, in fact, that I may be falling for Katherine Gibbs." Q said the words nonchalantly, testing out the way they felt in his mouth even as he winced at the idiocy of two sportsmen plowing straight into each other.

Mason raised an eyebrow. "Where you at with that?"

Q shrugged. "Anxious and borderline pathetic. Not sure I really want to own it, if you know what I'm saying."

"I guess if you told her, she'd just forget?"

Q flinched. "She wouldn't forget," he mumbled. "It would just be as if I'd never told her. It's not the same."

Mason shoved a couple of potato chips into his mouth. "I can respect that," he said through the mouthful. He finished chewing and swallowed. "Um . . . is there a conflict of interest? Do you think it's going to be a problem?" he asked.

Q turned and looked at him. "Only if I can't get her out."

The two men contemplated each other. Finally Mason said, "The computer should be done checking the stats I fed into it. We should be ready to try crossing the wall tomorrow."

Q gave him a chin nod. "Nice."

"I owe you an apology," Mason added.

Q gave him some space.

"It, uh . . ." Mason cleared his throat. "I, uh . . ."

Q calmly took a swig of beer, still following the game.

"I'm the asshat," Mason finally said.

Q could feel his stare, so he looked over.

"I'm the asshat. *I'm* the asshat."

"You're the asshat," agreed Q helpfully.

"Roxy wants this more than anything, and I have to sit on the sidelines while another guy gets to be the hero." Mason shook his head. "I wanted to be the one to do this for her. And I don't get to be. So I act like an asshat." He held out his closed fist. "It's not something I wanted to do, but I've done it."

Q stared down at the fist, then up at Mason, then realized that this was as close to "I'm sorry" as the guy was going to get, and that some sort of reciprocal hand motion was needed to recognize the apology for what it was. He decided that he could live with it, stuck out his hand, and they pounded knuckles.

Then they both turned back to the game and watched in companionable silence until the referee blew the final whistle, and the winning team engaged in the usual butt-slapping good times. Q cleared his throat.

"Sliceball game starts in twenty. You spliced in future cable yet?"

Mason perked up. "No. I've got a router, though. You got the tools?"

"Do I have the tools?" Q chuckled. "I *always* have the tools." They got up and Q brought his duffel to the table and began to lay out some equipment on the surface. Mason pawed over the gadgets like he was tanked up on catnip: Q was definitely cutting-edge. He crossed the room.

Q noticed a small black metal calibration device affixed to the wall with studs that he hadn't noticed earlier. "This Roxanne's work?" he asked, peering at the screen.

A smile quirked up at the corner of Mason's mouth. "She took the multidimensional coordinates you filtered and coded them against the firewall."

The numbers scrolled by so fast they looked like a blue neon blur against the gray background. Q nodded, peering at the screen. "How long has it been running?"

"Three days."

Q frowned.

"Yeah, I know," Mason said. "He's got a serious byte-fence now."

"Hmm. You've got a long history with this guy. Do you think he's figured out we're hacking? Or does he still just think the loop's weak and breaking down?"

Mason shrugged. "Seems to me he's either figured it out

and is pretending he hasn't, since we're basically providing him with some seriously high-caliber Q-and-A opportunities, or he thinks the loop's not working and he's throwing the kitchen sink at it. I've been going through my archives and reviewing every move he's made to date that I know of."

"And what's your professional opinion?"

"He doesn't know yet. But if we successfully hack this bytefence, or if he detects that someone's in there trying, he will, and then it'll be a whole different ball game."

"Someone seriously needs to figure out how to make a phone call between layers of time. We can go from one to the other, but we can't be in the ether of the two at the same time."

"There's a reason there's no such thing as a paradox specialist."

Mason laughed. "I can't tell you how much this pains me to say, but if anyone had it in them to solve a time paradox, it'd be Leonardo Kaysar." The two guys looked at each other, suddenly uneasy. Then they stared off into space, each lost in his own thoughts.

Mason finally said, "Hey, uh, you have good anniversary-present ideas?"

"For Roxy? Don't get her a smartie cartridge of any sort—not even if she's been talking about it. In fact, don't get her any sort of equipment, electronics . . . not even if it's from the future and doesn't exist yet for anybody else. Women don't dig that. Don't get her—"

"What *should* I get her?" Mason asked.

Q shrugged. "Why are you asking me? Has she mentioned anything she wants?"

"Nothing besides her friend back. That's why I'm asking." Mason sighed and shook his head.

We all want that, Q thought as he watched the lovesick fool stand up and wander off into the kitchen. Louise was right; watching two people in love act in love when you didn't have that for yourself was one of the hardest things in the world. He'd never realized that before.

In fact, Q was more than a little unnerved that he'd told Mason earlier that he might be falling in love with Kitty. Partly because it was odd for him to just come out and share something like that, but more because saying it out loud forced him to think hard about the truth of his words.

Might be falling in love with her?' Who are you kidding, Q? It's already too damn late.

Q just tipped his forehead to rest against the wall and groaned.

CHAPTER EIGHTEEN

A few days later, Q stopped in from the future to find Vesper on the couch and Mason, Roxy, and Louise seated around the dining room table, which seemed to have transformed into a set for a forensics show. A Bunsen burner was on, the flame bobbing and weaving beneath a copper bowl in which bubbled a small quantity of cloudy white liquid. Mason carefully squeezed in a single drop of blue substance from an eyedropper. Next to him, Louise's face was pressed down on the tube of an electron microscope. Next to her, Roxanne was preparing and labeling a set of glass slides and petri dishes.

Mason stirred the bluish substance with a glass rod, then turned his attention back to the control dish. Roxanne glanced up at Q.

"This is a very interesting set of compounds," she said. "It appears to be a kind of reverse-engineered hallucinogenic with a dampening effect. We're hypothesizing that it makes the brain somewhat more malleable, extra susceptible to the power of suggestion. The brain then begins to take suggestions as reality, while blockers work to prevent reality from seeping in to contradict the suggestions."

Mason lowered the petri dish and frowned. "Or not." He sighed. "Let's run the test battery again." Roxanne nodded, put on a pair of large plastic goggles, and went to work.

Mason walked up to Q and leaned against the bar top next to him. "It sounds similar to bovine spongiform encephalitis, in the sense that the pill makes 'holes' in the brain, if you will, and then allows those holes to be filled by whatever is most influential to the subject. Which would explain why the more she is with you over the course of the week, the less Kaysar is able to control her. And likewise, why, when he spikes the loop for a new week, she loses much of the learning she had with you. But since your continued influence trumps Kaysar's overall, she's in better shape than she was from Monday to Monday."

"Influence?"

"Her subconscious likes you better," Roxy explained. "Meaning, what you're doing is working."

"Kaysar's constantly losing ground?" Q asked.

"Exactly. For us, it's one step back, two steps forward. We can take as much time as we like, it seems to me—until Kaysar figures it out. Of course, if he figures it out we're screwed. Best case, he'd build a new firewall and bytefence and we'd start from square one. Worst case, he'd cross her wires again and we'd lose her forever—and possibly screw up some of the relationships in this room."

"No," Roxanne said. Everyone looked at her. "Worst case is he kills her."

"He could always bring her back by recrossing. He did it once," Mason spoke up.

"He wasn't exact. He couldn't have been. He crossed her wire before he killed her in the past, but he could have picked any number of points from which to start. And what if he's changed other things? No one would even be

able to figure out the general span of where he crossed."
She looked at Louise and Q.

Mason looked at the siblings too. "Either one of you
ever been able to find the exact fragment of time a wire
crosses and go back? My personal experience? No. We
can't get exact enough. A fragment of time can't be precisely duplicated when punched—not precisely, not with
the technology we have. And we tried, remember? You're
the best test we've had, Roxy," Mason said. "And thank
God you were, because otherwise getting Kitty wouldn't
be an option, Leonardo wouldn't still be in trials, and he'd
be dominating the world."

"Okay," Q said. "So, what's the bottom line? What's the
deal?"

"It's this: the pills don't just affect her brain. It's physiological and . . . physiotemporal. It's why she couldn't be
punched out in the normal way. Have you ever wondered
why some of the guys, some of the ones you'd think
would be great wire crossers, the ones who set up perfect
calculations but never get past that, never land accurately?
Or sometimes when they do, they arrive crippled?"

"Yeah." Q nodded. "Sure. Sometimes it surprises me
who's good at what."

"Well . . . these tests we're running are pointing to
something really interesting. That there are some people
who simply don't have the genetics to successfully time-
travel."

Q stared at Mason. "Really?" He looked away, trying to
process the implications of the discovery. "And . . . maybe
Kaysar is trying to isolate those genes? Which would suggest that Kitty isn't merely an experiment of the mind;
she's also an experiment of the body. Really, it makes control of the mind merely a means to the ability to control
the body."

"This analysis of ours, the tests we know to run, the
most minute details we can isolate—we're still missing the

answer. Because we can't find what we don't know to look for."

"Why would figuring this out be especially useful to Leonardo Kaysar?" Vesper asked from across the room. "I mean . . . he can travel. And he can fire people who can't."

"Here's the deal," Roxy said. "Mason and I got mixed up with Leo when he wanted to steal back some technology I'd developed that ended up being a key component of time-based technology. If he'd been able to, he'd be the only one who could manipulate time in the ways wire crossers do now. But he couldn't get it from us. So what does he do? He takes another tack, attempting to control not the technology itself, but the technology's ability to work on certain people. That's where the genetics and the pills come in.

"If he can make it impossible for wire crossers to do their jobs because the technology won't respond to their genetic structure, then there's no one capable of maintaining reality's original intent, and he can cross all the wires he wants to with no one to stop him. Right there is the power to change the world at will. It's what he's always wanted."

"Whoa," Vesper muttered.

"Yeah. Whoa," Roxy agreed.

Q pushed at the throbbing in his forehead with his thumb. "I wish I could be with Kitty more. I need more access, but Kaysar's a perceptive man. If she starts acting in unexpected ways, and I'm around and not blending in enough, he'll figure it out."

"Well, this is all very promising," Louise said, removing her goggles and sitting back in her chair. "At the very least, we know we don't want these damn pills in her system. How we get her to stop taking them is another matter."

"Maybe I can help you!" Vesper said, leaping from her

chair. "I got this new job and it was going to be a surprise but it's—"

"You got a job? That *is* a surprise." Louise was staring at her, all nose, glasses, and bug eyes.

Vesper compounded her mistake by looking nervously at Q, who leaned back, his eyebrow cocked, not sure what she was talking about. He was in no rush to bail her out.

"Oh. Okay. Right, well, here's the thing. I have something I need to tell you," Vesper admitted. "And really, when I tell you, you're going to be very excited."

The rest of the team looked at her with different magnitudes of alarm.

"You've been skipping class," Louise accused.

Vesper looked a bit scared. "Um, could you restate that in the form of a question?"

Louise tossed her smartie onto the table. "We had an arrangement. What am I supposed to tell your parents? You're running off on your own, using our tech to—"

"What parents? I'm a test-tube baby," Vesper interrupted.

Louise rolled her eyes. "Don't sass me."

The intern looked down. "Sorry. But that's so not the point." Her head snapped up, and she gave a wide smile that increased the group's magnitude of alarm threefold. "The point is . . . Here's the thing . . . You're going to *love* this. I'll be a part-time Kaysar Corporation smartie pusher! I'll have some dreary job in a back room, totally undercover. It's fantastic! I've infiltrated the system!"

"Oh, my God," Q said in horror.

Vesper paused, as if waiting for congratulations and gratitude. All three of her peers just stared at her in dismay. Then they looked at Louise, who seemed to have gone into shock—or rather, into some sort of personal DEFCON 1.

"Have you *started* this new job?" Louise asked very, very calmly.

"Nooo . . ." Vesper looked around the room for support. "I found out—"

"How accurately did you fill out the application papers?" Louise asked, still very, very calmly.

"Not very accurately," Vesper said, more in the form of a question than an answer. Then, somewhat more belligerently, she asked, "Am I seriously in trouble again?"

Mason and Roxy looked at each other. "Hey, Rox, you wanna help me with that thing upstairs?"

"Sure."

"Louise, I need to get back to Kitty. Can you . . . ?" Q looked wearily at Vesper and then shook his head.

"I've got this one. I'll fill you in later," his sister said, never taking her eyes off the intern.

At which point it began to dawn on young Vesper that she *really* wasn't going to be congratulated or thanked. She put her hands on her hips. "Oh, come on. How is this bad? I'm not directly linked, so I can't throw off the wire, and there's no way anyone's going to figure out I'm a double agent. The most you ever let me do is squeeze fresh orange juice!" Vesper's voice grew louder and more petulant, to the point where she essentially yelled, "I'm better than orange juice!" at the top of her lungs. "I bet I could get Q whatever props and costumes he needs to blend into whatever he needs to blend into. How does this not make sense? How does it not help?"

Still Louise remained calm. Too calm. She took a sip of water and pondered, letting Vesper stew in her own over-adrenalized juices. "Number one, there is no excuse for taking such a drastic step without consulting one of us. I should fire you at the end of this conversation."

The blood drained from Vesper's face.

"Number two, you should be in school. It's not okay to bail out of school for this. Number three, I don't appreciate wanton expressions of independence. I am the project manager. You have ignored my authority on numerous occasions. That makes you a bad team player and a danger to your teammates. We have to know at all times what everyone is doing. You go off script and you could be putting any or all of us at risk. This isn't just about keeping you safe. You've jeopardized the lives of five other people, and, for all we know, we haven't even begun to see the results that flow down the wire as a result of what you've been doing."

Vesper's lips trembled, and she blinked hard to keep back tears.

"Make no mistake," Louise continued, "you've gone too far this time. That you would be so thoughtless about the safety of others only proves your unreadiness for being a major player in this profession. Every little move affects every other move, Vesper. I'd like you to please go home now and spend some time analyzing the ways you might have jeopardized the wires that each of us walk. Because one more screwup, and you're out for good. I mean it." Louise got up without another word and went upstairs.

Vesper began to sniffle. She raised her smartie and punch—if she was going to bawl her eyes out, she'd rather do it in the future.

CHAPTER NINETEEN

In the thin strip of time where everyone believed she was snug in her loop and didn't need "directioning," an unmedicated Kitty walked down the street with her face turned up toward the sun. "Forgetting" to take her pills didn't seem to be as dire as she thought it might be. Though she knew it was silly and that no one could possibly be manipulating the weather, the warmth somehow felt better—more real, perhaps—than she ever remembered. Perhaps it was because she'd never really remembered before.

Things were different now. Everything had a texture, a vibrancy. She felt an inherent familiarity in everything she saw. *Oh. My. God. Oh, my God. Omigod. Oh, my God. This is really me. This is me! I'm me, and I'm right here!*

She paused on a busy corner downtown, positively beaming as the world jostled and bustled and bumped around her. The motoways spiraled and curlicued, with smoke and geetane belching from the assortment of vehicles traveling around and above—and Kitty couldn't have been happier.

Neon signs and building trim dropped ribbons of light through the sky. She slowly raised her arms, palms outstretched, and turned in a circle, laughing without reservation, uncaring of the shocked stares and giggles of the passersby. "Hello, world!" she yelled.

The urge to experience everything all at once and as quickly as possible impelled her onward. Kitty dropped her hands and walked, her mind overloading in the best possible way with sights and sounds and smells. She practically skipped along the pathway she knew she'd walked many times, until one window display stopped her full in her tracks. . . . It was a funny little outlet of a shop with a narrow storefront and stairs leading to an underground entrance. Without hesitation, she bounded down the stairs and stepped into the shop. It smelled like damp earth and greenery, a scent obviously emanating from the heat lamps shining down on a row of plants in the back.

The walls of the shop were lined with bottles and vials and jars and urns full of spicy-smelling powders and what looked like dried leaves and twigs. The proprietor looked as old-fashioned as her product—Kitty immediately guessed the fabric of her dress was made out of cotton or hemp. It was so delightfully retro! This must be what people had worn when they still played actual vinyls on those record-playing machines.

Kitty declined assistance and wandered the shop on her

own, sniffing and tasting the samples as she went along according to the directives by each container. Something about it all reminded her: *I've always been interested in this stuff.*

She stood there staring at everything around her, and scenes began flashing one after another in her brain. Scenes with people who didn't exist in her life with Leo. *My friend Roxy?* These were scenes with the people Q had said cared about Kitty.

Q! Kitty touched her fingers to her lips. She remembered. She remembered kissing him, and how it made her feel alive the way she felt right now. She remembered everything. Gesturing to the proprietor, Kitty made a sackful of purchases and left the shop with the herbs and twigs and spices that seemed so familiar. She went running toward the place where she remembered going for her "appointment" with Q, sprinted down the block, ran up the stairs instead of waiting for the elevator, and flung the door open.

The man inside looked up, startled.

"Hello, Q," she blurted, her chest heaving as she sought to catch her breath. "Please take me home and tell me who I am."

CHAPTER TWENTY

Ignorance is not bliss, Q repeated to himself over and over as Kitty ran around her apartment investigating all her belongings as if she were seeing them for the first time. She might feel as free and as joyful as she'd ever felt before, but he was terrified. He struggled against the fear, watching Kitty's face register the reality behind . . . well, reality. She ran to and fro, from one room to the next in a frenzy of delight, peppering him with rhetorical questions he couldn't have answered even if he'd wanted to.

"Before my brain went kaput, what kind of person was I? What are my real interests? Do I really have this much style? Was I smarter before? Funnier? Did I lose anything in the translation? Did I have a different favorite color? What's my favorite band? Am I strong? Brave? Do I let people walk all over me? When I fight, do I yell or pout?"

Q followed her into the bedroom and waited while she practically demolished the closet while looking at every piece of clothing and every tag on every piece of clothing. Then she bolted out of the bedroom without a word. He followed her into the kitchen she'd never used and watched her pull open all the drawers and cabinets.

While she examined a pair of salad tongs for clues about her true personality, Q went back to the foyer, dug Roxy's photo album out of the bottom of his bag, and slipped it onto a chair at the dining room table. Kitty's shopping sack sat on the tabletop. He couldn't help but sigh.

Don't step on her rapture yet. She deserves to feel happy.

But Kitty had come up behind him and begun poking around in her sack. "Oh, it was the most interesting thing! All of these herbs and powders for different cures and such . . ." Her voice faded away when she looked up at Q's face. "I can't keep it; that's what you're thinking, isn't it?"

Q looked into the sack, then gently pushed it away from her. "Roxy will keep it for you. You can't have anything new that would give Leonardo cause for concern."

"Leonardo," she echoed, taking a seat with a glum look on her face. "This is really hideous. You kissed me and I kissed you back. I have a fiancé and I kissed you back. Am I a bad person in real life? Do I cheat on people? And if I cheat, do I care?"

"First of all, none of this kissing stuff is your fault. And second of all, murder trumps infidelity," Q said. He was cross with both himself and her.

She didn't understand, and it still seemed a bit premature to explain that in the past, on a different wire of reality, she'd actually been shot dead, and the man to whom she was engaged was her murderer. "Consider this," he said, "How can you be unfaithful to someone you never *chose* to love?"

"Did I not choose him?" She looked lost. "And even if this is all . . . odd, it's not like he's done anything terrible, has he? 'Murder trumps infidelity'? What is that supposed to mean?"

Q went cold. Where to even begin? "Have you ever heard of wire crossing?"

"Of course." Kitty said, suddenly studying the tablecloth as if it were the most fascinating thing she'd ever seen. "Some people think it's all a lot of hooey, but I know there's a whole division for it in Leonardo's company, and I know the government worries about him. It's all there in the employee handbook. Full disclosure and all that."

Full disclosure, my ass, Q thought. Everybody in the business had a copy of the Kaysar "employee handbook," and it was nothing more than official, watered-down public relations spin.

"After all," Kitty continued, "he *is* the world's leading expert on time-based technology."

Q winced at the note of pride in her voice. "So you understand how it works?"

She rubbed the tablecloth fabric between her fingers. "Is this really my taste? This feels like a synthetic. Do I like synthetics?"

"Kitty, could we . . . ?"

She clasped her hands together on the table, but her eyes kept tracking the various furnishings in her apartment. "Sorry. Do I understand . . ."

"How wire crossing works."

"Well, not precisely. I mean, I don't really understand the technology itself, but I get the general premise. Reality consists of an infinite number of wires. You can splice them in different ways now. You can change people's fates. I think you can make it so people don't even know it's happened. It's really weird. I don't want to think about it too much, because it's kind of sad."

"Leonardo Kaysar is not a good man. He's using you as an experiment. . . . You know he's capable of murder, don't you?" Q blurted.

"I can't imagine that!"

Q sighed. He didn't know what he should tell her. "Okay. Maybe he's not a murderer—not as you know him—but are you suggesting that what he's doing, all the projects he runs . . . are you suggesting that it's the work of a misguided, good-hearted guy?"

Kitty sat straight up. "I've seen many things, and I know that he's capable of being a perfectly nice man."

"Oh, Kitty," Q said. "There are . . . an infinite number of situations in this world, and I'm hard-pressed to think of a single one where Leonardo Kaysar comes out as anything other than a complete and utter menace to society. But maybe you don't see that." He hesitated for a moment, then just went for it. "Have you considered the possibility that he has wire-crossed you at some point?"

"Oh, good Lord," she said with a dismissive wave of her hand. "He wouldn't wire-cross *me*. That would be absurd!"

"Not in the usual way." Q took a deep breath. "You're actually a study in the next generation of time-based technology, one that adds a much stronger component of biology and physiology to the equation. For God's sake, do you *want* to think of him as a good guy?"

She thought for a moment and then glanced up at Q. He saw from the look in her eyes that she wasn't as dismissive as he'd thought. "You're not the one who has to sleep with him," she said.

Q reeled back as if struck. "Is this about your not wanting to feel guilty?" he asked. "Because you have no reason to feel guilty." Then he shook his head. "Not *you*."

Kitty studied Q's face as if she were finally focusing in on him for the first time, and he couldn't hide a goddamn thing from her. He knew it was all there for her to see: his anger, his disgust, his jealousy . . . perhaps even his love. He looked away in a wash of confusion.

"Oh. Oh, my," she said. Then after a pause, she added, "You really believe Leo is awful, don't you?"

Q cleared his throat and stared down at the photo album on the chair next to him.

"Well, what if he thinks what he's doing is for the best?" Kitty asked. "What if he thinks he's helping people? Isn't it important what made people what they are? What if . . . what if Leo had a really horrible mother who . . . who beat him with a Crock-Pot? Or what if he saw something unspeakably terrible that scarred him for the rest of his life? What if love was his undoing? What if some tragic episode of loss in his past has made him—"

"More like the bots he creates than the bots themselves?" Q interrupted. He snorted. "In my line of work I can't honestly believe that I know anything about anyone—not for sure. And yet I know this: you are good through and through, and there's no excuse for Leonardo putting you in this situation. And I know that he's done that too."

Kitty stared off into space, her brow furrowed as she seemed to struggle with the idea of the same man having two such different sides to him: what she had implanted in her head, and what seemed more readily apparent.

Q abruptly stood up and grabbed the album with one hand, and then went to Kitty and held his other out to her. "I've got proof," he said. "I've got the proof right here. So if you're ready . . ."

She looked at the album and slowly stood up, taking Q's hand, following him into the bedroom. Q tossed the album on the bed, and then wrapped his arms around her waist. "This is the truth, right here. This is your reality. It's

waiting for you." After a moment Kitty leaned back against
him, resting her head on his chest. He smiled, burying his
face in her hair for a moment, then pressed his lips to her
ear. "Ready?"

He felt her nod. It was time. He hoped it was time. Q
plopped down on the bed and waited for Kitty to sit down
next to him. He leaned against the pillows, and Kitty suddenly scooted back, cuddling into his open arms. He
could hardly stand it. And yet he nonetheless found
courage and found himself pulling her closer, and then
with his arms around her he opened the album on her lap.

Roxy obviously hadn't tracked the entire record of
Kitty's life, and it did occur to Q that the memorabilia
contained within the album were based on the last reality
they'd all had together in the nanosecond particle just
before—or concurrent with—her death in the past. It was
the only way for Leonardo to avoid rewriting history for
all of them. The life reflected in this album was as real as she
was ever going to get. It was one containing all the people
who cared most about her, and it was at least enough to
give Kitty back more of herself.

"Roxy asked me to give you this," Q said, pointing to
the envelope sticking out of the inside pocket.

Kitty slowly reached out and took the envelope. *To
Kitty from Roxy,* it said.

"Kitty," she repeated. "That's where it comes from. That's
why it sounds right when I give in to the feeling. *Kitty.*
That's what they called me there." The corner of her
mouth quirked up as she opened the envelope and pulled
out two pieces of folded paper: one printed, one handwritten. "It doesn't sound so strange to me anymore."

She selected the printed one and read it in silence. Q
studied the hard set of Kitty's jaw and the way she blinked
her eyelashes against her tears as she read the first part,
Roxy's plea asking Kitty to come home, followed by a list

of some trigger memories and a promise to tell her anything else Roxy could think of when Kitty got back.

Kitty picked up the handwritten page, and then looked at Q, her face a question mark.

"*That* is what Leonardo Kaysar did to you," he said. "I wasn't there. Only Roxy saw. She wrote it out exactly how it happened."

She seemed to steel herself, read in silence for a moment, and then started to read aloud.

"'. . . I swear to God, for once time stands still. I can still see her blond hair swinging as she turned to look at me over her shoulder, her hand on the doorknob. It would have made for a hilarious anecdote: me, arms and legs flailing in midair, knocking the vase of flowers off the counter. It could have been absolutely hysterically funny, except the bullet hit her in the chest.

"'Kitty went down, bleeding out, just bleeding out all over the apartment floor. *My friend,* I said. That's all I said. *My friend.*

"'I remember someone from down the hall poking their head out and screaming into a cell phone for an ambulance. I just knelt in the blood and held her hand. *My friend,* I said, squeezing it. The kohl around Kitty's eyes ran as she turned her face to me, and the tears slipped from the corners of her eyes.

"'"My *friend,*" she said.

"'The gadget Mason gave me blinked. The red light next to my name went out. The sweet spot. Out of time. Case closed. Kitty sucked in a quick breath and squeezed my hand. Then she died.

"'So . . . that's what happened. I swear it, Kitty. On a wire in the past, Leonardo Kaysar literally put a bullet through your heart in front of me, and on this wire he's trying to take away your soul. Please, please trust in Q and do whatever you can to come back to us. We miss you. Love, Roxy.'

"Roxy . . ." Kitty nodded, and a surprised little laugh suddenly burst out. "Oh, I do remember Roxy." She folded both pages and slipped them back in the envelope, then just stared down at her name scrawled across the top. Q watched the play of emotions on her face. It was as if she were pulling memories from the dark one by one to see if she could find herself in them.

Suddenly Kitty pursed her lips and frowned. "You know, I used to beg Roxy all the time to let me take her shopping. She has horrible taste in clothes. God forbid she should wear anything but black." She raised her index finger. "Although, I will confess I had this phase in college . . ." She giggled.

"What phase?" Q asked, laughing, finding it impossible to resist the contagious joy in her voice.

"I dyed my hair black. Completely black. I wore it in ponytails and went all faux-Goth. But, I assure you, I was still very chic in my way. It didn't last that long. I went on to another style. I've always liked fashion, and it was fun to try out different looks, different clothes." She glanced up from the photos, her gaze softening. "I guess I was still trying to figure out who I was, who I wanted to be. . . ."

Kitty shook her head, then turned to Q and unfurled a brilliant smile. "Oh! And I remember I made Roxy soup a lot. She had a hard time after college, and I ended up moving in with her. I'm a crappy cook, but she was just always so glad when I made soup. It was really nice to be appreciated. That's the thing most people don't realize. It doesn't take much, really. And I've never met anyone so loyal. You can't buy that, you know."

Such a heart, Q found himself thinking. He gazed at her face as memories flooded through her, so touched that his eyes watered. She leaned back against him without any artifice at all and flipped to a page of the photo album, one with a picture in which she and Roxy were mugging for the camera: Roxy was sticking a fake tiara on Kitty's head, and Kitty was curtsying, with her pink skirt raised above the ankles.

Kitty nodded at the photo and chuckled. "Roxy's always been my best friend," she said. And as suddenly as she'd laughed, her face crumpled and she burst into tears.

Q pulled her close, and she turned and put her face into his chest and cried. He simply held her and did his best to make the pain a little bit less.

It took some time for her to collect herself. It involved an entire box of tissues, a mug of tea made out of something from her purchases that looked to Q like glorified dirt, and lots of silent embracing.

At last, when she'd stopped crying and the tea was all gone, Kitty padded off to wash her face while Q flipped through the album again from the beginning. Doing so, he paid particular attention to the details, trying to learn as much about this girl he couldn't help but love, even though she couldn't remember his name half the time. And he had to know her enough for the both of them.

Kitty came back and sat down next to him, looking at the album over his shoulder. Q hesitated for a moment; then, before he could second-guess himself, he flipped the pages quickly to the end. To the pages Roxy had left blank. He'd put his own photos there.

Kitty immediately placed her hand on top of Q's to stop him from turning the page back. She was right to do so; he was already losing his nerve. He felt oddly exposed as she studied the pictures. There were only a few. Well, he owned only a few. How strange to view scenes of his own life from a distance: Q and Louise as young kids, when they still had a nuclear family. Q graduating from the academy; with some freelance buddies; at one of Louise's birthday parties . . .

"You remember that I'm not really a doctor, right?" he said, suddenly more scared than he ever remembered being in his life.

Kitty's hair blocked her face, and Q couldn't gauge her reaction. *I've lied. I've lied to her just like everybody else.* What could he possibly say? "Please believe that my lies were for a better purpose than those others"? Everybody had been telling her that whatever they did, it was for her own good. What could possibly make her believe that he cared and wasn't using her, that he just wanted to help? Was it possible for anyone to trust so blindly?

"I know," she finally said, fussing with the business of pressing down on the spots in the album where the plastic cover was lifting off the page. But her face was hard.

"Please believe me, I—"

"Don't."

Q winced.

"Can you just do your best—your absolutely, positively most accurate best—to explain what's happening to me *now,* and what you think Leo is doing? Just tell me what you think is happening and what you think I can do about it. Then I'll decide what to believe."

Q took a breath, aware that this was quite possibly one of the most important moments of his life. "The deal is this. You're having a really great week. In fact, it's probably the best week of your life. You have a great job, great friends"—he had to force himself to continue—"and a great boyfriend. You have money, clothes, popularity, respect . . . everything you've ever wanted. Monday morning you wake up and you can't wait to start your week. You go to Kaysar Corp and work on the new collection. Everybody loves your ideas. Tuesday is fantastic too. Wednesday . . ." He didn't really want to describe what he really thought he knew about Wednesday, so he allowed himself to hedge just a bit. "Wednesday you realize you are more in love with your boyfriend than ever. Thursday he proposes. Friday your friends throw a party. Sunday you'll go to brunch and do the girlie thing with the girls.

In between you see a psychiatrist for your so-called brain problems and do a myriad of other scheduled tasks programmed into your smartie. You're happy in your week. It's what you know. You have no reason to want to leave." He watched her carefully. "But it's not real. You're living a life that Leonardo Kaysar has created for you so that he can take out as many variables as possible for time-technology experimentation."

Q felt Kitty recoil, processing. He unfurled one arm and covered her hand with his, trying to provide a comforting gesture. He wasn't very good at it, but slowly she threaded her fingers through his, and that trusting movement touched him.

"Well, one day," he continued, "there's a small crack in the system. For less than a nanosecond, you blink and catch something that doesn't sync with your understanding. You ignore it, but it doesn't go away. Like thin, transparent slices of impossibly small moments in time are building up into something that cannot be ignored. And this mysterious inevitability . . ."

Kitty squeezed his hand really hard, as if willing herself not to freak out. He continued.

"You catch it from the corner of your eye, sense it just as you turn away from the mirror, miss your footing as it flashes too quickly from somewhere through the crowds in the street."

Kitty sucked in a quick breath. "I know that feeling. All those times when there's a strange little disconnect between what I think I see and what someone tells me is there. It happens all the time." She nodded for him to go on.

"At first you ignore it, because life is good and change carries no guarantee. But your brain is recording these moments, and something is building up in there, and you won't be able to stop yourself from questioning it much longer. You won't be able to stop yourself from wanting to know the why and the what, and what about the when, does where really matter, and if there's a who . . . and if the who is still really you."

Kitty turned her face toward his, and Q trailed his lips across her temple.

"Just when you think you're onto something, you get to the end of the week and Kaysar resets everything," he said softly. "The tech has never been perfected. Leonardo Kaysar is trying to do just that. It's a test, and you're in the middle of it.

"So . . . my team—your friend Roxy and her boyfriend, Mason, and my sister, Louise—we don't know everything about this tech. We know it's a physiological construct, not just messing with your thoughts but your body, and not just one time but many. It's not just physics; it's biology and chemistry too. That's where those pills come in."

He paused, not sure how she was feeling about his explanation, but she motioned for him to continue. Her silence made him nervous.

"We're working on breaking this hold he has on you and preventing an endless number of resets. We're trying everything we can, from bulldozing layers of time to breaking down the chemistry of those pills. We're trying everything." Q placed his fingers under her chin and raised her gaze to his. "Most important, you need to know there's an endgame out there somewhere, but we haven't been able to get you out against your will when you're deep in the world Kaysar has created for you."

"So what do I do?"

"You do your best to remember everything you can about the real Kitty Gibbs, even when Leonardo's doing his best to make you forget, and be ready to push through the lies the next time we get an opening to get you out, or . . ."

"Or?"

Q wished he hadn't gotten as far as an or. "Or you can succumb to someone's version of bliss for you and be ignorant but happy. At least until the man who's put you there doesn't feel like maintaining the loop anymore." He couldn't keep the bitterness out of his voice.

Kitty's face showed nothing but pain. She looked away.

Q gently pressed his hand against her cheek. "I don't know exactly what's going to happen next. I don't know how, when, or where the loop is going to take you, or what Leo will do, but if you want out, I need you to know something. You need to know this: that someone on the outside is exploiting the crack like a chisel on the outside wall, breaking things down—that someone is me. If you can just try to remember me always, no matter what happens, we're going to be okay. If you can just work on that, well . . . one day I won't even have to ask you to try."

"I will try," she said. "I'll try as hard as I can. Do you . . . do you have any idea how long this is going to take?"

He shook his head and moved away from her to the edge of the bed. "Before we can get you out? I don't know, but I'm starting with those damn pills. We're going to figure out what to do about them without everyone catching on, and in the meantime, I'm going to work on being wherever you are as well. Every event you go to, look for me. Always look for me. Remember me."

"I will," she whispered, sniffing back tears. "You're going to leave me now, aren't you? I wish you wouldn't go."

Q looked away, feeling sick. He didn't want to go either. "I'll see you soon," he said; then he leaned over and gently pressed his mouth against her temple. Her hand slipped up to his cheek, her fingertips caressing his skin. Q closed his eyes. He could feel his body react to her and pulled away.

Kitty looked up. There was no expression on her face at all. "Leo killed me," she said woodenly. "Leo killed me." She and Q sat there for some time, hand in hand in silence, with him on the edge of the bed and Kitty staring blankly in front of her. The sound of water gurgling in the pipes and the faint buzz of the hover-ads outside filled the void.

"The idea of kissing Leonardo makes me want to vomit now," Kitty blurted. "The idea of me not realizing that kissing Leonardo makes me want to vomit, makes me want to vomit more."

"Imagine how it makes me feel," Q blurted.

She looked at him. "How does it make you feel?"

Q pulled his hands away. *Don't tell her something you don't want to follow up on. Just tell her to remember.*

"Q?"

"What I meant was that . . . I mean, it's hard for me to know that you're being forced to do things against your will. I feel responsible for you now, and you know, it's, well . . ." He averted his gaze and rose, wandering around and looking for his smartie to cover his confusion, cursing himself in the same moment for his cowardice.

He caught a glimpse of her face and did a double take. She looked so forlorn, sitting there on the bed all alone, hoping to get some sort of meaningful response out of him.

"I feel very . . . bad about all this. I feel responsible for you," he said again, relieved to find his smartie on the bureau. He picked it up and fiddled aimlessly with the calendar function. "Look, I think about you all the time. Every day of the week. You can't imagine what my Sundays are like, when I know the reset is about to kick in. I just start thinking about whether or not you're going to forget about me again, and if so, how much." He managed a wan smile. "At least we now know I've been having some sort of cumulative effect on you. It was hellish in the beginning."

They looked at each other. "You've definitely been having some sort of effect on me," Kitty said softly.

Though Q stood perfectly still, he felt as if he were

jumping out of his skin. Kitty looked at him, chewing on her lower lip with a slight wrinkle in the center of her forehead.

He set his smartie back on the bureau and released the breath he'd been holding. Kitty didn't move from where she sat, but she might as well have been breathing down his neck. His hands trembled on the wood surface, and Q curled his fingers into fists. Then he looked up into the mirror and caught her gaze.

"I need to go," he said, his voice clogging.

Kitty tore her gaze from his and looked away, her expression tight.

"You're being really brave," he said.

"No, I'm not," she replied, still looking away.

He gently touched her chin to make her look at him. "Yeah. You are. If anyone knows what's going on here, it's me. You're the bravest woman I've met—and I'm not just saying you're fabulous."

She managed a smile.

He heaved a sigh and added what he least wanted to say: "You're going to have to keep it up. I know you can do it."

A look of dread passed over her face. "Do . . . what, exactly?"

"Fake things for just another small while."

Her mouth became a grim line. "You're not suggesting . . . !"

Q reeled back, horrified. "No, no. That's not what I meant. I mean, not exactly." He shook his head, trying not to consider what would have to be done. "I'm just talking about . . . well, maintaining continuity as best you can."

Kitty shuddered, clearly reliving something Q didn't know. He wondered what it was—though he could guess. God, he hated Leo. "I'm so sorry," he blurted.

She stared blankly into space.

I'm hurting her again. Someone's always hurting her. The pressure was getting to him. Q forced himself not to comfort her, and escaped into the bathroom, where he leaned against the door for a moment to calm down, and then splashed cold water on his face.

You don't do relationships because they disappear so easily, he reminded himself. *It isn't a terrible policy, no matter what Louise says. Keep it together. Focus and keep it together.*

Kitty's cosmetics were lined up like little soldiers along a shelf by the sink. Gold and silver mixed with pinks and purples and blues. Q had to quell the urge to just take his arm and sweep the whole lot to the ground and say, "To hell with continuity." Instead he carefully picked one lip-stick out of the lineup, uncapped the tube, and wrote a sin-gle letter on the mirror.

" 'Remember Q,' " he whispered with a hint of a smile. "You know I'll remember you." And then he replaced the cap and put the lipstick back in the same exact way in the same exact spot on the shelf.

CHAPTER TWENTY-ONE

The waiter smiles and bends slightly at the waist as he refills her glass. Katherine excuses herself to touch up her makeup.

When she leaves the room, everybody relaxes: you can feel it in the air, though they don't dare break character when I'm on set. Ah, yes. She returns, pleasant as always, such a pleasure to be with, though still blank. Odd, though. She's not like the other girl, my first fiancé, and she should be. I would expect them to be equally blank, interchangeable. Does that mean something's not working? Or does it simply mean that I feel differently about them, when I should feel exactly the same? Is it Kitty who's be-having differently, or is it that my feelings are different?

I stifle the urge to look at the time, knowing it's probably around nine p.m., as it always is when she excuses herself. Like clockwork, and I make these notes. I never thought she would last this long. The experiment holds; the subject is contained in the loop. The implications of this technology . . . it could open up a whole new world. Perhaps the Kaysar Corporation will have the last laugh after all.

Leonardo practically had to lug Katherine back to her apartment after the engagement scenario was complete. She stood in the middle of her living room, the peacock blue dress shimmering under the lights as she wobbled on her heels and stared down at the enormous diamond on her left ring finger. She'd had quite a bit of champagne.

He walked up behind her, gently moved her hair aside, and pressed his mouth against the side of her neck, giving her the illusion of a loving kiss.

"Omigosh. Why did I drink so much?" she asked with a giggle.

"It's not every day you get engaged," Leonardo murmured against her skin. His hand slipped around and folded into hers. He pulled, unwinding her body until she faced him, and he tried to concentrate. It was difficult. It had been a dreadful day at the office. A dreadful day, a dreadful evening. How ironic that he could cycle Katherine Gibbs's thoughts and actions so that everything seemed fresh and as if it were happening for the very first time for her, but he couldn't maintain any of it for himself.

Perhaps I'll skip tonight, he thought. *She's drunk, anyway.* Maybe that meant that taking things to their expected end wasn't entirely necessary. Would there be any damage to the experiment?

Of course, he had to admit that odder than his lack of desire to seduce her was that she hadn't seemed to want or even expect it. She should have expected it on some level, because that was what they'd always done—and she also should have wanted it because that was who she thought she was: a girl who loved and wanted Leonardo Kaysar.

As if reading his mind, she smiled sweetly and moved in

close, giving a loving brush to remove what she seemed to think was lint from the shoulder of his tuxedo. "I'm so happy with you, Leo," she slurred. "I must be the luckiest girl in the world."

Ah, much better. She still loves me. A strange wave of relief swept through him, a sensation with which he wasn't particularly familiar. *Rather, she still* thinks *she loves me.* Leonardo trailed his fingers across her collarbone and down her arm. He caressed her left breast through the smooth satin fabric of her dress and rested his palm gently over her heart, which he felt beat against his hand. She gave a sly smile, but all the same he had an odd feeling of distance.

"Katherine?" He lifted his palm to her cheek, then her forehead. "You're very warm." She'd been drinking entirely too much champagne, he reminded himself.

"Mmm," she replied. "I think I need to sit down. So much excitement."

Leonardo led her to the bedroom and eased her onto the bed. Katherine's head had only just hit the pillow when she went out cold. She was still lying on her back when her mouth dropped open and a very unladylike snoring sound began buzzing in and out.

Leo sat down on the bed next to her and studied her face. His Katherine Gibbs had never gotten drunk to the point of unconsciousness. One might think she'd drunk so much tonight for the specific purpose of getting totally soused. One might think . . .

He stood and began to search the apartment, even though that, too, wasn't part of the weekly protocol. But this time he didn't look for the existence of the things he expected to see, but rather he looked for the opposite: anything that might have been planted, something changed for appearances. Something planted by someone who was meddling. Or maybe the experiment was breaking down on its own.

He couldn't find proof. There *was* no proof.

Leonardo wandered into the bathroom, studied the cos-

metics lined up perfectly along the shelf, and reviewed the
contents of the medicine cabinet. There was nothing unexpected. He shut the cabinet and stared at himself in the mirror, touched his finger to the glass, and drew a line
diagonally across his reflection. And then his focus shifted
and he stared at a slightly filmier gray spot; his finger had
caught oil.

He contemplated the mirror for a few moments more,
then reached under the sink and pulled out a bottle of
cleanser that had never been used. He unsealed the top
and sprayed the substance over the mirror. The cleaning
agent adhered most strongly to the greasiest sections,
trickling quickly down the rest. Appearing upon the glass
was the distinct impression of a single letter.

Q

Leonardo stared calmly at the symbol, and then his gaze
refocused a bit more to follow the slash his own finger had
made. Studying the spot, he gently reached out and
rubbed away the greasy tail of the Q. The symbol was
now:

$\emptyset$

As he stared at the naught sign, his mind clicked in with
a clarity of purpose that had recently been flagging.
Something odd was happening, something more than either coincidence or happenstance. Something that wasn't
part of any natural breakdown in technology he might
have expected. Leonardo backed away from the mirror,
blew past the snoring Katherine, and went directly to his
office.

Q. All night the symbol taunted him. He simply could not
interpret what it meant. He racked his brain for traditional

code, Morse or perhaps wartime systems, ancient hiero-
glyphics, anything he could think of, but by the time he'd
fallen asleep with his head on the desk, he'd still come up
with nothing. It was only when he woke that things were
clear. He sat straight up in his chair, his eyes bloodshot, his
hair askew, an inkblot on his crumpled left white sleeve.

"They must be *insane*. They couldn't possibly be that
stupid."

He grabbed the smartie off his desktop and hit the
hotkey for Ariel. She answered immediately. "Two
things. I want to see the chemist. Get him into the lab immediately . . . whoever worked on the pills," he ordered.
"And then schedule an all-day with the best bloody code
jockey we've got. One with maximum security clearance."

He didn't wait for her answer, just swiveled violently in
his chair to stare out the window. Why was Katherine slipping away from him? Was it a natural degradation of the
experiment . . . or were his nemeses, Mason Merrick and
Roxanne Zaborovksy, back in the picture? Had they figured out where she was and come after her at last? His eyes
searched the cloverleaf maze of mototracks, the antlike
streams far below, as if there were a possibility he could actually find them. But he knew they couldn't be there.

Both chill and fever swept through his blood as he
racked his brain for the possibilities. They couldn't logi-
cally be involved, manipulating Katherine from another angle. Her early life was far too intertwined with Roxanne's,
and by extension Mason's; he'd made sure of it while setting this up. Mason would risk losing Roxanne forever by
coming here and attempting what Leo suspected, and such
an outcome would go against everything the man had already worked so hard for. And yet . . .

Leonardo Kaysar was rarely caught by surprise. Even an
unexpected outcome wasn't often a surprise. Unexpected
outcomes were the norm; they were what he reacted to,
were catalysts for his new ideas. But this . . . this scenario

was something else. He didn't know what to do with himself. He paced his office like one possessed, compulsively rolling up his sleeves and rolling them down again. He'd known that one day his enemies would figure out where Katherine was, but he had not counted on the fact that her two friends would actually risk themselves and their relationship to get her back. Nor had he intended to bring Katherine in as close to himself as he had.

No, Mason and Roxanne hadn't risked crossing the wires. They wouldn't—and couldn't. If they came to Kitty and got involved, it wasn't just risking their relationship; all of them might be tossed into chaos, and Mason was much too principled for that. He and his fellow wire crossers were committed to the theory of original intent: Time was to travel in a straight line whenever possible, and wire crossers made only small changes—usually defensive ones—to keep the original version of reality in place. The man was damn lucky his original reality had included Roxanne.

Both palms against the glass window, Leonardo hung his head. He was too tired to think straight. This needed focus, concentration, but he had none.

He wrenched away from the glass and went to the bar table, pouring himself a Scotch, straight up. The alcohol had a bracing effect, though it didn't seem to make things any clearer.

Think. Think!

It would be simple to let Katherine go—it would, in fact, be safer. He had plenty of data, had logged all of the problems in the technique, and it seemed she was beginning to frag out. Ending the experiment was the logical, rational thing to do. With the next girl, he would adhere strictly to the law of diminishing returns. Bloody hell, that was really what he should just do: send Katherine the way of the last girl and start over, building further upon what had been already learned from both of them.

He should have ended this experiment a while ago. Failure was a natural part of science. He didn't enjoy it, but he always learned from it. And keeping Katherine in a decent loop was a pain in the arse—it had become that way some time ago, and the only reason he could think that he'd expended so many resources and spent so many sleepless nights to keep her beyond what a useful experiment really, truly required was that . . .

He simply didn't want her to go.

Leonardo groaned. What was this nonsense clouding up his brain? It was if a coin had fallen into the lining of his suit jacket that was equally impossible to find or ignore.

Once more he moved to the bar table, this time pushing the lid off the insulator and scooping out a slice of cold-stay, which he pressed to his forehead. The coolness, his ability to focus once more, both had a calming effect. Leonardo returned to his desk and pulled forward his smartie. He raised his stylus and began asking himself a series of questions and bulleting the facts as he understood them. Finally, one paragraph stood out.

> I would not take the risk of mixing with Mason and Rox-anne, and nor would they with me. If one presumes that they are not stupid enough to cross wires and/or insert them-selves into a situation where they risk losing each other and original intent, they must be working with someone else.

"Mason and Roxanne are using someone else . . . and God only knows how long this person has been poking around!"

A burst of adrenaline filled Leonardo's system. He grabbed his suit jacket and stopped short of the door, took a deep calming breath, and stepped into his large executive bathroom. The sight in the mirror was something of a shock. He hardly recognized himself, almost as if he were breaking down in some way along with Katherine's loop.

Fanciful notion, man. A fanciful notion. He took the time necessary to clean himself up properly, lit a clove cigarette, and smoked until the trembling in his hand stilled, and when he calmly and confidently stepped out through his office door and into the hallway, only someone truly close to him would have noticed the fraying around his edges.

And there was no one truly close to him to worry about.

CHAPTER TWENTY-TWO

Kitty had been pacing her bedroom for the better part of an hour. She was remembering things. It was pretty damn thrilling, to say the least, and Q had to work to keep his mouth shut and just let her experience her memories and thoughts as they came spilling back into her mind.

"It was awful. It was horrible!" Kitty held up her palm. "I had to drink so much that I was still toxic for three hours the next day, but he didn't touch me, thank God. I'm doing my best, but I don't know how long I can keep faking everything. He's already suspicious. I think he did an extra continuity check."

Q winced as the gigantic diamond in her engagement ring flashed under the lights. "It's going to be fine," he said, suppressing the urge to rip the ring from her finger and flush it down the toilet.

"It's *not* going to be fine," she argued. "I don't love him. I don't want to love him. I know it's not really love. I mean, I can't be sure what he wants me to be feeling, what all these loops have done, but I just have to believe I know the truth. On some level, I'd know if this were real, and it's not. I know what love is, Q, and that's not it."

Q stared at her, not sure what to say.

"Do *you* know what love is?" she whispered.

"I don't want to know," he replied, though it was too casual, even to his own ears. "Doesn't fly right in my line of work," he explained awkwardly, trying to step out of her way.

Kitty stepped back in front of him. When Q tried to walk around her, she blocked his path. "Don't run away," she said.

"Let me," he begged.

"Coward."

Q winced. "I'm no coward," he said. He pressed his palm to his forehead and shook his head. "What do you *want* from me?"

"I want everything. I want to know you, and I want you to know me . . . I'm sorry," Kitty said in a clogged voice. "I'm sorry. You can go. You should go. I just thought . . . Never mind."

Q looked into Kitty's eyes for a long, long time before he finally murmured, "You just kill me, Katherine Gibbs." Then he sat on the edge of the bed and stared down at the floor between his feet. "My sister and I . . . we didn't have . . ." He shook his head and looked up at the ceiling, and then tried again. "Things have changed so much from the way they used to be.. There's a lot of stuff you don't know. Things are . . . we're running out of things . . . it's hard to hold on to things. . . ." He looked into Kitty's face; she was trying to understand. "The technology we have now is amazing, and it's easier to cure things now, but there are also more ways to die."

Kitty frowned and chewed on her lower lip. She sat next to him.

Q managed a wan smile and shook his head. "This is not helpful, is it?" He cleared his throat. "Time can be a very bitter enemy. It can take things away so easily and so fast." Fighting his own tears, he looked into Kitty's eyes. "It can take people away so easily and so damn fast. A couple of times I thought maybe I'd try to get to know people better. You know, make some really good friends. Maybe . . . maybe find someone to love." His eyes turned steely. "It never lasts. Someone always goes away. One splice and they're gone. And maybe it wasn't even your splice. Maybe it was someone on a wire-cross job somewhere else whom you've never met. They don't mean to, maybe, but one damn splice and everything's different and you're gone." He cradled Kitty's face in his hand. "You're just gone," he said hoarsely.

She pulled his hand away from her face and entwined her fingers in his. "Not forever. Not everyone. You're bringing me home. I was gone, wasn't I?"

He pulled his hand away and stood up, walking to the bureau, where he absently ran a thick gold chain through his fingers. "Chances are you won't remember this in a little while. You won't remember what I said, and you won't remember me."

"Look at me," Kitty said.

Q didn't move. He just let the chain slip through his fingers again and again like liquid gold.

She stood up. "Look at me!"

He finally turned. They just stared at each other for a moment.

"Damn," Q said softly, shaking his head. "Damn it." He crossed the room and took her roughly in his arms. "You won't remember," he said bitterly.

"I'll remember," she said. "It stays inside me somewhere. I'm sure of it."

He blinked, warring with his emotions. Kitty held his gaze, refusing to give in. Q shook his head angrily, but his mouth came down hard on hers.

Her lips parted instantly, and Q's body reacted as if he'd been shocked as he slid his tongue into the sensuous heat of her mouth. She tasted like heaven. Almost too perfect. Too much to allow himself to have. Q jerked his head away, panting. "You won't remember this."

Kitty slid her hand slowly up the side of his neck and gently brought his mouth back down to hers. She bit gently at his lower lip. Q tried to keep his wits about him, but he felt as though he were going completely blank to everything but pure sensation. "You won't remember this," he repeated one last time in a kind of surrender, and the words simply disappeared between them.

With a gasp, Kitty threw back her head as Q trailed his lips across her collarbone. She grabbed the neck of his T-shirt, pulled it over his head, and sent it sailing across the room. Careening wildly off balance, Q twisted Kitty around and they fell onto the bed together.

Oh, how he wanted to burn the images of all others from her mind and body. He wanted to take her with everything in his heart and teach her the difference between the touch of an empty man and that of one entirely filled with love for her. He inhaled Kitty's scent and buried his face in her silky hair while his fingers searched for bare skin, clawing at the luxurious fabric of her dress. Too much was covering her, too damn much. He pulled off her dress and she removed his clothing; it all vanished in a hailstorm off the side of the bed.

He moved his mouth over her skin, and hearing her moan he imagined that his passion for her was hot enough to brand her forever in a way she'd never forget. If his kiss truly meant something—oh, what he might do for her! "There's just not enough *time*," he murmured, running his mouth along her curves.

Kitty whispered his name and then arched her back, pressing herself against his body. He slid the straps from her bra down her shoulders. Her chest heaved, the lace cupping her breasts coming away to reveal rosy nipples. He pulled the bra back and took off her panties, leaving her clad only in stockings that came up to her thighs with a teasing froth of lace. She moved her hands over his back and down, and then suddenly froze.

Panting, Q pulled away and looked into her eyes, but he couldn't get a read until suddenly she removed the diamond ring from her hand and flung it across the room. Then, with the speed of a gunshot, they moved together, unable to keep the slow pace that had reined them in earlier even if time had been on their side.

Kitty gasped in delight as he slid one hand down the length of her stocking and parted her legs. He rolled atop her, entering her damp heat slowly, trying not to let his intense desire force him to drive brutally into her. But rough passion had already taken *her* over. She wrapped her long legs around him and bucked upward, and in a kind of frenzied passion they made love as if it were the last day of the world.

In the aftermath, they lay curled together in a tangle of blankets, their skin streaked with sweat. Q couldn't take his eyes off her, couldn't believe that he'd ever thought he wouldn't need to feel this. And when their breathing evened and their bodies calmed, Kitty talked to him about new memories from her old life that had come back to her out of the fog. Q only interrupted to capture her face in a kiss every now and again. Everything she did enchanted him, from the way she wrinkled her nose when she laughed to the way her fingers stroked his chest as she spoke.

She looked at him as if he were the best sort of reality she could have ever thought up, and they made love again, gazing into each other's eyes this time, unwilling to rush one moment together even as the nanoseconds drained away.

Q kissed the top of her head and hugged her closer, wishing he weren't so aware of the time. "Kitty," he whispered.

"Mmm?"

"I just wanted to say . . . I just wanted to say that I'll always be here. Mind, body, soul. Whether you can see me in front of you or not. I'll be with with you." He pressed his mouth against her temple. "And no matter what wire you're on or what I have to do. I'm not going to quit until you're free."

She turned her face and nodded, obviously undone. And when she kissed his mouth, a hint of salt from a single tear stung his tongue. Finally, he pulled away.

"Tell me you don't have to leave yet," she whispered.

He frowned. "Gotta get back in the game. Gotta find a way to save you." He rolled out of bed and walked into the bathroom.

Kitty climbed off the bed and followed him. Q had turned on the faucet but was just gripping the sides of the sink with his head bowed. He suddenly splashed water on his face and then looked over his shoulder at her, the droplets obscuring what might have been tears.

And if she hadn't been watching him quite so closely, she might have missed the first time that he literally flickered like a broken light.

"What's wrong?" he asked sharply.

"You did that," she said in confusion.

"No, you did that. I'm right here. What's wrong? You're . . . fading on me."

Kitty wrinkled her forehead and looked down at her palm. It wasn't him flickering; it was her. The light in the room dimmed, and she felt herself vanish inside herself for a moment, as if she'd fallen asleep for a split second and lost a millennium. She fell to her knees.

"What's wrong?"

She opened her eyes as wide as she could, fighting the clogged sensation in her head. "What time is it? Is it Sunday? It's not time yet. It's not even night!"

Q put his hand on her cheek; she was *sure* he had. But like a hologram, he physically wasn't quite there. His form flickered, the pressure on her face was too light, and then she thought she heard him gasp as if someone had just punched him in the stomach.

"Oh, God," he whispered. "He knows."

In one sweep of her eyelashes, a simple blink, he'd vanished again. With a sinking feeling Kitty staggered to her feet and looked through the doorway at the wall clock. It was spinning erratically backward and forward.

Q seemed to appear and reappear all around her, translucent and hesitant, always trying to speak, always reaching for her, never finishing the thought before he was gone again. And with each successive appearance, his voice became less certain, his motions less sure. His very presence on her plane seemed to be substantially weakening—everything about him but the look in his eyes, which had never been more intense. And every time he reappeared, it was as if he were chasing her around the room.

She felt in a way as though she were standing still, doing nothing while he did everything, though the amount of time passing was minimal. The room faded, and it seemed she was in a black universe. In one moment Q was standing there in complete detail; in the next, the outline of his body was blurred and he was gone. He'd reappear somewhere else in the apartment, slammed against a wall, his jaw set and his fingers madly punching at his smartie.

Then he'd be back. Sometimes his face looked perfect; sometimes it was tender and bloody. She guessed from all he'd told her that he was whipping back and forth through fragments of time, clearly playing defense against Leonardo's offense, responding as best he could. But superior technology and the upper hand were on Leo's side.

"Listen to me, Kitty," Q said when he'd returned what seemed like the fortieth time. "I—" His words cut off as the space in front of Kitty blurred and he vanished again.

She whirled. "Q?"

A light flashed, followed by a loud, otherworldly scraping. Kitty blinked and screamed, but the sound of her own voice disappeared in a vacuum. Q was in front of her only in static, his body seemingly rendered in outlines and shades of fluorescent blue light. His form flickered in and out, his mouth emitting only her name before his very existence was once more extinguished.

She could feel pressure all around her body. Her head grew heavy, as if she'd taken a sedative. When she screamed, no sound came out. When she tried to reach forward, her limbs wouldn't move.

"Don't do this, Leo. Don't do this to me again," she begged.

In the end, all she could do was watch. Q appeared in one last sequence, fighting to reach her. He seemed farther and farther away, and the pressure on her felt as if she were being pulled farther and farther back, though she never moved at all.

Oh, God, Leo's unraveling time, she thought. *Unwinding the wire, reeling me in.* If Kitty could have dug her heels in, she would have, because all she could think was that if he pulled too hard she'd be somewhere Q had never existed for her at all. And then, as if it were just another end to just another day, Leonardo pulled the trigger on her loop.

There was no soft bed to gracefully fall back on. Kitty slammed her head against the bathroom wall as she fell to the tile.

CHAPTER TWENTY-THREE

"Psst. Louise, check this out." Mason dropped a newspaper on the table in front of Louise right smack on top of the plans she was working on for infiltrating Kitty's world and swapping out her pills. Not that that was important or anything.

She poked at the scruffy-looking wad of newsprint and glanced at the date. "It's an old newspaper."

"This is not any old newspaper. This is memorabilia.

Romantic memorabilia. I dug it out of the files back from when Roxy was our case. This newspaper commemorates the very day I found her again." He gazed up at the ceiling, an inscrutable look coming over his face. "I remember it distinctly. She was wandering down the street on her way to the 7-Eleven in the middle of the night wearing those god-awful sweatpants. It was windy . . . stuff was blowing every-where, newspapers, Big Gulp cups . . . and then I saw her face again for the first time since I'd lost her." He looked right at Louise. "It was the best moment of my life."

Louise smiled. "Oh. That's so . . . cute." She sniffed loudly, but didn't comment on the obvious musty smell. "What are you going to do with it?"

"I'm going to wrap Roxy's ring in it. She'll think it's really romantic and sentimental and shit, and I'll get extra brownie points, and she'll say yes."

"I think she'll say yes without the newspaper." Louise leaned over. "Besides, there's a crusty glob of peanut but-ter on it."

"You don't have a romantic bone in your body," Mason said, carefully folding the newspaper up and pushing it out of the range of her coffee cup.

"So does this mean you found a ring?" Louise asked, pointedly ignoring the statement.

Mason grinned at Louise. "Vesper said she'd price some for me in the future, but she's made it clear your orders are first priority."

Louise nodded; then, almost in spite of herself, she reached out and touched Mason's arm. "I'm really happy for you, Mason. You waited a long time to find Roxy."

Mason gave Louise a look to silence her as Roxy came bounding downstairs. He hastily buried the newspaper under a stack of files and opened the top file, pretending to be engrossed.

Roxy put her hands on the banister at the last bit, swung her legs in the air, and hit the landing with a massive bang.

The team all glanced up at the same time. Roxy looked down at her feet in surprise. "I don't think that was all me." She jerked her head up and then stared over at the door. Everyone perked up and listened, but no follow-up sound came, so Roxy went to the door and peeked through the keyhole. "There's nobody there," she said. Shrugging, she turned back to the table, but then she heard what sounded like scraping against the wood.

As far as Roxy was concerned, there was no such thing as a scraping sound on the outside of the door that had positive connotations, so she gestured back to the table. Mason pulled out a weapon and crept forward. Louise and Vesper moved out of the door's sight line and watched from the kitchen. She discreetly pulled a butcher's knife from the knife block and held it behind her back.

Roxy took a deep breath and forced herself to open the door. She opened it very suddenly, and leaped to the side at the same time. The figure of Q lying in a heap took all fear away—at least, fear for herself.

Louise focused in on the body and ran to her brother with a horrified cry. She gently tipped his face toward her to get a look. He was a mess.

His swollen eyes shifted. "Have to help . . ." was all he could muster before passing out.

Mason gently lifted Q's shoulder and slipped his arm under the man, while Louise, her face stonier than ever, did the same on the other side. The two picked Q up and half dragged, half carried him to the sofa, where Roxy was already tossing off extra pillows and moving the coffee table out of the way.

"How many times did he make the leap?" Vesper asked, coming in from the kitchen with an enormous first-aid box that was much wider than she was. "And why is he so banged up?"

Roxy and Louise immediately set to tending Q's wounds. Every now and then he'd make a sound, his eyelids would flutter, and he'd try to speak, but it was simply too much; he never quite managed an explanation.

Mason pulled a small light from the first-aid box. "Sorry, man," he mumbled to Q, then pressed up each of Q's eyelids and studied the man's pupils. He lowered them gently and checked out a few of the other bruises.

Louise looked up. "He's fried."

"Yeah. It's like time-travel suicide. Except he didn't do it to himself."

Vesper elbowed her way into the circle and looked woefully down at Q. "Will somebody please tell me what's happening? Is he going to be all right?"

"Look at this," Mason said, cradling Q's arm in his hands and slowly bending the limb slightly forward and back. "Total loss of flexibility, muscle cramping, slowed blood circulation. They're all symptoms of too much punch travel. This is straight-line stuff. Since he's still here, my guess is that Kaysar was working the time line back and forth in pretty quick succession. Q could easily have just done the equivalent of a dozen trips back and forth in something like a minute. Bad news."

He took a loose piece of string from the box and held it up taut between two fingers. "See this?" When Vesper nodded, he moved his hands and grabbed the piece of string closer to the center. "Still the same wire, but a sub-set." He jiggled the string so that the segment between his two fingers went from loose to taut to loose again. "Kaysar's trying to throw him without affecting time on the either end. He just wants to change the middle. But Q wouldn't let go."

"Ouch," Vesper said. She moved to Q's feet and started to untie his combat boots. Q's head lolled from side to side, his parched lips just barely moving.

"I'll get him some water," Roxy said, gesturing silently for Mason to join her in the kitchen.

They met over the sink. Her boyfriend pulled a glass

down and handed it to her, and she turned on the faucet. He said, "The guy's strong, but he's just been through the wringer. We need to find out what's become of Kitty."

Roxy nodded, grabbed a clean kitchen towel from the shelf, and brought the water and towel back to the couch. She dipped the towel in the water and pressed it to Q's mouth.

Q's eyelids fluttered. He managed to part his lips. "Have to get her . . . out."

"We're going to get her out," Louise said, crouching at her brother's side and gently stroking his hair.

"Don't . . . can't . . . wait anymore," he croaked. "Kitty . . . she never . . ."

"Shush. We think we've got something." Louise frowned, probably to avoid crying. "We're going to replace her pills with placebos as soon as we can. So don't you worry. She's going to stop forgetting you. Okay?"

Q nodded weakly. "What . . . time is it?" But before anyone could answer, he closed his eyes and again passed out.

Q came to consciousness with bones that felt loose under his skin and a searing pain in his thigh. "Kitty?" he whispered hoarsely. With a grunt and a wince, he moved one aching arm up toward his head and pushed against the wall to give himself the space to rise.

He rose too quickly, tearing a cry of pain from his lips. His knees shook uncontrollably, every muscle in his body seemed too tender, and he felt uncomfortably delicate—as if his legs might go to pieces underneath him and shatter the rest of him to dust. From battered, swollen eye sockets he searched the room before him, finally placing his location. He was in the spare bedroom in Roxy and Mason's apartment—he'd left Kitty alone in the future.

Q crept to the door and moved out into the hall far enough to listen in on the conversations downstairs. He heard the urgency in their voices, but the words "placebo" and "strategy" didn't impress him.

I'm lying in bed catching Z's while Kaysar's terrorizing my girl. I have to get to her . . . now.

Muttering a litany of curses under his breath, Q turned back into the room and found his stuff on top of the bureau. He wanted to break down more than just a door or a wall. Q wanted to rage against everyone and everything. Struggling against the exhaustion that threatened to pull him under, Q staggered backward and had to lean against the wall to keep from falling. With shaking hands, he keyed his smartie, unclipped his punch, and jammed the needle in his neck.

CHAPTER TWENTY-FOUR

"Katherine! Wake up! Katherine!"

Through a haze, Katherine felt the dull pain of someone's palm swatting her cheek. She was lifted up and seated on the edge of a bed. Falling backward, she was then flung forward once more and propped up before flopping over the bend of an arm. Leonardo Kaysar's arm. A litany of curse words exited his mouth, entered one of her ears, and drifted out the other.

Katherine looked up and couldn't decide whose face she was seeing, if it really was Leonardo . . . or maybe it was Q. But Q would never swat her face, and he'd certainly never take her nightie off without asking.

Lying sprawled naked on her own bed, Katherine lolled, staring up at the ceiling.

"Oh, hello, darling," she said as the face loomed nearer. Its owner seemed to be trying to get a nylon thigh-high stocking up one leg.

"Hello, Katherine. We need to get you to work. If you'd cooperate . . ."

She giggled. "Cooperate being me?" she asked.

The face froze. All was silent until the scratchy sound of a fake record player could be heard. Katherine turned her head to look at her sound system, wondering why it was still on.

She scratched an itch on her face, only to jab herself with something attached to her left hand. She stared at the enormous diamond protruding from her ring finger. "Good Lord! Is that what I think it is?" Then suddenly Leonardo was trying harder with the stocking.

"Damn it," he said.

She turned her head to the side and saw he was getting all red and angry at the silly little stocking. "Did it run?" she asked.

He didn't answer. He just left the stocking as it was with a bit of extra toe flopping at the end of her foot and went to work on the other leg. He loomed over her once more.

"Hello, darling," she said again.

"Katherine, I need you to listen to me. You need to get dressed."

"*You* need to get me dressed," she said, choking on laughter. "I didn't take my pills and it's made me loopy. I feel like spaghetti. I'm cold turkey and my head hurts." She laughed hysterically.

He froze. "When did you stop taking your pills again?"

She flapped her hand in the air. "Oh, whenever. I don't remember."

"More than a day ago?"

"I don't remember. Which is odd, since usually I don't remember things when I do take them. Isn't all this so very odd?"

Leonardo stood back. He brushed his hair off his forehead and tried to keep his shit together. "Why didn't you take them in the morning like you're supposed to?"

"My smartie forgot to remind me."

"Well, let's get you back on schedule. That's the most important thing." He turned to her bureau and rummaged around.

"Is it?"

Leo looked over his shoulder in surprise. "What do you mean?"

"Is my schedule the most important thing?" Katherine raised her fist in the air. "I am not an animal—I am a human being!" she pronounced.

Leonardo's hands stilled wrist-deep in her panty drawer.

"I'm a person. I'm not a bot!" she continued. "I have a personality. Somewhere. I've just forgotten what it was." Then she giggled and her arm fell down to her side.

Leonardo approached the bed with a pair of pink hipsters edged with delicate white scalloped lace, which he proceeded to slip over one of her feet and then the other. A shocking sense of revulsion passed through Katherine's body. Her nakedness should have been nothing in front of her fiancé, but she felt exposed, mistreated, sickened by his touch. She flinched and then froze.

"Leo?"

"Yes?"

Flashes, images of another time raced through her brain, as if her synapses were struggling to the death to communicate a truth she wasn't supposed to know: She put one hand to her head and grimaced at the view down the barrel of a gun. Then she focused in on Leonardo and screamed at the top of her lungs as his hand moved away in a motion as though he'd just discharged a bullet.

"Katherine! Katherine!"

She blinked, registering her Leonardo fiancé of today, who wasn't truly pointing a gun at anybody.

"What is the matter with you?" he asked through gritted teeth.

She didn't say another word as this stranger of a man

she was supposed to love more than anyone touched her intimately in the course of dressing her. "I don't think I'm up to work today," she whispered up at him, but he continued to button her into a crisp blouse that was taking on more wrinkles with every errant move.

"Nonsense," he said briskly. "We need to get you back on track."

"I need to be left alone," she said. Only it seemed as if the words never actually came out of her mouth.

She let Leo dress her, feeling like a corpse being readied for a funeral. The sense of wrongness loomed in every cell of her being, yet she couldn't put her finger on the problem and thus could not fix it. "It starts with a Q . . . what is it . . . something about my Romeo . . . I think somebody out there loves me," she mumbled vaguely. She looked up at Leo. "But it's not you, is it?"

"You're talking nonsense," her fiancé said, finally losing his cool. "You've agreed to marry me. Of course I love you. And you love me, and everything shall be perfectly wonderful."

He proceeded to finish dressing her as best he could, though it was difficult with her every muscle clenched in horror and refusing to assist the process in any way. "Damn it, your makeup," he muttered. "We'll have Deirdre do it."

He gently placed one hand behind her neck and one under her knees and lifted her to a sitting position at the edge of the bed. Her head lolled back and he pushed it onto his shoulder. "Katherine, look at me."

She opened her eyes extra wide.

"It's Monday morning. You're going to work now. You're going to get a cup of coffee and work on the fall collection. Yes?"

She smiled and nodded, her head collapsing to the side. Leonardo propped it up and lifted her to her feet, swearing as he apparently remembered she wasn't wearing shoes. Dragging a spacey, limp Katherine to the closet, he reached

down and randomly grabbed a pair of stiletto heels, made
a futile attempt to get them on her feet, and then finally
just tucked them under his arm and dragged her out the
front door.

The motolimo ride gave Katherine a chance to recover
a bit from the fuzziness that had filled her brain. By the
time she reached the office, she could actually stand on her
own two feet. Leonardo dragged her into Dee's cubicle.

"Hello, Dee!"

"Hey, Katherine," Dee said, staring at Leonardo in alarm.
Ariel stood up and looked over the wall of her cubicle.

"Call an all-hands meeting," Leonardo said. Ariel's head
disappeared back below the wall.

"Deirdre, please help Katherine with her . . . look," he
said, gesturing to her unmade-up face. "Then pick up the
schedule and go forward as normal."

"Yes, Mr. Kaysar."

And with that, Leonardo dumped Katherine into Dee's
arms and vanished into his office.

"Let's go get you fixed up," Dee said quietly, one hand
on Katherine's elbow to steer.

"Oh," her ward said as they stepped into the bathroom.
She stared at her image in the mirror as Dee pulled a small
makeup bag from her purse and laid out several items.
"How interesting. I just remembered my dream." Her
sunny expression turned dark. "Ohhhh. It wasn't a good
one, was it?"

"What did you dream of?" Ariel asked, briskly stepping
into the bathroom.

"He shot me. Leonardo *shot* me. Oh, goodness. That's
twisted. I obviously have darkness in my soul."

Her friends didn't answer.

Dee and Ariel looked at each other. Ariel elbowed Dee.
Dee elbowed Ariel.

Ariel cleared her throat and applied some concealer under Kitty's eyes. "I think it's about loss."

Katherine froze.

"It's about loss?" she echoed, eager for a reasonable explanation.

"Yeah, it's about loss!" Dee agreed enthusiastically.

Ariel nodded. "Loss," she intoned a final time.

Katherine tried not to be impatient with her friends. "What *about* loss?"

"You want him so badly that your mind is showing you ways you might lose him."

Dee nodded vigorously. "See? It's about loss."

"There's been only one way—the way in which my fiancé shoots me in the chest and I bleed out on the floor with Rox—"

"With *what?*" Ariel asked. "What were you going to say?"

With Roxanne holding my hand and crying. "Rocks. You know, like I'm lying on the ground bleeding to death or whatever and rocks and stuff are digging into my back." She waved her hand dismissively. "You're right. It's about loss. No big deal. I'm going to get a coffee." She turned on her heel and headed out the bathroom door.

My friend Roxanne. Where's my friend Roxanne? Who's my friend Roxanne?

"Why am I here?" she muttered to herself.

There was a pause, and then Ariel and Dee said in unison, "We're putting mascara on you." They had followed.

"Oh." Katherine's eyelids spasmed. "Of course. Just a minute." Her body relaxed, and she turned to the kitchen bot and put in her order.

"Is there a Roxanne on the cast list?" she heard Ariel murmur behind her. "Or does she remember her?"

"This is wrong," Dee replied. "We're going to hell for this." She turned to leave the room.

Ariel grabbed her by the wrist. "What are you thinking? You want to give up the year-end bonus? We're almost there."

"What happens to *her* at the end of the year?"

"She marries Kaysar."

"In her mind, Dee. The mind we've helped fuck up. I'm done. What if this were you?" She wrested her arm away and vanished through the door.

Ariel ran after her. "Do you need a mental flush? She's not really your friend, you know."

"Neither are you," Dee snapped, her voice clogged with tears. "And to tell you the truth, if push came to shove I'd rather be friends with her."

Katherine focused her dull gaze on the back of the kitchen bot's head, but she listened with all her might to the conversation behind her. If only . . . if only she could put two thoughts together and make sense out of them. But as the smell of the roast coffee filled her senses and the sound of the percolation swept through her eardrums, her body and mind settled into Pavlovian bliss. She had her coffee. It was time to work on the fall collection. Her life was perfect. She headed back to her desk.

Funny how the office seemed to be in disarray. Her friend Dee was standing over at her desk with a bot from HR. "What do you mean, I can't quit?" Dee asked in a high-pitched voice.

Katherine took a sip of coffee and let it slip down her throat. She closed her eyes to enjoy that sheer pleasure.

"This is insane!" Dee shrieked. Katherine opened her eyes again and looked over. Dee took a stack of papers off her desk and tossed it into the air. A flurry of pages rose above her cubicle like a snowstorm. The girl in the cubicle behind Dee—whose name Katherine couldn't remember, if she'd ever known it—whimpered.

"Is something wrong?" Katherine asked. She couldn't see anything then, because all of her other coworkers were suddenly gathered in front of her cube blocking the scene.

"She's losing her shit," the girl behind her mumbled.

Oh well. It would pass. It was time to finish up with the

design of the fall collection. Blue security lights flashed overhead, throwing fluorescent stains across the illustrations papering her workspace. Such a lovely blue. Cornflower blue. She'd have to remember that color when it was time to work on spring again.

Q landed inside his apartment in the condo next to Kitty's. Winded and in pain, his knees buckled beneath him and he was forced to kneel down on the floor for a moment to gather his strength.

I should have said more when I had the chance. When we were together that day. I showed you, I made love to you, but I never said the words. Well, he'd say it all now. He'd say it as soon as he had the chance. He was no longer a person to delay speaking his feelings, or to deny them.

His heart pounded in his chest as he climbed back to his feet, grabbed his bag and headed for the door. Maybe she was waiting for him. If Leonardo had harmed one hair on her head . . .

As Q stepped out into the hallway, he saw the door to Kitty's apartment open a second later. She didn't see him as she turned to close the door.

Just tell her you love her. Rush right up and tell her you love her and you're never going to let Leonardo separate the two of you again. We're so close to figuring this out.

His emotions just about bursting right out of his chest, he realized that the pain and suffering were all worth it: Kitty was worth taking the chance on. He finally understood.

"Kitty!" he called.

She stopped halfway down the hall and looked over her shoulder. She didn't answer him, didn't even make a sound, and a swell of fear prickled at the back of Q's neck. The toolbag on his shoulder felt incredibly heavy and Q wanted to sink down into the floor along with it.

He moved quickly down the hall toward her. "Katherine," he said this time, fighting his sinking feeling. She blinked at him uncertainly as he walked right up to her and looked down into her eyes.

Q literally had to brace himself against the wall. "Do you remember me?" he asked hoarsely.

She pressed her lips together and flicked a glance toward the elevator. "Um . . . you're . . . ?"

No. She didn't remember him.

The dull monotone of her voice should have been enough evidence, but Q still couldn't accept the truth. "We've . . . spent a lot of time together," he said in anguish.

"When?" she asked. She took a step backward.

Q's mouth went completely dry. *When I last held you in my arms, for starters,* he thought. "From before," was all he could muster.

"I . . . No . . . I mean . . . I'm not sure." She seemed confused. "Why?"

The roar in Q's brain swamped his senses. He ran his hand over his T-shirt, clutching at the place his heart used to be.

She looked squarely at him with those blue eyes, so earnest, and wrinkled her nose. "You know, I'm beginning to think maybe it's possible we've met before. Do you work at the Kaysar Corporation?"

"No," he said. But a spark of hope filled him.

"Maybe in another life," she said with a laugh, smothering the spark. "I'm sorry. I have to go. Good-bye." And then she turned and stepped into the elevator.

"Good-bye, Kitty," Q whispered as the doors closed on her. And he meant it.

He didn't have a plan for this. There was no plan for going back to square one. Q turned and headed back down the hall. He had not a frown on his face and not a

tear in his eye. He never should have opened his heart in
the first place; everybody knew that. But it was fine. He'd
be fine. Because going numb was the easy part.

In a kind of robotic daze, Q stopped in front of Kitty's
door.

How does he do it? he was asking himself. *How does Leo
keep getting her to come back to him?*

He scanned the code he'd lifted from Kitty's smartie
into her lock and stepped into her apartment. Nothing
looked much different. He allowed himself no leeway, ignoring the visions of their night together that struggled
for his attention. And then, pulling his crowbar out of his
bag, he turned toward the bathroom.

What he wouldn't give to see Kitty standing there by
the wall, calling him by his name like she knew exactly who
he was, waiting for him to set her free. What he wouldn't
give to smash that goddamn wall into oblivion.

Q pushed open the door. Inside, standing by the bathroom wall that had turned black, wasn't Kitty.

"Why, hello, Mr. Walter 'Q' Sheffield," Leonardo Kaysar
said, overenunciating each syllable. "My word, don't you
look a bit roughed up," he added too innocently.

"Why are you holding on to her so damn hard?" Q
blurted out.

Leonardo didn't answer.

"She's nothing to you. Not really. You're a businessman,
and a good one. You know you don't keep pouring resources into a lost cause. This whole project is getting away
from you, and yet you just won't let go. You know better
than this. You take what you learned and you put the
knowledge into a new iteration. *Why are you holding on so
damn hard?*"

Leonardo covered his mouth, and Q couldn't tell if he
was laughing or about to cough.

"This isn't just about revenge and power, is it? You can
only hold out for so long—I know."

Leonardo's gaze drilled into him. "Hold out? What the hell are you talking about?"

"She doesn't love you. You understand that, don't you?" Q said, hiding the trembling of his hands by clenching them into fists at his sides.

Leonardo shrugged. "That was never the point."

"Wasn't it?"

"No," he said. "Love. The one girl? The point is so much bigger."

The way he spoke of Kitty, disposing of her in two flip words, made Q grit his teeth. "You don't love her either. Is it that you enjoy pretending you can be a normal human being?"

Leonardo narrowed his eyes. "I believe the conversation portion of our meeting is over," he said, drawing a pair of leather gloves from his coat and pulling them on.

"Protecting your baby skin from cuts," Q growled as he squared his shoulders and raised the crowbar. "How sweet." He'd already put up a hell of a fight and been walloped, considering he'd been rocketed back and forth through a thousand layers of time, but he hadn't seen his opponent during that battle. Now, face-to-face . . . well, Leonardo wasn't reputedly the best fighter, so Q thought maybe he'd be up to the task of a beat-down.

Q took offense and lunged for Leonardo's smartie, the surge of Q's adrenaline camoflauging much of his fatigue at first. The crowbar whipped over Kaysar's head as he ducked. Q swore and fell forward, taking Kaysar down to the floor where they wrestled on the bathroom tile; Kaysar was as shitty a fighter as they said, but the ace up his sleeve had nothing to do with fists or punches and kicks.

Every time Q swung the crowbar or raised a fist, Kaysar punched a hotkey on his smartie and bounced a laser of the degrading black temporal ooze of the wall against one of Q's limbs. Q felt like he was taking in time-travel fatigue without making the journey.

He had to get at Kaysar's smartie or it was all over. With a loud war cry, Q lunged at Leonardo once more, sending a shower of hard blows raining down on the man's chiseled jaw. The crowbar made contact with Kaysar's ribs, a thick, meaty sound as it smashed into his body. Leonardo struggled, successfully dodging more of Q's blows than he had to withstand. *All he has to do is wait me out*, Q thought with alarm as his knees gave out and he crumpled to the floor.

From the corner of his eye, he saw Leonardo flick a laser off his smartie directly into Q's eyes. Q reeled back, only to receive a fist in the next nanosecond. The man landed a good one, snapping Q's head back and sending spatter from his cuts flying against the parquet tile. "There's more to a fight than just blood and guts," Leonardo said into Q's ear. "But I have a reputation to work on, so if you don't mind, I'll take a few more." His words were followed by a ringing blow to that same ear.

Woozy, now, Q pushed himself to his hands and knees and managed to stand, blood dripping from his mouth. His body ached everywhere, even in places Leonardo hadn't actually touched. *I'm failing you, Kitty. He's got something I've never seen before.*

He'd barely risen when Leonardo grabbed him by the front of his shirt, slammed him against the wall, and raised a finger punch to his neck. It confirmed to Q that he might not win this battle; Leo again had tech on his side. Nonetheless, he summoned all the strength he could, and with a cry of rage twisted his body and slammed his elbow into his opponent.

Kaysar's punch went flying. Both men went for it.

Leonardo came out the winner over the battered, spent Q. His breath coming out in heavy pants, Kaysar stuck his boot on Q's back, pressing him down against the ground, and entered something into his smartie. He placed it so close to the black muck, Q wasn't entirely sure he hadn't

actually touched it to the ooze before Kaysar's other hand
came down on Q's collar. "Get up," the man bit out.

"Don't hurt Kitty," Q said. He couldn't beat him now.
The man could sap his strength with a flick of his wrist
and a button. He'd do better to save his energy . . . find a
weapon—

"Get up!"

"Just don't hurt Kitty!" Q staggered to his feet.

Leonardo looked up at him, made a long several nanoseconds of contact, and then smiled. With one hand on his
smartie and the other gripped around a handful of Q's
shirt, Kaysar pushed a button and shoved Q straight
through the seething black wall.

The only thing Q could say for his pathetic performance was that he had the poise to grab his goddam crowbar on the way out.

CHAPTER TWENTY-FIVE

"Q?" Louise called, just as she'd done every time a door
opened or anybody's smartie alarm went off.

"Sorry! Just me," Roxy answered as she burst through
the door of the apartment with two enormous sacks of
groceries in her arms. Mason immediately dropped the
pile of files he'd just picked up back on the table and pretended he'd been about to feed the fish.

Vesper looked at him suspiciously through her safety
goggles as she adjusted the Bunsen burner, but before she
could process his behavior, Roxy dumped her purchases
on the table.

"Watch out!" Vesper squawked, throwing her arms up
defensively around the flame. "These are the last of the
pills."

"Sorry," Roxy said, giving Mason a noisy smack on the cheek. She peered over Vesper's shoulder at the white bubbling foam. "Anything interesting?"

"Nah. Just grunt work. Since we needed the capsule casings for placebos, Louise told me to liquefy the rest of the pill contents so we'd have more fluid to experiment with. I gotta tell you, this stuff has some seriously strong vaporage. For a minute, I thought I was back in junior high." Vesper turned off the flame.

Roxy laughed. "You're doing a great job." She looked around the room. "Has Q checked in yet?"

"No," Mason said.

Roxy grimaced. "Oh. Man." She looked at Louise. "You okay?"

Vesper poured Kitty's liquefied pills into two small heatproof jars to cool. The steam was so hot, she just sort of dropped the lid on top of the jars without screwing it on.

Over on the couch, Louise still hadn't answered Roxy.

"Are you *okay*?" Roxy asked again loudly.

Louise stopped typing but still appeared to be staring at her keyboard. "He'll be fine," she said, finally putting the laptop aside and coming over to the table with the rest of the team.

Vesper pretended she was totally engrossed in putting the Bunsen equipment away. Team drama was always so much better when the tension wasn't directed at her.

"Man, you are *cold*," Roxy muttered. "I'd be totally freaking out." She moved to dump Mason's coffee mug in the sink, but Louise grabbed her wrist.

"Don't even think about making a judgment like that, Roxanne," she said, a grim intensity about her. Grabbing a stack of archived files, she headed off with them. "You're just a straight-line girl living in a straight-line world."

"Louise, I—"

"Well, send someone after him if we don't hear from him soon," Louise said, uninterested in apologies or commiserations. "I'll be right down." She went clomping up the stairs.

Roxy looked at Angus, and muttered, "Straight-line world, my ass."

"She's just worried about her brother. Don't take it personally," Mason said.

"I know." Roxy managed a smile. "It's cool."

"Hey, Louise, any day now!" Mason yelled.

"I'm getting my jacket," Louise answered from upstairs.

Vesper hastily removed her protective goggles and tossed them on the chair next to her, along with her heat-proof gloves. "Where are we going?" she asked eagerly.

"Black-market sale. We're going through a lot of cartridges," he explained. "Need more."

"Here in the present?" Vesper asked, grabbing her jacket. "Awesome!"

"Sorry, but I need you to stay," Louise said, clumping back down the stairs. "Since you're done with the chemistry, you can get started on the transcriptions." She followed Mason and Roxy to the door, and the latter two gave the intern a sympathetic look.

"Hold the fort, Vesper," Mason said not unkindly. "We'll bring you something back." And out they went.

Vesper got up and closed the door. " 'Hold the fort, Vesper,' " she mimicked. She grimaced and walked back to the table, slumping heavily in her seat. *How much action do they think can happen here?*

Zero. Vesper knew she'd screwed up and Louise had made it clear Vesper was out of chances. And yet even as the intern sat alone at the dining room table categorizing and annotating Q's boring reports for the official file, the back of her mind was still cycling and imagining and planning—all for the greater good of the team, of course.

So while Vesper's fingers were moving on the keyboard of the laptop, her eyes were focused on the wall and the crack there. Something about that crack was too hard to resist.

She should have simply waited for everyone to get home and then reported it, and she knew that, but she felt like a hospital intern dying to get into open heart surgery and being denied time and again. Always the complaint was the same: You're too inexperienced. But she could gain experience only if they let her get some. What a catch-22.

It was for that reason—in the interest of education and self-improvement—that she justified approaching the wall and poking at the crack therein. And she did this more than she really ought to have done. Of course she poked too hard and too long, and her finger broke through. When she drew it back, it was covered with black, gummy slime. And the worst part was the fingerprint she left behind. Then it got worse.

With a squeak of horror, Vesper flapped her hand in the air until the black goo was flung off her finger back against the wall, and then she darted back down in front of her keyboard. Sweating, her heart palpitating, she told herself to focus on inputting Q's reports, but as she glanced at the screen she realized that some of the words from the paragraph she'd been typing had literally vanished from the document she'd just been working on.

Vesper wrinkled her nose, staring at the screen and then the keyboard. She frowned at a bit of the black globby stuff still stuck to the knuckle on her index finger, and then poked experimentally at the touch pad to see if the computer had crashed. It was fine. She read another few lines of the report. She leaned back in her chair, studying this latest entry as a whole. Ten minutes she must have stared at the screen; no more words disappeared. But nor did the missing ones return.

Slowly, as if drawn against her will, Vesper looked over

her shoulder at the hole in the wall. Then she got up and walked back to it. Chipping away just a smidge at the loose fragments directly around the original hole, she took her thumb and pressed it even farther into the black. A fist-size area bowed inward. Vesper sucked in a quick breath, but nothing more happened. Contemplating the total lack of drama that ensued, she finally shrugged and walked back to her keyboard. There again was the transcription she'd been working on, but all the words were jumbled.

seems to be a collective advance during the course of week. Each successive week she is more cognizant Unfortunately, subset of "Kitty time, than the week of the herself. Formerly, not was of the loop conscious prison. least cognizant at beginning of brought back speed to some extent over the course of the sev

"Oh, shit. Oh, *shit!" What did I do?* she wondered. *What was I sticking my fingers into?*

Vesper looked at her hand and then looked wildly around the cluttered table. She pushed at the stacks of files with her forearm to find something that wasn't critical. She grabbed an old copy of the SF *Chronicle* with which to plug the hole, and in the process of ripping off the front page, struck one of the jars of liquefied Kitty pills. The lid went flying; the contents spilled out.

"Holy Shiiiiiittttttt! This is not happening, this is not happening . . ." Vesper intoned as she threw the front page down to soak up the spillage and prevent it from reaching her laptop.

As the fluid absorbed into the newsprint, Vesper glanced back at the wall in panic, and then sprinted to the kitchen. "I'm so screwed! We're talking massive quantities of evidence of complete and total ineptitude!" she cried out unto the heavens since no one else happened to be around. Thank God.

She scrabbled around in the drawers, grabbed a thin metal frosting spatula from a drawer, and then darted back into the living room for a can of spackle from the supply box they'd used in earlier restoration attempts. She'd simply make it all go away.

She passed the table, U-turned and grabbed the sodden newsprint and turned back again for the wall. *Just make it all go away.* "It's gonna be okay . . . it's gonna be okay . . ." Repeating the mantra over and over, Vesper raised the spatula in the air . . . and froze. She didn't dare scoop out more black. This was delicate.

"Fill and smooth. Fill . . . and smooth," she muttered to herself. She gingerly raised the clump of newsprint to the hole; the corner of the page touched the black—

"Gah!" Vesper cried as the greater part of the paper sank into the ooze upon contact. She stared at the lumpy black area and told herself that at least the section wasn't so indented and all the evidence was concealed.

Vesper delicately swiped her knuckles across the last bit of newspaper still above surface until the black on her hand adhered to it rather than to her. As she did so, it sunk completely under. She grabbed the can of spackle, flung a blob right at the lump, and used the spatula to spread another scoop of white spackle over the whole thing.

Five minutes of careful smoothing later, she was finished. It seemed as though all the black had gone back to where it was supposed to be. Vesper took everything to the kitchen, washed the spatula, threw it in a drawer, and washed her hands.

Terrified, she ran back to the keyboard and sat down in a sweaty heap. Before her was:

seems to be a collective advance during the course of week. Each successive week she is more cognizant. Unfortunately, within the week subset of "Kitty time, than the week of the herself. Formerly, she was not even conscious of the loop prison. she is least cognizant at the beginning of the week brought back up to speed to some extent over the course of the seven days. The ramp-up time, while increasingly shorter from one week to the next, is still significant enough to slow progress and prevent full extraction.

Well, it was better than nothing, better than before. Vesper leaped up and grabbed the rest of the front section from the paper she'd ripped apart and stuck it way down into the garbage under the sink. She ran back and plopped down in her seat once more. She leaned over and wiped her sleeve on the dampish remnants of the spilled chemical, and then tipped half the contents of the first jar into the second jar and screwed on both lids. And just in time, because the key turned in the lock of the front door. They were back already?

"You have to jiggle it, Roxy," Mason said from the other side.

"I *am* jiggling it. What does this look like?"

"It looks like jiggling to me," Louise said.

Vesper looked at the wall in total and complete panic. She'd done an okay job on the spackling, but it wasn't completely undetectable.

A bit more scuffling and confusion came from the other side of the door before it burst open. Roxy, Mason, and Louise barreled in on top of one another. "We're like the Three Stooges or something," Roxy grumbled. Mason grabbed her around the head and landed a loud kiss on her cheek.

"My little Stooge," he said.

"Oy," Roxy groused, though she was clearly loving it.

"Can you save it for happy hour or something?" Louise complained. She tossed their purchases neatly on the sofa and then looked at her intern. "What's with *you*, V?" she asked.

Vesper had tried her best to look as normal as humanly

possible, but she could feel her eyes bugging out and her throat closing. *Shit, if trace amounts of Kitty's medicine make me feel this whacked out, she must have felt like a total basket-case.*

"Vesper?" Roxy and Mason turned to stare at her. Vesper hiccuped.

Louise smacked her hard on the back a couple of times. "She's fine. Just choked on her own spit. So, Vesper, we've got a lot on our plate this afternoon. Can you take care of some of that report transcription backlog? Oh . . . you've already started. Good. 'Cause there's always more." Louise pulled a spiral pad from the back pocket of her jeans and ripped off an index card, handing it over. "Record this."

Vesper took the card. "Anything else?"

"You and I need a sit-down. I'll be right back."

A sit-down? Shit! As Louise headed upstairs, Vesper looked down at the index card she'd been given.

Incident start time 2:07 p.m. Headed from apartment, standing outside in the parking lot talking. Weird sitch. Three of us forgot what the hell we were talking about and what we were planning to do next. Not sure if we were coming or going, but we were still cognizant of predicament with no loss of context. Several theoretical minutes later, situation clarified and proceeded forward with no loss of forward physical time. Log as Leonardo wire- cross attempt. End time 2:07 p.m.

Vesper dropped her head on her arms and groaned.

"Tired?" Louise asked, coming up behind her.

Vesper sat up whip-straight. "Nope! Just thinking. What did you want to talk about?"

Louise became very quiet and very still. Then her fingers started tapping on the table. Then she looked straight into Vesper's eyes. "You've been really working hard. There have been several times . . . several times when I really questioned your ability to follow instructions and act as part of a team. I feel you've made great strides. You've earned the right to take on more responsibility."

Vesper swallowed hard.

Louise looked her straight in the eyes. "I know you think that all I do is tell you to stay out of the way, and I know that you want to get more involved. So let's get you more involved. Sound good?"

Vesper was really wishing right about now that she hadn't poked the wall.

Louise put a large plastic bag full of what looked like Kitty's pills on the table. "These are the placebos. It's going to be tough to get them everywhere they need to be since everyone around her seems to have some available the moment she appears to have a functioning brain cell, but we have to start rolling them in somewhere."

"Okay," Vesper said.

Louise frowned. "That's it?"

"I'm ready for the job," Vesper said, hoisting one fist in the air with as much enthusiasm as she could muster.

Her boss gave her a suspicious look. "Great. I'll wire what we know about her current pill supplies to your smartie. Give it a think and we'll talk about it."

Vesper nodded. "Okay." Louise headed for the living room, glancing over her shoulder at the intern with a befuddled look on her face.

Counting herself luckier than she had any right to be that her mess-up hadn't been discovered right away— apparently there hadn't been *much* effect of her wall poke . . . or at least she hoped not—Vesper gave herself a nanosecond to silently freak out before getting back to work.

CHAPTER TWENTY-SIX

Katherine was looking forward to seeing her psychiatrist again and discussing the state of her brain. In spite of the fact that he always confirmed that something was, indeed, wrong, she always left feeling better than she had felt coming in. She was beginning to think that Dr. Van Heusenfleugen might actually be curing her, because she could remember that she'd seen a Dr. Van Heusenfleugen last week and that he was very handsome, what with his dark hair and eyes. Not that such details were relevant in any way, considering that her boyfriend was equally if perhaps differently handsome.

Katherine stared down at the red laser keyboard projected onto the spongy finger pad and tried to force herself to stop obsessing about seeing her psychiatrist. It was slow going. She'd spent the better part of an hour trying to type up a very simple request for extra budget to provide the bots with a wider range of hair accessories. Her finger hovered over the q in requisition, and as she paused just before clicking down, a synapse in her brain misfired again.

Ariel popped over the side of the cubicle. "Is quagmire m-i-r-e at the end? Or m-e-r-e?"

"I," Katherine answered.

"Thanks."

Katherine looked down at her keypad again, but was

interrupted by a knock on the side of her cubicle. It was
Dee with a face so pale it was practically transparent and
dark circles like half-moons under her eyes. "Good morning," she said woodenly to Katherine.

Katherine leaped up from her chair and grabbed Dee by
the elbow. "Good God! You look terrible. Let's get you a
cup of coffee."

Dee let Katherine steer her into the break room, where
they put in their orders with the refreshment bot. Katherine put a comforting hand on Dee's shoulder. "Should I
switch the order to a cup of hot soup? I think soup makes
everything nicer, don't you?"

"No soup," Dee said nervously. "I'm fine. I just need a
vacation. HR said I could have a vacation. Very soon. So
I'll be having a vacation very, very soon."

"That will be nice." Katherine took the coffee from the
bot and handed the cup to her friend. "Just take a sip and
try to relax. You know you can talk to me about anything."

Dee stared at her over the rim of the coffee mug. She
swallowed and said, "Everything's fine."

Ariel ran up to the doorway of the break room. "Hey!
How goes it?" She gave Dee a funny look, and before
Katherine could say anything, Dee just walked out of the
break room.

"Question," Ariel said.

"Shoot," Katherine said as they headed back to the
desks together.

"It's about production on the summer line. We've run
out of white ribbon, which was supposed to go with the
chocolate brown fabric. There's plenty of lime, but we'd
decided it was sort of too *lime* and, you know, made the
palette just too browny green. Although it does comple-
ment the pale yellow chiffon in the second line. Very color-
block summery, and all that."

Katherine cocked her head. "Well, we need the dresses
to go out on time. Can't get around that. I want to know

how we ended up running out without a reorder, though, so do check into that. In the meantime, let's make up whatever we're short with the green combo. We have a quo . . . a qu . . . a qu . . ."

Ariel raised an eyebrow.

"Wow. Sorry. Total misfire," Katherine said. "*Quota.* We'll just tell them we're experimenting with a variety of offerings."

"Quite." Ariel turned away.

"What?"

Ariel turned back. "What?"

"No, I mean, what did you just say?"

"I said 'okay.' "

"No, you didn't."

Her friend shifted her weight. "I guess I don't remember."

Waving her hand as if to dismiss the entire issue, Katherine smiled. "I'm just hearing what I want to hear, I guess."

Ariel nodded and went back to work.

Katherine sat down at her desk. She looked at the unfinished document on her computer screen and tried to focus. *Okay. Where was I? Requisition. R-e-q . . .*

Q . . .

Across the row, Dee waggled her stylus in the air. "Quick! The beta samples are here."

Katherine tried to quell the queer . . . *Good God!* "Dee, is it weird to be fixated on a letter?" she asked.

"Someone sent you a letter?" Dee replied with a laugh. "How deliciously retro. What did it say?"

"We need a quorum, people!" Ariel waved them over to the conference room, and the two girls complied.

Soon Katherine, Dee, and Ariel sat three abreast in what they referred to as the judging chairs. The bots stood in a line before them, holding a carefully edited series of poses.

Draped on their perfectly molded bodies were pieces from the fall collection. Katherine regarded them in an uncharacteristically dark mood. She didn't love the designs. She pressed the tip of her stylus absently against her cheek.

"Well?" Dee asked. "Can we sign off on it?"

Kitty frowned and twirled the stylus. "No, I think the ox-horn buttons are too masculine for the lace edging, and the juxtaposition doesn't look intentional."

Dee and Ariel frowned likewise—at Kitty. "But it's the contrast that makes it work," Dee insisted.

"It totally works," Ariel said firmly. "I've never seen such a collection. You're brilliant, Katherine. Brilliant. You did a fantastic job with this one. You're fabulous."

Katherine shrugged the compliment off, unaware that she should have been smiling humbly and thanking her complimenter profusely, because that was how Katherine Gibbs of the Kaysar Corporation had always responded to such matters. But something was brewing inside of her. Something surprising and peculiar that she wanted to explore. There was something claustrophobic about the way Ariel and Dee sat so closely on either side of her. Of course, they were her best friends and she adored them, but their incessant compliments and reassurances were having a dampening effect. Didn't she ever make a bad choice? At least pick an unpopular shade of green? Was she really that good? Maybe she *was* that good!

She closed her eyes, took a deep breath to relax, and told herself to ease into a kind of comfortable, liquid acceptance. She looked at the bots and pointed to the one with the ox-horn buttons. "I think my first instinct was probably correct. The one with the ox-horn buttons is better."

Even as she said it, she felt a roar sweep through her insides, a kind of screaming. It was as if the ox-horn buttons really hadn't been her first instinct, as if the ox-horn buttons were competing with her first instinct—the leather-wrapped ones with the tiny brass centers—but that thought couldn't make it up to her brain and out of her mouth.

Quagmire question quota quite quick quorum . . . Her mind searched out the words, amplified them, tried to listen to what they were telling her.

"No, wait! The leather! The leather! I like the leather better!" Her breathing was coming out in pants as a strange panic enveloped her.

Ariel leaned forward, very close, and stared into Katherine's eyes. "The leather buttons are ugly," she said firmly. "Aren't they, Dee?"

"They're the ugliest buttons *I've* ever seen."

Both women went silent . . . waiting?

Katherine searched Ariel's eyes. *You're supposed to agree.* She smiled gently and in a stilted voice said, "The ox-horn will be great."

She barely heard the rest of the conversation, nodding in agreement to the questions put forth by Dee and Ariel that didn't seem to be questions so much as prompts. If she waited just a few seconds more before answering, she could easily figure out what it was they wanted her to say. And when she tried experimentally once more to go with what felt like the real instinct behind the suggestion, her friends seemed to reroute her with a fluidity and sense of agreement and understanding between the two of them that made Katherine almost jealous.

"Katherine?" Dee asked gently.

"Mmm? Oh. What was that?" Katherine blinked. "Where'd Ariel go?"

Dee leaned forward and covered Katherine's hand with her own. "Relax. You'll be back on track very soon."

"Why would you say something like that to me?" Katherine asked quietly.

"What do you mean?"

"I mean, why are you always treating me like a small child?"

"It's never bothered you before," Dee said haltingly. Her eyes narrowed. "And what do you mean by 'always'?"

"You're always reminding me that something's wrong with me."

"I didn't think you . . ." Dee didn't finish her sentence, and Katherine started obsessing about all the words Dee could have used before the period.

Noticed? Minded? Remembered? Or maybe something that started with a Q. Questioned? "I want to see my psychiatrist," she whispered, her voice clogging up with tears. She looked at Dee. "Can you . . . ?"

"You're already scheduled."

"Did I know that? How would I know?"

Dee starting chewing on the French tip of her thumbnail as she stared at the smartie Katherine held loosely in her hand. Katherine followed her gaze and suddenly the screen produced an alert.

"Oh, there's your car now," Dee said, leaping to her feet in a show of unbridled relief. "Let's go back to your cubicle and get your things."

Katherine frowned at Dee's outstretched hand. "I'm not an invalid." She ignored the proffered help and headed to her cubicle, where she gathered her things together, stuffed her smartie in her purse, and grabbed her coat, putting her arms through the sleeves as she headed toward the elevator.

Down in the lobby, she felt her heart beating harder without her even really knowing why. And then the doors opened into the lobby and she stepped out. The lobby receptionist looked up and smiled, then away. Katherine continued to the front door, and the doorman held it open.

Outside, a motolimo was parked at the curb; the driver opened her door. "Good afternoon, Miss Gibbs."

"Good afternoon." She slid into the backseat and tried

not to make anything out of the sound of the door slamming, and they were on their way soon enough. Katherine didn't know how to ask her question without alarming the driver in addition to her friends, so she worked her way around it. "Screen down," she said. The driver glanced into the rearview mirror as the glass between them slid open. "How long have I been going here?"

He knitted his brows. "Long time, Miss Gibbs. How are you feeling today?"

"I feel fine," she lied.

He gave her a sympathetic look. "Well, best to be sure, I guess."

"I guess," she murmured, wondering whether either of them knew what conversation they were really having.

The motolimo didn't have far to go. It was a fifteen-minute drive; then she walked into a building, up to the receptionist with another roundabout bunch of statements and questions to find out where she was supposed to go, and then up to an office that didn't seem familiar at all.

" 'Dr. Greeley,' " she read off the sign on the door. *Why doesn't that sound right? Why doesn't that feel right?*

A throat cleared behind her. Katherine whirled around. A gray-haired gentleman tipped his head to one side, examining her like a specimen on a petri dish. He smiled the sort of smile that didn't get as far as his eyes and ushered her into his office, which was very lush, with a Freud-friendly, indigo velvet–covered settee, but he ushered her to a guest chair at the desk. He went around to the proper side, then clasped his hands on the wood and leaned in. "Are you feeling all right, Katherine? It's been a while. Mr. Kaysar and I have been talking about making these check-ins part of your weekly schedule. Perhaps that would be best. You seem to be getting a bit . . . sidetracked in your recovery."

She just blinked up at him, afraid to say the wrong thing.

"Anything unusual happening?" he prodded.

Odd question. It was becoming apparent that as far

as everyone else in her life was concerned, she was acting strange. Trouble was, she wasn't sure which actions
were the oddities. Best not to lie. "Well, actually, sometimes I find myself . . ." How to put it without raising
too much of an alarm? "I find myself . . . well, I have these
dreams."

He looked most interested, taking her words down in
his smartie. "What kind of dreams?"

"I see things that seem very real but that are, of course,
entirely fantasy."

"How long has this been going on?"

"It's a fairly recent development."

"Days? Weeks? Months?"

"Days, maybe?"

He didn't seem concerned in the least. "I think your
body is still adapting to . . . changes. You've had some recent changes in your medication."

She looked up at him in surprise. "I have?"

"I'd say we'd do well to increase your dose."

"Of my pills?"

He looked up from the plate in surprise. "Yes."

She nodded slowly. "Because of my brain damage."

"That's right."

She gave him a bright smile. "Excellent."

He pushed print, ripped off the paper tab that chugged
out of the side, and then signed his name to the bottom.
He folded it before Katherine could see anything about it,
then slipped it into a brass slot in the wall. He opened the
drawer at his side and pulled out a curvy amber-colored
glass pill bottle and pushed it across the desk at her. He followed it with a second.

Katherine slowly took possession of the first bottle,
rolling it in her fingers to reveal the personalized tag already affixed to the glass in sepia ink. *Ms. Katherine Gibbs.
30mg Exonofin pluribumus. Take 1 per day, orally. May cause
disorientation.* "So, let's bump it to three per day, yes?"

"Yes," Katherine said automatically, the sepia ink blurring in front of her eyes.

"You're certain your smartie alarm is set properly?"

She narrowed her eyes at him. "I've been taking my pills, doctor. This just changes the dose."

His gaze swept over her face. He pulled one of the bottles back, unscrewed the top of the vial, and shook three pills onto a doily resting on the silver tray on the side of the desk. He poured her a glass of water from the pitcher, put it on the tray, and pushed the set toward her.

Katherine looked down at the capsules. She picked one up, pretending to position it properly for ingestion, but couldn't find any marking. One thing was certain: she sure as hell didn't want to ingest it, no matter what position it was in.

"Is something wrong?" the doctor asked.

Yes, something's wrong, you unbelievable moron! "Nope." Katherine popped the pills in her mouth and drank them down with some water.

"A pleasure, as always," he said, standing up.

"Likewise," she said, fixating on the two bottles and attempting not to heave on the spot. She looked up at him and fiddled nervously with her gold bracelet.

They blinked at each other, and his bland expression melted into a slight frown. "That's all there is."

Katherine managed not to make too much of that. "That's all there is," she echoed, dropping the bottles into the recesses of her purse. They vanished into the silk lining, cradled in the bottom of the bag. She got up and walked to the door, the hairs on the back of her neck rising as she sensed him behind her. He opened the door and stood aside as she walked through.

She walked with a measured gait, disgust and fear raising her temperature. She headed for the restroom, but someone swung in just ahead of her, so she kept moving to the elevator, sensing the eyes of the doctor on the back of the head. Her body was sweating by the time she stepped into the waiting motolimo, an intense panic welling up as she imagined the pills dissolving and permeating her entire body like a wave running through her bloodstream.

Now. She glanced up at the rearview mirror. *Now!*

"Screen down! Pull over! Pull over!"

In the mirror, the driver's eyes widened in fear. He swerved across two lanes, just barely missing a pair of mechanical tuk-tuks moving herky-jerky two abreast in the next lane. He hit the brakes. Katherine lurched forward, the seat belt cutting into her as they slammed forward. She unhooked her seat belt, put her foot on the door, and slammed it open. She lurched out. As the traffic whizzed by on the overpass and drops of condensation fell from the motoway above, Katherine stuck her finger down her throat and vomited on the pavement.

The sound of the driver exiting the car freaked her out. With the heel of her shoe she ground the remnants of the partially dissolved pills into the concrete and stepped back, leaning on the side of the motolimo. Shaking, sweaty, the acrid taste burning her mouth and throat, Katherine desperately wanted to cry. The driver held a box with Leonardo's monogram. He opened the box; it contained a neat collection of odd bits and pieces: a multifunction knife, a small cartridge of bullets, a spare smartie battery, a small package of first-aid supplies, a syringe punch, a clear envelope of travel-sized toiletries. The driver handed her a toothbrush and a handkerchief, along with a bottle of water from the minibar. Then he discreetly left her alone and returned to the driver's seat.

Katherine took everything without a word, cleaned herself up, brushed her teeth, and thought of an explanation. She crumpled the soiled handkerchief in her fist and then tossed it into traffic and got back into the limo. The screen was still down, and the driver was carefully avoiding her eyes. He put the car into motion and merged back into traffic.

They drove in silence back toward the office. "I'm sorry you're not feeling well. I wish I could drive you home," the man blurted, a miserable look on his face.

"Yes, I'd really like to go home," she said.

He glanced up then, and she could see the sadness in his eyes. "Got to take you back to the office."

"Why?" she blurted.

He didn't answer. Katherine looked out the window and sighed, wondering if he would tell someone about her puking, and if it would be considered a matter of national security, as everything about her seemed to be.

As they wound their way along the familiar route, which was not back to her home, Katherine stared unhappily at the city whisking by, feeling displaced and lonely. At last they reached her office.

"Katherine! Are you sick?" she heard immediately as she entered. Ariel and Dee, both standing up in their cubicles, were looking rather frazzled. Katherine wearily took in that everyone else around them had stopped working and was watching.

"I'm just really tired," she said truthfully, plunking her stuff down and easing herself into her chair. Dee and Ariel crowded the doorway. Kitty dropped her head and rubbed her temples, wishing they would just give her some space.

"I think I'm in some kind of crisis," Katherine whispered.

"What do you mean?" asked Dee.

She swiveled in her chair and looked up at her two best friends. "Do you guys want to go out tonight? Grab a drink? Talk?"

Dee's mouth didn't move. It just hovered there, gaping. Katherine shifted her gaze to Ariel, who compulsively licked her lips.

"It's not a trick question," Katherine said softly. *Please be real. Please be true.*

"I can't," Dee said. "I've already made plans."

Ariel stared at Katherine with what read as total alarm. "I can't go either," she finally said, after weighing the simple question for what seemed like an eternity.

"I really need you guys tonight. I'm having a horrible day." Tears slipped from Katherine's eyes and flowed down her cheeks, making dark blobs on the fabric of her skirt. "Please be there for me."

"We'll have brunch on Sunday," Dee said. The stricken look in her eyes didn't seem fake. Ariel nodded, and she took Katherine's hand. "I'm so sorry, Katherine. I just can't tonight. Sunday. We'll have a big ol' breakfast. It'll cheer you right up. You'll have your granola and yogurt, I'll get hash, Dee will get her frappucino, and everything will be right in the world."

Katherine gritted her teeth and stared at them with desperation. "I'm crying. You're my best friends in the world and I'm crying and you won't come out with me tonight?" The girls were silent. The entire room was still silent. Why couldn't everybody just mind their own business? She pulled her hand away. Then she took a tissue from the box on her desk, wiped her face, and pulled her makeup kit out of her purse. The concealer from the wand she dabbed under her eyes went all runny with tears that wouldn't stay back. Katherine tossed the tube back in the kit with a cry of frustration and grabbed her lipliner.

She lined her lips, more of her attention focused on watching everybody in the reflection of her travel-sized makeup mirror watching her, than in the precision of her application. *Why can't you all stop staring at me?*

She shifted her gaze back to the reflection of her mouth and froze as she stared at the tip of her lip pencil pressed against her lip. *I drew a tiny Q on the inside of my wrist with this lipliner. A Q. Q.* With a sharp inhale, she tossed the pencil back along with the rest of her touch-up makeup and zipped it all up.

"Katherine?" Ariel asked suspiciously.

Katherine forced a smile and turned around. "Sunday, then. You're right. It can wait until Sunday." She turned back to her desk and opened the file sitting on top, pretending to read the contents. Out of the corner of her eye she noticed Ariel vanish without another word.

Katherine immediately stood and started out of the cube. Dee popped her head up from her own workspace.

"Where ya off to?" her friend asked, her gaze dropping to Katherine's purse.

Katherine circled her face with her hand. "Mascara's stinging my eye. I should use waterproof," she said. Dee babbled some words of sympathy, but Katherine's focus had switched away from her.

Katherine headed first toward the bathroom, but at the last moment turned quietly toward the exit. She was interrupted by, "Hey, Katherine! Mr. Kaysar wants to see you." It was Ariel.

Something strange happened, then: it was as if a cog in her brain had worked free of the grease clogging it and managed a quarter turn. Katherine stopped in her tracks. Her eyes fixated on the row of lights lining the threshold of her escape. The funny idea that she'd be shocked if she tried to cross the building exit occurred to her, but also the notion that walking out now might be the wrong thing to do. She couldn't figure out which idea was natural—or more correct.

"I have to pee," she blurted. "I'll be right back." And she forced herself to turn slowly around and head back to her original destination.

When she made it into the restroom, she locked herself in a stall and sat down on the toilet seat. *He killed me. He killed me. Somewhere, sometime, he killed me.* These thoughts were bursting through her mind. Kitty lifted her knees and rested her shoes on the toilet lid, wrapping her arms around herself and rocking, her mind racing. She started to work on separating reality from fantasy, wondered for a moment if it mattered as long as she could pick the one she liked best, and then realized that it wasn't hard at all. It was surprisingly easy.

Yes, she still had to dredge up the memory from out of the fog, but once she had the idea in front of her . . . she just knew under which category it fell. Real was real, fake was fake, and the problem was that she was living with one foot in each world.

This is not my life. Leo doesn't love me and he's not my fiancé, and he killed me, and that means I'm fucking the man who killed me. And he's fucking me on a weekly schedule like a board meeting. I've got to get out of here. I cannot do this anymore. I wake up and I open my eyes and I see the ceiling and my music goes on and I get up and go to the bathroom and I . . . and I . . .

What's my music? Kitty searched her brain, rocking her body desperately. *I'm supposed to remember. It's so important. It will help me. Think. Think! My music goes on. My music goes on. . . .*

She took a deep breath and tried to calm herself. She brought her mind back to that morning and the sound of her alarm going off and then that Gershwin music switching on.

I've got a crush on you, sweetie-pie
All the day and night-time, hear me sigh
I never had the least notion
That I could fall with so much emotion
But you had such persistence,
You wore down my resistance:
I fell, and it was swell
You're my big and brave and handsome Romeo. . . .

Oh, Q! I remembered. Please, please, come and get me away from here. Save me. Save me!

All Katherine wanted to do was run, but she had to go back. Just for show, since they were obviously waiting with bated breath for her to return from her mascara mishap. For the next hour, she shuffled papers at her desk and made sure to smile at Ariel and Dee at regular intervals.

But once an hour had passed, the first moment she wasn't being scrutinized, watched, or spied on, Katherine escaped. She slipped down the stairway, hailed a motolimo, and didn't dare look behind her until she'd made it all the way home. She ran as fast as she could up to the complex and nearly burst into tears waiting for the elevator to deliver her to her floor. She ran down the hall and practically launched herself into her apartment, slamming the door behind her as if that would make a difference.

Katherine dumped her purse at the door and went straight to her bathroom where she stared in shock. It was a disaster area. Red, white, and black, in the most terrifying design. Blood on the walls and floor, plaster everywhere and a wall comprised of black, churning muck. *What's happening? Maybe they're right and I'm going crazy. I can't live like this. I can't do this anymore. Q? Where are you? I need you,* she thought. But she didn't know how to find him. Her legs shaking so hard it was all she could do to make it to the bed, Kitty backed out of the bathroom into the bedroom. And then she sat there and waited for Q. She waited and waited and waited some more. But when she'd waited so long her legs had totally cramped and her neck hurt, she realized that ignorance was, indeed, bliss, and she was happier when she knew no pain and things didn't go horribly wrong and blood didn't mar the white tiles of her floor. If everybody else was faking life and love, why shouldn't she? The argument was at the least, reasonable, and at the worst, no worse than her reality.

In a complete daze, Katherine went into that bathroom

and without looking at the hellish black and the red drops, opened her medicine cabinet, took out the bottle and shook out what little remained. It didn't matter that they weren't the new stronger dosage from the bottle in the hall; the small pile of pills in her hand was still far beyond her normal dose. She filled her water glass and stared down at the capsules, noting that they didn't have the bitter smell she remembered. God, she must be so used to them it was like eating a snack. This was intolerable. Half in and half out of reality? To know love and to be unable to have it was worse than anything. Oblivion was better.

Leonardo Kaysar's Katherine Gibbs was a happy person, as far as she knew—which wasn't far, she admitted. But being a deep person wasn't all it was cracked up to be. Why feel pain if you didn't have to?

Even so, she waited. She turned her back on the horror and returned to her bedroom, stripped down, and put on what she knew was her Thursday teddy, then pulled the comforter off the bed and went into the bathroom and sat down in the middle of the muck facing the wall. She closed her eyes. *I love you. Don't you understand? I love you, and I promise I will never forget you again,* she said. But nobody was listening and nobody heard. And when Romeo still hadn't shown by eleven fifty p.m., Juliet took her poison and cried for exactly ten minutes.

She sat there waiting for the reset to kick in. Waiting . . . waiting . . . and at last her weary mind and body were accepted into the darkness. But her plan didn't go as expected. The one time she truly sought oblivion was the first time the pills were unable to affect her brain. When Kitty awoke this time, she knew why she was on the floor wrapped in a blanket. She remembered what she'd done before and how her day had come to this end. She remembered that everything seemed to have failed and that she'd taken the pills expecting to go back into Leonardo's dark world.

Failure had never felt so good. Kitty was only just beginning to understand what it meant that she could remember everything and everyone when she heard Q calling her name.

But the sound of his cry was not one of joy, and Kitty's own smile faded away. Slowly she climbed to her feet and let the blanket fall to the floor. She turned to the black oozing wall and faced the fear in Q's voice.

CHAPTER TWENTY-SEVEN

Blackness rumbled all around Q, and his chest constricted in fear, making it hard to breath. Q had not passed straight through the layer as he might have expected, and the hole through which he'd been shoved had closed behind him. *Kaysar,* he wondered, *are you that good? Or are we both in uncharted waters? And if I can't get to you . . . how do I get to Kitty?*

Using the crowbar to pry and bash at the cracks and divots in the wall, Q paused only to recalculate his angles and wires before doing it again and again; he tried anything he could think of to weaken and break down the nanoseconds imprisoning him. It was systematic, brutal, the most intense assault on time he'd ever made.

Q's adrenaline surged as he attacked the wall from the inside. "Kitty!" he yelled desperately. Opalescent chips sprayed everywhere, slicing into his exposed face and arms. Black spattered around him with every blow. The black spurred him on; it was a sign of degrading time. It was a sign of vulnerability in the time mechanism.

And then suddenly Q noticed a low sound underneath all the other noise. It was the sound of time matter churning and mixing; an area where time was degrading the most would be the easiest place to break through. He isolated the sound in his mind and traced the center to an area slightly to his right just below waist level. He forced himself to focus his vision on the spot and saw a portion that seemed more textured and raised than in other areas. Q lifted his knee and pressed at the area with his boot to test the give. A wad of matter that seemed to be at the center of the soft spot dislodged and slid down toward Q's feet, revealing a lighter-colored area in its wake. As the wad slowed, the black around it immediately began to swirl and degrade, but Q was already focusing on the soft spot above.

Leaning back for momentum, Q lurched forward and then jammed the heel of his boot directly at the grayish spot. He lurched back and felt solid wall behind him, but a wave of claustrophobia struck as he realized he could not proceed more than four strides and that his vision was even more limited than before; he was in some sort of channel between layers. For all he knew, it could go on and on like this; Q punching through layers only to find himself imprisoned in a new one.

Reaching out like a panicked mime, he tried to assess the qualities of his container, but, working blind, he could only speculate. There wasn't enough width in this prison to hold a tool horizontal, either. He looked up, but without a strong light source he couldn't even see if the composition of time matter above was different from below, in front, or behind him.

The only thing that kept him from losing complete hope was her. Kitty, his love for her and his fear that she needed his help.

"Kitty! Kitty, can you hear me?" he called in desperation.

He thought he heard her voice. Maybe he just wanted to believe, but he could have sworn he heard her voice. The walls on either side of him began to close; Q could feel more than see it. He lodged his crowbar between the barriers, and it worked enough—though the metal began to bow and the squares of light on his crowbar's electrical meter flittered into the red zone. His clothes were soaked with sweat, and nausea began to set in. His body temperature fluctuated wildly. He pressed his forehead against a strangely pliable substance before him and swallowed hard, taking long, deep breaths.

The crowbar trembled violently, then bent further. Q placed his palms before him and knocked his forehead against the wall in despair. His right fist pounded uselessly at cheek level. If he could just pretened Kitty was right there on the other side, it wouldn't be so bad to go like this.

The odd sound of the rhodium crowbar losing its battle against the dual pressure of past and present time was like the ticking of seconds. Each cracking noise made Q think it would simply break and that would be it; he'd be squashed flat. He'd never met an anomaly he couldn't best, but then again, he'd never *been* the anomaly.

"Q," a voice said softly, tremulously. "Are you there?" *Kitty!*

Tears pricked at his eyes. "I'm here."

"Tell me what to do."

The strain in her voice told him they'd come to the end of the road, on every level, from every angle, in every plane of the infinite number of highways running through their lives. At times, just before he fell asleep, he thought about having a lifetime of Sundays with her. He'd never lost confidence in his abilities. He'd never for one moment thought Leonardo Kaysar would have the last word, throwing up this last roadblock with him trapped inside, crushed by the firewall. *I am the firewall,* he thought. *And I can't hack my way out of this.* The crowbar groaned.

"Q? Tell me what to do," Kitty repeated, obviously in tears.

"Kitty, listen to me. Listen to me. It's going to be fine. Just hold on tight and listen."

Kitty made a strangled sound, as if she didn't want him to hear her cry.

Q cleared his throat. " 'I've got a crush on you . . . sweetie-pie,' " he sang. " 'All the day and—' "

The crowbar was now at almost a ninety-degree angle, an inconsistent flickering of lights running up and down the control panel as its electrical system tried to make sense of impossible instructions. Q's prison illuminated, and somehow, in the flash of light, the barrier became semi-transparent and he saw Kitty on the other side. She pressed herself forward, her fists clasped to her chest and tears streaming from her eyes.

Remember Q, he mouthed to her. He managed a smile. The crowbar went into autoshutdown and the light vanished. Time constricted. Q took his last breath. In the darkness a song seemed to echo.

"I fell . . . and it was swell."

CHAPTER TWENTY-EIGHT

To say that time had become unstable would have been an understatement. Vesper gripped the exposed springs of the sofa as its pillows flew around in midair. Mason was yelling all sorts of instructions involving anchoring to things, as if they were all drowning.

But we are *drowning,* Roxy thought. *We're drowning in blackness.*

The air was clogged, thick and warm, a vaporous white cloud streak the only thing that gave any depth perception at all. And then reality came back. It had been blinking on and off while the entire apartment whirled in place.

Louise and Roxy clutched each other, but centrifugal force had them, their bodies spinning in parallel to the ground. Louise went sailing, smacked face-first into the far wall, then went spinning off again, her body sagging as she lost consciousness. A streak of books spun off the shelf and dove through the apartment window. Mason threw his body on top of Roxy's as the shattered glass swirled toward her. His weight, flung on top of her, dropped them both down; the glass flew over their heads and shredded a whirling pillow. Vesper was vertical now, her hands still gripping the sofa springs, but her legs flying up in the air.

"Louise!" Roxy yelled, though there was no sound; it seemed the entire room had been put on mute. Her colleague was still unconscious and was being battered by knickknacks and flowers and binders and whatnot, unable to defend herself. Imploringly Roxy looked at Mason, who nodded. He would try to help her.

Roxy whirled past the coat closet door and grabbed the knob. In a moment of inspiration she opened it and shut herself inside. But . . . *Clunk. Clunk.* It didn't help. The world continued to turn, and Roxy was thrown from one wall to the other. The door was flung open again, and Roxy braced her legs on either side, hanging on to the bar. The apartment spun again, and the door slammed in her face.

Suddenly it was as if someone had put on the brakes: everything in the apartment settled. All was silent save the sounds of settling papers and furniture coming to a halt.

It took a good ten minutes before the team members trusted the pause. And when they all let go of whatever had been stabilizing them and Roxy crept out of the closet, they each went straight to the wall.

Louise had regained consciousness, and she heard the persistent text-message beep emanating from her smartie. She scrambled over the wreckage and found it under a throw pillow. She checked the message with trembling hands and looked up at the rest of the team with a stricken expression. "SOS," she whispered. "Walter *never* asks for help."

Mason gently took the smartie out of her hands and studied it. The message log was scrambled and blinking; they were lucky the unit had survived at all. "It was sent from two different times!" he said.

"What do you mean?" Roxy asked.

"It says this message was sent on both Sunday and Monday."

No one said, "That's impossible," because they'd all stopped saying that a long time ago. But each of them wanted to say it.

"Walter!" Louise yelled, pounding on the wall. She looked wildly around at the others. "Do something! Shake him loose!"

"What do you want me to do?" Mason asked. "If he's not in Sunday and he's not in Monday . . . where exactly do we find him?"

"But then, he's just gone?" Vesper wailed. "There's no such thing as Smunday!"

"Yes, there is," Roxy said, grasping at straws. "Time is infinite. The days of the week are an arbitrary construct designed by humanity so that they don't go running hither and yon, confused and unable to interact, all working at counterpurposes. So there's a Smunday if we say there's a Smunday—which means that if we find the borderline of even just a particle containing the seconds in between these two days, he'll be there."

"If a time particle has a borderline, doesn't that mean it's finite?" Vesper asked.

"Er, not necessarily?" Roxy mumbled. Everyone looked at her dubiously.

Everyone but Louise, who nodded. "Roxy's got a lead, at least. If we find a particle, we'll have a better chance of finding where he went—whatever 'day' it is—and maybe we can follow his path." She looked around. "Anyone have any ideas for hacking into this 'Smunday' when we find the particle?"

The group was silent. Louise added, her face grim, "We need a time-anomaly specialist. I know a great one, but he's already *in* Smunday."

"Maybe he's hacking toward Monday," Roxy suggested, with as much perkiness as she could muster. "Maybe we can meet him there?"

"Maybe," Mason said. "Or maybe it's like *Charlie and the Chocolate Factory* and he's momentarily just particulate matter out in the ether somewhere. Like Mike Teavee."

Louise's face crumpled. Her chin wobbled.

Roxy elbowed Mason and turned to Louise. "Don't cry, Louise," she said sternly. "You don't do that. Your brother would be disappointed."

"Nobody's crying," Louise replied, pulling herself together.

Vesper rubbed her back. "Don't you remember, Louise? In *Charlie and the Chocolate Factory*, Mike Teavee *did* come out the other side in the end. . . ."

Louise stared at the intern. "He came out *two inches tall.*" Her pale face was bright red. She turned and dropped her forehead on Vesper's shoulder. The intern patted her and looked helplessly at Mason and Roxy.

"Mason, you've got to turn time back. You've got to reverse this, cross a wire," Roxy suggested.

"I think that's a bad idea. This is already so screwed up. And we agreed that any involvement from us would mess things up historically. Tell me you're not second-guessing *that.*"

Roxy swallowed. "I don't know! At least we'll all still be alive. Continuity is busted anyway. Do you have any idea what Leo could do to Kitty if he realizes it's over? He despises us. What does he have to lose by killing her? He's probably planning—"

"Good Lord," Louise said.

The other three turned toward her and saw for the first

time what degradation had done to the wall. The surface area in play had expanded threefold, at least, and appeared to be compromised of the unstable black molecules that had degraded out of the very layers they'd been trying to breach.

Louise groaned. "My brain already hurts, but let's break this down. Here's what we've got: We've got a wall that acts like a portal. Time supports the physical wall and this theoretical portal. Something has weakened the support system. . . ."

As Louise continued to break things down, a sick feeling worse than the nausea brought about by what had just transpired began to seize at Vesper's throat. Louise had moved to the wall with a ruler she was using as a pointer. She referenced the jagged edges and the more oozy section in the center that had generated from a circular . . . hole. The sort of hole that might have been triggered by . . .

Vesper made a nervous squeaking sound, but nobody seemed to notice.

Louise suddenly crouched down and jabbed the ruler at a goopy black wad down just below floor level that was protruding slightly from the ooze. Careful not to touch anything for fear of removing nanoseconds, she didn't dig it out.

Vesper swallowed hard as the rest of the team moved in and peered at the wad.

"There's probably a lot of insulation and sandpaper and stuff floating around in the walls," Roxy said. "Mason, what do you think we should do?"

Mason went to Q's tool kit and rummaged around, tossing a variety of instruments and tools out behind him. "You know in movies, when the pilot dies and some dude in the passenger seat comes forward and says that since he drove a corn thresher or whatever as a kid he'll be able to extrapolate from those controls the ability to fly the plane?"

The team remained silent.

"Sadly, I never drove a corn thresher," he muttered, shaking his head at the unfamiliar remnants in Q's stash.

"And the pilot's not dead!" Louise shrieked. "We have no evidence the pilot's dead. I thought we agreed he was particulate matter, and at the very worst he'd come out two inches tall!"

"This is starting to get out of hand," Roxy muttered, steering Louise toward the kitchen for some tea or drugs or whatever would ease her unhappiness.

Mason was left holding the bazooka. "So, what do you think, Vesper? Should I just pick this up and try to blast through the wall again?" he asked.

"Q's done plenty of bazooka blasting with little enough result," Louise said. "We need to think outside the box." She seemed to war with her emotions for a moment, but stayed strong. "We need to remain calm. We know Q is out there and needs our help, but we've *got* to remain calm. Let's throw out some new ideas. Anybody? Anyone?"

Vesper was having an internal struggle. *Should I tell him? I should tell him. But there's no point in telling him if there's nothing we can do about anything. But we don't know if there's nothing we can do about it unless I 'fess up to—*

"Vesper? You're never going to learn if you don't participate. Don't worry about whether it's right or wrong; just put it out there. You never know," Mason prompted. "And giving an opinion is better than making orange juice."

Vesper coughed to hide her panic. "Um . . . uh . . . that would probably be an excellent idea if we didn't think Kitty might be standing in the spot we'd want to blast. Or Q."

"But if it could blast through, maybe we could break the tech."

"Yeah, and Kitty or Q might have a giant bazooka-size hole through their torso, which would sort of negate the whole purpose of the exercise."

Mason grimaced. "I can't solve this. This is totally emasculating."

"I wouldn't worry about it," Louise said dryly. "You've still got Roxy, and she still thinks you're the bee's knees." She seemed to have put her emotions back together.

Roxy put her arms around Mason and rested her neck on his shoulder. "Being able to admit you can't do something is very macho, actually," she said. He rolled his eyes in response, but gave her kiss on the cheek.

"I was hoping we'd have everything done by today," he said absently as she turned and headed for the stairs.

Louise watched Roxy disappear to the second floor. "*I* was hoping we'd have everything done weeks ago."

"Today's the day Roxy and I came back into each other's lives." Mason actually blushed as he said this. "You know, the day I fought for Roxy against Leonardo by the 7-Eleven."

Vesper turned, shocked. She actually felt the blood drain from her face. "That's today?" she choked out.

Mason nodded. "Yeah, it's the anniversary. Weird, though. I was talking about it this morning with Roxy, and, well, you know, we were sort of revisiting our history. . . ." He cleared his throat sheepishly. "And it was strange, because neither of us has the details exact anymore. I was going to go double-check the time line, run some tests to see if Leonardo was meddling with us . . . but he usually doesn't, because he knows that our paths have crossed so many times that when he tweaks me, he tweaks himself."

"Oh. Well . . . maybe he's figured out some other way to play with time. What do you think he might have done?" Vesper asked.

"Beats me," Mason said. "But I'd swear there's a pin-prick in the time line. And that worries me more than anything—even the fact that I still haven't come up with the perfect proposal speech," he joked. He took a deep breath and released it. "By the way, I . . ."

Louise raised an eyebrow.

Mason cleared his throat. "If you see that newspaper I was saving for Roxy's proposal, let me know."

"You lost it?" Louise asked with an incredulous laugh.

Vesper stared down at the floor.

"Is it absolutely necessary to give me shit for this?" Mason asked irritably.

"That's just so . . . you." Louise cackled.

Mason rolled his eyes. "Just let me know if you find it. It's here somewhere. I put it somewhere and—"

Louise's persistent laugh made it impossible for Mason to continue. He shook his head and looked at Vesper. "Keep an eye on things down here." And with that, he bounded upstairs after Roxy. Louise shook her head likewise and followed up the stairs more slowly.

Vesper turned back to the table. She started cleaning up, then sat for a moment basking in the horrible realization that Smunday was very likely her fault. She went through the steps in her head. She'd poked at the wall, and swirled the black time matter a bit. Then she'd stuck in the newspaper to plug the hole—to add insult to injury, it was Mason's special newspaper he was going to give to Roxy.

Okay, yeah, so that was all very bad. Especially because it was probably responsible for pushing time around to the point where it created space between layers, and that was how Q got stuck in between. But still . . . the space had stretched to a channel, a crevasse in time. Was it infinite? Or did it have a destination? What connected it all together?

Vesper tapped her finger rhythmically against her temple as she wracked her brain for answers. She had introduced a foreign element—the newspaper—into the particles of time between the present and future layers. And that element was from a particular day in the past . . .

Vesper bolted upright. What connected it all together

was the stupid chemical spill which got Kitty's brain pills all over the newspaper. The newsprint had absorbed most of the liquid, and then gone into the wall where the time holding barriers between the layers of past, present and future was degrading nanosecond by nanosecond.

She swallowed hard as tears suddenly came to her eyes. She'd degraded time on Mason and Roxy's anniversary. She'd created a path on the one wire that none of them— not the team, not even Leonardo Kaysar—wanted access to.

What if she didn't get it back and Roxy and Mason were parted and Q disappeared on Louise and Kitty because he got stuck in some amalgam of mixed-up time zones that was Vesper's fault?

Her hands poised over the keyboard of her laptop, she slammed them down and began to type. When she'd got down all she wanted, she pushed away from the table and walked slowly to the wall.

The hole was still there—all the way to the floor now, writhing and bubbling blackness. It stretched out far, or at least it seemed to; Vesper couldn't exactly tell what was beyond the dark. She put her toes up to the edge. Her stomach quaking, she looked into the blackness, then back into the apartment.

It's my fault. I screwed up the timing of everything, and I didn't tell them when it counted, so now I have to set things right. If I don't get the newspaper back, nobody—not Mason or Roxy or Louise or Q or Kitty—can be certain of being together and maybe Q will be stuck in some weird little pocket of untime forever.

She shuffled her feet a little farther and felt herself teetering on the edge of a precipice. The blackness was bubbling around her toes, but she couldn't feel it.

Everything's fine. This isn't going to kill you, she told herself. *Even if Leonardo's got the know-how, he doesn't know*

*you're here, so he can't crush you between days like a Wookiee in
a trash compactor. Besides, Mason said that Wookiee didn't technically get crushed, and even though I think that's really a matter
of semantics, since both walls were moving in, which is therefore
the act of crushing, in this case I'll give him the benefit of doubt
because . . . oh, quit stalling, V, and jump already!*

She shuffled forward another smidge, the blackness bubbling even further. She teetered, pinpointed the center of
the channel, and then bent her knees and did a perfect swan
dive into the crevasse. Her body vanished without a splash.

CHAPTER TWENTY-NINE

Kitty knelt on her bathroom floor, her tears dried up. A
spiderweb of cracks mottled the wall in front of her like a
network of highways with no ultimate destination. A pile
of plaster cluttered the floor, black splotches scattered
erratically across the white.

I'm blank without you. I'm nothing. She tentatively raised
her index finger and traced one of the cracks. More white
plaster fell away, and the black beneath was soft, smearing
her skin like ink. Kitty stared down as it sank into the
ridges of her fingerprint.

What happens if I break through time? she wondered. *I
might end up in some random historical period in time. I can deal
with that,* she decided. *Or I might go forward into the future. I
could deal with that too. Or I screw up the lives of my friends.
Not so much.*

Or I could die.

Good Lord.

She drew a black smear down the face of the cracked
white wall. In the minuscule slice of time behind this, she
knew, and in front of Roxy's living room wall, was Q. Or

at least she hoped that was the case. She prayed he was okay.

Kitty slowly climbed to her feet. She made a fist, drew back her arm, and smashed it straight into the plaster. Pain radiated from her knuckles. White plaster rained down on the floor, burst from an imprint in the wall, a shallow divot.

She looked down at her hand. Blood welled from the cuts across the top. And in the calmest voice she owned Kitty said, "I hate you, Leonardo Kaysar." She pulled back her fist and slammed it forward again, this time with all her strength. Then again. And again. And again. Eyes narrowed, teeth gritted, focusing all of her anger and hate on the black, red, and white mess in front of her, she ignored the pain. "I *hate* you!"

A giant black spot radiated from the center of the wall. Again and again she punched, striking as if it were Leo himself. She fought the loop. She fought her prison. But it was no good; she got nowhere. Blood ran down her inky black hand and wrist, falling to the ground in drops that shone with grease.

"I hate you! I hate you! I *hate* you!"

With both hands she clawed at the blackness, the substance breaking off her fingernails, sticking underneath them, staining her clothes, smearing her face as she swiped at the sweat stinging her face and neck. She stared down at her hands and considered. "This is . . . time? This is infinity. This is where he is." She flung the black globs to the ground and attacked the wall with renewed fervor.

I'm coming, Q, she thought. *Just wait for me. I'm coming.*

Kitty stared at the opalescent area she'd finally cleared away. She saw a man on the other side, someone who looked vaguely familiar. *M . . . Mason, maybe?* She wasn't sure. She reared back her arm and smashed her fist straight into the plane. Across time and space, mirroring her exactly, he did the same, at the very same time.

Time collided. Everything went black, and totally, completely bonkers.

It seemed to Kitty as if the world had slipped off its axis and was spinning out into space. All was pitch dark. Her apartment spun as though it were on its way to Oz. Every piece of furniture in the place went flying, caught up in some eddy of who knew what. The sink ripped free of the floor and came at her. Kitty screamed and closed her eyes, but the porcelain basin went flying in the opposite direction just at the last moment, for the apartment had tipped on some axis and flung everything to the opposite side.

Then Leonardo appeared from nowhere, his fingers clamping around the thick gold bracelet hanging from her wrist. As he used the link to drag her into the blackness of the wall, Kitty screamed. Her eyes and mouth seemed to gum up. She coughed but no sound came out; nothing happened at all. She couldn't understand how it was possible to feel as if every part of her were compacted, and her throat full, and yet still be able to breathe. The idea of what was going on made her want to gag— or at least the idea of what she *thought* was going on— and it also overwhelmed her with a sense of virtual paralysis. She swayed in a state of dimming consciousness, stumbling and falling to her knees, crying out in soundless fury.

Light flickered. Ahead of her Leonardo stalked across the black plane, the metal of his cuff links reflecting occasional eerie opalescence from the walls around them. Kitty hung her head, trying not to panic, trying to . . . tolerate. And through the claustrophobic muck of her dulled senses a violent ringing sound penetrated, as if sound waves had drilled a path directly to her eardrums.

She lifted her head again and saw a kind of smoky pearlescence and the shadowy form of Leonardo. He was beating against the side of the tunnel with very controlled and consistent underhand motions, with something that appeared to be a crowbar. A sudden blast of white exploded in toward him, showering everything with white powder. The material almost immediately turned to darkness.

Leo turned to look back at her, his face smeared with white, his eyes expressionless. Kitty forced herself to her feet and watched as he stepped toward the billowing white powder and the outer wall, and . . . then he vanished.

Kitty tried to run, to follow, but she could make only slow, short strides. Watching the white flecks waft outward, she noticed there wasn't as much volume; all movement was slowing, and the hole, the archway—wherever it led—was closing. She could see Leonardo on the other side, a curious look on his face. They stared at each other, Kitty rapidly blinking against the white flecks now sticking to her eyelashes.

He wants to leave me here, she realized.

A kind of hatred built up inside her, pushing at the void around Kitty. She didn't make a move as the white vapor from the outer world continued to thin, but a smell like wet plaster seeped into her senses, and the doorway to freedom again began to narrow.

Whatever he saw in her eyes then, Leonardo seemed to fight against. The cold hardness of him warred with something softer. At last he reached out and grabbed the bracelet she wore around her wrist and pulled her through and out. The metal cut into Kitty's skin as she was tugged, a bit of blood from beneath smearing her. The look of it, all medieval dungeonesque, made Kitty feel nauseated.

The two of them stood together, covered with white, the black void looming before them once again. Kitty didn't want to move away. Yet the rift was closing. She watched Leonardo's face as he punched things into his electronic crowbar, asking him a question that had no sound; then she watched as the white evaporated into the black and they were enveloped once more. Whichever way Kitty looked, she saw a long tunnel-like void with black walls.

And yet Leonardo did not lead them onward. He stalked to and fro in the blackness, talking to himself. His chiseled face was all tight angles, the muscles in his jaw twitching, and Kitty came to a new conclusion: he hadn't meant to take them here. Whatever he'd programmed hadn't worked.

For the first time in ages, the fear Katherine felt wasn't about Leonardo Kaysar. It was about death—or worse, conscious oblivion. Eternal nothingness. Because that was what this felt like.

Conscious or unconscious, she thought bitterly, I'm always stuck with the same question. Would it be better to know she was unhappy, or remain blissfully clueless to the truth?

Katherine experimented with the black walls, leaning backward and bumping her spine against a barrier, then turning and seeing a tunnel before her and the walls in new locations. What did that mean? Was this the way she was to take—forward? Was it the way out? Of course, "out" was not a given. Everything was both a path and an impenetrable wall, depending on how you looked at it, and there was no assurance of exit. Escape might not even be possible. Not even for Leo.

He gestured suddenly for her to follow, urgent in his motions. She tripped again complying, and he was merciless, yanking on her bracelet to pull her up.

Yet for all his seeming brutality, the oddest thing occurred to Kitty. It wasn't concrete; it couldn't be proven, but she and Leonardo had a bond that would never go away. However fake their relationship had been, she could read him. And, reading him, she knew that he was having trouble compartmentalizing his emotions toward her. That was something she could possibly use against him when the time came.

At that moment Leonardo yanked her forward. Kitty crashed into him. She couldn't understand his change in behavior, the sudden urgency, but then a noise sounded. It was a noise that terrified her, for it was reminiscent of a huge wave at the seashore, an oncoming wave that was growing bigger and louder. Kitty wanted to bury her face in Leonardo's back and wait for it to go away, but instead she looked behind her. A medium distance back, the black plane upon which they stood was breaking down, the edges softening and falling away in thick globs.

Leonardo's face was grim but focused. He let go of Katherine's bracelet, unhooked the electric crowbar from his belt once more, and pressed in some sort of code on the number pad. As he swiped his smartie over the crystal panel, the red bar code flashed across his face, lighting up the surroundings for an instant.

Katherine looked around in a panic, but there was no visible way out. She put her hand out to the side and came away with a handful of black like that of the material falling away from their platform. It seemed to be absorbing into her skin, sliding down her body like a thick, hot sweat. She couldn't speak; it was as if her throat were again clogged with the substance.

Leonardo swung the crowbar like a hammer, his teeth gritted and a fire in his eyes brighter than she'd ever seen in them. The bar struck the wall, sending out a shower of rainbow-colored sparks and glassy shards that sank into the ooze as if it were quicksand. Katherine looked down at her feet; she was up to her ankles in the lugubrious black.

Leonardo drew his next swing back so far that Katherine felt the breeze of his effort on the side of her face. His lips parted in a silent cry of angry desperation, and he slammed the crowbar again into the wall—which cracked like ice on a warm spring day. Not wasting a moment, he pulled her forward and through, the jagged edges of the exit scraping bloody lines in his hand and eventually trails through the black covering Kitty's body.

They emerged in bright splendor, and Leo turned to face Kitty in the crisp and clean tuxedo she'd once adored on him. She looked down and found she wore the peacock blue satin gown of her engagement night, which was pristine; her shoes were sparkling. They were in the foyer of the restaurant in which he'd proposed. She could breathe again; the clogging claustrophobia and the heavy blackness were gone.

Leonardo swore and pulled her into the restaurant dining room, with its carved ebony panels and embroidered chinoiserie. The place was empty, but . . . Katherine's work cubicle sat where the bar should have been. Leonardo pulled her toward it.

Oddly, right at the entrance to the cubicle, what looked like thin air was solid, and he bounced off some invisible layer with a wince. Katherine looked toward the door of the restaurant, then back at him, gauging her chances of escape. Leo took hold of her bracelet again and started working on the see-through wall across her cubicle entrance, using his tools, his smartie, and an endless stream of code.

Katherine watched a drop of sweat slip from his neck down the collar of his tuxedo. The back of his black satin bow tie was soaked through. *He's struggling,* she realized. *He doesn't entirely know what's going on.*

She looked down at her bracelet in his hand. As he worked on the cubicle, the scent of cooking food wafted through the room, as well as the invisible rumble of fellow diners who weren't really there. Katherine carefully, slowly prepared herself—and then she wrested her bracelet from his grip and gave him a shove with all her might.

Leonardo went sailing off his feet. He pitched forward into the clear wall separating them from the cubicle, and he slammed his head. He called Kitty's name, a warning shout. But Katherine was off and running, holding her hem high and weaving through the tables and chairs with their suddenly strange red-and-white-checked tablecloths from her brunch and not her engagement, and she found the door and opened it and . . .

At the last minute she felt Leonardo's hand grasp the fabric at her waist, but it was too late; she pitched forward into the previous blackness, plunging in an endless waterfall of ebony water, trying to surface to keep from drowning, feeling Leonardo's grip on her the whole while. And then she did surface, her head rising into ambient white, and she was disoriented but staring at a strip of red.

Along that strip were the soles of shoes treading the red carpet at her engagement party. The area on either side of the carpet was like clear acrylic, and she reached out an ooze-covered arm from where she was treading blackness. Stilettos, men's dress shoes, the sweep of the trains of evening gowns, these all passed. The voices—she could hear the voices, but the pull of the black was still too great. And another pull: Leo. She reached out and yelled for help, but then was dragged under once more.

Suddenly the tension let up and she knew she was free of him. Gagging as black slipped down her throat and began to fill her lungs, she pushed upward, swimming hard, and she broke through to air once more and began vomiting black. She looked up, reaching out, trying to shriek with a voice that no longer worked.

A bot from her office smashed down on the acrylic between her and the red carpet, then another and another; her fall collection was obscuring her view of whatever was going on above. Another and yet another fell, their limbs breaking away from their torsos, fabric spilling everywhere until she could no longer see anything but gray. Katherine was treading water, her body pulling her under more often now, her limbs giving way, but she still tried to spit out the black that filled her mouth each time she went under.

And then she was tugged backward and up suddenly, her other hand held by Leonardo's. He had captured her—and now he was rising out of the onyx sea, black as night himself, and his crowbar was bouncing off the ceiling, sparks flying everywhere. She saw he was tiring, but his grit would conquer. He was nothing if not dedicated. And then, without his doing another thing, thin rivulets of light formed in a grid on the ceiling.

Leonardo's gaze narrowed as he stared at the fiery grid erupting above. Then that grid replicated multiple times. She saw one of them seem to slip free from some tenuous mooring, and it hurtled toward them like a falling elevator. It moved as if in slow motion, the layer descending toward them.

Leonardo burst toward her, and with his hands on her head he pushed Kitty under, down, down, down until her lungs filled. Her skirts were engorged, also pulling her down. Flecks of silver showed through the shifting blackness all around her, perhaps the silver of metal, and Katherine found peace somehow in watching. Then a tremendous tsunami erupted as the grid struck, splashing into the black water, its edges glowing like metal in a fire—metal so hot it was white. That white sizzled as it hit the black; then it vanished and there was nothing left.

I'll never see Q again. I'm going to die, she thought.

Try to relax. It will be over soon. Think of something cheerful.

She found Q's face in her mind's eye, found an image of the two of them together in her bed. Laughing, sharing. . . . It was one of her most pleasant memories ever. And, of course, there was the memory of them making love.

She felt Leonardo's arm slip around her chest and under her armpit, and then she felt him push for the surface. Her lungs were now completely filled with black. She should have been dead, but her mind still pulsed even if her body had weakened to a paralyzed state.

Suddenly Leo was holding her by the arm, dragging her

out of the black, ooze dripping off her skin. He'd somehow managed to get a grip. It was a miracle he had the
strength to keep both of them from going under forever.
He pulled her onto a white platform, and Katherine collapsed in a heap on the floor, half-dead, struggling against
unconsciousness. Beyond where she lay, other slabs of grid
fell, crashing into the sea of black below.

Kitty turned to the side and heaved up a couple lung-
fuls of black. This hit the white floor and vanished. Kitty
closed her eyes and once more found herself—albeit a
weakened version of herself.

A persistent clicking drew her attention. She opened
her eyes, dizzy, lifted herself onto her feet, lurched, and fell
back . . . against the wall of the elevator at the Kaysar Corporation. Leonardo was pounding on the button to a specific floor, barking his name in an effort to order the
machine to obey. The elevator was rising.

He's lost control of the situation. He's lost control of the loop.
Kitty couldn't help sneering in derision.

She grabbed the rail on the wall and steadied herself on
her feet. The elevator's mirrored wall showed her with not
a hair out of place, her makeup perfect, the fabric of her
wrap dress as smooth as it ever was on a regular afternoon.
She looked down, recognizing her Wednesday outfit. But
her eyes were different—the *look* in her eyes was different.
This was not a time or place to make love. And this was
not the man she'd want to be doing it with.

Katherine glanced up at the camera she knew was there;
a blue light was blinking on and off. Katherine raised her
face and screamed for help at the top of her lungs, but the
elevator continued to ascend.

Kaysar backed up against the mirrored wall, his body
curled around her side, his mouth at her ear, so close to
how it had been on so many previous days—yet so different. "Don't move," he said, and a wave of shock passed
through her. His voice sounded almost . . . personable. As

if he cared about her as much as he cared about the experiment Q had explained, as if he'd been protecting her as much as the work he'd put in.

The elevator jolted to a halt. Kitty sucked in a breath, feeling Leonardo's body flinch in similar surprise. He pulled himself off her, the bracelet around her wrists held loosely in his grip as they both turned to the door. It didn't open. The silence was deafening, save for the low panting of Leonardo's breath and her own gasps of terror.

Leonardo reached out a tentative hand and touched the elevator door. His fingers slid across the metal surface, which was solid. Katherine almost laughed, half expecting his fingers to sink through.

A *ding* sounded, and the elevator doors slowly opened. With Katherine following, Leonardo stepped boldly . . . into her usual Friday set, or some variation on its theme.

Leonardo breathed a sigh of relief. Katherine looked around for inconsistencies, but it seemed as if they'd managed to settle into the actual middle of a week—albeit in a different location: they stood in the dark, empty club that normally hosted her engagement party, and there was nothing odd about the location. Even the elevator they'd come in had disappeared.

Both Katherine and Leonardo stayed frozen in place, each waiting to see if time had finally settled. Kitty turned her head and looked right at Leo. His grip loosened, and then his hand fell away and he reached slowly into his suit jacket, drawing forth his smartie.

Something didn't feel right here. Kitty just stared at Leo as if her feet were glued in place. The ambient air seemed to pulse and press around her.

"Kitty!" *Roxy's voice!*

Kitty tried to whip her head around to determine where the voice might have come from, but she couldn't seem to do so quickly enough to catch the direction. In a panic, she looked to Leonardo for help. He stared at his smartie, a finger punch drawn and at the ready but a look of bewilderment on his face.

And then it hit her. She felt it strike her like another wave: every fiber of her being was pushed hard. Leo had a similar reaction. Disheveled, his hair falling into his eyes, one cuff flapping and undone, his lip curled and teeth gritted, he struggled with his equipment. And just as Kitty felt that she might be pushed right into another dimension, as if all the wires of the possible versions of her life were reaching out to her . . . Leonardo slashed her across the neck with his punch.

The blackness became visible again as both she and Leo were overwhelmed. The blackness was again a flood. Kitty felt the punch's nanoliquid working its way through her body. Helpless to do anything even if she wanted to, she watched Leo get swept in a different direction, bouncing among mixed-up scenes of her life that passed before her eyes like changing scenery on a rotating stage. At last they parted ways and became invisible to each other.

Whether she faded to white or he faded to black, Kitty couldn't have said; all she could do was wonder whether he'd been trying to kill her or save her.

CHAPTER THIRTY

Vesper landed in the past, in a Dumpster on a questionable segment of San Francisco's Market Street.

Why is there always a trash bin at the most inopportune locations? she wondered. *There's always a trash bin and never a mattress. This is so gross! At least Mason was right about the Wookiee and I'm here in one piece. Uncrushed. Excellent.*

The intern pulled herself out of the bin and noted that she wasn't covered in black from the transit, but examined herself anyway to make sure there was no truly disgusting slime on her. She found just what she was looking for on the side of one tennis shoe—something gelatinous and indistinct from the trash. She scraped around on the pavement until it was gone.

The wind picked up, blowing errant bits of garbage and paper around. A piece of newspaper fluttered up from the bin and began blowing down the street. With a start, she looked down the street at the blowing trash and ran toward the missing piece, hoping it was what she'd come for. The damn thing seemed to have a life of its own. It blew around a corner, Vesper lunging and missing in pursuit, lunging and missing.

Vesper turned the corner and immediately saw something she didn't expect. Slamming herself against the side of a building, her chest heaving, she watched in controlled silence as Roxanne walked by a short distance away and in the middle of the street. The moment she'd recognized the woman Vesper had almost called out, but then she'd choked off the word and prayed her voice would simply float away on the wind: If there was one thing Louise had bored into her, it was that you never, ever interrupted the past life of a person with whom you were linked. At least Vesper ought to know *that* lesson by now, even if she'd failed the other stuff about not meddling.

Roxanne paused, looked around, then kept going. Vesper frowned. This woman seemed different from the version of Roxy in the future: she was sort of hunched and nervous, as if she wanted to melt into those lumpy sweats of hers and completely disappear.

Vesper checked her watch. It was approximately two a.m. If Roxy would just keep walking, maybe Vesper could dart out and grab the newspaper and return without having changed a thing.

"I've got her!"

Vesper pressed harder against the wall. That had been Mason Merrick's voice.

"No, I've got her!"

Holy crap. That was Leonardo Kaysar's voice. No way could she get involved in this situation, not while they were still in the area; she'd throw the whole lot of them off their wires. She'd therefore have to wait it out.

Vesper slid down the wall until she was in a sitting position and wrapped her arms around her knees. She kept one eye on the newspaper she was chasing, but every part of her wanted to get involved as Mason and Leonardo ran toward Roxy and started scrapping. Next, Mason and Roxy walked off together toward . . . was that what was now their apartment? Nice. How could you mess with a love affair this fabulous? You couldn't.

She waited a moment more to be sure no one remained; then Vesper stepped out of the shadows. She looked around and saw her newspaper blowing down the street, then turned and bumped directly into the suddenly present chest of Leonardo Kaysar.

He looked down at her with a slightly puzzled expression on his face, and then a spark of something flickered in his eyes. "You're a wire crosser, I presume."

Vesper swallowed hard, wondering if he had any idea who she was or that she was working against him. "I recognize you, Mr. Kaysar. It's an honor."

Leonardo gave an amused shake of his head.

"What about if I point out that every second you stand here with me now is screwing up everything we know to be true about the present and future?"

Leonardo produced his smartie. Snapped onto the gadget was another candy bar–shaped gadget with blue lights. "I know where those seconds went," was how he replied.

Vesper's eyes lit up. "New invention? Yours are the best."

A look of pride swept Leonardo's face. "It's not that new," he muttered.

Vesper leaned forward to get a peek, and she was sure he almost moved to show it to her before catching himself at the last second and slipping it back into his pocket. Which was when Vesper stopped herself and realized she was essentially geeking out with the enemy. She licked her lips and took a small shuffle back. "Do you think . . . ?"

He raised an eyebrow.

"Do you think people are inherently good?" she asked, suddenly just *really* not wanting him to be the enemy.

His expression shifted, and his gaze seemed to bore right through her. "No."

"You don't think *you* are?"

"No," he said.

"So you think you're inherently evil, then."

"I never thought about it. May I ask the reason for your line of questioning?"

"Dunno," she replied. "I've just been thinking a lot about our line of work. It does seem to beg a lot of these sorts of questions."

"Who do you work for?" he asked, something unknowable shifting behind his eyes.

Vesper played it cool.

"Oh, heh. You know. I just . . . dabble. I'm still in high school."

To her surprise, he relaxed a little, seeming to accept her answer.

" 'Kay, then," she tried. "So . . . um, how about I just go do my thing and you just go do your thing, and we'll, um, call it even."

Leonardo frowned at her for a moment; then suddenly he laughed. It was hardly the evil cackle Roxy's description of him would have suggested. Vesper decided the best policy was to laugh with him.

"We'll call it even, then," he said.

"Fab." Vesper held out her hand.

Again, Leonardo seemed surprisingly nonplussed. But he extended his hand anyway, and they shook. Vesper cleared her throat, stepped past him, turned, and walked backward toward the newspaper she was chasing.

"Great . . . excellent to meet you, Mr. Kaysar," she said. She raised her palm in a kind of awkward farewell. "Gonna take off now. Heh. Gotta go, um . . . deal with . . . stuff."

She walked another couple of backward steps as Leo stood in the street casually watching her, his hands in the pockets of his suit, which was traumatized from the earlier scuffle with Mason. There was no air of evil about him, no sense of impending danger or attack. Maybe it was because he knew that her bosses couldn't afford to let Vesper do anything more than run straight through the situation and out again. Maybe it was because he didn't really know who she was working for.

Vesper and Leonardo looked at each other across the distance of the street. He inclined his head and swept his fingers delicately to the side. She heard him chuckling as he walked away.

She immediately turned her attention back to looking for the newspaper she'd chased. It had fluttered up against a building. Vesper grabbed it before it could fly away again. She knew before she looked at it that it would be Mason's front page of the SF *Chronicle*, but she still heaved an enormous sigh of relief when she saw it was the same.

Folding the whole thing up in her hands, she heard the sound of shoes clicking against the pavement and whirled back around. This time it was Leonardo Kaysar wearing a tuxedo, a bracelet dangling from his grasp. He looked a bit dazed, a bit older, and he blinked a couple of times and stared at Vesper. He didn't say a word.

"Hello, again. Didn't I just see you wearing a regular suit?" she asked.

"Did you?" he replied.

"Yeah." She pointed into the distance. "You went that way, wearing a regular suit. Right after Mason beat the living crap out of you. And then I turned around and here you are in a tuxedo . . . coming from *that* way."

Leonardo stared at her. "Dear God."

Vesper widened her eyes. "Did you . . . did you just make a temporal *loop*?"

He brushed a lock of hair from his face, a weary motion, and Vesper noticed that his face was no longer bruised from any fight. Nonetheless he said, "I certainly hope not. And while I would appreciate the irony of a loop, I certainly would not welcome it."

"*Duuude*," Vesper said. "Did you get yourself into a paradox?"

Leonardo was rustling around in his pockets. He pulled out his smartie and looked tensely down at the blackish, barely recognizable remnants of his technology.

"Mine's gone," she said hoarsley, looking in her pockets for her smartie. "Maybe it fell when I jumped."

Leonardo's smartie was clearly not in good shape. Vesper craned her neck to try and catch a glimpse of his screen and from the little she saw, it was definitely on the fritz. He glanced sharply at her, and she could see the wheels in his head turning. Which made the wheels in her head turn. Which made her realize that they might both be kind of screwed.

"Is there juice on that thing?" she asked hopefully.

He didn't answer, and Vesper knew that it wasn't because he was ignoring her.

Finally he said, "There's not enough for a full leap at this time," he said, obviously choosing his words very carefully.

"How about a half-leap," she joked. "A half-leap could get us somewhere else, at least."

No answer as Leonardo poked at his smartie with his index finger; apparently his stylus was gone. "It's possible there's enough for a partial leap if I use the exact same portion of wire."

Vesper chose to ignore his use of the prounoun "I" instead of "we." "Did you jump into the black?" she asked.

"Not intentionally," he replied, looking up at the sky.

Vesper's face lit. "That was my crevasse of time you fell through!" she said proudly.

"I suppose you just saved the day, then," he said sarcastically, looking down at the concrete. To Vesper's surprise, it was disintegrating around their shoes to take the form of black ooze.

She tried lifting her own foot, except that it wouldn't lift; her boots were stuck. Fear prickled down her spine. "Oh, *man*." She looked up at Leonardo. Behind him, the neon lights from the 7-Eleven seemed to have been extinguished by a sea of black.

A faint glow emanated from Leonardo's smartie, but all the screen showed was a stream of numbers scrolling across the screen. "That's not going to be able to save us, is it?" she asked.

"I don't think so," he admitted, slipping the smartie into his breast pocket.

Vesper swallowed hard and shifted her gaze back to Leo's face. "Is this *it?*"

Leonardo looked up, and an odd expression swept his face. The expression told Vesper that: a) whatever was about to happen was unexpected, b) it wasn't good, and c) the man most likely to have a solution had none.

The city behind him was disappearing quickly, as if someone had taken a paintbrush and were applying black oil paint to a canvas. Vesper shot a look behind her shoulder and saw the same thing. She looked down at the newspaper in her hand, crumpled into a tight wad and damp from her sweat. What if she never got it back to them? What if, without it, she'd disappear them all from one another? She looked up at Leonardo. "Do you think we'll be able to get back?" She unfurled her hand and he looked down at the newsprint. "I have to get this to Mason and Roxy," she said, on the verge of tears.

The muscles in Leonardo's jaw quivered as he surveyed the encroaching darkness. Was it fear? Panic welled up inside Vesper, either way.

"Mr. Kaysar, you're not all bad, are you?" she asked.

"That's unlikely," he replied.

"What were you going to do with Kitty Gibbs . . . in the end?"

Kaysar looked down at Vesper in surprise. "I don't know. What do you do with a lab rat . . . in the end?"

Vesper's heart pounded as she felt the blackness pass her knees. "I think something in you tries to be a jerk, but maybe there's a good person inside you trying to get out— almost like with Kitty's real personality."

He'd stopped fighting and gazed at her with turbulent eyes, as if he were trying to appear emotionless and cold but was breaking down in the very same way the time they were in was breaking down. "I don't think about that sort of thing," he said quietly.

"Well, I choose that you're good, okay?" Her voice trembled, but Vesper held back her tears and raised her chin defiantly. "Will you hold my hand?"

Leonardo looked at her as if she were insane, and then something in his face softened. She saw a dark shadow move through his eyes; then a flaming grid appeared in the sky over them.

Leonardo Kaysar faced Vesper and took both of her hands in his. His right hand curled over the wad of newspaper in her one palm and his left hand gave the other a squeeze. She looked at him and managed something of a smile as she squeezed back.

"What's going to happen?" she whispered, still holding on tight.

Leonardo looked down at her. "Everything . . . and nothing."

They stood there without another word, sharing an end, and that end came crashing down upon them along with the beginning and the middle. All was smashed into one layer of time.

CHAPTER THIRTY-ONE

Smunday, as it turned out, was not really "Smunday" per se, as Roxy had opined. It was simply nontime, or untime, depending on one's point of view. It was every February 29 in years that weren't leap years, all the moments that vanished when a civilization switched from one calendar to another, the particles of the days lost when traveling to a different time zone, the difference between the Earth's rotation and the precision of an atomic clock . . . In other words, Smunday was the collection of every time anomaly one could think of; it was both everything and nothing.

If one ever found oneself in the position of not actually existing, or existing only between nanoseconds currently in use, one had better hope one was a time anomaly specialist. From Q's vantage point—which fortunately still existed even as he floated like a bunch of pixels in a non-temporally affixed reality—that was the good news: it gave him a limited understanding of what was going on, or at least an intuitive guess at where he was. Unfortunately, even though he remembered himself and his love for Kitty, he had no way of getting back to the physical reality where any of that existed. On any wire anywhere.

What do you do when you've become a figment of imagination, when you think but therefore you aren't? You cling to something true. You find whatever matters most to you, and you bind yourself to that—even if it has no physical form either. What Q needed most was Katherine Gibbs.

Q envisioned himself in full human form. He imagined Kitty all the different times he'd been with her, and how in spite of all the forces working against them, their true feelings could never be denied. Love conquers all, they say. *It's so true. What's real inside can't be suppressed or denied and it transcends mere words or even physical presence. I don't have to say Kitty's name while standing in front of her for her to know I'm calling for her.* And in his mind, he began to sing their song.

Kitty knelt in the middle of her apartment staring at the gray and black rivulets streaking the walls. She didn't know if everything looked so dull and dilapidated now that she could really see things as they were, on her own, or if something new had happened.

She'd been kneeling on the floor there, just staring, for quite a while. Her legs seemed to not want to work anymore. Since Leonardo Kaysar had essentially deposited her back in her apartment, all Kitty had been able to do was tremble and cry and wait for something else to happen to her. It was small consolation that she was keenly aware of how useless that sort of behavior was in the situation and how disappointed in her Q would have been had he known.

And finally, after she'd sat there for some time, crumpled on the living room floor waiting for her world to come to a definitive end, Kitty heard a sound. First one note, then two, followed by three. She lifted her head. A song began to unfold note by note, line by line, verse by verse. Q.

The music wasn't in the air around her; it was inside of her, as if her heartbeat were the metronome keeping time. Kitty pressed her palm over her heart and closed her eyes.

She took a deep breath and stumbled to her feet. *I'm right here . . . where are you?*

Q's singing, tremulous at first, seemed to gain strength from her thoughts. He drew her through the apartment as if he'd physically reached out and taken her hand. Kitty curled her hands into fists to stop the shaking and walked toward her bedroom. She stepped carefully from white square to white square on the parquet, avoiding the black harlequin squares that seemed to have sunk into themselves and were pulling at the white edges like black holes sucking in everything around them.

Kitty stepped over the threshold and walked into her bedroom, trying not to make too much of the way an even thicker ashy black covered the walls there. Her closet door was open; half of her clothes had fallen off their hangers and lay in sparkly, cheerfully colored piles on the floor. Perfume bottles and trinkets from the top of her bureau were scattered about the room. It was as if the apartment had been jerked off its axis; one great jolt had put the brakes on and sent everything flying.

". . . how I won you, I shall never, ever know . . ."

"Q?" Kitty ran across the bedroom and stepped into her bathroom. The wall was nearly gone, the edge of it melting away like ice cream dropped on hot pavement. There was nothing in front of her, nothing but blackness. She bit down on her lip to stop herself from crying, then looked into the dark. "Q? Are you there?"

". . . oh, my heart grew active . . ."

Q's voice was so much louder now. Kitty could feel the strain and fear in his voice throughout her entire body. "I'm coming, Q. Wait for me." She took a deep breath and steeled herself before lifting her foot and stepping to the last stable white square closest to the wall.

"Kitty? Is that you?"

She closed her eyes and forced her mind to see Q as if he were physically in front of her. *"It's me,"* she answered.

"*Don't stop singing our song!*" Kitty's white square suddenly buckled; she looked behind her and took a hasty step backward, taking care to place her feet squarely on the next best white square back from the black.

She was running out of time. If she didn't act soon, she'd be as nowhere as Q was—and all alone. A rivulet of sweat streaked down her temple. She swiped it away, her hand freezing in midair as she noticed something odd sticking out of the blackness just in front of her. It looked like metal—a sharp metal point. As the blackness shifted around it, moving the point slightly to one side, more of the object was revealed, and she could see the colored buttons of a code input box.

"*I fell, and it was swell,*" Q sang.

The floor beneath Kitty slipped, jolting downward an inch. She grabbed on to the towel rack, putting her weight on it long enough to reposition her feet on a safer square. One of her shoes fell off, the toe sinking into the black square next to her. She looked over her shoulder to find the metal point. The object had keeled over, revealing a handle of some sort. A wood-and-metal handle. Kitty blinked her stinging eyes until the object came into focus and she saw that it was a pickax.

"*How I won you I shall never, ever know . . .*"

Q's voice seemed to be in every part of her. Spurred onward, Kitty gripped the towel rack hard with one hand and reached out toward the tool. Her fingertips grazed the handle, but she lost her chance as the towel rack sagged. One screw popped out of the side and sank into the floor. "I can't do this," Kitty burst out, tears streaming down her face, sweat stinging her eyes.

"*Yes, you can.*"

"Q?" she cried. "Help me."

"*I can't help you from where I am. You can do it. Try again.*"

Kitty stared at the handle, shifting slowly with the tide of black. Any longer and it would sink back in. She

reached out her hand, then closed her eyes and imagined
Q standing in front of her, waiting just beyond the black
veil.

She clenched her teeth, focused on the handle bobbing
in front of her, and kicked off her remaining shoe. She put
the sole of her foot against the wall and pushed off into
midair. Kitty caught the handle in one hand and sank
straight downward as her weight dragged the pickax down,
and then could only watch as her momentum took her
straight into the blackness.

Kitty closed her eyes and screamed as she plunged
through the edge of the layer into what felt like a column
of air. As the blackness closed behind her and her apartment vanished from sight, the pressure in the column
changed. As she hung suspended from the handle in complete darkness, she felt in her body that it was as if Q had
just been kicked in the gut; his thoughts just seemed to ex-
tinquish all at once.

Kitty's legs swung beneath her as she held on to the end
of the pickax with both hands. "Q?" she squeaked. "What
do I do now? Q?"

He didn't answer. Kitty started to panic. Her muscles
were burning, and she could feel the blackness pressing in
on all sides. Her sense of Q's physical presence went in
and out of focus in her mind; it was as if he were having
trouble maintaining consciousness, and if he couldn't imagine himself whole, neither could she.

"Q?" she yelled. "Q, come back. Don't fall asleep on
me!"

Her hands were slipping. Desperate, Kitty lunged upward for a better grip, and her fingers struck the control
panel of the pickax. Out of the darkness a line of lights
turned on, sending a welcome surge of adrenaline through
Kitty's body. "*Q, there's a tool here, and I think it still works,
but I don't know how to use it. Tell me what to do.*"

He didn't answer.

"Q, this really isn't the time to disappear on me," she said firmly. Nothing. Kitty moistened her lips as her sweaty hands slid away from the control panel. *"You had such persistence, you wore down my resistance,"* she sang, the line broken and tentative.

"Hotkey Roxy." It was an abrupt thought.

"What? What did you say?"

"Hotkey Roxy."

"What's a hotkey?" Kitty cried. She could feel Q struggling to stay focused, to keep her in his mind. He was so weak. *Oh, God. I should know this. I'm sure I should know this. Think, Kitty. Think for yourself.*

Kitty gripped the handle hard, and then closed her eyes against the darkness and focused inward. *Hotkey. Hotkey is an automatic smartie function, isn't it? It's something that's programmed to do something automatically on a smartie. The same something. Does this have the same thing? Oh . . . I hope I know how to use this thing. . . .*

She opened her eyes and stared at the glowing control panel. "Call Roxy?" she said in a tremulous voice. Nothing happened. "Call Roxy!" she yelled. "Hotkey Roxy! Go to Roxy?" She tried the whole thing over, using "Roxanne" and "Zaborovsky," but the panel didn't so much as blink in response to her voice commands. "Q? It doesn't understand me. It doesn't recognize my voice."

She could hear him again, crooning gently, his voice so weak she wanted to cry. He'd never give up. He'd try to the very end. Kitty let Q's song fill the space all around them, allowed him to draw what had been true and real in her life in the present into focus. *You know a lot of things. You can do this.*

Kitty yanked down hard on the pickax; the embedded tip pulled a deep groove in the blackness as it moved. She took a deep breath and shoved as hard as she could to press the arched side opposite into the blackness so the handle would stick out perpendicular to the black wall. Then she slung her body over it so that she was resting on it like a chin-up bar, her arms slung over the handle. The pickax's control panel faced up, the screen still glowing.

With shaking hands, Kitty reached over and pressed the menu button on the screen with a finger she couldn't even see until it moved into the halo of light. She scrolled through menus and drop-downs, parabolic graphs and coordinate sequences, and just when she was beginning to give up hope, she found the address book. "It's just a button." A burst of her own nervous laughter filled the silence.

Her finger hovered over a hotkey button labeled, HEAD-QUARTERS. Not too early, Kitty told herself. He needed to come to her. Q had to come to her. "Follow my voice," she said. She sang a verse and he answered. Another verse, and he felt closer than ever, until with her eyes closed she could imagine him standing next to her. "Put your arms around me," she said. "And hold on really tight."

Kitty imagined Q putting his arms around her. In her mind, she turned her face into his chest. Then she pushed the hotkey.

Leonardo grabbed at the wall of the apartment, his greasy black fingers slipping and sliding all over the whiteness. He'd just managed to burst his head and shoulders through. His mouth was coated with black, his eyes blood-shot and wild. He saw his enemies.

"Where's Kitty?" Roxy screamed, battling against Louise, who held her back. "You bastard! Where's Kitty?"

Mason ran to the wall. He grabbed Leonardo's wrist and his nemesis returned the gesture, their fingers trying to get a firm purchase despite the slipperiness caused by the ooze. The two men looked at each other, but they never had a chance to speak. Whether Leonardo Kaysar would have begged for rescue, whether Mason would have truly given it to him without knowing where Kitty was would remain a mystery.

In the shards of a nanosecond, the hold between them slipped. Leonardo's eyes widened, and he flailed out to regain contact; he managed nothing. At the last moment he fell backward but left one thing to remind them of him: a crumpled wad of newspaper stuck between the black and plaster. Then he plummeted out of sight, spread-eagled. None of them saw his face again.

Kitty and Q blasted through the wall into the living room of Roxy and Mason's apartment. Q's arms were wrapped tightly around Kitty; her head was buried in his chest. The vacuum sound behind them of time contracting and expanding between the two layers roared so loudly they had to cover their ears. The lights in the apartment flickered and spat as the energy fields shifted, and then everything finally settled. Kitty and Q slowly opened their eyes. The pickax lay before them, smoke coming out of the panel.

Kitty pressed her face into Q's neck and just breathed, taking in the warmth of his body and focusing on the fact that it wasn't just in her mind: these were his arms wrapped around her; these were his lips gently pressing against her skin. He was really here with her.

Q lifted her chin and looked into Kitty's eyes. "I love you," he said. Kitty sniffed back tears. "I love you too."

Q brushed her hair away and kissed her mouth. He kissed her over and over again and then started laughing. Kitty started laughing too, and they just lay there in each other's arms on the floor laughing and kissing until Q rolled over and pulled her on top of him . . . and then went completely still, staring upward just beyond her.

Kitty swallowed her laughter and slowly followed his gaze. Louise, Roxy, and Mason stood there, bodies frozen in place, and various expressions of complete shock on their faces as they watched the two of them rolling around on the floor.

Louise had obviously been holding a sheaf of documents;

they lay all over the floor where she'd dropped them. Her mouth was hanging open. Mason's finger was poised over his smartie, as if he'd been in the middle of making a call. Roxy was standing stock-still, her eyes open so wide she looked catatonic.

Q got to his feet and helped Kitty up, then stepped back as Kitty limped up to Roxy. Roxy just kept staring, apparently unable to speak.

"Hello, Roxy," Kitty said softly.

"Oh, my God!" Roxy shrieked as she hurtled forward, leaping between Kitty and Q to give her best friend an enormous hug. "I'm so, so sorry. You have no idea how sorry I am!"

"Rox?" Kitty looked nonplussed at the excess of tears pouring down the woman's face.

"It's my fault you died!" Roxy wailed. "And were trapped!"

"I'm not dead," Kitty pointed out helpfully. "But *you* don't look so well. Do you want me to make you some soup?"

Roxy started laughing and crying all at once. Q walked up beside Kitty and took her hand. Mason slung his arm around Louise's shoulder. They stood in a circle in the living room with the wall blown out, in the present-day world, and lost no time reclaiming the nanoseconds of friendship they'd lost.

CHAPTER THIRTY-TWO

It was shortly after they all were eating soup that they processed Vesper's absence. Kitty and Q had gone upstairs for some privacy, and it was Louise who found the note on the laptop:

Dear guys. When you find this I will already be gone. . . .

"Oh, shit!" Louise screamed, her index finger pecking hysterically at the down-arrow key. "I should have let her do more! It's my fault. What the hell has she done?"

Mason gave her an odd look, and soon he and Roxy hovered over her shoulder, staring at the screen alongside her.

No big deal, it's just that I've jumped into the crevasse of time. . . .

Louise stopped reading and stared around at the others. "Who the hell would proactively, purposely do that? Why would *Vesper* do that?"

"She was probably sick of making orange juice," Roxy said.

It's a really long story, and I don't want to bore you. . . .

Mason stopped reading. "She doesn't want to bore us? She committed time-travel hara-kiri and doesn't want to *bore* us? What have we done to this girl?"

Roxy grabbed the laptop and continued to read:

Anyway, I messed up and I'm sorry and I'm going to fix things. The 2:07 p.m. situation? Totally my fault. I poked at the wall and messed it up and made a hole, and then I stuffed Mason's special newspaper in the hole before I knew it was special and the problem was that I'd spilled the melted stuff from Kitty's pills all over it and then after I stuck it in the hole I covered it up with spackle and everything seemed fine and I thought I'd fixed it, which is why I didn't say anything. I think that's part of what's messing things up. I'm going to go find it. I'll try to make it back for the barbecue.

"What was the 'two-oh-seven p.m.' thing?" Roxy asked, confused.

Louise stared at her with a stricken expression. "I'll have to look at our records. It was something I recorded on a card, I think."

Mason looked down at the floor, shaking his head. "Poor kid. She thinks she's gonna make it back to the barbecue? She might not make it back to this century. She has no experience, no tools . . . I'm not even sure she has a smartie on her."

"Well, she's resourceful," Roxy suggested, trying to make Louise feel less guilty.

"She's resourceful *in the present and the future*," Louise said. "What happens if she wakes up in the middle of the Spanish Inquisition?"

"Actually, I think she's doing senior-level Spanish," Roxy replied. "Not that that makes it okay," she hastened to add when Mason and Louise stared at her. "I'm just saying she's got a lot going for her. She's gotten an A in every weapons class too."

"Okay, fine. She can handle herself physically. What if she lands in the middle of the Black Plague?"

"Er, maybe we could cross wires and unsick her?"

"You're going to cross wires in the middle of the plague? Are you insane?" Louise asked.

"One of us is, apparently," Mason muttered.

Louise squared her shoulders. "Vesper is my responsibility. I have to go get her." She jumped up from her chair and ran to the wall, staring into the bubbling and boiling crevasse of blackness. Her eyes bugged out, and she wavered and swayed. "I'm going to puke. I have vertigo."

Mason and Roxy looked at each other. "How can you have vertigo if you can't see the bottom?" Roxy asked.

"Well, I'm *guessing* this crevasse extends a very long way down," Louise replied. "Psychologically I can see the bottom, and it's very, very far away." She closed her hands into fists and steeled herself. "But I gotta do it, for Vesper's sake."

Yet Louise didn't actually jump. She'd turned a peculiar shade of green and looked more capable of tipping haphazardly into the crevasse rather than leaping.

Mason and Roxy put out a hand simultaneously, each grabbed a sleeve, and yanked her back. Mason gave Roxy a signal, and she stayed with Louise while he approached the crevasse and looked down. It was just black; bubbling, boiling black that had no depth at all. It looked a little like tar that you could jump on and then bounce back off. It looked . . .

He raised an index finger. "Flashlight," he requested.

Roxy ran to the kitchen utility drawer and came back with what he wanted. Mason shone the flashlight across the crevasse. Then he looked at his girlfriend. Then he looked back down. "Do you see . . . ?"

"Oh, wow. Texture. I see texture."

"So do I," he replied.

"It doesn't make sense. We've reached across this thing. It was air. It was . . . oh."

"Maybe Leo changed the recipe or whatever."

"The recipe? What is it, key time pie or something?"

"This is the time neither for debilitatingly bad puns, nor for sarcasm, O light of my life," Mason remarked. "Either Leo changed the, er, recipe or—"

"Or it was like this all the time."

"Yeah. Maybe that. But . . . maybe the molecular structure, if you will, of time is deconstructing in some way."

"Hello, Mr. Science," Louise muttered from where she now sat.

"That does not sound good," Roxy said, ignoring her cohort's mutterings. "In fact, that sounds very, very bad. What does it mean?"

"It means we need to get Vesper back as soon as possible." Mason got down on his knees beside the crevasse with his flashlight. He tipped his head and looked at the substance lengthwise. The light bounced off the black, showing ridges and dips. Slowly he extended his hand and went to touch the surface with his finger.

"Stop!"

They wheeled around. Louise held a sheaf of printouts. "Two-oh-seven p.m. I wrote on an index card about that day when we were outside the apartment and lost track of time, and then suddenly it all came back to us. It wasn't Leonardo doing that. It was Vesper."

Roxy looked back into the blackness. "So . . . according to her message, she screwed around with the wall and accessed a mass of disintegrating time?"

"And then she tried to fix it with a spackle patch-up job using my newspaper," Mason said.

"Which got absorbed into the shifting, unstable time and created a channel," Roxy added.

Louise grimaced. "And she went after it . . . does it make anybody else extremely nervous that it was Leonardo Kaysar who brought it back? If Kaysar found the newspaper, where the hell is Vesper?"

There was the sound of footsteps on the stairs, and then Kitty and Q reappeared. Q looked around at everyone, gave a broad grin, and said, "Why's everyone look so dour?"

They explained the situation. Upon hearing Vesper's situation, Q's face paled. Kitty glanced at him and ran her finger down his cheek. She kissed him and gave him a hug.

There was a pause as they all processed what had happened, and then a kind of pall was cast over the room. Then Mason suddenly said, "So . . . if that time is missing, how has everything worked out okay? What did Leo mean by returning the newspaper?"

They all looked at one another in shock.

"Hey. Whoa. Are you all thinking what I'm thinking?" Mason asked.

Kitty looked suddenly ill. Q wrapped a protective arm

around her shoulders and pulled her closer. Had their enemy done something kind? Had he sacrificed himself to bring back that newspaper? And what were the ramifications of everything that had just happened? If anyone would know, it was Leo—and the last they'd seen of him, he was spinning off into Smunday.

And didn't this mean that he'd seen Vesper? He could tell them only if they found him. They'd have to save him.

"I don't think there's any other solution," Mason said, answering their unspoken agreement.

"Better the devil you know than the devil you don't," Kitty finally agreed.

"Oh, my God," Roxy said.

"Oh, my *God*," Louise echoed.

Mason went with, "Holy shit."

Q just shook his head.

"The irony of this is giving me heartburn," Roxy said.

No one seemed to know how to answer that.

Louise heaved a deep breath. "I must say, I'm really glad I didn't jump in that crevasse."

"Lucky for you it's Vesper who jumped then," Q said.

Louise turned on him, furious. "Vesper is the most resourceful person I've ever met. More so, even, than I was at her age. Assuming that Vesper did not, as we posited earlier, land in the middle of the Black Plague or on the battlefield during the Crusades, she's probably figuring out a way back as we speak. I'll grab a couple hours of sleep and start working on it from our end."

"You're assuming she landed in the past?" Q asked.

"Of course I am."

Everyone went silent.

"Why is that better?" Kitty asked, clearly confused.

Roxy gave her a grim look. "Because if she's in the future, beyond what we know of the future, then . . ."

"Then we probably can't help her," Q finished.

"At least not without Leonardo Kaysar," Roxy added

with a grim laugh. She didn't add that they needed to talk to him either way.

"She's *obviously* in the past," Louise said in clipped tones, clearly having decided that a declarative statement would make it so. "And she's quite possibly with the world's foremost expert in time travel."

"Oh, my God," Roxy muttered again. She was still processing what they had to do next.

"I'll start a file for Vesper first thing," Louise announced, stacking up the Katherine Gibbs file and preparing it for a permanent archive.

"She'll be all right," Kitty said.

Roxy nodded. Mason tried to smile. Q's jaw muscle twitched.

Louise pushed her glasses up the bridge of her nose. "Both of them will be okay. Lucky for Leonardo Kaysar, he's trapped in this mysterious and anomalistic black crevasse of time with our plucky intern—or at least, he'd better hope he lands back with her again. When we find them both, we'll kick his ass, okay? He deserves it."

Q frowned. "I don't mean to be a downer, but there's no closing the file for me. No matter what he did, no matter why we have to help him, he's still an asshat—if you know what I mean. I've . . . got unfinished business."

"Don't we all," Roxy said.

The tension in the air had ratcheted up a good three notches.

Mason sat heavily down on the sofa, a look of annoyance on his face. "Maybe it was always heading this way, but I don't think I really understood. He's forever intertwined with our lives now, and not just the past or the present. He's in our future, and I'm sure it's irreversible. Some relationships are." He looked at Roxy. "I can't lose you again. I *won't*. I couldn't bear it."

"Me neither," she said, a stricken look on her face.

Q looked at Kitty and took her in his arms. He held her

close, but he didn't say anything. Sometimes there weren't words for a feeling, and even if there were words, he didn't know that he had the strength to say them.

The wholesale embracing made Louise sigh wistfully and say, "I think this is where I make my exit."

"No!" Mason barked, pulling away from Roxy. "Stay. I have something important to say.

"I was going to make a big song and dance about this, Rox. I was going to wrap it in a copy of the newspaper from the exact day we met again on this wire, but . . . but obviously it's a little messed up now, and I don't think you'd want to risk getting a bunch of misplaced time on your ring, and, well, hell, we're with all our favorite people in the world, and every goddamned nanosecond with you is special. More precious than the next, you know?"

He rummaged through his messenger bag and took out a small blue velvet box. He got down on one knee and cleared his throat, a bit of a red flush climbing his face. "L. Roxanne Zaborovsky . . . will you marry me?" He opened the box. "I know this isn't the most original way to—"

Roxy squealed, ran over, and leaped on the sofa, bouncing up and down on the cushion, clapping her hands. Louise looked up at her as if she were out of her mind.

Mason was staring at her nervously. Roxy looked down at him and squealed and bounced and clapped some more.

Mason looked in confusion at Louise and Kitty and Q, then back at Roxy.

"Duh!" Roxy screamed. "Yes, yes, yes."

She leaped forward, barreling into him and taking him down to the floor with her. The velvet box went flying.

Louise caught the ring box neatly in one hand, grinning down at Roxy, who was now sitting on Mason, laughing and kissing him. She set the box down next to Angus's fishbowl, grabbed her purse, and slipped out the door with a wink to Kitty and Q. They knew she was headed to start a file on Vesper, no matter that she'd said she was tired.

Q took Kitty's hand with a grin. On this wire, in this time, on this layer, in this moment, the nanoseconds and seconds and days and hours and weeks had finally lined up just right. He had someone he loved, and he was never letting her go.

"For once," he said, leading her up the stairs, "our time is really our own."

"And only we know how we're going to spend it," Kitty whispered with a giggle.

"You know, when I was at that point when I thought I might not make it out, all I could think about was what things were like when I had everything—those fragments of time when I had you." He stopped, cradling her face in his hands. "They weren't enough, Kitty. I don't want to be just the guy who saved you. I don't want a brief time we spend together. I want something like Mason and Roxy have. I want you . . . I want you to learn to love me the way I love you. I want to make things permanent—at least as permanent as they can be in this crazy world."

"You want me to learn to *love* you? That could take a million hours." Kitty laughed. "Lucky for you I already lived them."

She kissed him gently on the mouth. "How lucky am I to be in love with a time-anomaly specialist," she said as he started pushing her again up the stairs. And when Q easily flipped her into his arms and carried her into what had once been her bedroom, she added, "Maybe you could figure out how to turn tonight into infinity."

Q laughed. "They say I'm the best."

He laid Kitty on the bed, followed her down, and wasted not one nanosecond making good on his promise.

SHOMI

An imaginative, new line of speculative fiction destined to break all the rules.

Visit us at:

www.rebelsofromance.com

and

www.shomifiction.com

to

 Preview upcoming novels!

Ⓔ View the latest cover art!

Ⓔ Learn about the authors!

Ⓔ Chat with other SHOMI fans!

Ⓔ Enter contests!

Ⓔ Sign up for the SHOMI newsletter!

And much, much more...

SHOMI

The future of romance where anything is possible.

Turn the page for a taste
of the titles in our SHOMI line,
edgy, speculative fiction
destined to break all the rules.

Be sure to visit us at:
www.rebelsofromance.com
and
www.shomifiction.com

The future of romance where anything is possible.

WiRED

LIZ MAVERICK

Seconds aren't like pennies. They can't be saved in a jar and spent later. Pluck a second out of time or slip an extra one in, the consequences will change your life forever.

L. Roxanne Zaborovsky discovers that fate is comprised of an infinite number of wires, filaments that can be manipulated, and she's not the one at the controls. From the roguishly charming Mason Merrick—a shadow from her increasingly tenebrous past—to the dangerously seductive Leonardo Kaysar, she's barely holding on. This isn't a game, and the pennies are rolling all over the floor. Roxy just has to figure out which are the ones worth picking up.

ISBN 13: 978-0-505-52724-0

To order a book or to request a catalog call:
1-800-481-9191
This book is also available at your local bookstore, or you can check out our Web site **www.dorchesterpub.com** where you can look up your favorite authors, read excerpts, or glance at our discussion forum to see what people have to say about your favorite books.

SHOMI
👁

PHENOMENAL GIRL ⑤

Lainey Livingston has just been made a member of the Elite Hands of Justice, the world's premiere cadre of superheroes. All her senses are extraordinary, and her great strength and ability to fly are equally remarkable. But no one gets a free pass to active duty, and Lainey's next test is going to be her hardest. She's to train with Robert Elliot, the Reincarnist. A magician who has lived multiple lifetimes, he's the smartest man in the world—and Lainey's last obstacle.

Lesson #1: Romantic entanglements among crime fighters are super exploitable, and falling in love with a man who "can't die" is like waving a red flag at a bull. Especially when the most fiendish plot ever is about to break over Megolopolis like a wave of fire.

A. J. MENDEN

ISBN 13: 978-0-505-52786-8

To order a book or to request a catalog call:
1-800-481-9191
This book is also available at your local bookstore, or you can check out our Web site **www.dorchesterpub.com** where you can look up your favorite authors, read excerpts, or glance at our discussion forum to see what people have to say about your favorite books.

Molly Anderson is built to survive.

RAZOR GIRL

It's been six years since she and her family escaped into a bunker, led by her conspiracy theorist father and his fore-knowledge of a plot to bring about the apocalypse. But her father's precautions didn't stop there.

Molly is faster, stronger, and her ocular implants and razor-tipped nails set her apart. Apart, when—venturing alone out of the bunker and into a plague ravaged, monster-ridden wilderness—what Molly needs most is togetherness.

Chase Griffin, a friend from her past, is her best bet. But while he and others have miraculously survived, the kind boy has become a tormented man. Together, these remnants of humanity must journey to the one place Molly's father believed all civilization would be reborn: the Magic Kingdom, where everyone knows it's a small world after all.

MARIANNE MANCUSI

ISBN 13: 978-0-505-52780-6

To order a book or to request a catalog call:
1-800-481-9191
This book is also available at your local bookstore, or you can check out our Web site **www.dorchesterpub.com** where you can look up your favorite authors, read excerpts, or glance at our discussion forum to see what people have to say about your favorite books.

☐ YES!

Sign me up for the Love Spell Book Club and send my
FREE BOOKS! If I choose to stay in the club, I will pay only
$8.50* each month, a savings of $6.48!

NAME: _____

ADDRESS: _____

TELEPHONE: _____

EMAIL: _____

☐ I want to pay by credit card.

☐ **VISA**   ☐ **MasterCard.**   ☐ **DISCOVER**

ACCOUNT #: _____

EXPIRATION DATE: _____

SIGNATURE: _____

Mail this page along with $2.00 shipping and handling to:
Love Spell Book Club
PO Box 6640
Wayne, PA 19087
Or fax (must include credit card information) to:
610-995-9274
You can also sign up online at **www.dorchesterpub.com**.
*Plus $2.00 for shipping. Offer open to residents of the U.S. and Canada only. Canadian
residents please call 1-800-481-9191 for pricing information.
If under 18, a parent or guardian must sign. Terms, prices and conditions subject to
change. Subscription subject to acceptance. Dorchester Publishing reserves the right to
reject any order or cancel any subscription.

GET FREE BOOKS!

You can have the best romance delivered to your door for less than what you'd pay in a bookstore or online. Sign up for one of our book clubs today, and we'll send you *FREE* BOOKS* just for trying it out... **with no obligation to buy, ever!**

Bring a little magic into your life with the romances of Love Spell—fun contemporaries, paranormals, time-travels, futuristics, and more. Your shipments will include authors such as **MARJORIE LIU, JADE LEE, NINA BANGS, GEMMA HALLIDAY**, and many more.

As a book club member you also receive the following special benefits:
- **30% off all orders!**
- **Exclusive access to special discounts!**
- **Convenient home delivery and 10 days to return any books you don't want to keep.**

Visit www.dorchesterpub.com
or call 1-800-481-9191

There is no minimum number of books to buy, and you may cancel membership at any time.
*Please include $2.00 for shipping and handling.